MEMORY GIRL

LINDA JOY SINGLETON

CBAY BOOKS
DALLAS, TX

From idea to published book, MEMORY GIRL has been a long journey that began nearly a decade ago. I wish to thank my family, Danna Smith, Linda Whalen, Verla Kay, my critique group and other supportive friends who never stopped believing that this book would be published.

Also, an infinity of thanks to Madeline Smoot, a good friend and amazing editor who is sharing this journey with me.

"Natural selection, as it has operated in human history, favors not only the clever but the murderous."

—Barbara Ehrenreich

PART
ONE

ONE

"Get down, Jennza—or you'll die!"

"Don't be dramatic," I call out to Lorelei, my fingers curling around steel mesh as I dangle midway up the Fence. "No one dies anymore."

Lorelei flips her raven-black braid over her shoulder while glaring at me. "Some do. If they're not cautious."

"I'm never cautious and look! I'm nearly touching the sky." My words sail on salty breezes, challenging the world to strike me down. Nothing happens, of course. Dying is so retro-century. I laugh and turn away from Lorelei, not wanting to waste a second of my last freedom. It's her last day too, so you'd think she'd understand. Guess not.

I swat aside a loose spiral of my too-curly brown hair as I look up. Only four more handholds to the top, which is strung with barbed wire to keep out the dangers roaming the rocky shore cliffs. I've never seen any dangers—only a sparkling sea spilling beyond the sky with mysterious possibilities. The view is amazing, breathtaking, and completely forbidden.

"Lor, you can see forever up here," I call down. "Climb up."

"Are you crazed? I have no wish to crack my bones." She folds her arms across her chest, rattling the tiny sand-shells she's sewn on her tunic sleeves. "Why must you keep ripping rules? Don't you think I notice when you sneak out? I never

1

tell the Instructors, but I worry until you return."

"You worry too much."

"And you don't worry—ever! If you won't listen to me, talk to him!" She points to a lanky figure coming up the cliff path. It's only Marcus, his fawn-brown hair shining with streaks of sun, his attention focused on something dark and wiggly cupped in his hand.

Lorelei stomps over to Marcus, then points toward me. "Marcus, tell her to get down, or she'll fall and break her neck."

"Get down, Jennz," Marcus says in a distracted tone, his hair sweeping across his forehead as he studies the crawly in his palm.

"Heya, Marc!" Balancing carefully, high over my born-mates, I cling to steel mesh with one hand and wave with the other. "What are you holding?"

"A hybrid of lizard." He taps the squirming creature in his hand. "Its back is smooth with fish scales, not rough like the lizards I typically find."

I could tell him where there are more scaled lizards (I call them "swizards" because they swim). But telling Marcus would lead to questions I don't want to answer. After the Celebraze today, there won't be much left that's completely my own, so I hold tight to my secret.

"Where'd you find it?" Steel presses hard lines into my back as I lean against the Fence.

"On a decaying log."

"Put him in water. Soon."

"Why?"

"So he'll survive."

Marcus lifts his hand over his eyes to shield the rising sun as he gazes up curiously. "How do you know?"

I am saved from answering by Lorelei, who turns on Marcus, knuckling her hand into a fist, her obsidian ring flashing like her dark, angry eyes. "Can you stay to the topic? Or don't you care that Jennza is over ten meters high?"

"She's no more than four meters," he replies.

"But she shouldn't even be climbing the Fence! We should be studying the Name Books so we'll be prepared for our new names."

"We're getting more than new names," I say, that familiar tightness squeezing my chest. I've never confided to my friends how much I dread joining a Family—leaving everything I've known to become someone else. So much is changing. Too much! After tonight, I won't be allowed to call my friends by their youth names, and no one will ever call me Jennza again.

"Finally our lives are beginning." Lorelei's anger melts into a dreamy smile. "Since learning of memdenity I've wondered who I'll become. Today I'll find out."

"I already know who I'll be," Marcus says with a shrug.

"Don't be demental," Lorelei scoffs. "You can't know which Family will Choose you."

"Oh, I'm sure."

"How?" Lorelei asks.

Marcus runs his finger along the swizard's scaly spine, his cheeks reddening. "I—I visited them."

Lorelei's mouth falls open, speechless, which would amuse me if I weren't also stunned. She doesn't ask which Family; that would be completely against the rules. Even I won't ask, but I can guess because, well, I know Marcus. He's fascinated with farming, bees and gardens, and while most Families grow their own crops and gardens, only the

3

Sarwalds raise bees.

Who allowed this unusual visit? I wonder. Not our Instructors, surely, as they are rigid about rules. Was it the Sarwald Family leader? As Grand Leader in ShareHaven, no one holds a higher regard in the community than Grand Sarwald—except the scientists who gave us immortality.

"You're both ripping impossible." Lorelei stomps over to the trail, then turns back to me. "Jennza, I refuse to cover for you this time. Get down now!"

Instead, I climb up. Steadying myself on a steel post, I duck my head to avoid razor-sharp barbed wire that stretches endlessly in both directions. This should be an impossible barrier to cross but I know the flaw. The wire above me snapped two years ago, and instead of the usual repair, someone twisted it back together for quick escapes.

I was that someone.

Beyond the Fence a steep cliff trail winds through boulders and dense brush down to the shore. I inhale a deep breath of sea and courage. I've been doing this for two years, but it's still tricky—throwing one leg like a hook, heaving myself close to the razor-barbs, clinging to a post with one hand while I untwist wires into a narrow gap of escape.

Fingers clutching wire mesh, I rear back with my leg, swing upward, and ....

Smack.

My leg smashes against steel.

Pain crashes through me. My hands slip and my arms flail.

Dizzily, I hear Lorelei yelling my name. A blur of movement below and she's rushing toward me. Marcus drops the swizard, following. Lorelei reaches the Fence first, her arms

4

lifted, with no doubt that she's strong enough to catch me.

But I don't fall. Sweat soaks my clothes and blood trickles from a jagged cut on my arm. Glancing down at Lorelei's pinched face, I swallow guilt. She cares about me, not only because we're born-mates but because we're friends.

"No worries. I'm okay," I call down with apology in my voice.

"You're bleeding," Lorelei accuses.

"Only a scratch." I shift on my wire perch to hide my arm.

"It'll need curing ointment. Hurry down."

"No." I shake my head. "I can't explain where I'm going, just trust that it's important. Afterward, I'll join you for reading or studying or anything you want."

"I want you to follow rules!" She throws up her arms. "By climbing the Fence, you're risking all Three Dangers."

Marcus lifts his hand automatically, like every morning in Instruction when we recite the Safety Pledge. "Protect your body from the Three Dangers: head trauma, heart puncture, and drowning."

Lorelei glares at me. "If you fall to your death, I'll never forgive you."

I try not to laugh at her unlogic. My theory is that Instructors invented the Three Dangers to control us. My born-mates have no trouble avoiding danger, but Instructor Penny says I have a rare talent for rule breaking. I don't set out to break anything—I just find more interesting things to do. Like today during study session. While the others studied Name Books or planned Celebraze statements, I staredreamed out a window, imagining I was a storm gull soaring over the sea. Skimming foamy waves, air-dancing in salty

5

drizzles, feathers fluttering on gusty breezes. Without planning, I'd jumped from my work station and run outside. I knew the Instructors wouldn't object since it's our last day. But I didn't know Lorelei and Marcus would follow.

Marcus peers up at me, suspiciously. "Why *are* you up there, Jennz?"

"Why do you think?" Two years ago, I'd invited him to climb the Fence with me, excited to share my discoveries with the only person who would appreciate them. But he refused to break rules. I never asked him again.

"I think you should listen to Lorelei," he says stubbornly. "Reaching fifteen comes with responsibilities."

"I'll be responsible later."

Marcus frowns. "Jennz, don't do this. Our days of youth-playing are over. Today is for growing-up."

Wire bites my skin as I grip the Fence. "What if I don't want to grow up? I like who I am. I don't want to change."

Marcus shakes his head, as if I've spoken in a language he's never heard before. "You're not being sensical."

"It makes sense to me. I like sharing days with you, Lorelei, the other youths, and our Instructors. Why should I be forced to take someone else's name and memories?"

"We're not *forced*," Lorelei argues. "We'll be welcomed by our relatives and take a contributing role in ShareHaven. How can you not want that honor?"

Marcus nods. "It's why we were born."

"I know," I say, so softly my words are autumn leaves withering and falling to the ground.

Lorelei puts her arm around Marcus, and they stand unified against me. I know they're right. I should be preparing for my new life and excited like my fourteen born-mates.

But how can I give up everything I've been until now? After today I may never touch the sea again.

I feel a prick of wetness on my arm. The cut from the barbed wire still bleeds. It's only a thin pink-red line, but it reminds me I'm not danger-proof. I'm a caretaker of my body—not the sole owner—and it's my duty to be careful. Soon I'll have a Family, a new name, and a forever role in ShareHaven society.

But will I still be me?

"I have to go … I'm sorry," I say and turn my back on my friends.

I untwist the wires so they fall to the sides like the open mouth of a jagged-toothed monster. I've grown up with warnings of claws and snakes outside ShareHaven. But while I've heard roars beyond our boundaries, I've never seen monstrous creatures. Day by day, I only see the same eternal faces.

Everything except my face will change when I belong to a Family.

I don't want to think on this and push through the narrow opening, legs dangling as I balance precariously on wire. I'm only a jump away from the forbidden side of the Fence.

They are no more warnings from my best mates. I'm tempted to look behind me. Instead, I lift my gaze to the gray-blue horizon that stretches forever. Chilly sea fills me with an ache so deep I want to cry, although I have no idea why. Am I flawed somehow? Why can't I behave the expected, dutiful way, like Lorelei, and be studious, like Marcus? Why am I always yearning, frustrated, even angry sometimes for no sensical reason? Why can't I accept all I've learned from the

Instructors? Instead I am tormented with questions.

My mind slips into familiar groves of wonderings—whispers shared in darkness about belonging to a Family. Since our birth, we've been on the same path with the same destination—to reach age fifteen, join a Family, and receive memories of a Lost One. There's a retro word that comes to mind: recycling—when rare resources like metal or plastic are melted and reshaped into something new.

Why can't I stay in this shape?

With a fierce look at the sky, I suck in salty freedom. I look over at the safe side of the Fence, relieved yet a little disappointed too. No one is there.

In the distance, I spot Lorelei and Marcus walking away.

Clinging to the wire, I whisper over and over, "I am Jennza … I am Jennza … I am Jennza …."

I spread my arms wide.

And jump.

TWO

I land on a rock shelf on the forbidden side of the Fence. Slowly, I wind down the steep, rocky trail. Warm blood droplets trickle on my arm, and I swipe them away. The cut isn't deep, but it reminds me of that heart-stopping moment of falling. Balancing on a boulder, I dig into my front panton pocket for a cloth rag and wrap it around my arm.

Shivering, I gulp in deep breaths. Why am I fearful? I've climbed down this cliff often, even in the night-dark, and never came close to falling. I sneak out early morns when winds slumber and waves softly sigh in their sleep. It's only me, alone, with a friendly sea. Now the sun is bright, breezes swirling sand and salty droplets. I shut out fearsome thoughts and continue down the path.

Foamy waves splash, and my leather boots sink into the damp sand. I glance over my shoulder at my sunken footsteps trailing me like stalking shadows. Smiling at my imaginings, I throw out my arms to embrace the sea, sky, and morning. Rocky outcroppings teem with life, storm gulls fly overhead, and tiny sea creatures dive into bubbly sand holes. Despite warnings of claws, venomous snakes, and savage sub-human Nocturnes lurking outside the boundaries, I feel safe here. In this hidden shore, I can just be *me*.

Usually, I throw sticks in the surf or hunt for sand shells, but my time is running out. So I hop over rocks and streams spilling into the sea until I reach a steep rock formation, so impassible that anyone else would have retreated in surrender.

On my first trip over the Fence, I nearly did turn around. But I was curious, so I splashed in the waves, delighting in the giantness of the castle-like rock. I tossed driftwood into the surf, then laughed when the sea flung it back to me. A gift from my sea minions, I imagined. I flung the stick until a gusty wind hurled it high at the rocky cliff. I waited for my stick to bounce off the rock back to me. Only it never did. I threw another stick at the same spot. And it vanished too.

That's how I found the cave.

My cave.

Now I'm visiting for the last time. I won't have the same freedom in a Family, and my new memories— memdenity—will change me too. I may not even *want* to play in the sea, although that seems impossible. But the Instructors say thoughts, habits, and even tastes change when a youth receives a Lost One's memories. I ache to think of never coming here again and forgetting what I love most. Yet Instructor Penny, whom I love dearly, says that memdenity will grow stronger with maturity, like heavy blankets layering over my Jennza memories.

As if I can run from these thoughts, I climb like a monklee up the steep rock castle, pressing myself against the craggy surface. Tufts of green moss stain my fingers. The stain will wash off, so when I stand on the podium at the Celebraze today, I will appear no different than my born-mates.

The shadowed cave is camouflaged by darkness. My feet find the plateau, narrow but wide enough to perch on as

I enter the tunnel. It slants down, seeming to plunge into oblivion.

When I first discovered this opening, I could hear Instructor Theo's voice in my head warning of dangers.

Do not stray from the paths.

Do not touch anything unnamed.

Do not venture beyond boundaries.

I always roll my eyes when he goes on and on about safeguarding our bodies. He isn't worried about us but about the Lost Ones whose memories won't live again if we're damaged. *Don't I matter too?* I want to ask. But I already know the answer and rebel by growing more reckless. With near zero chance of dying, what is there to fear?

Still that first time at the cave, I took a deep breath before crawling into the unknown. Now I know every shadow and secret of my cave.

This morning is cool with chilly air breezing through my cotton shirt and denim pantons. While youths usually wear tunic shirts over dark-gray pantons, we also have some treasured old-made garments. Instructor Penny gifted me with black denim pantons—sturdy fabric that's flexible for climbing. Of all the Instructors, I'll miss Penny the most. She's the only one who feels like … well … family.

Sighing with the sadness of good-byes, I descend into darkness, my echoing footfalls surrounding me. When my eyes adjust, I smile at tiny crawlies creeping on the narrow passage walls. Once I turn the corner, the tunnel lightens from high ceiling holes that let in golden rays. I nearly slip on a patch of moss but grab a protruding rock. The narrow tunnel drops, then rises, opening into an amazing chamber. Rock walls slither and shimmer with small, slimy creatures. I don't know their species names but have given them names of my own: swizards, finshines, and rainbells. High on the ceiling, purple vines and crystal bubble chains dangle like luminescent wind chimes. Every time I come here, awe bursts inside me.

Except I sense something different today.

The air trembles with a disturbance.

My gaze sweeps the circular chamber, yet I see nothing— until I look down at the sand sprinkled rocky floor and jump backward.

The indentation is unlike any footprint I've ever seen. Three times my hand-size with round, giant toes. A half-print disappears in the stream pouring into the deep pool at the end of the cave. I named it the Lavender Pool because green-blue sea becomes sunset-purple when it streams through the tunnel, as if the chameleon water is adapting to its shadowy environment.

I stand still as if I'm made of rock. Usually I'd go to the Lavender Pool and visit my tiny crawly friends. But I'm not sure what else I might find. Who—what—made the footprints?

Reaching down, I trace my finger inside the deepest curving footprint. Something very, very, scary-large stepped here. What if it's still here? Hiding behind boulders, waiting for me?

I want to keep going, yet warnings haunt my thoughts. Avoid the Three Dangers: this mantra has been ingrained in me. *Sticks and stones may break your bones, but the Three Dangers will surely kill you.* No one grows old and dies like in retro-century but there are rare accidents: drowning, falls, and tool mishaps. It's my born purpose to protect this body, a duty impossible for even me to ignore.

I'm turning to leave when I hear a familiar tinkling-glass sound.

"Petal?" I call out. When we first met, I mistook her— green-gold, curled within her shimmery tail—for a floating water petal. So tiny and defenseless. My stomach clenches to think of her alone with a massive-footed monster.

I hurry to the natural-formed crystal bridge arched over the Lavender Pool and whisper, "Petal?"

The sense of wrongness sharpens.

A weapon. Yes, that's what I need. Fumbling in my pan- ton pockets, I find a pencil nub, paper scrap, and comb. Nothing useful.

When I hear Petal's tinkling cry again, I run across the bridge. Above the pool, a rainbow-glistening ceiling shines with fluttery winged creatures that sing when they fly. In the deep water below are swirling fish with many eyes and long, feathery fins. I usually find my tiny Petal on the ledge at the pool's edge. She's sweet and unique; like no other creature. I imagine a giant monster crushing her in its monstrous hand.

But when I look down into the Lavender Pool, the misty water is calm and undisturbed. There's no monster. Only Petal perched on her ledge.

She's no bigger than my palm, except her tail is twice her length. She's light as feathers with bright black eyes and velvety lashes, but instead of fur, she has leathery bris- tles, and her limbs are webbed, so when she swims, she's as quick as a fish. I don't know what species she is; all I know is that when I tickle her belly, she tinkles with laughter, and I love her.

"Petal!" I scoop her up in my hands. She rubs her face against mine, purring a musical sound that is part hello and part fear. I can feel her tiny heart racing.

"Graces good, you're safe," I say, kissing her head.

She blinks up at me, her dark eyes so bright with intelligence that if she could talk, we'd have the most fascinating conversations. We communicate in a language of sounds and gestures, and often I think she reads my mind. Yet when I ask her about the footprint she only blinks, then wiggles through my fingers and dives, whiskery nose first, into the water.

Petal makes a gesture with her webbed limb for me to swim. But after seeing the footprint, I don't want to take off my coverings. I shake my head. Playfully, she splashes at me, and when I lift my arms to shield my face, my arm stings. The cut I got while climbing the Fence has reopened; the cloth around it loosened. Droplets of blood drip down my arm. A drop plops into the Pool, spreading dark red circles on lavender water.

The fish, always gentle and friendly, suddenly merge together in a frenzied swirl. Dark, gray, brown and silver fins dart toward the blood droplets. I've never seen the fish act so strangely, storming together in a cyclone around the bloody drops. Petal scampers up to my shoulder, her cries chiming alarm.

Another blood drop splashes into the pool.

A fish shoots out of the water, changing its shape. Growing and stretching larger than the monster footprint. Three knife-fang teeth jut from the usually toothless fish mouth. Buggy eyes burn fire as the fish opens its jaw wide. The vampire fish is flying. Coming straight at me ....

Whoosh!

A splinter-sized object shoots over the pool, striking the attacking fish mid-air. Ruby-black blood spills from one of its eyes. With a shriek, the fish shrinks to normal size and plops into the water.

When I turn toward the front of the cave, there's a human-shaped monster with arm-like tubes dangling along his body and giantness flipper feet. Impossible! I've been told we're the only humans on this island. So what is this creature? A male, I sense. He has no face—only a head-sized glassy bubble. Beyond the mask, there's a blur of human features, and I realize the bulbous tubes aren't living limbs but devices connected to the mask. Also, his pale hand is very human as he holds a cylindrical object. Is this the weapon which speared the fish? Is he going to spear me too?

"Stay away!" I clutch the slash on my arm so tightly I stop the blood flow.

The glassy head tilts with a simpleness that reminds me of youth monklees when they are scolded but don't understand what they did wrong. The glassy-faced creature says nothing, as if dull-witted and primitive.

He lifts the round spear weapon.

No place to run. I'm surrounded by rocky walls on three sides, and the only way out is the tunnel—which he's blocking. I press against cold, damp rock, ready to dodge if he shoots at me like he did the fish.

Instead of aiming his weapon, he tucks it into an opening in one of his tubes. He extends his palm out like a wave. Is it an offer of friendship or an order to surrender? I breathe again, deciding maybe he isn't dangerous.

In fact, he may have just saved my life.

Green, slimy algae clings to his dangling tubes and flipper feet. Where did he come from? I've never heard of sea-dwellers, but I know so little about what lies beyond the Fence.

"Who are you?" I ask. When he doesn't respond, I point to the Lavender Pool, which is calm again, with no ripple of sharp-toothed danger. "Do you come from the sea or another island?"

No flicker of comprehension. I get more reaction when I talk to Petal.

"My name is Jennza. What are you called?" I ask slower and louder. "Are you understanding me? Can you speak?"

He stares blankly, as if he's not an intelligent species. He doesn't seem menacing though, so maybe he'll let me leave—which I need to do very soon. But what if he tries to follow me over the Fence? He'll be captured or executed. A simple-minded sea creature would have no chance against our Uniforms.

"You have to go back to your … um … home." I gesture beyond him to the tunnel. "It's not safe here for you."

He still makes no move to leave.

"You must leave now." I sweep my arm as if shooing a small fly instead of a man-beast. When he takes a step backward, relief flows through me. "Yes! That's it. Return to the sea."

But he only takes a few steps then stops. Turning back toward me, he lifts his glassy mask. I'm startled by the most dazzling sea-blue eyes I've ever seen. And these amazing eyes shine bright as his full lips stretch into a smile. He's not only human, but he's about my age and extremely stun-looking.

"Next time you're bleeding, it would be wise to avoid blood-sucking vampfins." He speaks more intelligently than some Instructors. "I'm Nate. It's pleasing to meet you, Jennza."

He clasps his hands over his heart, then out toward me. The mask falls back over his face and his flipper feet make no more sound than a breeze.

And he's gone.

THREE

I return along the rocky path and climb the Fence. Balancing near the top, I stare back toward the sea, thinking of Nate—his hands clasped over his heart, reaching out to me as if offering something like friendship. My gaze sweeps across waves, searching for the glint of a glassy mask. Is he out there? Where does he live? Are there others like him?

What I wonder most, I'm embarrassed even to admit to myself.

Will I ever see him again?

Of course not. Even if he returns to the cave, I won't be able to come back. The Celebraze will bind me to a new life, and I must accept my fate.

Jumping down to the safe side of the Fence, I wonder which Family will Choose me. With only fifteen youths and twenty-two Families, it's a certainty my name will be called.

Instructors assure us we'll be welcomed with affection and gifts. Still … it's hard to imagine living anywhere else, being someone else. I've been told what to expect in a Family, but words are only a frame without the texture and shape of the true picture. Only fifteen Families will Choose a youth. Our highest leader, Grand Sarwald, will have already selected these Families, basing his decision on necessity, communal contributions, and each Family's number of Lost Ones. Some Family Name Books (or as I call them:

Unusual and Terriful Ways to Die Books) are giantness! It's ripping amazing how many lives have been lost due to accidents in over three centuries.

But thanks to our four life-giving scientists, the dead are never truly lost, their memories born again in the body of a youth.

"Like me." I stomp a spike-weed growing where the dirt trails meets the smooth gravel path leading to the Edu-Center.

While my fourteen born-mates are eager to bond with a Family, I only think of what I'll be missing: my cave, the sea, Petal, Instructor Penny, and my close friendships with Lorelei and Marcus. As ShareHaven citizens with separate Families, my best mates and I will never play games of seeking or have a box lunch in our tree platform. Youth ends today, and tonight I will leave everything I've known.

I am *so* not ready for the Celebraze.

It's ripping unfair that youths are expected to study all twenty-two Family Name books. That's like hundreds— thousands!—of Lost Ones. I suggested to the Instructors that the Celebraze change the rules so youths are told in advance which Family they'll join. Studying only one Name book would be much easier. But apparently centuries of tradition are more important than a logical process, and no one cares to hear my ideas.

Lorelei says to stop complaining and Marcus keeps handing me Name Books, urging me to read. But I grow quickly bored when reading of Lost Ones, who seem less real than characters from fictional retro-books. Only their manners of death stir my interest.

Still … I *will* have to stand on the stage and Choose a

Name. I wanted to bond with the Hu Family, since they dwell near the sea—until I discovered they raise the largest hoxen and woolly grazer herds, and nine of their female Lost Ones (yes, I counted) died in bloody accidents involving stampedes and piercing horns. Ouch. Besides, I itch when I get near wool—a fact noted in the medi section of my chart.

I also considered the Dallow Family. They dwell near City Center and offer the most interesting female roles, several involving solar energy research. But they place great value on study scores and will surely Choose Merry or Charles. Also cross off the Ying Family, since I have no patience for stitchery, and over a dozen of their Lost Ones crafted artistic coverings for ShareHaven. Lorelei, who is clever at stitching, hopes to join the Ying Family. And Marcus is sure he's going to the Sarwald Family.

So where does that leave me?

Sighing, I glance up to the sharp-angled roofs of the Edu-Center, dusk-brown buildings reaching for the soft blue sky. The weather, usually chilly in late autumn, has calmed for Celebraze. I feel no calm though, only unease twisting my stomach. There's something else too—a sense of wrongness. My neck itches, and I stop to scratch. A sound as close as a whisper stuns me in place. From the corner of my eye I catch the swish of a leathery tail across my shoulder.

"Petal! Not again!" I reach through my thick tangled curls for my tiny stowaway. "I've told you not to hide in my hair!"

She wiggles in my grasp, licking my neck and purring as if proud of herself.

"Oh, Petal." I offer her my arm so she can scrawl down to my hand. "What am I going to do with you?"

Petal blinks up at me, her way of smiling since her tiny mouth has no teeth, nor does it stretch sideways. I am both mad and happy to see her. Clever Petal, hiding so well I didn't know I had a hitchhiker. My hair is thick enough to conceal the largest Name Book and so wild I usually tame it in a scarf.

"Petal, you can't stay with me."

She licks my hand. "No," I say firmly. "You must go back now. Last time you left the cave for too many hours, you nearly shriveled to bones." Her tail encircles my wrist like jewelry. I sigh, knowing I must return her to the sea.

I'm turning back to the Fence when I hear my name called. Spinning around, I see Lorelei racing up the path toward me. Her milk-white tunic rattles with the small shells, now polished into beads, and the coral spirals twisting in her long black braid.

"Graces good, you're here!" She bends at her waist, breathing deep to catch her breath. "I feared I'd have to break more rules than I have bones to find you!"

"I wasn't gone very long, and there are still hours before the Celebraze," I say casually, as if I'm not concealing a small creature in my hair.

"Instructor Penny requests us all to gather in the reading room." Lorelei's dark eyes shine with excitement as she tugs me forward. "Right now!"

I shake off her grip. "But I can't go."

"Why not?"

"I—I need more time to ... um ... study Name Books." Claws dig into my neck and I mind-talk to Petal, *Be quiet and don't move.* I'm not sure she understands, but her claws ease their grip.

"You should have thought of that before you climbed that ripping Fence this morning. Instructor Penny has a surprise for us. It's all very mysterious, and I'm bursting to find out. Nothing will be revealed until we're all together."

"I have something to do first." I try to ignore the claws on my neck. "Cover for me, okay?"

"No, it's not okay. If you don't come, I'll tell the Instructors about the broken wires on the Fence. I will hate myself for hurting you, but I will do it." When her lips press into a stubborn line and her crescent-shaped dark eyes narrow to slits, her mind is set firm.

"Well … um … okay. I'm curious about this surprise too." I think quickly. "But you go ahead. I—I need to use the privacy room."

Lorelei frowns. "Seriously?"

"Desperately." I wiggle my hips for emphasis. "I'll be quick."

"You'd better." She arches her brows doubtfully.

"I criss-cross thumb promise," I say, crossing my thumbs together—our secret sign of friendship. Lorelei hesitates, then crosses her thumbs too.

I watch Lorelei leave, waiting 'til the dorm building door closes behind her.

"Stay hidden," I whisper to Petal.

Instead of the privacy room, I go to the kitchen, where I pour a bowl of water and rummage in the dry goods cabinet for sugar sticklets (Petal's special treat). I sneak her into the storage room behind the torium—the largest building in the Edu-Center with a stage and wings of seats that rise up near the ceiling. I performed here in minor roles as a tree or toad, leaving the dramatical roles to those with acting skills,

22

like Asha and Homer.

The storage room is crowded with boxes, wooden sets, and hanging costumes. No one ever goes here between plays, so it's a good place to hide Petal. Her tail thumps a complaint when I set her near the water bowl. I wish I could give her salty seawater. When I offer her a sugar sticklet, her tail dances and she tinkles a happy sound. She's safe ... for now.

As my quick footsteps tap on the path to the study room, I try to guess what the "urgent" meeting is about. With only hours before the Celebraze, it must be highly important to interrupt our preparations—unless the Celebraze has been postponed? This thought floods me with relief. Another day, perhaps a week, even a month, of staying here would be a welcome surprise.

When I enter the study room, high ceilings shine with light-tubes, and sun streams through windows. I ignore the accusing looks from my born-mates (as if being late is so unusual?) and take my assigned station, the one with the black ink stain on the seat from my unfortunate finger-painting incident at age nine. How could I know puha berry ink would not wash clean?

"About time her royal lateness decides to show up," Homer says, laughing as if he's told a clever joke. *Not even close to clever*, I think. He's a twig-tall boy with large teeth and a laugh harsher than a squawking crow-hawk.

"I offer my apologies," I say turning away from annoying Homer to give a respectful nod to Instructor Penny, and instead of anger in the gentle angles of her olive skin, I see forgiveness. Tightness eases in my chest.

"Apology accepted, Jennza," she says, and I think how good my name sounds from her lips. I will miss that.

"Now that we're all here, I'd like to introduce my surprise." Instructor Penny gestures to two figures seated in chairs beside her. "Please welcome our guests, Monroe and Greta Hu."

Not one, but two guests! Indeed this is a rare surprise, as we're seldom permitted contact with the community. Monroe and Greta radiate a sense of maturity like all of those who have ceased aging at the communal age of twenty-five. Monroe is of short stature, with high cheekbones, slim shoulders, and dark amber skin. His sturdy pantons and thick woven shirt are patched and faded as if his work role is outside climate-maintained dwellings. He taps his pointed-toe boot with nervous energy, while Greta gazes serenely around the room. She's roundly built, clothed in a bright blue tunic, with short, honey-brown hair waving from a scarf.

"I've invited our guests because many of you have come to me with questions about what happens when you leave here," Instructor Penny tells us. "We've been like a family, but now it's time for you to take your roles in our communal Family. It's been an honor to teach you, and I will miss you all." Her voice catches, and she leans against an edge of her workstation, as if needing the extra support. "While I have told you my own experiences about bonding with a Family, I thought it would be helpful to hear of others' experiences. So I asked Greta and Monroe to share their unique perspectives with you."

"We're honored to be here," Greta adds with a polite head bow.

"I taught Greta over twenty-five years ago." Instructor Penny bends toward her former student, no longer separated by youth and Instructor status, both bearing the smooth, attractively mature faces of age twenty-five.

"It seems much longer since I've been here," Greta says.

"Enough time for you to grow into a fine, respected citizen," Instructor Penny says warmly. "Greta was in the last group of youths—only her name wasn't Greta."

"I was called Abigail, and that was my study station," Greta says, pointing to where Merry sits in the front row. "I've changed much since then. Abigail was a timid girl, never raising her hand to answer questions, much less standing in front of a group as I'm doing now. As Greta, I have gained much confidence and happiness with my Family—especially Monroe. My husband."

At the word "husband" I suck in a gasp, as do several other youths. Our Instructors taught the basics: math, communication, history, science, faith, citizenship, and Family relationships like sister, brother, and parents. But even though most Instructors have marriage partners in their separate Families, they don't discuss their intimate relationships. When youths ask what goes on privately between a husband and a wife, the answer is always, "You'll understand with memdenity." Still, rumors of shared beds and nakedness cause much whispering after dark in my dorm room.

"Abi—I mean, Greta—please tell us about your Celebraze experience," Instructor Penny says, then slips into her chair.

"I was a youth much like you, eager to bond with a Family," Greta says, pushing up her scarf, embroidered with the Hu Family emblem—tiny hooves curling into the letter H. "I read every Name Book, and the Hu Family was my top choice. At my Celebraze, I was joysome when the Hu Family Chose me, and I proudly Chose my forever Name—Greta Hu."

"How wondrous to get your top choice," Lorelei says

with a wistful sigh.

"It was. But the best moment came when I met my dearest husband."

Monroe smiles shyly at Greta, saying nothing, but the way he looks into her face says more than words, as if his dark eyes see only her.

Bob, a freckled youth with cropped-short red hair and a stubby nose, raises his hand. "Did it take long to adjust to living in a Family?"

"No. They were very kind to me. Although before my first memdenity, when I knew nothing about my role, I worried about disappointing them."

"You were perfect," Monroe says quietly.

"See how sweet he is?" Greta beams. "I expected to love my Family but not to have the deep love I feel for my husband—even before my first memdenity."

Merry, who sits in the front row, raises her hand. "Did memdenity hurt?"

"Not at all!" Greta chuckles. "It's like going to sleep and having wondrous dreams of new people and experiences, then waking to find these experiences really happened to you—at least through memories. My second mem was the best. That's when I remembered all my firsts with Monroe: first meeting, date, and our beauteous wedding."

"Ooh, I hope it's like that for me," says Polly, a quiet youth who shares my interest in reading retro-books. Many rainy days we've sat together in the reading nest, a cushioned seat surrounded by curved windows, traveling to faraway places with words.

"Blah! Too sappy," spits out Homer. "Tell me exciting memories, like in retro-century when people went brain-crazy or the Attack on ShareHaven. If I'd been there when that the terror-mob Attacked, I would have ripping kicked those—"

"Homer!" Instructor Penny slaps her hands together, a gesture for silence. "You will not speak rudely."

"But I want to know about—"

"Homer!" She rises in her chair warningly.

He opens his mouth as if to argue, then slumps his shoulders. "I apologize," he mumbles.

Marcus, in the chair beside me, lifts his hand. "May I ask a question?"

Instructor Penny nods, clearly relieved. "Please, do, Marcus."

"I was wondering about the other youths from the last born-group," he says slowly, as if carefully choosing each word.

"Yes?" Greta says, turning toward him. "What would you like to know?"

"You each went to different Families. Do you still see them?"

"Oh, yes." Greta nods. "At City Center, faith service, and Sunday Fair."

"But is it the sameness?" Marcus gnaws his lips. "Are you still friends with all fourteen of your born-mates?"

Her tawny skin pales as she glances over at Monroe, who gives a terse shake with his head. Greta's smile stiffens as she answers, "I am friendly with all of my community."

Marcus's brows knit together, and he picks at the dirt under his thumb like he always does when troubled.

Greta goes on to describe her community role in the Role Assignments Office, where she organizes communal work hours, and her daily Family chores of tending livestock and gardening. She glows when she speaks of her Hu Family relatives: three sisters, a brother, five nieces, seven nephews, and a grandfather who is the only Family member who appears older than twenty-five, a founding member of ShareHaven who didn't cease aging until the rare age of fifty-two.

"Gramps refuses hair shading," Monroe adds with a pearly grin that dimples with humor. "He says he earned every one of his gray hairs."

"He certainly has." Greta grins back at her husband.

"I've met many of our founding citizens and they are so wise in experience," Instructor Penny adds, then glances at the wall timepiece with surprise. "Graces good, we're out of time. This has been such an inspiring talk. Thank you so much for sharing with us."

"I've enjoyed coming here. I know I learned much here, but I remember little of those youth years." Greta gazes around the room, from chairs to work stations to the large table stacked with Name Books. "When I think of my childhood, I visualize a tall building in a faraway place called Chicago. My home was a two-bedroom apartment on the ninth floor, with a balcony blooming with potted flowers and a sparkling blue view overlooking the lake."

"But you've never left the island," I blurt. "What of your Abigail memories?"

"They aren't important," she says with a toss of her scarved head.

I want to argue that youth memories *are* important; fifteen years together makes us a family too. But Instructor Penny is giving me the *look*. I remember her harsh tone with Homer and don't want to ruin our last day together.

"It's unhealthy to dwell on the past," Greta adds with smiling conviction. "I have a fulfilling role with my Family—especially my darling Monroe, and I could not be happier. Monroe is more than my husband. He's my soul mate."

Soul mate?

In the retro-books I've read, the idea of soul mates—two people destined only for each other—seemed to be made of fantasy, like unicorns and wishing on a star. How can one person be mated to another by a soul? An unsensical concept with no scientific proof. Our faith lessons teach that science created a circle of life and death—the natural way for thousands of years—until our scientists discovered the cease-aging process, transforming life's circle into a line of infinity. Belief in a soul is merely a myth from long-ago religions. There is no physical organ on the human body labeled "soul."

Yet the way Greta and Monroe look at each other, as if they're touching even when they sit apart, gives me a strange longing.

"It's so romantic," Lorelei whispers.

"Confusing," I murmur, but she doesn't hear me because everyone is clapping. Chairs scrape the floor as my born-mates gather around our guests, following them to the door, asking questions about Family meals, clothing, work assignments, and other ordinary topics.

But it's the unordinary, unasked questions that trouble me. I stay in my chair, thinking. What if the soul truly exists? Is it physical like blood and skin? Does everyone have one? When someone has an accidental death and their memories are saved, is a soul a part of those memories? Does that mean the souls of Abigail and Greta now share the same body?

I concentrate on my own body, aware of my beating

heart, my skin's heat, and a faint stinging from the cut on my arm. My mind churns through memories and knowledge, conscious of thoughts. But I sense more to me, something deeper than thoughts and emotions. Could this be a soul? If so, where does body end and soul begin?

Glancing over at Monroe, who shadows close to Greta, I think about the first Greta. If she hadn't died, she'd still be his wife—or maybe she still is his wife. Reborn inside of a youth who was once called Abigail. Is Monroe in love with one woman or two?

And I wonder what will happen when I take on the memdenity of someone else. Who will I be?

"Jennza!" A voice jerks me out of my thoughts.

Startled, I look up at Marcus. I'm even more startled to realize we're the only ones left in the room. "Where did everyone go?"

"To the dorms. Didn't you hear Instructor Penny announce it was time to prepare for the Celebraze?" he asks.

My cheeks burn as I rise to my feet. "I must hurry to my dorm—"

"Wait, Jennz." His voice lowers. "I want to speak to you."

"Aren't you already doing that?" I say lightly.

"No, I mean ... I have something to give you." He pushes his waving hair from his eyes, furrowing his brow. "But not here."

"Oh?" I stare at him, puzzled by his intense expression.

"No one else must know." He tugs on my arm. "Come with me."

FOUR

I follow Marcus down the hall to the boys' dorm, where I hear rushing footsteps and excited voices behind the door. While Marcus goes inside, I wait in the hall, since girls aren't allowed in the boys' dorm, nor are boys allowed in our dorm. I impatiently tap my boot, unable to guess what Marcus wants to give me.

The door bursts open, and there's Marcus, clutching a rolled paper.

I eye the gray hemper, a paper used commonly for youth lessons. "What's this about?"

He glances up and down the hall, then even though no one else is near, he lowers his voice. "I've wanted to … um … talk to you, but Lorelei is always around."

"There's nothing you can't say to me in front of her."

"Oh, there is." The paper rustles in his hand. "Remember when you asked me to climb the Fence with you?"

I stiffen, hurt feelings rushing back. "Two years ago." I press my lips together. "You refused."

"I wanted to go but couldn't break an important rule. Still, I kept your secret."

"I know, and I'm grateful," I say softly.

"Rules are important to me, but that doesn't mean I don't want to have fun too. My best memory is of carrying boards with you and Lorelei into a tree and making a platform and

31

watching a bird build a nest. After that you started collecting feathers."

I laugh. "I wanted to fly and thought I only needed to build big wings."

"I believed you could do it," he says solemnly. "You always surprise me with things you say and do. I'm ready to join a Family, but it makes me sad because I'll miss you."

"You'll miss Lorelei too," I add.

"Yes, but not the same way." He clears his throat. "Lorelei isn't you."

I suck a sharp breath, aware of Marcus as if we were strangers meeting for the first time. Do I truly know him? I'd never guessed he favored me over Lorelei, especially after that awkward "kissing" moment when we were younger that he pretended never happened. I didn't even tell Lorelei, embarrassed and heart-stung.

"I'll miss you too," I finally say, swallowing a lump in my throat. "I dread leaving here and going to different Families. We won't spend days together."

"Maybe we can," Marcus says mysteriously. "I've put much thought on this and researched the relationships in Families. In retro-century, Family relationships were a product of DNA and age. A youth couldn't care for itself, so the parents took a nurturing role and the responsibility for their children. As the parents aged, roles reversed—children caring for their parents. Family structure was a means of survival, the stronger caring for the weak."

"But no one grows old in ShareHaven," I say with the same pride for community I hear every day from our Instructors. "Everyone, except founders and youths like us, are age twenty-five."

"Exactly. Our roles have changed—and so have the rules. In retro-century, it would be illegal for a brother and sister to marry. But now any unmarried person has the freedom to marry a Family member. Edward Salazar, a youth from three groups ago, married his own mother. There have even been allowances for unmarried people to marry into another Family if the Leaders approve. So it's important to belong to a Family with a forward-thinking Leader. There are ways for us to stay close, but it depends on the Family you join."

"Which I have no control over," I remind him.

"So you need to be ready with the best Name."

I stare down at a floor tile with a scrape mark like someone slid to a sudden stop. "You know I'm not ready. I've barely studied."

"That's why I studied for you." Marcus pushes the rolled paper into my hand, his proud smile reaching deep inside of me. "Here's a list of suitable Names from the three Families most likely to Choose you."

"Oh, Marcus," I say, humbled that he broke a rule to help me. "You shouldn't have."

"I wanted to … for you," he adds softly.

"But how could you know which Families to study?"

"There are patterns in the selection process, like patterns a bee hive displays in the presence of its queen. I analyzed records of past Celebrazes to come to my conclusions. Besides, I hear things," he says with a secretive lift of his brows. "Wait till you're alone before reading the list. Then memorize it."

"I will," I promise, suddenly lighter, as if the paper in my hand is made of wings. "Thank you so much, Marcus. You're the best best-mate ever."

"I hope to be more than that … someday." He looks into

my face as if searching for something, then steps away and disappears into his dorm room.

I stare at the closed door for a moment, puzzled and pleasantly warmed inside. Is he hinting at what I think? I stare down curiously at the hemper in my hand, rough-edged paper, smooth in texture and smelling rich in leafy pulp. In retro-century, paper was created from trees, but most of the trees on our island are on the dangerous side of the Fence, so tree paper was replaced with hemper.

Footsteps from a near hall make me jump and remember I must get ready for the Celebraze. The hemper rustles in my fingers and teases my curiosity.

When I reach the door to girls' dorm, curiosity wins.

Furtively looking around, I decide it's safe to peek at Marcus' list. Written in slanted precise letters, there are only three Names, each long with sentences of details. The Lost Ones had different roles, histories, and manners of death.

But they each shared one thing in common.

All three Lost Ones never married.

FIVE

Opening the door to the girls' dorm room, I find a whirlwind of frantic changing of coverings and hair-brushing.

Lorelei rushes over to me, her black braid whipping like an agitated snake.

"Jennza, where have you been? Why must you always be late?" Lorelei cries as I enter a room scented floral by hair cleaners and body fragrances. Only two other girls are still getting ready, Merry and Asha; the others have already gone. Lorelei wears her Celebraze tunic, but she waited for me.

She offers to help me prepare for the Celebraze, but I assure her I can dress on my own. With a stubborn purse of her lips, she refuses to leave me and helps me button my tunic when my back buttons are out of reach.

Even with Lorelei's help, I'm last to dress and wrap my hair in a traditional white scarf. White symbolizes youth, and at the end of the ceremony, we burn our scarves as a gesture of leaving our childhood for new roles in the community. We'll be gifted with new scarves with symbols of our Families.

Tension builds as all fifteen of us—eight girls and seven boys—gather in the Communal Study, which is circular, with curved rows of chairs and luminous lamps. Floor-to-ceiling shelves overfill with books, most hemper-bound, but some are from long ago, with brittle yellow pages that crackle with each turn.

Homer jumps atop the center table, his black hair wagging like a hoxen tail beneath his white scarf. He quotes poetry—something retro about the passage of youth—as if he's on a stage and we're his audience. His dramatical need to be the focus of attention annoys me, and it's satisfying to share an eye-roll with Lorelei. She's not a Homer fan either.

I look around at the born-mates I've grown older with. After we join a Family, we'll never learn together again. I don't want to think on this, but it's hard not to when others talk about what will happen in the next hours.

"I hope, I hope, I hope," Lorelei says as she scoots her chair closer to mine. "I hope to be in the Ying Family."

"Sewing will give you squinty eyes," I warn.

"I am willing for the risk," she says with a furrow in her brow that tells me she does not appreciate my teasing when she is being serious. "My top Choice is Flavia Ying—she was brilliant with design and fashionizing."

"Didn't she die in a freak scissor accident?"

"I will not run with scissors. Fashionizing would be my perfect forever."

"You'll have to make boring coverings like this," I point out, plucking at my itchy tunic. "And needles hurt when they stab fingers."

"Only for you, clumsy Jennz," she teases.

"I'd rather do something exciting."

She arches one eyebrow. "And your idea of 'exciting' is?'"

"I don't know."

"If you listened to the Instructors instead of window gazing, you'd be better prepared. I love you, Jennz, but learn discipline or you'll never adjust to a Family. I have worked hard on my stitchery and will do well with the Ying Family—if I'm lucky and they Choose me."

"They will be lucky to Choose you," I say. Lorelei's crafting skill transforms coral into hair frivels, cloth into coverings, and shells into luminous buttons. When I gift her with coral and shells, she pretends I found them within boundaries, although she knows they come from the sea. She's very loyal that way.

"Seam work is my dream community role," she says with a passion I envy. "So much more fun than office duties, repairing machines, or dirt-digging."

"I'm all for dirt-digging." It's Marcus coming to join us, taking the seat on the other side of mine. When I catch his gaze, he winks at me.

"Your filthy fingernails prove that," Lorelei teases him.

"Heya, I just scrubbed them!" He wiggles his tanned fingers that I have never seen so clean. "I can't wait to muck out animal pens."

"You're the oddest boy ever." Lorelei flips her braid, then adds in a lofty tone. "I still want to know how you visited the Sarwald Family without us knowing. Did the Instructors allow it?"

His gaze shifts away. "Some may have."

"Vagueness is a form of lying." Lorelei wags her finger at him. "It's unlike you to keep secrets and break rules."

"Not break … bend. Jennza is the rule breaker." He playfully taps my shoulder. "But I'm learning too."

"If I don't agree with a rule, I'll find a way around it."

"You can't, Jennza," Lorelei argues. "It'll dishonor your Family."

"What can they do? Return me?" I say recklessly.

"Shhh!" Marcus glances around the room. But the other youths are too busy talking to notice us.

"I was only joking," I tell him, shrugging. "Returning is a scarytale."

"It's real, Jennz—even if Greta Hu won't admit it," he adds bitterly.

Lorelei's jaw falls open. "What do you mean?"

"Greta lied to us." Marcus narrows his brown eyes to slits. "She said she was still friends with *all* of her bornmates. But that's impossible."

"Why?" I ask.

"Because one of them was Returned."

Lorelei nearly falls out of her chair.

"Are you sure?" I ask him.

Marcus nods. "The youth, Carlos, was bonding well with his Family until he suddenly stopped talking. One morning when his cousin told him to help with kitchen chores, he sliced her face with a knife. He was Returned."

The way Marcus says "Returned" chills me. No one knows what happens to the Returned, only that they're never seen again.

"Who told you this?" I demand. "An Instructor?"

"No. I heard it from …." His brows furrow, as if he's reluctant to say any more. So I stare him down, challenging him to finish.

"Scientists," Marcus finally admits in a hushed voice.

"No way!" Lorelei smacks his arm.

I find it hard to believe too, although I can't remember Marcus ever telling an untruth. It's just that the scientists are so … so mystical. Only Grand Sarwald is allowed to consult with them, and for this, he must travel to the highest peak

38

of our island where the scientists live in a mysterious compound seemingly invisible to ordinary eyes. Every morning it's customary to arise, look to the east, and recite the Faith Pledge: *I pledge to honor Family, community, and the miracles of the scientists. Peace and safety forever.*

"You did *not* talk to scientists," I say skeptically.

"Ripping impossible," Lorelei adds.

"But I did." Marcus speaks so sincerely I know he's truth telling.

"Seriously? You met them?" I'm still shaking my head. "But the scientists keep to their compound."

"Not always. You already know I visited the Sarwald Family." He glances around nervously. "They asked me to dine with them, and during dessert, two visitors arrived—a man and woman in purple and gold robes."

"Scientists." The word tastes mysterious on my lips. The four scientists seem almost magical, more thrilling than ordinary humans. If the scientists had a Name Book, I would have been eager to study, dreaming of wearing gold and purple robes. A secret wish I have, not even revealed to Marcus and Lorelei, is to go to the top of our island where the scientists live.

Lorelei's eyes widen like dark moons. "Are they really aged beyond twenty-five? With wisdom lines and hair shining like stars?"

Marcus nods. "Scientist Lila's hair has more silver than her brother Scientist Daniel's, but the wisdom lines are deeper on his face. It was hard not to stare. When Scientist Lila noticed, she ordered me out of the room. I left but could still hear when she shouted, 'There's nothing wrong with the process!' Leader Sarwald argued, 'Then why did that youth attack his cousin? We need to be sure these new youths aren't a risk or there will be more Returns."' Marcus breathes hard as if he's run a long distance. "They stopped shouting, so I couldn't hear any more. But later I asked my sister—my future sister—what happens when a youth is Returned, and she told me they cease to exist."

Cease to exist? I wonder. *As in dead?* What would cause a youth to go crazy, and why would Leader Sarwald blame the scientists? We've been told over and over that we're precious gifts to ShareHaven. With only fifteen youths born every twenty-five years, Families treasure us. Yet a youth was Returned.

Could it happen again?

Marcus looks so miserable, and I know it's because he broke rules by repeating a private conversation. I squeeze his hand to remind him he's with friends. I clasp Lorelei's hand too. No matter who we become, we'll always be best mates.

"It's right you told us." Lorelei also squeezes Marcus's hand, so we're now a circle of friendship. "But no worries. Our Families will love us."

I smile at Lorelei. "Your Family will love you so much they'll shower you with gifts."

"I only want one thing. Can you guess?"

"What?" Marcus and I both ask.

Lorelei sits up straighter. "Memdenity. All three mems right away."

"Not a good idea." Marcus frowns. "Memories must be carefully timed over a year for proper adjustment."

I nod. "Or your brain will explode."

"Don't exaggerate," Marcus says, pretending to be annoyed.

"It could happen." I shrug. "Maybe."

"I'll more likely explode from waiting." Lorelei twists her white scarf. "A whole month before the first mem—and then I'll only have up to age fifteen memories. Torturous! I want to know everything from fifteen to forever about my new brothers, sisters, cousins, parents, aunts, uncles, husband and children."

"If we have children in our new role, they'll already be age twenty-five," I say, my uneasiness returning. "I read in a retro-book that youths used to be grown by genetic parents."

"Not in a lab?" Lorelei's brows arch. "That's ripping random."

"It was nice in the book. Youths had mothers and fathers." I idly tap my hand on my chair. "It'll be strange to be called *mother.*"

"It won't happen if you Choose a Lost One who never married or had children," Marcus says with deep meaning.

"I don't care if I have a zillion children. I just want the Celebraze to start now," Lorelei says, with a frustrated look at the wall timepiece. She throws up her hands, her shell-bracelets jingling. "Why haven't they come for us yet? It feels like I'll be a youth for centuries. I'm tired of being treated as if I'm brain-lacking because I'm only a youth. I'm still growing too, but not in places where I want to. And I found a pimple yesterday."

"Really?" I look closely at her face. "I don't see anything."

She touches her nose. "I clear-creamed it away. But what if it comes back and brings friends?"

"I see it," Marcus says, pointing at her chin.

"No!" She jumps from her chair and rushes over to the wall mirror at the far side of the room.

"You're a wicked boy," I accuse Marcus, not sure whether I'm angry or amused. "Her face had no mark."

"My mistake." He grins with no apology. "So did you read it?"

I nod, well aware we're no longing speaking of Lorelei.

"And memorize the names?"

I humph, insulted. "There were only three."

"Recite them," he orders, clearly doubting my study skills.

"Seriously?" I retort, annoyed by his superior attitude.

"Unless you can't remember ...." He says this slowly, taunting me.

"Oh, I can," I reply with a wicked-sweet smile. "Agnes Candras was trampled by a team of hoxen. Vesper Sanchez drowned while collecting algae samples in her role at our water system. Hilda Treveno died from falling off a cliff and landing on a deadened tree limb that pierced her throat."

Marcus rolls his eyes. "Why do you focus on life endings rather than life accomplishments?"

"Morbidity interests me," I say to annoy him, although in truth I found Hilda Treveno's community role interesting. She's my top choice, concocting herbal cures that boost immunity systems and spiced up her salsa. I've found unusual plants in my cave and would be interested to learn more about them. If the Treveno Family Chooses me, I'll be ready.

Lorelei returns to her seat and starts to say something but stops at the click of a door opening. The room goes silent.

Instructor Ivan appears in the doorway, a tall cornstalk of a man with a thick thatch of bark-brown hair on a long, sharp-boned face. He gestures to us and says in a deep booming voice, "Now."

Marcus gives my hand an encouraging squeeze while Lorelei jumps up with a squeal. I look around the room at my born-mates grinning, rising, and moving to the door.

It's time.

Six

I've attended many events in the torium but never any so grand as the Celebraze. I step away from my born-mates and Instructors to peer through the doorway. My breath catches at the tiered seats, streaming banners representing each Family's colors, and a stage adorned with banners and ribbons grander than on Haven Day, the anniversary of the Fence's completion.

I am dazzled. Excited. Uneasy.

My too-long white tunic drags on the tiles as I line up according to my Edu-grade ranking: *last*. Grades are an unsensical way to define someone. I've learned more by exploring my cave, swimming with sea creatures and gathering shells, than from brain-dulling lessons. I'd rather be in the cave with Petal.

Poor little Petal. Alone in the storage room. How will I get her back to the cave? My only chance will be after the Celebraze, when I'm allowed to gather my belongings and say good-byes.

"Jennza!"

Startled, I look up at Instructor Penny. The line has started to move.

"Don't be so sluggy, Jennza." My Instructor's smile takes the sting from her criticism. Her bark-brown tunic is styled similar to mine, but it fits well, not dragging. She's tall and willowy, with shiny dark hair curled high on her head, reminding me of an elegant yet sturdy oak tree. Her gray eyes always sparkle with humor, making her seem more like a youth than a mature twenty-five.

"I'm hurrying," I tell her.

She touches my cheek softly. "Don't be afraid," she whispers.

"Me, afraid? Never."

"No need to pretend with me, Jenny."

I shrug, looking down at the dusty hem of my tunic. I don't care—I don't want to care—yet I do. I don't mean to voice what I'm desperately trying *not* to think about, so it's a surprise to hear myself say, "No one will Choose me."

"Of course they will."

"Last." I spit out this foul-tasting word.

I expect Instructor Penny to argue. You'll be wanted and loved, she'll assure me. But she slips her arms around my shoulders, saying nothing, only holding me tight. Soon I'll walk to the stage to be judged among Family Leaders.

I will be chosen last. There's no one to blame except me.

As I follow the others down the center aisle I hear flutters as the audience flips through booklets citing our grades, good habits, poor habits, health history, photos, and recommendations from the Instructors for placement.

"Lift your head; smile." Instructor Penny pats my arm. "You'll never forget the day you meet your Family. They'll love you as I do."

She is being kind and we both know it, but I lift my head with a forced smile. Being last doesn't matter. Someone has to Choose me. Right?

Musicians perform on the stage, their string and pipe

melodies soothing. Belonging to a Family is an honor, not a punishment. So why do my hands shake? I have no fear of high climbs or exploring darkness, yet leaving everything I know is scarifying. I tell myself it's the natural way for youths. I'll become a useful member of society, restoring lost knowledge, and gaining a Family—all connected to me by memories.

Someone else's memories.

My own memories will be pushed aside like outgrown clothes buried in a closet corner. But I'll hold tight to my important memories, reminding myself of them so often they'll never fade. It's possible because I've tried it already.

At age ten, we had our first memdenity lesson. Instructor Ivan said, "Raise your hands if you can remember something that happened when you were age six." We all raised our hands. "Age four?" he asked. Only a few hands were raised. "Age one?" I looked around and saw no hands raised. So I raised mine.

"Are you sure, Jennza?" He arched one bushy black brow, doubting me.

"Yes." I nodded. "When I was learning to walk, I fell on a big rock and cut my knee. It was a deep cut and bled and bled. There's still a little scar."

The next day I was taken to the health-keepers. They dabbed clear-cream on my knee until there was no trace of the scar. But whenever I look at my knee, in my mind I see the tiny scar.

New memories may crowd my mind, but the important memories, especially my friendships with Lorelei and Marcus, will never fade. Instructors say stubbornness is my worst trait, but my stubbornness will keep me always Jennza.

So bring on the Choosing!

The music stops abruptly when all fifteen of us reach the stage. We line up in our white tunics while the Instructors, draped in dark-brown, file to their seats in the audience.

Grand Sarwald steps on a block of wood behind the podium. He has a scruffy white beard and no hair on his head. I've heard scientists are working on a hair growth pill but haven't succeeded. He clears his throat, silencing the audience. Not even paper rustles.

"Welcome, Havenites. Has it already been twenty-five years since I last stood here to welcome youths into our Families?" He chuckles. "Time used to govern our existence; now it's only visible in the aged faces of your founders." His deep-set eyes crinkle with humor as he rubs his bald head. "On this joyous day, we welcome our newest Family members." He sweeps his hand toward us. "It is my honor and pleasure to introduce our fifteen youths!"

Applause thunders through the room, and my pulse jumps with an unexpected thrill. ShareHaven has waited a long time for us; we're as treasured as the rarest plastics. To be accepted and loved could be, well, nice.

"Also we're fortunate to have our esteemed Instructors to teach our youths. They have worked hard to shape these fine youths and may now return to their Families until their roles are needed again." Grand Sarwald gestures to the Instructors, each Family in the audience clapping louder for one of their own members. I clap loudest when he calls Instructor Penny Dallow.

More introductions: each Family Leader. I've met a few Leaders on rare trips to City Central Museum or to pastures to observe cows, wooly grazers, and hoglets. Youths stay separate from the community to avoid favoritism at the Celebraze, which is why Marcus's visit to the Sarwalds is so unusual.

I'm itching from the tunic but can't scratch—not with hundreds of gazes on me. Grand Sarwald pauses, and I think he's finished with his speech until he gestures to the back of the room. "We are much honored today with a rare appearance from our revered scientists," he adds. "Lila Farrow, Daniel Farrow, Martyn Scallag, and Kataya Jovovich."

Scientists! Here? Graces good! I shift in our lineup for a better view of the audience, peering at four figures shimmering in purple and gold robes: a twig-thin man with stooped shoulders, a taller man with midnight-black hair, and two women of contrasting seasons—strawberry summer and silvery-frosted winter. Silver hair? She must be the scientist Marcus overheard being warned by Grand Sarwald, "If we don't change, there will be more Returns."

Now on the podium, Grand Sarwald beams a gracious smile, founder lines deep on his aged face. "We owe much to our fine scientists," he says. "Never forget our beginnings—over three centuries ago, when scientists from many countries came to this island to work together for the betterment of humanity. When the mind-plague struck, they searched for a cure. Sadly, they failed. But untrue rumors spread to the outside that we had a cure—which led to the Attack." He grimaces. "Hundreds killed, research destroyed, and buildings burnt."

I know our history well, yet his words bring it alive in vivid images of fire and blood. There's a hush over the audience, their heads bowed.

"But out of chaos, the surviving scientists gave us immortality and memdenity," Grand Sarwald continues. "We are protected in ShareHaven, safe from beasts and Nocturnes, sharing memories, resources, and respect for Family. We are not divided by warring religions as were retro-societies; instead, we're united in the shared faith of science miracles. Some might say ShareHaven is utopia, where life is forever and not even memories die ...." He clutches the podium, doubling over with a hacking cough. "Dry ... throat," he murmurs, sipping from a water glass. His coughing ends quickly and he lifts his head, once again smiling. "As I was saying, we are a strong society, but societies can't thrive without growth." He sweeps his hand toward us. "Our youths bring hope for the future."

Applause echoes so loudly that I long to cover my ears.

"I hold fifteen tiles in this bag, each representing a Family who will welcome a youth," Grand Sarwald declares. "The first Family to Choose is ...."

Tensing, I hold my head high and struggle to hide the fear from my face. I am torn between wanting it over and wishing time would stop.

If aging can stop, why not time?

When Grand Sarwald pulls out a tile bearing his own Family name, I am not surprised (nor, I suspect, is anyone in the audience). I'm glad for Marcus, who proudly steps forward to announce his new Name: Neil Sarwald.

Once Marcus, it's hard to think of him as Neil, leaves the stage with a tall dark-skinned woman who wears her hair in a tight knot on her head, the room goes silent.

I'm holding my breath. Waiting ...

Another tile drawn. The Candras Family.

Agnes Candras, I think with a rise of hope. One of the Names from Marcus's list. If I'm called, I'll have a Name ready for this Family.

Leader Candras, a rounded woman with wispy sun-streaked hair, steps up to the podium. She glances at the booklets with our information then moves toward us. I remind myself, *You're going to be last.*

With a lift of her arm, Leader Candras points to Jane, a shy, freckled girl who is a skilled swimmer. "I Choose you," Leader Candras says, not using the youth name because "Jane" no longer exists.

Formerly Jane jumps excitedly. This is the Family she hoped for.

"Have you Chosen a Name?" Leader Candras asks the traditional question.

I hold my breath, waiting for Jane's answer. Watching the Celebraze unfold is stunning—not a lesson anymore but real life.

Jane shows no hesitation as she declares herself. "Hillari Candras." I know of Agnes Candras but all I recall of Hillari Candras is her death from falling from a high window.

Another tile is drawn.

I cross my fingers, hoping it's not Sanchez or Treveno, so my top choices are last. Like I will be.

But Leader Sanchez is next, and he Chooses Merry. Never one to wait until the last minute for studying, Merry is quick with her Choice: Vesper Sanchez.

The Sanchez Family sits in the front, so I'm able to watch Merry (oops, Vesper) being welcomed. A woman hugs her, tears streaming down her face as she ties a scarf around Vesper's head. A man offers Vesper a lily bouquet and another woman gifts Vesper with a wrapped box. Many arms reach to embrace Vesper. So much love and acceptance .... My heart tightens.

Only one Name remaining from Marcus' list.

I clench my hands into fists at my sides, relieved each time a name is called that isn't Treveno. Our line grows smaller as several more youths are led down the aisle to join their new Families.

When the Hu Family is called, I'm sure they'll select a boy since most of their Lost Ones had strenuous roles tending livestock. No surprise when Leader Hu points to Bob, who becomes Benjamin Hu. His welcome is boisterous, back-slapping with whoops of joy. A sparrow-like dark-haired woman embraces him so passionately I suspect she's his wife.

Next Charles becomes Kirk Dallows, and I'm sorry for him because I know he hoped to join the Hu Family. Polly becomes January Salazar. Asha is Noelle Burrecia. Simon is Tyler Jones. And Barbara is Chosen by the Hale Family, but she's too nervous to remember a Name, so her new Family Chooses for her: Alexandria Hale. I remember Alexandria's gruesome death—while practicing fencing, a sword pierced her heart.

Lorelei shines brighter than night stars when she's Chosen by the Ying Family. Her top choice! Graces good!

Only three youths remain.

I've dreaded this moment—standing at the end, knowing that the tiles are randomly drawn so I have no idea who will Choose me. But I am hopeful, because the Treveno Family hasn't Chosen yet. They may have preferred Hillari (Jane) or Charles (Kirk), but there are only Clark, Homer, and me. Clark, who is muscular and strong, hopes for the Cross Family, since many of their Lost Ones had roles in construction, and jokester Homer is suited for the dramatical Starr Family.

Homer *is* Chosen by the Starr Family. After Choosing his name, he twirls to the audience and gives a dramatical bow.

Two Families remaining …

Longingly, I watch Leader Treveno, who waits her turn on the stage, a wide-boned woman with laughing eyes. I could easily bond with her and become Hildy Treveno, lost to drowning seventy-three years ago. Leader Treveno holds a pink box, a gift for her Chosen youth. I imagine opening the pink box, finding jewelry or a hair frivel, and oohing with delight. "Although a gift isn't necessary," I'll say with appropriate humbleness. "Being Chosen by your Family is gift enough."

Please Choose me, I think. *Please!*

The next tile drawn is for the Cross Family. *So I will be last*, I think with a resigned sigh as I wait for Leader Cross to Choose muscular Clark.

Leader Cross, a tall, grim-faced, tawny-skinned man, steps forward, his hand raised with decision.

"I Choose her."

He points to me.

SEVEN

No, no, NO!

There has to be a mistake!

But Leader Cross clearly said "her," not "him," and he stands before me, tying the red scarf with the Cross Family insignia around my neck.

I have been claimed.

Shock-stunned, I'm unable to move. I want to run to Leader Treveno and beg her to Choose me. *I'll work hard and follow rules. I'll do whatever you ask with no arguments. I'll be a great fit into your Family.*

But Leader Cross looms before me like an impassable mountain.

"Have you Chosen a Name?" He asks the traditional question.

What can I say? I never even looked at the Cross Family Name Book. Everyone knows they only select boys to replace Lost Ones who had labor roles, like digging ditches or hefting crates. Me? A laborer? Crazy!

"Your Name?" Leader Cross prompts.

"Jennza," I say before realizing my error.

"Your Chosen Name," Leader Cross says sternly.

I can only shake my head.

Fifteen years led to this moment. Why didn't I spend fifteen extra minutes reading the Cross Name Book? I blink back tears. A Name is more than what I'll be called—it's my forever role in ShareHaven.

Grand Sarwald comes over beside Leader Cross, his expression less than kind as he regards me. "You don't have a Name prepared?"

"N-no." I suck in a breath of shame.

"Then as is customary, Leader Cross may Choose your Name."

I know, I think miserably. *Oh, I know ….*

So I become Milly Cross.

Mind-fogged, I follow Leader Cross off the stage. He's unsmiling. As we reach the rows assigned to the Cross Family, a woman with thickly coiled black braids at each side of her head opens her arms to me. She offers me a wrapped gift, then embraces me, smelling sweetly of fresh bread and flowers.

"Milly, oh my dear sister," she says, tears shining in her black eyes as if I'm a living miracle. "I can hardly wait till you remember everything. I've missed our talks so much … for so long."

Her affection should ease my disappointment, but I don't know this woman or any of the Cross Family. I'm not Milly. Not yet anyway.

The microphone booms loudly around the room. I look up to the stage where smiling, sweet-faced Leader Treveno joyfully declares, "I Choose you!"

Clark is Chosen last.

Once I take a seat in the audience with the Cross Family, the braided woman—Rosemarie one of the men calls her—urges me to open her gift. I unwrap a silver utility knife. It

54

unfolds into useful tools: pliers, a nail file, and tiny scissors. I almost smile because while Lorelei would have hated this, a tool suits me more than jewelry.

I speak the expected respectful phrases. My new Family has seven members present: five men and two women. The men acknowledge me with disinterested nods. Only Rosemarie hugs and offers words of welcome. Her overwhelming emotion, though, makes me uncomfortable, as if in that quick moment of Naming, I have become her Milly. I prefer the more honest hostility of the other woman who ignores me, her emotions hidden behind a curtain of black hair sweeping across one side of her face.

As white scarves burn in a ceremonial pot at the center of the stage and Grand Sarwald declares closing words, I stop worrying about my new life because this is the moment for good-byes and I have a bigger problem.

Petal.

I must return her to the sea. But will I get a chance? Once I enter the Cross compound, I'll be bound by their rules. I may never visit the sea again.

Rosemarie is reluctant to part with me, but I convince her to wait with the others outside the dorm building while I gather my belongings. I hurry ahead of the dense crowd, breaking into a run. I can only think of sweet Petal. Her skin will be dry and withery without seawater.

I take the path to the communal building where dorms are split, boys on the left and girls on the right. A familiar voice calls behind me and I glance over my shoulder. I groan—it's Lorelei, coming this way with her new Family. She gestures for me to wait. But I pretend not to see her and race to my dorm room.

A dark curl snags in my red noose-scarf, and I untangle it, then yank off the scarf. As I reach for a comb, I bump the dish of my sea treasures but catch it before it topples to the floor. Agates, sand-coins, coral spirals, and shining shells. My favorite star-shaped shell, tiny as my thumb, glimmers blue.

Blue like Nate's eyes.

Sighing, I tuck the sea-star shell into my tunic pocket.

After retying my scarf, I see myself in the hanging wall mirror where I've grown taller over the years. How different will it be to share a Family dwelling instead of a room with seven girls? I gaze around at identical wood-framed beds, cabinets, and dressers topped with personal items like brushes and hair decors. I've been happy here. But the Edu-Center is closing until the next group of youths, and I must bond with the Cross Family.

Or I could run away, right now, grab my belongings and hide in my cave with Petal. She's taught me to forage for edible sea scrubs, shell-slugs, and flowers. I could survive better in her world than she could in mine.

But I am fooling myself.

No one ever leaves ShareHaven.

I sneak out of the dorm through a back door, then keep to the shadows until I reach the storage room. Petal scurries over to me. Her tinkling greeting rumbles a purr as I gently stroke her leathery back. Her skin is flaky, and when she opens her mouth to lick my hand, her tongue is dry. The water bowl I left for her hasn't been touched.

"I'll take you to seawater," I promise, offering her my arm. Petal scrawls up to my neck, then burrows inside my thick hair, beneath the Cross Family scarf.

"Hold tight," I tell her, although it's not necessary because

56

even weak, she's skilled at hiding.

I move carefully to the door, turning the handle until I hear the click. I peer out, then gasp. Two purple-and-gold-clad figures stand a few meters from the door—blocking my escape.

Two scientists! The brother and sister, Daniel and Lila Farrow, both tall with proud faces lined with wisdom; Lila's silver hair contrasts against her brother's shining black head, yet their straight noses, strong chins, and slim lips are alike.

I draw back into hiding, my hand gripping the door so it stays open a sliver. They are so deep in conversation they don't notice me.

"—can't fool me," Daniel says in a smooth and pleasant voice which doesn't match the anger in his expression. "Give up this ridiculous interest in youths."

"Is it ridiculous to want to save lives?" she argues.

"My research proves there is no cause for alarm," he says calmly.

"And my research proves otherwise. Matters will only worsen unless we can find new resources." She gestures with her hands as she talks, and I'm awed by her shimmering fingernails, gold with purple tips, like flowers blooming.

"No!" His eyes narrow at her. "I agreed to attend today at your insistence, but I won't interfere in community affairs."

She shakes her head. "The community relies on us. We can't wait another twenty-five years to find what we need."

"Is this another attempt to prove your superiority over me? One miracle discovery wasn't enough for you?" His voice rolls low and smooth, as if he's complimenting instead of criticizing. Only his glare hints at his anger.

"I know we've had differences in the past, but this is

about our future—all of our futures. I need your support."

"You need nothing from me. Everyone knows how much more clever you are," he says coolly. "But I warn you, stay away from the youths—unless you're in the need of another droll."

Droll? I've never heard this word but it sends fear quivering through me.

"End this nonsense now, Lila," Scientist Daniel adds, turning from his sister. "I'll be in the solar-cart with the others, and if you don't join us soon, I'm sure you'll cleverly find a way back on your own." His footsteps smack sharply on the pavement as he strides down the corridor.

Scientist Lila stays so still I can't tell if she's breathing. She stares after her brother, then sighs, her expression so sorrowful my heart aches for her. Slowly, she walks in the opposite direction toward the dorms.

Making sure Petal is securely hidden, I hurry from the storage room to the path. Can I reach the Fence and return without being missed? Doubtful. But I try.

I run, pushing aside branches, breathing hard. I'm far enough now to see the glinting steel of the Fence. I run faster, muscles in my legs screaming for relief. A dip in the ground takes me by surprise, and I stumble. Grabbing hold of a boulder, I steady myself, then stop at the sound of a snapping branch. My pulse jumps. I dive behind a gnarled tree trunk. Peering through shadows, I see nothing, but I sense a living creature nearby, stalking. I shiver at the thought of claws, snakes, and primitive-human Nocturnes. I peer through thick bushes, all senses alert. A sweet roseberry blossom scent swirls in the air, and a flash of gold rustles in the bushes. Is someone—something—out there?

When a bird bursts from the bushes, I laugh at my fears and resume my hurried pace. I can clearly see the Fence now, glistening silver-gold in the setting sun. I slow to a stop, although my heart continues to pound fiercely like the waves crashing below the cliff.

"We're here," I tell Petal as I reach up so she can climb on my hand. "You'll be safe once you reach the sea."

She blinks up at me, making no move to jump off my hand.

"Go on, Petal."

She clings tighter. I sense her reluctance to leave me.

I shake her off my arm and she falls onto the soft dirt, landing gracefully on her four webbed feet. I point to the Fence. "There isn't time to take you to the cave. Squeeze under the wire and go down to the sea."

Petal curls her tail around herself, the way I sometimes wrap my arms around my shoulders. But she doesn't move.

"Don't be stubborn. I want to go with you, but I can't. Everything has changed. I'm going to change too, and I can't be with you anymore." My voice chokes. "Please, don't make this even harder."

I carry her to the Fence, the sound of lapping waves a bittersweet song.

"Go and don't come back." I speak harsher so she knows I'm serious.

She crawls closer to me, away from the Fence.

"No. You must crawl through the wire."

She shakes her leathery head. How can I convince her to leave? If the Instructors or my new Family realize I'm missing, an alarm will bring a search team and Uniforms with sniffer hounds. There is no hiding from the sniffers.

"Go away!" I shout at her in my fiercest tone. "Now!"

Her silky pink tongue curls from her mouth, like when she lick-kisses me. She paws my leg, poised to jump into my arms. But if I hold her again, I won't have the courage to let her go. l must be strong for both of us.

"Petal, go to the cave! I don't want you here! Get away from me!"

Her eyes shine liquid hurt, but she doesn't move.

I gulp in sea-tasting air then do something I'll never forget or forgive. Reaching down to the ground, I pick up a rock. It's heavy in my palm. Sharp-edges stab my skin. I pull back my arm and—

"Don't!" someone shouts.

The rock drops from my fingers. I whip around, not seeing anyone until I peer beyond the Fence. A figure steps out from behind a boulder.

My gasp startles Petal, who winds her leathery body around my ankle. I hardly notice her, staring at Nate, stunned by how goodly he looks without the bulky tube costume. I thought he'd left hours ago. Why is he here?

His hair, shining black like wet sea pebbles, is pulled back into a long rope that trails over his shoulder. But his skin is a sharp contrast, pale as winter clouds, as if he is from a world of water and rarely touched by the sun. There are scars—jagged slashes near his mouth and above his left brow, and deeper, redder marks on his hands. His eyes—oh, those amazing eyes—pull me into a gaze bluer than the sea behind him.

He frowns at me. "Were you going to throw that rock?"

"I—I wasn't …. I would never …." I hang my head, ashamed at what I almost did. "I didn't plan to hit Petal, only scare her away."

"I believe you," he says softly. "You were very gentle with her in the cave. Yet you want her to leave you. Why?"

"I love her." My voice breaks, and I hate how close I am to tears. When I caress Petal's bristly skin, dry flakes fall away. "She's withering."

"Sea creatures belong in the sea," he says with a nod of understanding.

"Right. But I don't have time to take her to the cave, and she refuses to leave me. She … she knows I won't be coming back."

He tilts his head, his black rope hair swaying. "You're going away?"

"To my Family. Today was the Celebraze."

"What's a Celebraze?"

"You don't know?" I stare at his odd clothing—black pantons of rough fabric, stained and worn at the knees. His snug shirt misses top buttons, revealing a curl of chest hair.

"There are many things I don't know," he admits. "But I'm eager to learn and to help. I'll take your Petal back to the cave."

"You will?" I almost sink to the ground, relieved.

"I'm already on this side of the Fence—unlike you. Also, I know the way into the cave." His scar creases into the curve of his smile. "Hand her to me."

We kneel at our separate sides of the Fence, worlds of wire apart.

Nate holds out his arms. "She's small enough to squeeze under the wire."

"Go with him," I whisper to Petal.

She tries to escape my grasp. "Petal, don't fight. Please,

you need the sea." I kiss her whiskery face. "Go now."

Petal lick-kisses my cheek, then looks curiously at Nate. He reaches beneath the fence. I see chipped nails, his up-turned palms callused and strong. Our fingertips brush as I pass Petal to him, heat shooting through me. My heart rushes like strong winds, blowing me somewhere I've never been.

Petal curls into Nate's arms, and I wonder if they've met before. How long has Nate been coming to my cave? I want to know so much more, like where he lives and what his people are like. I thought he came from a sea society, but without his bulky tubes, he looks so … well … normal.

The sinking sun reminds me I'm running out of time, so I speak quickly. "I won't be able to come back to the cave. Will you visit her?"

"I promise," he says, clasping a hand over his heart. "I wish you weren't leaving. You're the most interesting girl I've ever met."

"You must not have met many girls." My cheeks heat like a sunburn.

"Oh, I know many—but no one like you. If things were different I'd take you to my …." He stops abruptly, frowning.

"Your what?"

"Nowhere. You have your side of the Fence and I … I can't ever be like you." His eyes shine blue sadness. "I hate good-byes."

"I hate them too," I say softly.

Abruptly, he turns from the Fence with Petal. With agile moves, he climbs down the trail to the sea. I watch until the tangled brush swallows him.

For the second time today, Nate is gone.

And I still know nothing about him.

EIGHT

It's not cold outside, but I'm shaking. Wrapping my arms around my shoulders, I leave the Fence.

My heart is heavy stone, yet I must hide my emotions. I slow at the sound of voices. Families gather in groups outside the dorms, talking.

Ducking into the bathroom, I splash water on my face and pluck off orange-red leaves from my tunic. These sticky leaves only grow on the trees near the sea—which could lead to dangerous questions.

In my dorm room, I hurriedly finish packing, since the Cross Family will expect me to join them with my belongings. I yank open drawers and toss clothes, shoes, and everything else into a leather bag. I wrap my sea treasures in clothing, careful with each precious shell, coral, and polished rock. Grabbing the bags, I hurry to find my Family.

My Family. I still can't wrap my thoughts around my new role. Milly Cross. Once I have Milly's memories, the name will seem familiar. If I had more time, I'd go to the learning room and read the Cross Name Book. I know the braided woman is Milly's sister, Rosemarie, but I don't know if Milly has a spouse or children. I don't even know how she died.

"Where have you been?" When I turn, there's Marcus. He's carrying two bulging bags, heavy with all his notebooks and nature collections. There's a dirty smudge on his chin that makes me think of our mud battles and frog races. This is the last we'll be together as Jennza and Marcus.

"I was in the girls' dorm," I tell him.

"Not twenty minutes ago."

"You know better than to go into the girls' room." I muster up outrage to stop his questions. "That's completely forbidden."

He snorts. "As if you never do anything forbidden? You went back there, didn't you?"

"I don't know what you mean." I press my lips tightly. "I wasn't feeling well and have been in the privacy room vomiting."

"Oh, Jennza." He hangs his head. "I never thought the Cross Family would Choose you. I was sure they'd want a boy. I am so sorry. If I'd researched them, at least you would have been ready for a better Name."

"It's not your fault," I touch his hand reassuringly. "Besides, I will do well with the Cross Family. I have a sister, Rosemarie, who is very sweet. She even gave me a gift. Don't worry about me. Enjoy your joy at becoming a Sarwald."

"I am," he says with a sudden smile. "I expected work with gardens and orchards, but I just found out my mem-denity will bring knowledge of pollination techniques. The first Neil was an apiarist—a honey keeper."

"That's great." I try not to sound envious.

"I'm sorry you didn't get the Family you expected, but the Cross Family dwells near the Sarwalds, so we should be able to meet often."

"Still, why did they Choose me instead of a boy? I don't understand it."

"You're not large or muscled, but you're tough. When

you tackle a project, you never give up."

"Never," I say, forcing a grin.

"Remember when we raced and you stumbled in a hole and sprained your ankle? You were in last place but even when the winner was announced, you didn't quit until you crossed the finish line." He gazes at me with something like admiration. He's different tonight—more confident and full of purpose, as if his new identity has matured him, while I'd rather stay a youth and play games with my best mates.

But I know Marcus cares about me, which means a lot. "I'll be okay," I tell him again, perhaps more to reassure myself. "Thank you for everything, Marcus."

"Neil," he corrects.

But to me he'll always be Marcus.

We don't talk any more as we leave the dorms of our youth to join our Families. The Sarwalds, a large group of ruddy, tanned men and women, surround Marcus with back-slapping and rowdy voices. His bags are snatched by Grand Sarwald, who pats Marcus on the shoulder. "I'll carry them for you, Neil."

Beyond them, I see the Cross Family—the men standing with arms folded as if bored and Rosemarie peering around anxiously, clearly looking for me. I don't see the unfriendly woman.

"There you are," a soft, lyrical voice calls behind me.

I stop, stunned, recognizing that voice. When I turn, I'm facing Scientist Lila, dazzling in purple and gold, her silver hair shining too bright for an ordinary human. But then a scientist is far from ordinary.

"Me?" I gasp, dizzy to be so close to a real scientist.

"I'm so glad to meet you, Jennza," Scientist Lila says

warmly. "No one knew where you were, and we nearly called the Uniforms to search for you."

"I was packing," I say quickly.

"Of course you were." Her gaze captures mine with humor I don't understand. "This is an exciting day for you, and I'm sure you're eager to join your new Family. But I've spoken to them and gained permission to talk with you privately."

Graces good! Am I hearing right? Why would a scientist want to talk to me? I have never heard of anything so awe-making ever happening to a youth.

My hands tremble, so I clasp them together. "Have I done something wrong?"

"My stars, no." Her laugh is music, and I'm drawn closer, wanting to touch the silky fabric of her tunic. "Will you walk with me?"

I nod, even more confused when I remember her brother warning her to stay away from youths. Yet here she is with me.

"Jennza," the scientist says once we have turned a corner of the dorm building where no one else in near. "We don't have much time, and there's something of importance I need to ask you."

My head spins. What does a scientist—*a scientist!*—want from me? The only thing I am sure of is that it can't be good.

She's staring at me with an intense gaze, one hand lightly on my shoulder. "I need you to be honest with me," she says solemnly.

"I never lie," I say automatically.

"Never?" she challenges.

I glance away. "Well … not without a good reason."

"Now that's an honest answer I can respect." She chuckles. "Some lies are necessary, but knowing when to be truthful is necessary too."

"Has someone been talking ... about me?" What has she heard? That I have poor study habits and lose my temper? (Homer deserved a bloody nose for releasing Marcus' earwigs collection into the girls' dorm).

"It's nothing like that." Lila flicks her purple-gold fingernails, flashing a sapphire ring that dazzles as brilliant as stars. "I'm concerned about your future."

"You are?" My mouth drops open.

"The reasons you were Chosen trouble me."

I bite my lip. "I don't understand."

"You weren't Chosen because of your skills but because of your lack of them. They have always selected boys, so usually only the boys are prepared with a Cross name. Not the girls," she says angrily. "You had no real Choice. Leader Cross was swayed by his cousin Rosemarie who still grieves for her sister. They want to replace Milly."

"Rosemarie is kind," I say, well aware I'm talking to one of the most powerful people in ShareHaven. "I'll do my best to be a good sister."

Lila touches my cheek softly. "You don't belong with the Cross Family."

I stare at her, relief rushing through my veins. It's a mistake! I won't have to go with the Cross Family. I was tricked, and a powerful scientist is on my side .... But why is she interested in me? She seems sincere, but her brother's words push down my hope. *Stay away from the youths.* What was he warning her about? Could speaking to her be dangerous?

I twist the edge of my red scarf. "The Crosses are my

Family now."

"Is this really what you want? To perform mundane duties rather than stretch your mind and discover your true potential?" She draws closer to me, and I'm drowning in perfume and uncertainty. "Do you want to bond with the Cross Family?"

"If I answer truthfully, I'll dishonor my Family."

"I will tell no one how you answer," she assures.

"Why are you interested in me?" I finally ask what's troubling me most. "You're a scientist."

"Scientists care deeply about youths. Did you know there were only two youths born in the first group?"

"Why so few?" I ask.

"Scientists were in charge of youth creation in the early stages, and we only had limited resources. This was decades after the Attack, over two centuries ago, which may seem like a long time when you're only age fifteen, but my memory stretches far." Her gaze drifts across paths and buildings, as if winding into the past. "I had expected people to be content once they ceased aging and no longer feared wrinkles or death. Yet once they realized a side effect of immortality was infertility, there was a rush to get pregnant for those still under twenty-five. The sudden population increase drained our resources."

"You mean people in ShareHaven gave birth the retro way?" I say, wide-eyed. Instructors had never told us this.

"Oh, yes, it was quite archaic," she says with a chuckle. "After much trial and error, we calculated that fifteen youths every twenty-five years creates harmony among Families and restores an adequate number of Lost Ones."

While this is interesting, I still have no idea why she's

talking to me.

"Sorry for rambling on," she says with an apologetic smile. "You must be wondering why I've singled you out from the other youths."

"Well ... yeah," I admit.

"After speaking to your Instructors, I know you have unique talents."

Being the worst student ever is not a talent, I think guiltily.

"You enjoy walking, often early in the morn, which is an activity I find invigorating too," she goes on. "My compound borders the cliff, so I take walks at the edge of land and sea. Where do you usually walk?"

Is this a trick question? So I'll admit I regularly break rules?

"On marked trails," I answer carefully, bending the truth.

"Those trails only circle around buildings." She spreads her arms wide. "If I lived here I would want to explore wilder places by the sea."

"That would be against the rules."

"But I would go anyway," she says, leading me away from the building to a dirt path winding into thorny berry bushes. "Scientists make their own trails."

I am unsure what to say, confusion rising. What does she want from me?

Scientist Lila stops at a berry bush, its shiny, red-gold leaves hiding prickly thorns. She reaches into a berry bush and plucks a juicy red berry.

"No!" I shout, rushing to her side. "Don't eat that!"

"Why not? It looks ripe and delicious." She lifts it to her mouth.

I slap the berry from her hand. "It's poisonous!"

She raises her brows, not alarmed as I had expected but smiling. "How do you know about puha berries?"

"The leaves are distinct." I point to the reddish leaves, the only way of telling the safe berries from the poisonous ones. There's an antidote, but if not taken soon enough, paralysis could linger for a week. I made this error once, and now won't even eat the safe green-leaf berries.

"Thank you for the warning." Scientist Lila twirls the red berry between her fingers. Her nails shine unnaturally with square tips. "Nature taunts mere humans, packaging the puha berry so it appears as safe as a verberry. But the puha berry is more interesting. If you crush it into a powder, it can heal infection." She tosses the red berry aside, then bends over a clump of wild grass, plucking a scruffy green weed. "Did you know common weeds can be used for medicines?"

"Yes," I say remembering the scarifying day I found Petal almost dead in my cave, moaning and barely able to move. I didn't know how to help her, but after a while, she crawled to the edge of the pond and nibbled on lavender sea grass. Within minutes she spit up, healing herself.

"Did the Instructors teach you this?"

I shake my head. "I learned from watching animals."

Lila's smile softens the lines in her face. "I knew we were alike, noticing small things that others overlook and stretching boundaries. Do you agree?"

"Uh ... it's possible. I guess."

"A good answer. Stay open to possibilities. Questions begin every scientific discovery. It takes a special person to answer the call of science."

If she's hinting at what I suspect—more than I ever

dreamed—I can escape the Crosses and live at the scientists' compound. No one will call me "Milly."

She grasps my hands, and I can't look away from her. Her flowery perfume mingles with my dizzy thoughts, making it impossible to think. "Your curiosity and resourcefulness would be wasted on menial jobs," she says. "I'll only ask you once more: Do you want to live with the Cross Family?"

Absolutely not, I think. But the scientists' compound is so isolated, its mystery and secrets separate from ShareHaven. Only Grand Sarwald knows how to journey there. Would I be trapped there in a cage of secrecy? Never seeing Marcus or Lorelei again?

Still, it would be thrilling to learn science and create miracle discoveries. And once I'm a scientist, I can make my own rules. I'd find a way to see my friends. A wondrous future is within my reach. I only need to say yes.

I breathe in hopes and dreams and Lila's flowery perfume. My gaze sweeps down from her silvery hair to the dirt-stained hem of her shimmering purple robe. I jerk away, clasping my hands to my chest.

And I say no.

Scientist Lila Farrow's expression reveals no emotion. My answer must shock her, yet she doesn't question me. Twining her fingers together to form a hand temple, her gaze props me under a microscope and dissects my thoughts.

"Thank you," she says simply. "I wish you much joy in your new life, Milly."

She turns away, a swirl of silver and purple with a fragrance of orange blossoms. An orange-red leaf sticks to her shoe. A leaf only found near the sea cliffs. I smelled her flowery scent when I returned Petal to the sea—after glimpsing golden movement in the bushes.

Scientist Lila was in the bushes.

Spying on me.

NINE

Leader Cross drives the solar coach with the confidence of someone used to being in charge. A stout man with a shaggy brown beard sits beside him. The hostile woman whose hair half hides her face has taken a back bench, avoiding contact with me. I sit beside Rosemarie, across from the three men who have similar sand-brown hair and stubby noses.

"My sons." Rosemarie introduces them proudly. "Tyler, Tomas, and Titas."

The men smile, then talk among themselves about repairing a windmill. Rosemarie joins in, and I don't understand much of what they're saying. I turn away from them, pressing my face against the cool glass window. It's a dark night; heavy fog billows in from the sea, reminding me of what I'm leaving. No more mornings wading in the sea or swimming in my cave with Petal. And if Nate returns to the cave, I'll never know.

Conversation drizzles around me like mist, touching the air but not reaching my thoughts. I wonder again about Lila. How much did she see when she followed me? Nate? Probably not, or she would have alerted the Uniforms. But she surely heard me shout at Petal. I cringe, replaying the heaviness of the rock in my hand and the hurt in Petal's liquid eyes. Lila must think I'm cruel. Yet when she spoke to me, she said nothing of following me. Instead she asked if I was happy with my Chosen Family. But when she returned me to my Family, not even Rosemarie asked any questions. They obviously care little for me. Why is Lila, an important scientist, so interested?

My Family is polite but distant, as if Choosing a youth is of no importance. Shouldn't they want to know more about me? Or do they only see me as a vessel to bring back Milly's memories? Who I am should matter too.

As if Rosemarie Cross knows my thoughts, she slips an arm around my shoulders. "I'm so happy you're here."

I sense she hopes I'll say I'm happy to be with her too. But I say nothing.

"We'll share kitchen duties as before," she goes on, not looking at me but at our blurred reflections in the window. "I thought you'd be more comfortable staying with me until after your memdenity, so I readied my room."

"You planned to Choose a girl?" I ask, remembering my conversation with Lila. "Usually boys become laborers."

"We took a boy last time," she says with a shrug.

I glance over at her sons, wondering if one of them is a replacement like me. But I decide it must have been a different man since these men share their mother's rounded cheekbones, olive complexion, and rich, shiny black hair.

"I've rearranged the furniture and brought in a bed for you," she goes on cheerfully. "It's been quite a house-craft, clearing out cupboards and the closet."

"You're very kind," I say.

"Selfish, more likely. I don't want to share you yet." She giggles, which makes her seem closer to my age of fifteen, although she looks twenty-five and has experienced two, maybe three centuries of life.

"I want you to feel comfortable," she goes on. "I know you won't remember much until the memdenity, but I hoped you might enjoy some of the same things as Milly. I hung her favorite painting on the wall over your bed—a lovely scene of a summer garden your—I mean, her—daughter Daisy painted."

So I have a daughter. Not unexpected, but I shift uneasily on the hard wood solar cart bench. What will it be like to meet Milly's womb-born child? An adult now, of course, so she'll appear ten years older than me.

I really, really wish I'd studied the Cross Name book.

Tall poles with glow-lights brighten the dark roads, and other lights shine too, from buildings in the distance. I press close to the window, squinting at white streaks of fences that stretch over the rolling hills where the Hu Family dwells. I visited the ranch once on a lesson trip, and a tall man wearing a wide-brimmed hat explained the importance of fencing in livestock.

The terrain changes, flat as flapcakes, then rising into ghost-pale domes like giant bubbles. Distant lights shine like land-trapped stars, and I realize these multi-dwellings must belong to the Sarwald Family. The domed climate-controlled buildings contain acres of vegetation, our prime food supply. And it's where Marcus is. I already miss him and Lorelei, but I am glad they got the Families they wanted. I won't be able to see them often, and when I do, I'll have to call them Neil and Flavia.

The glass is cool against my cheek. Fields and orchards pass by as my thoughts travel to my new Family. Aside from kitchen duty, what chores will be expected of me? I have no labor skills, although I am quick with my hands and a good climber. My stomach knots as I imagine being ordered to lift crates and other muscle-aching chores. Doing what I'm told: not my best skill. And I dread the memdenity. My head is already too full of thoughts. Why can't I make my own memories like retro-century people? Sure, their uncontrolled societies caused war, disease, and death, but at least no one had strange memories crammed into their brains.

Of course when ShareHaven was first created, no one lived forever either. The development of memdenities strengthened our society, preserving memory knowledge like ripe fruit canned in jars for future usage. My lessons come back now, and I can almost hear Instructor Heath's deep voice explaining how ShareHaven began as something called a "think tank" for scientists. Dozens of scientists were brought to this island to work in isolation on medical research. When the mind-plague struck and people all around the world were stricken with an airborne memory-wiping disease, most scientists left ShareHaven. The scientists who remained brought their families. Outside ShareHaven, civilization crumbled as fear and death spread. A false rumor that our scientists had a mind-plague vaccine led to the Attack: a violent, desperate mob, armed with guns and explosives, stormed ShareHaven. Buildings, research, and lives were destroyed.

Survivors put up the Fence to protect us. And when the scientists developed the cease-aging patch, they gave us immortality.

Living forever could grow boring with a dull Family. I think of the solemn way Scientist Lila stared at me, as if seeing inside my thoughts when she asked, "Do you want to live with the Cross Family?" I was going to accept until I realized she'd spied on me and couldn't be trusted. I wonder what would have happened if I'd answered yes. Instead of heading for the Cross Family multi-dwelling, would I be on a different road?

"Aren't you eager to see your home?" Rosemarie nudges my arm, so I turn from the window toward her.

"I, um, guess." I want to remind her I don't have Milly's memories yet, so "home" is only a word I've been taught at the Edu-Center.

"We're almost there. I have so much to show you! We've made many improvements since you ... well, since Milly was there. Milly hated being so close to my sons' room because Tyler's snoring is worse than a claw's roar. But the boys have their own dwelling now."

She says "boys" as if they're youths, but they're clearly age twenty-fives like their mother.

"You, Arthur, and I have rooms on the top floor," she continues. "But Arthur has temporarily moved in with my boys."

"Arthur?"

"He wanted to greet you today but had to oversee a constructing project. He was sorry to miss your Celebraze." Rosemarie speaks with such affection that I guess Arthur is her husband.

The solar coach turns into a lighted entrance with an archway sign announcing "Cross" in large flowy letters. The road is bumpy, rougher than the paved road we left. We pass dark-wood square dwellings with corralled livestock, barns, and gardens. Rattling, rumbling, and an occasional bump lead us farther down the road until we curve and rise toward red-trimmed wood buildings: not one dwelling, but three squeezed together.

The solar coach jerks to a stop, and a spotted, short-haired dog chases over to us, tail wagging.

"Felix, you sweet boy!" Rosemarie says, scratching the dog's head.

I reach out to pet Felix, but he sniffs at me and growls, baring his teeth.

"You're not fooled by her, are you?" the unfriendly woman says with wicked delight, kneeling beside the dog.

A dog lover, but a Jennza hater (or is it Milly she hates?), the dark-haired woman ignores me as she hurries up a stone trail and into the house, with Felix scampering after her.

"Guess I'm not her favorite person." I say wryly.

"She needs time to adjust," Rosemarie says apologetically. "This is all confusing for Daisy."

"Daisy? You mean ... Milly's—*my* daughter?"

"I thought you knew."

No, I did not. But I'd rather die than become her mother. Just strike me down now with all Three Dangers.

I sense someone coming up behind me and turn to find Leader Cross, so I give him the customary head-tuck of respect.

"We're gratified to have you with us, Milly," he says with a smile that doesn't touch his eyes.

My new name feels wrong. "I'm honored to be with your Family."

"Your Family now," he says. "Come inside where we can sit down and introduce ourselves properly. Do you play chess?"

I shake my head. "I tried once with a friend, but I wasn't very skilled."

"Pity." He shrugs. "Still, you will find my collection

of chess sets fascinating. My oldest dates back to 1820, Chinese-carved, a rare ox bone chess set. Chess is a strategic game like a civilized war, placing men in the line of fire and never underestimating your opponent."

There's a gleam in his gaze that makes me hope I never become his opponent. Smiling politely, I follow him up steep wooden steps into a house with ceilings twice as tall as Leader Cross. Walls are painted white and decored with stunning, realistic retro photos. One photo shows Leader Cross, standing tall and proud in a blue uniform with military patches. There were only a few photos on display in the Edu-Center. I read in a lesson book that a chemical for photo processing isn't on our island. But this is no loss since faces never change after age twenty-five.

As I go down a hall, I stare at sculptures of machinery and tools. On one wall is a quilt made of work gloves. The furniture is heavy, dark wood. When we enter a dining room, there's an elegant oval table with fourteen chairs. Leader Cross pulls out a chair for me, then sits at the head of the table. Others take positions around the table too—except my hostile daughter. Glances shift toward a closed door, and I realize they're waiting for someone. I hope not for Daisy.

When the door opens, a woman hobbles in on a cane. She's wrinkled, with dark bruising spots on her blue-veined skin, and her back is humped.

"Grandmother," Leader Cross says in a gentle, respectful tone, "allow me to help you into your chair."

She snorts, slapping his hand. "I don't need help." She hobbles to a chair, leaning one gnarled hand against a handrail, before sinking down into a chair so only her shoulders and head are visible.

A real living elder person! Not merely over twenty-five like Grand Sarwald but body withered and bent with a vast age. To see one up so close and hear her speak, well, it's amazing. I can't take my gaze from her. Blue veins rise on her hands like swells in a rough sea, and dark spots dimple her face, arms, and hands. I can hardly believe she moves and speaks like a normal person.

"I'd like you to meet our new Family member, Milly," Leader Cross says with a gesture toward me. "Milly, this is my grandmother, Ida Mae."

The old woman squints at me. "That's not Milly," she says, scowling.

Leader Cross shares a tired "do we have to go through this again?" look with the others around the table. "Gram, I've explained this to you."

"You don't need to explain anything. My eyes may not be what they used to be, but I can see clear as daylight that this scrawny child isn't my Milly."

"You will call her Milly," he says forcefully.

"I'll call her mud if I've a mind to, and I won't be bullied by a snit like you."

"I apologize for this rudeness, Milly. Forgive her poor manners. She forgets to take her medis and becomes unsensical." He turns back to the old woman. "Gram, we'll talk about this later."

"Talk all you want," the old woman says with a sly grin. "If you say something interesting, maybe I'll listen."

I cover my mouth so I don't laugh. Gram is one opponent Leader Cross should never underestimate.

Rosemarie enters the room, balancing a tray with steaming cups of cinnamon apple cider followed by a blond woman who carries a basket of warmed scones. I have no idea I'm hungry until my stomach rumbles. When I bite into a scone, buttery sweetness melts into my mouth.

Rosemarie sits beside a man with a red mustache, calling him Arthur. *Her husband,* I think. She glances at him, smiling, but she doesn't touch him intimately like "soul mates" Greta and Monroe.

No one talks for a while, and the only sound is soft chewing, until Leader Cross taps his fork against his coffee cup.

"As is customary," he says with a gesture to me, "we gathered here to welcome Milly back into our Family."

"I am honored," I say politely.

He glances down at his silverware, frowns, then rearranges the spoon and knife so they are positioned side by side opposite of the fork. He looks up at me with an assessing gaze, as if trying to gauge my position too. "Your records show a lack of preparation and low marks. Still, you seem bright enough. What do you know of Milly's history?"

All eyes fall on me. "Um ... not much. But I can learn."

"Certainly you will," he says. "Our Family is respected for our strenuous work. We repair community roads, machinery, roofs, and pipes, and we maintain the Fence and the Gate. We rise early and work till dark."

I nod, pressing my lips tight to hide my anxiety. I look at the men, their deep tans and rugged hands. The fair-haired man with a reddish mustache is especially muscled and nice-looking, with a dimpled chin and pleasing smile. Even the dark-haired woman beside Leader Cross has strong hands and broad shoulders. Only Rosemarie has softness to her slim figure and smooth skin.

"Rosemarie will explain your role," Leader Cross goes on. "Your duties will be split between communal and home. Communal duties aren't scheduled until your trial period ends, but you'll begin house-crafting duties tomorrow."

"Milly was highly skilled in cookery," the red-mustached man says.

"My sister could whip up fabulous recipes of her own invention," Rosemarie adds with a wistful glance at me. "I've tried to recreate some, but it's not the same."

I have zero cookery skills. I was barred from the kitchen after the cinnamon cookie incident. I had no idea stove fires spread so quickly.

Rosemarie reaches for one of my hands. "I've been carrying a heavy load since you … well, since I've had to take care of duties alone. It will be wondrous to share duties with you."

"She won't be any help until after completion of all three memdenities." Leader Cross snaps a scone in half and plops it in his mouth.

"I'll teach her," Rosemarie offers.

"Still, it's inefficient to wait a month for the first memdenity." Leader Cross taps his fingers on the table. "I'll consult the health-keepers and request them to schedule an appointment soon."

"I don't mind waiting," I say quickly.

"Memdenity is painless," Rosemarie tells me. "There are only minor side effects with the first insertion. Did your Instructors explain what will happen?"

I nod. I had listened to that lesson without staring out the window even once, dreading my future, yet also fascinated.

Memdenity is a simple process: a device is inserted into the brain to transfer memories of a Lost One. The first insert contains memories to age fifteen. Next is fifteen to twenty-five. Third is the most important, from age twenty-five to death.

Knowing what will happen should make things easier—but not much.

Rosemarie squeezes my hand. "Once you have memdenity, you'll be as talented as Milly."

"Still, I need time to … well, to get to know everyone. I don't want to hurry the memdenity."

Leader Sarwald frowns. "Your opinion was not asked."

"I was just pointing out—"

"I make the decisions here!" Leader Cross smacks the table, silverware clattering. "Milly would never argue with her Leader's decision. Didn't your Edu-Center teach you respect for Leaders?"

"Yes, but I thought—"

"You're here to serve your Family. Arthur will need to use a firm hand with you," Leader Cross says, gesturing to the mustached man.

"Relax, Ryan," Arthur says with a dimpling smile. "If Milly wants to wait, that's fine with me."

"Then I won't interfere." Leader Cross pats Arthur on the shoulder. "But say the word, and I'll schedule her first appointment."

Arthur twists the end of his red mustache, turning to me with an expression of longing. He's pleasing in appearance and manner, and I'm warmed by his attention. I've never had a twenty-five-age boy … man … show interest in me, as if I'm no longer a youth.

"Arthur there will be time for *that* later," Rosemarie says sharply, then turns to me. "Come along, Milly. I can see you're tired. I'll show you our room."

"Thank you," I say, suddenly aware of overwhelming fatigue.

I start to leave, but Arthur comes around the table, standing close to me. "Milly dear, before you go," he says seriously. "I have something for you."

"For me?" I ask, surprised. "But Rosemarie has already gifted me."

"This isn't a gift. It's already yours." His voice thickens with emotion. "I've waited long to return this to its rightful place."

Arthur grasps my left hand and slips a diamond and gold ring on my finger. A wedding band.

Arthur isn't Rosemarie's husband.

He's mine.

TEN

Staring at the ring steals my breath. So small, yet a heavy anchor dragging me somewhere I'm not ready to go. If only I'd been chosen by the Treveno Family where I'd have no marriage partnership.

"It's too big." Arthur sighs as he slips the ring off my finger, then tucks it into his pocket. His gaze sweeps over me with disappointment before he turns away.

Rosemarie, who has been tapping her foot impatiently, tugs on my hand and leads me out of the room, then up a stairway and through a maze of halls. I fix each turn in my memory. *In case of a quick escape*, I think, until I remember there's no escape. This is my new life. I will never see my cave again.

The second floor has so many similar doors I'll need a compass to find my way out. "I'll show you where you and Arthur will stay afterward," Rosemarie says, and I know "afterward" means after the memdenity.

She leads me to the second floor, passing through a narrow living room with a rectangular table, four chairs, and a bookshelf.

"Did Milly … I mean, I, like to read?" I ask, gesturing to the books.

"Cookbooks, although she rarely followed other people's recipes. She stirred up her own delicious creations."

"I don't know much about cooking."

"You will," Rosemarie assures.

I'll know much more, I think, with an uneasy glance at my ringless finger. What does being married actually mean?

Rosemarie stops before a door. "This is the room you and Arthur shared. But he moved in with my boys after you … after Milly left."

"How long ago?"

"Seventy-three years and four months." She clutches the door knob as she stares beyond me. "She fell from a ladder, striking her head on the stove. To lose her after we'd survived so much together made me wish I'd died too." Rosemarie looks directly into my face. "But you're bringing her back."

Her words squirm like crawlies in my gut. I want to argue that I'll only restore Milly's memories, not bring back the dead. Or does memdenity come with more than knowledge? Soul? It doesn't seem possible, but centuries ago no one believed immortality was possible either.

Rosemarie invites me into a spacious room with bone-white walls, two dressers side by side, plush brown chairs, a wardrobe closet, and retro-century cooking utensils fixed on the walls. Another wall has a gold-framed painting of a bride and a groom on a gilded platform beneath a shining white cross. The man is Arthur, looking exactly as he did today, and the woman, full-figured with olive skin and almond-shaped black eyes, must be Milly.

"Milly's wedding was beauteous." Rosemarie sighs as she gestures to the portrait. "Arthur made her so happy—he's a wonderful man, and you will find it easy to love him. I know he's thrilled you have joined our Family."

I'm less than thrilled. But how will I feel about this after the memdenity? Having layers of new memories—moments of joy, sadness, loss, and love—will change how I view myself and everyone around me.

Does that mean I'll love Arthur as a wife? When he stared at me, it was as if he was seeing through coverings and memories to the curvy body of the woman he loved.

My husband. The marriage contract will legally bind me to Arthur. My Instructors didn't explain what the contract included, but I'm not *that* innocent. I've taken my cycle pills since age twelve and, like all girls, when I reach age sixteen, I'll have the sterilization procedure. By then I'll have all three memdenity insertions and share nights with Arthur. I can't imagine it—and don't want to.

To shift my thoughts, I point to a jewelry box on a dresser. "Was this Milly's?"

"It's yours," she says with that questioning lift of her dark brow, as if she's surprised I'm asking permission.

I lift the curved lid to find pools of silver and gold necklaces, a ring with a stone so red I wonder if it's a ruby, and glittery bracelets with dangling charms. There's a tiny sandshell too, which makes me think of the sea—and of Petal. I'd give anything to be with her now, playing in the Lavender Pool and cradling her sweet body to my heart.

"Take whatever you want." Rosemarie's voice jerks me away from my cave and back to this bedroom. "The ruby ring will be too big, but you can wear a bracelet or necklace."

I shake my head. "They belong to Milly."

"But you're Milly." She smiles, then walks back to the door. "I can't wait for you to see how I've fancied our room."

"I'm coming," I say with a resigned shrug.

When I shut the jewelry box, my red scarf catches on an edge of the lid. As I untangle it, the jewelry box tips over and starts to fall. I grab quickly to right the box, but a gold necklace slips out from underneath the box and lands on the floor.

I pick up the necklace, admiring the four-point golden star dangling from a chain of fine gold. At the center, grooves spread out to repeat the four-star pattern, reminding me of the lines inside a shell. *A shell star*, I think as I slip it into my tunic pocket, then hurry to catch up with Rosemarie.

The top floor has low peaked ceilings, narrow halls, and so many windows, as if night is watching our every move. Rosmarie leads me past a combined kitchen-dining area and doors that she explains lead to closets, a pantry, and privacy rooms. Moving on, she opens a door and announces, "This is our room."

It's decorated in greens, yellows, and browns, with spacious windows, as if an outside garden has been invited inside. There's a desk, dressers, a tall mirror, and two comfortable-looking beds with bright pillows and handcrafted quilts.

Rosemarie gestures to the quilt on the bed she's prepared for me. "This is the first quilt Milly and I crafted together. We stayed up long nights cutting pieces. She stitched them so perfectly that Arthur thought we'd used a machine. He can be so serious, sometimes, and easy to tease," she adds with a chuckle.

"Lorelei would love to see this." I run my finger over the quilt's precise stitches. "She is more skilled at sewing than I'll ever be."

"You'll be surprised how well you can sew." Rosemarie tilts her head at me. "Who's Lorelei?"

"My born-mate. Only her name isn't Lorelei anymore. She's Flavia now."

"Oh, the Ying Family's youth. We considered her too." Rosemarie touches her chin thoughtfully. "But Ryan— Leader Cross—wanted you."

"He did?" I can't imagine anyone wanting me over Lorelei (impossible to think of her as Flavia). Lorelei even resembles Milly—if you add ten years and shorter hair. Of course, Lorelei had already been Chosen.

There's a tap on the door, and Rosemarie jumps up to answer with a big grin on her face. "He's here to see you," she says.

"Who?"

"Jarod." Her grin widens at the stocky guy with short black hair and wide lips against olive skin.

"Jarod and you have something in common," Rosemarie tells me with a pleased tone. "I thought you'd like to meet a Cross relative who understands what you're going through."

"That would be me," Jarod says, winking. "It's been fifty years since I came here as a youth."

"You were a youth?" I ask in surprise.

"You didn't think you were the only Cross newbie? My youth name was Adam."

He pulls up a chair and launches into his story of Instructors, pranks on his born-mates, and being so nervous at his Celebraze that he nearly wet his pants.

I lean forward on the edge of the quilt so I don't miss a word. Unlike me, Jarod was joyous to be Chosen by the Cross Family, although he admits to sadness at leaving his best mates and Instructors. But he sees them at Sunday Fair when Families gather for communal bartering. I'm loving his story until he mentions memdenity.

"Weren't you afraid?" I grip my hands together.

"Who wouldn't be? Only it didn't hurt, and afterward I knew more than I ever imagined. When I finished all three mems, I remembered life before ShareHaven, when I lived with family in Florida. I was in my senior year of college when the mind-plague hit. So many were lost—including my parents. I came to this island to escape sad memories and help find a cure as a lab assistant working for the scientists. We were close to a cure—until the Attack. Afterward I helped construct the Fence to keep out desperate people, beasts, and Nocturnes. When we settled into Families, I had no relations of my own, so I joined the Cross Family."

"You can do that?" I ask.

"I did." He grins mischievously. "Take a few hundred years and lots of things can happen. I could tell you some stories …."

Rosemarie, who sits in a nearby chair, clears her throat. "Jarod, keep to the topic," she says with reproach.

"Fine, fine." He winks at me. "So I'm a totally well-adjusted former youth, and you will be too. If you get bored, join a sports team or hobby club. In my free hours, I kick smack-ball. Two of my born-mates play too. And there are some sweet girls I see at every Sunday Fair. Never a dull day in forever-land."

I laugh, and something inside me lightens. He's doing a job he enjoys and kept youth friendships—confirming that not all memories fade.

When he leaves, I wrap my arms around Rosemarie. "Thank you so much for inviting him."

"I want you to be happy here."

"I am," I say, and for the first time I mean it.

Rosemarie has given me so much, yet there's nothing I can give to her—except the sister she misses. So I ask her to tell me about Milly.

I curl up on the quilt with a pillow and listen as she tells me sweet, funny, and sad stories of Milly. They were born in the retro-century and lived in a grand city by the Pacific Ocean called San Francisco. Her words paint images of cars, computers, school, and a magical way of communication called the Internet.

There was a brother too: Gregory.

"After he died from the mind-plague, our parents came to this island." A shadow crosses her face. "Things were wondrous for a while until the Attack, when my parents were killed. I was already planning my wedding to Jed, and Milly fell in love with Arthur. But you'll know this soon—I don't want to bore you."

"It's not boring. Milly is more real when you talk about her."

"I was closer to her than anyone—including Jed."

At the mention of her husband's name, I ask something I've been wondering. "Where is your husband? I've met your three sons, but not him. Won't he mind my sharing your room?"

"No." Her lips press tight. "He died."

I don't know what to say so I just nod.

She gazes at a framed retro-photo on a dresser of a smiling black-haired man with heavy brows and crooked teeth. "I thought we'd be together forever."

I wonder which of The Three Dangers ended their "forever." Wanting to comfort her but not knowing the right words, I repeat a phrase the Instructors say: "Accidents are tragic."

"It wasn't an accident," she says bluntly.

I blink at her, confused. "But then how … how did he die?"

Her lips press tighter. "My husband was murdered."

ELEVEN

I've been warned about accidental deaths for as long as I can remember but aside from The Attack I've never heard of an intentional death.

Murder.

How could that happen in ShareHaven? Violence is forbidden. Even a small offense like hitting is cause for Uniforms to step in with severe punishments. Clark was only age ten when he smacked Homer in the head with a stick. Homer wasn't hurt, but within an hour, the Uniforms arrived. They locked Clark away for a week.

Clark never lost his temper again.

Poor Rosemarie. She's suffered a terrific loss, yet she smiles as if she's eternally happy. I study her in a new way, creating a memory of my own.

Rosemarie offers me a nightshirt that is comfortably baggy, made of silky fabric. I crawl into my bed, which is made of softer cushions than I'm used to, but my mind won't relax. I glance over at Rosemarie as she reaches out to turn back her blankets. Only instead of climbing into bed, she kneels on the floor, and presses her palms together, her head bowed.

What's she doing? I wonder, breathing evenly so she won't know I'm awake. I can't see her face, but I understand some of her words.

"... am grateful ... second chance to ... right with Milly and forgive ...." Her voice falls to silence as she makes a gesture over her heart and climbs into bed. Something about her manner seems so private that I'm ashamed to eavesdrop.

When I close my eyes this time, I fall asleep almost before my head hits the soft downy pillow, and I dream ....

I'm at the sea, wading in the surf and flinging a stick in the waves. Petal clings on my shoulder. She tickles my neck, and when the stick doesn't return after I throw it, she dives into the foaming waves. She's so very tiny, smaller than the stick she's seeking, but she's done this many times before, so I don't worry.

The clouds darken, waves toss angrily, and Petal doesn't come up for air. She can swim like a fish, but she still needs air to breathe. I call her name over and over, running into the waves. The sea has become a wild monster, immense and black-hearted.

A glassy shape rises from the waves like a life-size monster. I try to run, but a tube-like arm snakes out, winding around my wrist. I can't breathe, sinking beneath the water, drowning. I'm going to break a rule—dying by one of the Three Dangers.

But the glassy shape peers at me with blue eyes, and the tube-arm becomes a human hand. When he lifts his other hand, he's holding tiny Petal out to me. She tinkles her bell laugh, then scurries up my arm.

"You came back," I say.

"To see you." Nate's smile goes straight to my heart. Stubble bristles around his jaw, and his cheeks are hollowed as if he doesn't eat enough. Yet he's all muscle too, and I can feel his strength through his gentle hand.

His shape shifts. Tubes sharpen into fins, scales cover his skin, and the smile glints with pointy-knife teeth. A human vampfish. I smell blood. The cut on my arm has burst open, bleeding swirls in seawater. And the creature that once was human aims fish fangs at me ....

I jerk up in bed. A dream ... that's all. Yet I'm startled by the quietness of the room. My first night away from the noisy whispers of my born-mates. I look over to the outline of Rosemarie underneath blankets. She snores softly, so deep in sleep not even my bad dreams wake her.

Dawn light creeps through the window, and I long to sneak out to my cave. Will Petal look for me today? She'll wait and wait, but I'll never come. Nate will comfort her, and she'll forget me. But no matter how many memories are crammed into my head, I'll never forget her.

There's no going back to sleep, so I change into a tunic. I'd rather wear comfy denim pantons, but I want to make a good impression on my Family.

Milly loves to cook, I think, as I slip out of the room. I don't have much experience cooking, but it can't be that hard. After only two wrong turns, I find the large kitchen downstairs. No one else is awake yet, thankfully. I'll surprise my new Family with a hot breakfast.

Flapcakes are the only breakfast food I know how to make. I've helped Instructor Penny crack eggs and whip a golden liquid into a creamy batter. I search cupboards for ingredients: flour, eggs, and milk. The eggs are fresh from the Hu Family chickens, and the milk is creamy. I find bowls and utensils, then mix and blend into a batter. But it's not thick and tastes bland.

Following a recipe book seems unimaginative, so I do

what I always do when tackling a challenge.

I go outside.

At the Edu-Center, it's a short walk into the woods to find spicy herbs. But this part of the island is rockier and thicker with brush. Beyond the Fence, dense woods with treetops stretch into the sky. I now live near the most dangerous edge of ShareHaven, where beasts roam beyond the Fence gate. As the only entrance into our community, it's locked and guarded.

A gravel path curves behind the vehicle storage building, toward neat gardens with row after row of vegetation. A golden-red glow softens the sky and warms my arms as I bend down, studying the plants. I recognize grape vines, corn stalks, and strings of green beans. I whoop with joy when I spot a red-stemmed plant. Cinnasweet is a hybrid of cinnamon and sugar. I sniff the rich sweetness, then pluck a few leaves and tuck them in my tunic pocket.

Smiling to myself, I head back to the kitchen.

I set to work, crushing the leaves then pouring them into my mixture. I add more flour to thicken the batter, whipping it with a wooden spoon until my arm aches. I smile at my creation, then flip flapcakes on a griddle. They're lumpy and more dirt-brown than golden, but they smell delicious.

Rosemarie's eyes widen when she sees setting utensils arranged neatly around the table and a steaming stack of flapcakes.

"Graces good, this looks amazing!" she exclaims. "Did you do all this yourself?"

I nod proudly.

"This is wonderful!" She hugs me like we really are sisters. "No one has surprised me with a hot breakfast since ... not since Milly."

"Really? Milly made flapcakes too?"

"She made *everything*."

"I only know how to make flapcakes."

"They smell delicious! And the setting looks lovely." Rosemarie walks around the table, admiring. "No one will want to miss this. They'll come, even if I have to drag them out of bed."

A short while later, everyone except Daisy and Grandmother join us.

"Milly, this brings back wonderful memories," Arthur tells me with tears in his eyes. I remember the bride and groom portrait and see him in a new way—as a loving husband who lost his wife. I don't want to let him see me naked or sleep with him, but I offer him a smile—and a flapcake.

"What's the unusual flavor?" Leader Cross asks, dabbing syrup off his chin with a napkin.

"A sweet secret," I say mysteriously. I envision creating meals, learning more about herbs, and inventing my own recipes.

The flapcakes are so warm steam rises from the plates. I haven't eaten any yet because I've been so busy. But there's not much work left, so I take a seat beside Rosemarie. I'm pouring golden syrup from a ceramic jug over a pile of flapcakes when I hear gagging.

Arthur clutches his throat, convulsing in his chair, his face mottled red, as if he can't breathe.

"Arthur!" Leader Cross lunges over to Arthur. But before he can reach out to help Arthur, he clutches his own stomach. His face pales, then flames as if on fire. He gags. He's not the only one. Everyone around the table is on their feet, doubling over and gasping in pain.

"Call ... the health workers!" Leader Cross manages to say before he vomits on Arthur's shoes.

All around the table, my new Family turns sick shades of green as they clutch their stomachs and vomit.

I've poisoned my Family.

I've been banished to my room.

The Family is having a meeting about me. Why can't I do anything right? How do I always cause trouble? I tried to fit in with the Crosses. But now I can't guess what they'll decide. I think Rosemarie will defend me, but my last glimpse of her was her back as she raced out of the room with her hand covering her mouth. She must think I'm a poor Milly replacement.

I don't want to be Returned like that crazy boy from the last group of youths. Where is he now? I've heard rumors the Returned are sent to the scientists' compound for secret experiments or locked into underground jails by the Uniforms. But I've always suspected they were sent outside the Fence. If the claws and snakes don't get them, the Nocturnes do.

Staring out the window, my gaze shifts off to the distant forest. A shadow flickers high in a tree, then vanishes into leafy limbs. It could be a harmless, gentle monklee. But I'm certain I've glimpsed something far more scarifying. A claw beast? Their massive jaws can crunch a hoxen in one bite and their razor claws rip through skin like it's cheese in a shredder. The claws only fear the Nocturnes—savage humans living beneath ground during light hours, then rising at night to hunt beasts. When I asked Instructor Penny how humans can be so savage, she said Nocturnes are monsters in human bodies, and while they're dangerous, they protect us by killing beasts and keeping outsiders away from our island. There is only safety inside the Fence.

Whatever happens to the Returned, I hope I never find out.

Poisoning my Family, although accidental, deserves a severe punishment. Uniforms could be on their way now to contain me. I gaze through the window and see no sign of solar coaches. They aren't coming to get me. Yet.

My skin aches with anxiety. I can't sit idly, waiting for others to decide my future. I'll go downstairs where decisions are being made.

When I reach the main floor, I follow the rumble of voices to a closed door. I press my ear against the wood and hear the sound of arguing.

"—wasn't her fault!" Rosemarie is shouting. "She used the wrong herb. It was clearly an accident!"

"I warned you not to trust another youth," a woman snaps.

"Don't be emotional, Daisy," Leader Cross says.

"It could happen again," Daisy warns angrily.

"No, it won't." Rosemarie's voice is soft and pleading. "Milly is nothing like *him*."

"That remains to be proven," Leader Cross replies. "She's not allowed to prepare meals alone until the completion of memdenity."

I can't blame them for not trusting me. Food poisoning won't kill you, but the antidote makes you wish you were dead.

"I should have been in the kitchen helping her. Blame

me, not her," Rosemarie says, and I vow that if I survive this, I'll work hard to be like Milly.

"I blame both of you."

There's a pause, then Rosemarie asks quietly, "Daisy, why can't you accept her? She may not be like your mother yet, but with memdenity she'll know everything Milly knew, and she will love you. You need to let go of your hate. Open your heart to your mother."

"You're delusional!" Daisy says fiercely. "She's only a youth and nothing like my mother. Memdenity can give her information, but my mother was more than her cleaning skills and recipes. I see her in dreams and feel her so close like she's holding me. She's gone somewhere else ... not into a tube of DNA. If you truly think that girl can bring back Milly, then you're fooling yourself."

"Enough, Daisy!" Leader Cross roars with a thud as if his fist hits a table.

"You're at fault too," Daisy accuses. "You insisted on bringing her here even though we voted against taking another youth."

"Are you challenging my decision?" His voice cuts like the sharp edge of an ax. "Rosemarie and Arthur will keep a close watch on the girl. Once she has all of Milly's memories, she'll be as pliable as Milly."

"You're a fool to trust memdenity." Daisy's voice shrills so she's almost screaming. "You may forget, but I'm marked forever. I'm warning you. Return her now, or we'll all regret it."

There's the sound of stomping feet. When the door flings open, I jump behind a corner. Daisy pushes her hair from her eyes and for the first time I see all of her face. Her words strike me with new meaning: *I'm marked forever.*

Marcus told me about a crazy youth who stabbed his sister.

Not a rumor—the truth marks Daisy's face.

From cheek to chin is a jagged scar.

TWELVE

I can't get Daisy's scar out of my mind. I've never seen anything like it. Faces are eternally smooth and perfect. Bruises, cuts, and burns are easily mended by health workers' medicreams.

So why hasn't Daisy had her scar removed?

Summoning sympathy for Daisy isn't easy since she's been so awful to me. But I dislike her less. My emotions tangle with what I've overheard. Daisy's words slam in my head: "We voted against taking a youth."

Yet they Chose me instead of strong, muscular Clark. I'd thought Leader Cross saw something worthwhile in me and was glad to add me to his Family. But the truth eats inside me like a poison I can't vomit out.

I've never heard of a Family deciding *not* to take a youth. Families wait so long for a youth that they're joyous to welcome us. Instructor Penny confided that some Families want to change the laws so youths are born every ten years instead of twenty-five. As decades pass, the Name Books grow thicker, and important knowledge is forever lost. There aren't enough youths born to carry on all memories. We're valuable and necessary to our community. Why blame all youths because of one crazy boy?

She can't be trusted.

This prejudgment is so unfair. Anger rips through

me … yet I'm hurting too, longing to be accepted. I don't need Milly's memories to be trustworthy.

I'll show them.

Instead of returning to my room, I detour through the kitchen and yank open the cabinet that holds rows of cookbooks, fluttering through pages until I find a chapter titled "Cooking Made Simple."

Not taking the time to study the Name Books before the Celebraze was my worst mistake. I deserved the shame I felt at the Celebraze on stage, unprepared for my own future. I didn't prepare then, but I will now. If I don't want to be Returned, I need to work harder to fit into my Family, starting off with learning to cook without poisoning anyone.

Although my recipe for redemption may be too late.

The Cross Family was poisoned against me long before I arrived.

Hours later, Rosemarie looks surprised when she finds me reading the cooking book in our room. She pulls up a chair beside where I'm sitting on my bed and points to the book. "My favorite recipe is on page 132," she says, as if there are no worries behind her smile.

"I'm not there yet."

"It pleases me to see your interest in cooking."

"I'm Milly, right?" I try to smile but fail.

"She never bothered with cookery books. You needn't either," Rosemarie adds. "You'll know everything soon."

I frown. She's referring to the memdenity, which I don't want to think about. I'm not even sure I'll be here long enough for new memories. If I make another mistake, I could be Returned. I'd probably already be gone if it weren't for Rosemarie.

"I want to learn so I can better help you," I tell her.

"By being here, you're helping me." She pats my arm.

"I wasn't any help this morning," I say bitterly.

"You had no way of knowing to use the cinnasweet roots, not the leaves. I explained this to Ryan—I mean, Leader Cross. A health worker administered the medidote, so everyone is well and able to attend to their duties."

"I want to make up for what I did." I close the cookbook. "I doubt any other youth poisoned their Family on the first day."

She chuckles. "But we didn't Chose those other youths. We wanted you."

When she hugs me, I hug her back, even though I know her answer is untrue. Rosemarie wants me to be Milly, and a majority of the Family doesn't want me at all. I touch my smooth cheek, cringing at the memory of Daisy's gruesome scar.

What happened to the crazy youth after he was Returned?

Is he still living on the island?

Is he still living at all?

I have to work hard not make any more mistakes. No daydreaming or breaking rules. I will become as perfect and useful as the real Milly.

The rest of the day flies by without any mishaps. Rosemarie leads me to the gardens and points out the prime herbs to use for cooking. Afterward, she shows me the cleaning cupboard, where brooms, mops, and cleaning bottles are stored. I soak in all this new information. Rosemarie accepts me as if I already have Milly's memories. I'm grateful yet uneasy. Despite Rosemarie's encouragement, I don't fit into this Family.

I don't fit in a literal way too.

When Rosemarie offers me Milly's clothing—tunics, blouses, and pantons in shades of garden flowers—they hang as loosely on my body as Arthur's wedding ring did on my hand.

"This won't do at all," Rosemarie says, tapping her finger to her chin, thinking. "You must have new fabrics. Can you stitch?"

"Um ... not my best skill."

"I'm only modestly skillful with a needle myself." Rosemarie pats my hand. "This is a prime opportunity for you to learn more about your duties. Have you heard of the Sunday Fair?"

Who hasn't? I jump, unable to contain my excitement. Whenever Lorelei found out an Instructor had been to Sunday Fair, she jabbed them with questions. What did they barter? Who was there? Did the artists sing, dance, or perform a play? What were people wearing? Was anyone in costume? Once Instructor Penny brought back lace headbands for all of us girls, and Lorelei wore hers constantly, even to bed, until she cut it up into lacy decors for her tunics.

"I'd love to go," I say wistfully. "But will Leader Cross let me?"

"I'll talk to him." Rosemarie waves away my concerns. "Bartering is the quickest way to get new clothes for you."

"He won't grant me any favors."

"I'll persuade him," she says with a confident smile.

Sunday Fair is rich with booths filled with all the crafts, food, and frivels imaginable. And I may get to go ... I hope.

The rest of the day, I learn to roll dough and cut vegetables into narrow slices. I help Rosemarie serve dinner and am so polite Lorelei would be impressed. Leader Cross ignores me, though, except to ask for a napkin. What do I have to do to earn his trust?

Before I crawl into bed that night, I spread out my favorite belongings on my quilt: a wood comb Marcus carved for me, a coral twist hair frivel crafted by Lorelei, the lacy headband from Instructor Penny, and a handful of sand shells. I touch each object, pieces of my life. I'm starting a new life now, and while I won't forget my past, I need to focus on my future. I add one new object to my special belongings: the utility tool Rosemarie gave me at the Celebraze.

An entire day passes into dark night without me poisoning anyone.

The next morning, Rosemarie tells me I'm allowed to attend Sunday Fair—if I keep out of trouble for three days.

I focus on my chores. I learn not to burn bread or leave egg shells in omelets. I dig vegetables from the garden and whip up a soup that tastes better than it smells. Each small accomplishment delights Rosemarie, and it feels good to succeed at lessons instead of daydreaming through them.

Leader Cross has stopped scowling at me, and I no longer feel like an unwelcome visitor at meals. I enjoy teasing with Jarod, who has a demental sense of humor. Rosemarie's sons are cordial too. But Daisy continues to ignore me, secluding herself with Grandmother. I'm avoiding someone too. Arthur, my "husband," is growing too attentive, pulling out my chair at meals, carrying my food trays, and brushing against me whenever we pass. He's appealing in looks, and my pulse races when he touches me, but I'm not sure if I even like him. After the memdenity, we'll share a room, and he'll have every right to touch me ... see me naked ... and my thoughts may long for him too.

Still I wish he'd stop staring at me like I'm on the menu.

On Saturday evening, I get through dinner without burning food or dropping plates. As I gather dishes from the table, I congratulate myself for keeping out of trouble for three days. In the morning, Rosemarie and I will rise early, prepare breakfast for the Family, then go to the Sunday Fair. We're taking pumpkin cupcakes to trade for coverings with the Ying Family. Leader Ying has a weakness for Rosemarie's baking.

When the last pan is dried and stacked in the cupboard, I wearily climb the stairs, exhausted but excited too. Sunday Fair, Sunday Fair, Sunday Fair! I'm almost singing with joy. I can't wait till the morning. I especially look forward to seeing Marcus and Lorelei, perhaps even Instructor Penny.

I'm feeling proud of myself for adapting so well to my new life—until I enter my room and find a tiny scaled creature curled on my bed.

Petal.

THIRTEEN

After the way I last treated Petal, she should hate me and never want to see me again. Yet she's come to me. At my cry, she swirls up on her curled tail, love shining from her precious dark eyes.

"Oh, Petal," I sigh. "You shouldn't be here."

She makes a purring sound, and I offer my arm so she can scrawl up to my shoulder.

"How did you come here from the cave and get in my room?"

She glances at an open window, blinking her silent answer.

"Clever girl." I shake my head. "But what am I going to do with you?"

The sea is miles away. Petal's skin already shows flaky dryness. How long can she stay out of water? A day, maybe two, I guess. She must go back, or she'll shrivel to bones.

If I start walking now—assuming I don't get lost in the darkness—I might make it to the cave and back by morning. But not likely. And If I'm not here by breakfast, the Uniforms will search for me. If I'm lucky, I'll only be punished with a few days in lock-up. If I'm not lucky ... well, I don't want to find out.

Why did Petal have to show up now? With Sunday Fair in the morning, I won't have any time on my own. Getting to the sea will be impossible.

"Milly," I hear Rosemarie call as she twists the doorknob.

She's back! I rush into the privacy room, locking the door behind me. I hear footsteps inside the room and call out to let her know where I am.

Her reply is muffled since I've turned on the tub water. "I'll be awhile," I raise my voice. "Go to sleep. Don't wait for me."

Petal makes a questioning squeal, the rushing water filling the tub muffling her sound. She wiggles down my arm, excited by the water, and dives into the tub. But she pops out almost immediately, spitting with her long pink tongue. Shaking off water, she slaps her tail angrily against the tub.

"It's not salty," I tell her. "You should have tasted it before diving in."

She shakes again, purposely dousing me with droplets.

"Don't splash me with bad attitude. You're the one who came here. I don't know how you managed or how to get you back to the sea."

She scrawls up my arm, dripping water all over me, and leaps back onto my shoulder. Her blinking gaze criticizes me—as if it's my fault humans don't have salt in their water. Hmmm ... maybe I could add salt to the water.

I'll wait till Rosemarie falls asleep, then take Petal down to the kitchen. If the salt-into-water recipe works, I'll bring a bowl of salty water back to my room and hide Petal under my bed. I'll make her understand she must stay hidden until I get back from Sunday Fair. Then I'll return her to the sea—even if I have to walk.

Not a great plan, but it's the best I have.

Rosemarie snores softly from her bed as I tiptoe from the room with tiny Petal hiding under my hair. We make it down the stairs, through the halls, and to the kitchen without meeting anyone.

I open the dry goods cupboard and take out the salt box, then sprinkle salt into a small bowl of water.

Petal sniffs the water and hisses. She slaps the bowl with her tail, tipping it over so water spills across the wooden floor. Sighing, I get a towel and clean up her mess. So much for my great plan ....

Petal rumbles a musical sound as she crawls to my lap. When I stroke her skin, dry flakes sprinkle off like dust. Petal doesn't seem sad, though, and rubs against me with her tinkling purr.

Leaning against a cabinet, I sink down to the floor and cover my face with my hands. I'm so frustrated I can't even cry. How can I save Petal? Would Rosemarie help if I explained? I'm not sure.

If only I had someone to talk to. I miss whispering with Lorelei at night, and I even miss how she bosses me around. I miss Marcus too—his curiosity and gentle voice that can charm even venomous crawlies. Marcus would know how to help Petal.

If only I could talk to him.

And I get an idea.

Sitting up straighter, I force myself to think logically. I don't rush into action impulsively like the old Jennza. Instead I sort through positive and negative details. It'll take careful timing and a few lies, but after much thought, I am confident it will work.

As long as I don't get caught.

Petal clings to the back of my neck, her tiny claws scratching my skin. I've wrapped my red scarf around my head so my hair falls thickly behind my shoulders, conceal-ing Petal. I take a seat in the solar coach beside Rosemarie, and she doesn't seem suspicious.

Daisy sits across from us, staring out the window as if no one else exists in her world. I ignore her too. I won-der, though, if once I have Milly's memories she'll become friendly. It'll just take time—like a century or two.

Leader Cross drives our solar coach slowly. Following behind are Rosemarie's sons with the hoxen driven cart, carrying baked goods and building materials for bartering. Everyone wears posh tunics—except me. None of Milly's coverings fit, so I have to wear the white tunic I wore to the Celebraze. It's embarrassing—it makes me appear more a child than a nearly grown woman.

Rosemarie turns excitedly to me. "You're going to love Sunday Fair—all the booths and food and people. I'll do the negotiating," she reminds me for at least the fiftieth time. "Stay close, and only speak when properly addressed."

I nod. Obedience is a small price for the honor of at-tending Sunday Fair.

"Youths don't make decisions about their coverings, but I'll allow you to choose one fabric. When you find something you like, point it out to me in a gesture. Don't be obvious. You must act disinterested."

I tilt my head, curious. "Can't I just tell you?"

"Bartering is a complex and acquired skill. The first rule is to never admit you want something. If you show interest, they'll ask for more in trade."

"Why don't they give us what we want?" I ask.

"That wouldn't be any fun." Rosemarie's face lights up with her grin. "You're no longer in the Edu-Center where the community replaces the coverings the youths outgrow. The system works well—quite different from the retro-century use of paper money and coins."

I nod, remembering these objects from a lesson trip to our history center. It seemed unsensical that retro-people would value strips of green paper. The coins were coolness, though, like shiny buttons. Once I found a copper coin and polished it until it shone like a winter sunset. Instructor Penny admired it, explaining that she'd been named after this "penny" coin, and I gifted it to her.

Still, it's puzzling why the retro-people didn't share or barter useful items. You can't eat a copper coin. I ask Rosemarie about this.

"Life was complicated in retro-century," she explains. "Some countries had abundant water and food, yet others starved. Our system is simple, balancing work hours with necessities. Leaders assign Family roles and community work hours. While this works fairly, there are frivels like hair ties or sweets or jewelry that we can trade among Families. On Sunday Fair, if you want anything, it's what you have to trade that matters."

"I can't wait to see all the—ow!" I cry out when a lurch of the solar coach startles Petal, and she digs her claws into my neck.

"What's wrong?" Rosemarie leans close, her face soft with concern.

"Only a bump to my elbow," I say, hiding my grimace.

I pretend to smooth my hair, but I'm reaching through curls to Petal's scaly skin, stroking her to calmness. Petal's tail wiggles across my ear, and I shift in my seat so Rosemarie won't notice. It's getting harder and harder to hide Petal.

The drive to town center—half of the distance to the sea—is longer than I remembered. It would take hours to walk. I can't return Petal back to the sea without a vehicle. Breaking rules is the only option.

And if it works, Petal will be safe.

After I talk to Marcus.

Not Marcus anymore, I correct myself. What's his new name? Oh, yeah. Neil Sarwald. How is he doing with his Family? They surely love him—how could they not? He's fun, kind, and brilliant. But he can be overly quiet. Lorelei has criticized him for this, but I think it makes Marcus more interesting. Sometimes we sit outside, saying nothing as we watch birds building a nest or study star patterns in the sky. He'll point out a distant constellation and tell me the name of each star. Once I teased, "There should be a star named Jennza." He didn't mock me but nodded as if considering this. "A star is a luminous mass of gas held together by its own gravity. Why would you want a gas named after you?" He doesn't always understand me, but he's a friend I can count on.

And I really need to count on him today.

But what if he's not at Sunday Fair?

The solar coach slows, dust spitting up as we turn into a vast field filled with tented booths. People are everywhere—they're a blur of movement against the colorfully decorated booths. Most people wear scarves or ties with the unique insignias of their Families. The Cross Family symbol isn't very interesting, only two crossed black lines on a red fabric. I'm expected to wear mine until after the memdenity process, which is tiresome. I look forward to selecting new coverings, but I won't be able to relax while Petal still digs her tiny claws into my neck.

As we step out of the solar coach, I plan my escape. Rosemarie watches me so closely it won't be easy to sneak away. I'll wait till she's distracted or busy bartering, then run down the aisles in search of Marcus. He won't approve of my plan, but he has a strong compassion for wild creatures. The Sarwald Family lives near the sea, so Marcus need only sneak Petal to the Fence. Then she'll find her way back to the cave.

If I can find Marcus ....

Rosemarie's hand rests lightly on my arm. We walk through an archway opening into rows and rows of an astonishing assortment of booths and offerings. Artists beneath one booth draped in silver curtains call out, "Sketch your portrait?" and "Paint flowers on your face?" and "Learn a fancy dance?" I want to answer "Yes!" to everything.

But Rosemarie guides me down an aisle of greenery in hanging pots.

"Isn't this wondrous?" she asks with a sweeping gesture.

"Stunning. I want to see everything."

"They'll be time after we fit you for new garments."

She picks up her speed, but I drag my steps, slowing so she's ahead of me. As I look around, I'm not only admiring the amazing booths, I'm also memorizing the crisscross pattern of the aisles, and mapping out escape routes. I reach up occasionally to stroke Petal so she knows I haven't forgotten her.

"Smell the delicious aromas." Rosemarie turns back to me. "Doesn't it make you hungry?"

"Very much," I say, smiling.

"Each Family has recipes from centuries past and offers samples to tempt barterers. There are contests too, awarding the spiciest chili sauce or sweetest jam. Milly loved to taste everything and raced from booth to booth."

It's hard to know what to say since I can't share memories I don't have yet. So I point to a blue-tarped booth with bottles in neat rows on wood shelves and a large cookery pot steaming on a counter. "That soup smells delish."

"Eliza Candras' soup wins honors every year. Would you like a taste?"

I sniff at unusual odor that reminds of me the sea. "What is it?"

"Creamed salmon egg."

Ewww. Fish is my least favorite food, probably because I'd rather swim with fish than eat them. "Uh ... no, thank you," I say.

Rosemarie gestures to a booth where pots and pans hang from a draped curtain. "Yum ... something smells good. Come on, let's have a taste."

I follow her into a booth where apples steam in a pan over hot fire, then bake until crispy in a sweet-powder batter. When I take the sample bite offered, my tongue burns at the heat, but the taste is sweet. I ask for more.

Afterward, we turn down a row with blue flags waving above a booth, when a horn blows and a strange procession comes into view. Cloaked figures with black masks glide down the aisle like storm clouds surprising a sunny sky. Their masks conceal all but their eyes and mouths. They blow into musical pipes, spinning and kicking up their heels in dance.

"A playrade!" Rosemarie claps, pulling me into the gathering crowd.

The sound rises so I have to shout. "What's a playrade?"

She leans closer to my ear. "A group of performers who parade around the booths until they reach the podium, where they act out a play, usually something from famous retro-stories by Shakespeare, Twain, or Rowling."

I clap along with her, as if I'm swept up in the gaiety of the crowd. But what I'm really doing is thinking hard—planning how to find Marcus. This could be my only chance to leave. I inch away from Rosemarie. She's focused on the playrade, swaying to flute music. I'm already planning what to say to her later: "I thought you were next to me. Where did you go?" I'll pretend she lost me. I've used this ruse successfully on my Instructors, confusing them before they can blame me. And when I accuse them of losing me rather than the other way around, they usually apologize to me.

I take another step away from Rosemarie, and a tall man shifts so he's blocking me from her sight. Now is my chance ....

Yet I pause. Not out of fear but out of a feeling of being watched. I glance over at Rosemarie, and she's still absorbed in the show, unaware of me. The hooded performers pause in front of us, twirling so their long, dark brown robes flare out at the bottom. It's odd to find such beauteous songs coming from such grimly masked performers. They should wear shades of rainbows, not gloomy darkness. I peer at each dancer as they pass, wondering if any are Instructors or members of my new Family, but their faces are hidden.

The watched feeling grows stronger. I swivel around, studying the crowd. There's nothing unusual until I turn back to the playrade—at the masked performer standing apart from the other dancers, staring directly at me.

When he catches me watching, he spins away.
But not before I see his eyes.
Unforgettable sea blue.

FOURTEEN

Impossible.

Nate can't be here.

Blue eyes are not uncommon—although I've never seen anyone else with such a stormy shade of blue. Still, the hooded dancer could *not* have been Nate. He can't be much older than me, and there are only fifteen youths in ShareHaven.

My thoughts spin dizzy circles, and when my head clears, the playformers have danced away.

"Here you are," Rosemarie says, coming beside me, her tone reprimanding. "I worried when I didn't see you. Why did you leave?"

"I looked up and you weren't there. I thought you'd left me."

"I would never do that, Milly." She slips her arm around my shoulders. "It's so crowded and noisy. Keep hold of my hand so we aren't parted again."

"I want to see more of the playrade." I gesture down the aisle where the last dancers are disappearing from view, sounds of music and laughter dimming.

"It was stunning, wasn't it? But that's enough for now. We'll see their performance later."

"Who are they?" I ask, breathlessly.

"The playformers? Oh, too many to name. It's one of the after-hours clubs that anyone can join, and the group changes often. Usually only those with both singing and dancing skills perform at Sunday Fair." She tugs on my hand. "Come on, Milly. There's much more to see."

I've already seen more than I expected. But I still need to see Marcus.

"Don't stand idle." Rosemarie points down an aisle. "We need to go to the fashionizers."

"Can we visit other booths first?" I ask, searching the faces in the crowd for Marcus. "You said that Milly loved to sample foods. I'd like to taste more from the booths."

"Fabrics now. Food later." Her smile is gentle, but her grip on my hand is firm. Arguing might make her suspicious, and then I'll never get a chance to sneak way.

The Ying Booth is draped in purple and amber chiffon swirls, like clouds of lavender fire. Tiny claws on my neck shift my thoughts back to Marcus. *I'll get help soon,* I think-talk to Petal. *Hold tight a little longer.*

As we weave through the crowd, I look around for Marcus. But as I pass booth after booth, my hopes fade. I'm not only looking for Marcus because Petal needs help but because I miss him too. Everything has been so strange since leaving the Edu-Center, as if nothing is real anymore, including me. So I'm startled when someone calls my name.

My real name.

I spin around—and beautiful, smiling Lorelei steps out of the booth billowing with clouds of fabric. Instead of wearing her scarf over her hair, she's wrapped it around her neck so the edges dangle like jewelry. Her braid captures her hair except for a few black strands waving across her face. She carries a roll of blue-striped fabric under her arm.

I start to run to her until I catch the subtle tilt of her head to the large bosomed woman beside her. Someone from her Family, I guess, hoping Lorelei won't get in trouble for using my youth name.

"Flavia, it's good to see you," I say in my most formal tone, aware that Rosemarie has come up beside me.

"It's pleasing to see you too, Milly," she replies so politely I almost burst out laughing. I don't, of course. Twinkling humor shines from her dark eyes. *We are still best mates,* I think with a rush of gratitude.

"That's a very lovely fabric." I point to the blue-striped cotton she's holding. It's actually puke-awful.

"Are you here for new coverings?" Lorelei asks with a formal gesture to nearby stacks of colorful fabric. No one else would know the twitch of her lips means this is all a game to her.

"Excellent suggestion, Flavia," the bosomed woman says. "We have a rose pattern that would be lovely with this young lady's dark hair."

I look pointedly at Lorelei. "Could you show it to me?"

"Don't get too attached to any fabric," Rosemarie says to me, but her gaze is on the bosomed woman as if seeking approval. "We don't need anything here."

"But you won't be able to resist our lovely fabrics. Go ahead, Flavia," the woman tells Lorelei. She folds her arms to her curvy chest, turning to Rosemarie. "You're not going to con me again, Rose. Your youth obviously has no suitable coverings and needs my fabrics. What can you offer in trade?"

Lorelei takes my arm and leads me to the back of the booth, loudly describing different fabric designs. She leans her head against mine and whispers, "I have so much to tell you!"

"I want to hear it all." I squeeze her hand. "You look happy."

"I am! I have my own room, two closets full of coverings, and my Family loves me so much they argue about who spends time with me."

My Family argues about me too, I think bitterly.

But I keep on smiling. "I'm glad for you, Lor."

"Do call me Flavia, dearest Milly." She giggles. "It's so ripping weird to have a new name. When we're alone like this, call me whatever you want. How's it going with your Family?"

I pause, willing Petal to stay quiet until it's safe to bring her out. I trust Lorelei, but she loves to talk more than she remembers to keep secrets.

"Rosemarie is wonderful." I select pieces of truth. "I wouldn't be at Sunday Fair if she hadn't persuaded our Leader to allow it. I can't fit into Milly's coverings. We're here to get new ones."

"I wondered why you wore this." She touches my white tunic, puckering her lips with distaste. "I'm glad Rosemarie is watching out for you. How is she related to you?"

"My sister."

"I have two of those. Having relatives is an odd concept—sister, mother, daughter, cousin. I don't understand why anyone cares."

"It has to do with sharing a past. Rosemarie has memories of her sister that no one else knows." *Except me—after memdenity*, I think uneasily. I gesture to the bosomed woman raising her voice at Rosemarie. "So who's she to you?"

"My daughter."

"You'll need to grow quickly to resemble her." I gesture

at Lorelei's small chest, teasing like we always have. But instead of teasing back, Lorelei frowns.

"Don't I know it?" Lorelei grimaces. "I have dark hair like the other Ying woman, but my skin is dark, not a lighter goldenrod. They assure me it doesn't matter that I look nothing like the first Flavia."

"You're much prettier."

"You don't even know what she looked like," Lorelei says.

"I saw her photo in a Name book."

"You studied?" She puts her hand to her forehead like she's going to faint.

"Don't fall over," I tease. "I didn't do it often."

"But why study the Yings? You were never interested in them."

"My interest was for you, Flavia." I emphasize her new name. "You're so obvious about everything, like you stitch your thoughts onto your tunic. When I found out Flavia Ying designed quilted tunics and led the trend for feathered scarves, I knew you'd Choose her. Flavia's death was gruesome, though. Do not *ever* stand beneath a shelf of scissors."

"You're so bad." Lorelei laughs. "I love—and hate—that about you."

"It's all love." I grin. "Admit it. You're bored when I'm not around."

"Maybe a little bored. I've missed you."

Glancing around to make sure we aren't being watched, I give her a quick hug. "I'll always be your best mate."

"You know that's not possible. Our memories will change us."

I fold my arms stubbornly over my chest. "I refuse to change."

"And I wish I could change quicker." Lorelei glances at her daughter, who skillfully slices scissors through fabric. "I'm not useful without my memdenity."

"You're perfect as you are—that's more than enough."

She shakes her head, frowning. I wish she could see herself through my eyes. She doesn't need someone else's memories; she's already smart, funny, and talented. If she could stay herself, she would achieve amazing things. I think I could too. And I'm more determined than ever to hold tight to my memories. I'll remind myself of them so often that they never fade. Like when I fell down while learning to walk. When I touch my knee, the scar is still in my mind.

Lorelei leads me to a heaping pile of fabric rolls, and I lean over for a close look at a green checkered cloth. Claws dig into my neck. Ouch. *Okay, Petal, I get the message.*

"Lor, have you seen Marcus?" I ask.

She nods. "Two aisles over. Selling jars of honey."

Relief flows through me. "I need to talk with him."

"Don't even try, Jennza. When I waved at him, he ignored me. I know youths are supposed to bond with their Families during our first month, but that doesn't mean we can't talk to each other. His rudeness really ripped me."

"He can be as rigid as a steel rod. I'm glad you're talking to me," I add.

"You're too much fun to resist." She drops her voice to a whisper. "So how are you adjusting?"

"I'm learning to be useful in the kitchen."

"You? In a kitchen?" Lorelei almost chokes. "Remember the fire you started when you tried to toast crumb-crackers over the stove?"

"I didn't know the rag I grabbed to wipe the mess would

catch on fire."

"It was a grease rag."

I shrug. "One mistake doesn't mean I'm a disaster with cookery."

"What about when you used bleach instead of soap to wash dishes? Your Family will be lucky if they don't get food poisoning."

"Actually ...." I feel my cheeks burning.

"No! You didn't!"

"Anyone can choose the wrong herb."

"Not anyone. It's an art form, and you're the master artist." She sets down a bolt of red flowered fabric. "I haven't laughed like this since ... well, since we were together. I wish I could feel as natural with my Family. Instead I feel ... like I'm lacking. I want to impress them, but there's so much I don't know."

"You'll learn."

"Not fast enough." She sighs. "I want my memdenity now."

"I'd rather wait." *Like forever*, I think with a shudder.

"Oh! My daughter is looking this way," Lorelei warns. "I need to seem busy. Hold this bolt of fabric."

I look down at the fabric, swirls of red in black night. "This would make a nice tunic," I say. "So how do I talk to Marcus alone?"

"It would look fine on you," she agrees, then whispers, "Don't even try."

"I'm going to talk to him with or without your help."

She sighs. "Your best chance is during the playformance. Booths shut down for two hours. He'll come to the show. Sneak in a quick convo with Marcus before the playformance begins—if he'll talk to you."

"I won't give him a choice." I add in a loud voice, "I'll take this one."

Lorelei lifts the heavy bolt, ignoring my offer of help, and carries it up to the front of the booth. Twenty minutes of bartering later, the fabric is ours.

Afterward, Rosemarie and I walk up the aisles, browsing the booths. I obediently stand aside while Rosemarie barters. She's quite good, pretending disinterest even if she admires something. I pay attention and learn to help her. I pick up a delicious-looking melon, smell it, then pucker like I just ate something sour. I shake my head at Rosemarie. "Not ripe enough." This causes the trader to drop his barter demand, and we walk away with not one but three melons. Rosemarie pats me on the shoulder, grinning.

Noises crash around me, and smells of savory, sweet, and spicy foods make my mouth water. When we come to a booth decorated with green vines and dried corn stalks, I peer inside, searching for Marcus.

He's turned away from me, long and lean, wearing a forest green shirt tucked into black pantons. I stare in surprise at his hair—his wavy wheat-brown hair has been sheared short.

"What would you like, Milly?" Rosemarie asks.

I'd like Marcus to be like he used to, serious but fun, with untidy hair and dirt under his fingernails. But that's not the answer Rosemarie expects. I tell her I'd like a sugar sticklet.

Rosemarie approaches a heavy man with black hair sheared like Marcus's. The man sets down the knife he used for carving a corncob into a sculpture and asks what she wants. She shrugs with disinterest—and the bartering begins.

Marcus won't look at me. He knows I'm here. I know he knows I'm here. I stare hard at the back of his head, willing him to look. But even after the bartering ends, he still hasn't turned around.

When I bite into the sugary sticklet, whiskers tickle my ear. *I know what you want,* I think to Petal. I break off a sugary piece and sneak it up into my hair.

Licking sugar from my fingers, I look at Marcus, then turn away reluctantly for the next booth. I only get a few steps before something makes me turn back. Marcus is staring at me. He quickly looks away.

We stop at so many booths that our burlap sacks swell with food, fabric, hair brushes made from hoxen hair, and a teeth-scrub cream. Music trumpets throughout the fair, and an excited rumble of voices rise around me.

"Playformance!" Rosemarie exclaims, sacks heavy in her arms as we stop by our cart to stow our goods. "If we hurry, we'll get seats up close."

Tiered rows of wooden chairs face an elevated stage with a pleated royal blue curtain. Will the playformance be as thrilling as I imagine? Instructor Theo often acted out lessons and boasted that he always received standing applause after his performances. But when he read to us, his voice shrilled like a squealing pig, and Lorelei and I had to bite our lips to stifle giggles.

While I'm eager to see my first playformance, I'd rather see the blue-eyed performer to prove to myself he's not Nate. Can *not* be him. My born-mates and I are the only youths in ShareHaven.

A claw jab in my neck jerks me back to the most urgent task: saving Petal.

"Where's the privacy room?" I ask Rosemarie after we're seated near the front by the stage.

"Near the vehicle park." She gestures past booths. "Hurry back."

I rush off before she offers to go with me.

Instead of heading for the privacy room—a wooden rectangular building with a compartment on one side for ladies and the other for gentlemen—I search for Marcus. If he refuses to even look at me this time, I'll kick him in the backside. I won't leave until he talks to me. But when I pass his booth, it's empty.

Sighing, I turn away, heavy with disappointment. But I've only gone a few steps when there's a tap on my shoulder

Spinning around, I discover I don't need to find Marcus.

He's found *me*.

FIFTEEN

All the conversations and companionable silences I'd shared with Marcus seem long ago. The boy I grew up with is ruggedly tanned, with taut arm muscles, and he seems taller, more confident. Shorter hair lengthens his face into sharp angles. I miss the unruly sweep of hair above his eyes.

"Heya, Jennz," he says in that familiar half-teasing, half-serious way.

"So you're speaking to me now?" I fold my arms across my chest.

"I couldn't before. Sorry."

"You should be."

"I was told not to speak to my born-mates."

"And you always do as you're told?"

"Clearly not, since I'm talking to you."

"Why now?"

"Because when I saw your face, I knew you were troubled. What is it, Jennz?" he asks with such gentleness that I can't hold onto anger.

Tiny claws tickle my neck. "I need your help."

"You've got it," he says with no hesitation.

"What I'm going to tell you can't be shared with anyone."

"I'm loyal to my Family." Conflicting emotions cross his face. "But you're like family too."

"You wouldn't look at me at your booth," I remind him

with a flare of anger.

"I was looking."

I arch my brows. "You didn't act like we were even friends."

"I'm learning to disguise my true thoughts." He lowers his voice. "My Family is welcoming, but they don't trust me. They watch suspiciously as if I'm a fanged snake that might bite them."

"How could anyone mistrust you?"

"It's not only me. Other youths are being watched closely, and I'm sure it's because of that crazed youth who attacked a Family member. I haven't learned which Family he was from, but I know it wasn't mine since Hector—the last youth—has been confiding in me. He tells me things I'm not supposed to know." He stops when two women in yellow tunics walk by. After they've passed, he lowers his voice. "We can talk privately in my cart."

I follow him beyond the privacy room to a wooden vehicle with a curved roof and boxes stacked in the back seat. He clasps my hand warmly. "It's good to see you, Jennza—oh, sorry. I should call you Milly."

"Please don't."

"Still resisting change?" His words would be critical except for his teasing smile. "When we're with others, call me Neil."

"But you're so not like a Neil."

He folds his arms across his chest. "Why not?"

"Neil sounds hard like nails. You can make me laugh even though you're serious too, thinking all the time."

"Thinking isn't a bad thing."

"No, of course not—it's a trait I admire about you."

"You admire me?" he asks, surprised.

"Always have," I admit. "I should be sensical like you and respect rules."

"This is a non-rule cart. Inside here, we're just Marcus and Jennza."

"I like that." I smile.

"And I like ... well ... if only you'd gone to one of the Families on my list. Now there's no chance for us to be ...."

"To be what?" My throat catches.

"Anything," he says, taking my hand.

His fingers. Touching my skin. A casual gesture we've shared many times, yet it's not the same now. He's looking into my face—sweetly, gently, longingly. My heart races like when I'm running with the wind. I'm breathless and shy with someone I've known since infancy.

I pull away, words failing me. I can't think now, and I must. There's so much I need to explain to him, but I'm incapable of clear thoughts. So in a sudden, swift move, I reach underneath my hair.

I show him Petal.

"What—what is that?" he cries, eyes wide as sand-shells.

"I don't know what she is—only that she's sweet and wonderful. I call her Petal." I cuddle her to my chest, aware of her fast-pounding heart matching mine.

Marcus holds out his hand, and after Petal sniffs his fingers, he gently strokes her scales. "She's amazing—like nothing I've ever seen."

"You would have seen her a long time ago if you'd climbed the Fence with me. Remember all those times I snuck out? I went to a cave—and that's where I met Petal. She didn't understand about my leaving and found me." I touch Petal's scaly skin, and flakes flutter down like papery rain. "She's drying up. I'm afraid she'll die if she doesn't return to the sea."

Marcus's gaze sharpens with interest. "Webbed legs, gills, claws, and horizontal markings. Leathery skin, but with bristles that are almost like fur, and webbed legs similar to wings. A fish-reptile hybrid. You say she lives in the sea?"

I nod, worry squeezing my heart. "But she won't live long without salt water."

He strokes her curled tail. "You're a beauty, little one."

Petal relaxes at his soft words, and I know she's accepting him, as all wild creatures do.

"Want to hold her?" I offer.

"Can I?"

"Here." I hold her out to him, and he takes her gently.

"Poor creature. Her skin is so dry."

"That's why I came to you."

He frowns. "I don't know how to heal her."

"I do." I fix him a challenging look. "She must go back to the sea. I can't take her there myself because it's too far. But your compound borders the sea."

He touches Petal lightly, but his gaze stays on me. "What are you asking?"

"You only need to take her to the Fence, and she'll slip through the wire."

He rubs his chin thoughtfully but says nothing for a while. Finally he blows out a long sigh and nods.

Marcus finds a bucket and fills it with water from a pitcher. Petal hisses at the clear water, and I tell her this is the best we can do. I explain through words and gestures, begging Petal to return to the cave and not to look for me again. I sense she understands—at least I hope so.

Still, saying good-bye—again—is difficult. I kiss Petal's soft leathery head. "You can trust Marcus," I say.

"I'll take care of her," he promises.

I nod, biting my lip. I won't cry. I won't.

He cradles the bucket with Petal in his arms, and I turn away.

It kills me not to turn back.

When I return to the playformance, it's crowded with hundreds of bright patches of Family colors. There are familiar faces—youths, Instructors, and members of my new Family. I'm surprised to see two scientists in the front row. Lila shines like a queen in gold and purple, sitting beside her brother Daniel. I'm tempted to go to Lila, to beg her to give me another chance. But I remind myself of her deceit.

"What took you so long?" Rosemarie whispers as I sit beside her.

"Sorry," I mumble. "I was feeling ill … something I ate."

Her expression softens. "Are you better now?"

I imagine Petal swimming in seawater soon. "Much better."

Grand Sarwald climbs up the steps to the stage, then takes the microphone, tapping his gnarled fingers on the podium. The echoing thud silences the audience. His thin lips fade into a pale, wrinkled face, and he seems more aged than I remembered, although that's impossible. Still he stands confident with an inner strength, and I understand why the scientists chose him for our highest leader.

"Welcome to Sunday Fair!" his gruff voice booms out. "I trust you've all enjoyed successful bartering."

The crowd explodes in applause, whistles and foot stomping.

"Our artists have prepared a fine entertainment for us. Let me welcome the playformers." He gestures to a royal blue stage curtain behind him, which slides open to reveal the dark-robed dancers.

The cloaked performers form a line at the back of the podium behind Leader Sarwald. I lean forward, searching each figure for blue eyes. But they stand in shadows. *I'm being foolish*, I tell myself. A boy of the sea has no place in ShareHaven. I only imagined Nate's eyes.

"A few announcements," Grand Sarwald calls out across the audience.

I'm glad Rosemarie chose seats near the podium so I have a good view.

"We have an esteemed audience," Grand Sarwald continues. "This could be the largest attendance yet for a playformance. I'm especially pleased to see our youths present. A round of applause for our newest citizens."

I glance around and spot Lorelei three rows behind me. She catches my gaze, and we share smiles. I don't see Marcus and guess he's farther back, hidden by taller heads.

"Pay attention," Rosemarie whispers into my ear. "Show respect for Grand Sarwald."

"Apologies," I murmur, and return my gaze forward, bringing my palms together as the audience explodes in applause.

"Much better," Rosemarie approves. "He's our Highest Leader, and it was kind of him to give tribute to youths. Gaining his notice is an honor."

I nod, noticing how Grand Sarwald's smile doesn't quite

reach his eyes, as if he's heavy with responsibilities. For a moment, I see beyond the smile to the old soul who survived over a century to reach this moment.

"ShareHaven embraces our precious new citizens," Grand Sarwald continues, moving his hands as he speaks. "The past is reborn again with each new cycle of youths. Precious resources are restored through these fine youths."

I smile, but my gaze shifts beyond Grand Sarwald to the playformers. A few have lifted their masks, men and women with tawny shades of smooth skin that ceased aging at twenty-five. Only one woman has blue eyes, but they're more gray than blue. I narrow down my search to two tall figures at the far edge of the podium. One leans to the other. I strain to see his face ….

"And our communal bounty continues to prosper," Leader Sarwald is saying. "I wish to thank the Instructors with us. Without our educators, our youths would be empty vessels. Let's give these fine men and women a round of—"

Leader Sarwald jerks back, gasping. He clutches at his chest. Blood spills through his fingers as he collapses on the stage.

It's all so fast. A blur of shouting. People rushing to the stage. Rosemarie's hand slaps over her mouth, but I still hear her scream. Loud, shrill, scared. My heart lurches. I want to run forward to help, but I can't move. Can't breathe ….

"Grand Sarwald has been shot!" someone cries.

"He's not breathing!"

"Dead!"

A wall of people swarm the front of the stage. While most gazes are fixed on Grand Sarwald, I climb on my chair and search the back of the stage where the playformers huddle together—except for one cloaked figure, backing away. Lights glint off a silver object in his hand—a blow pipe. As he shoves the pipe into his cloak pocket, his mask slips off.

I cry out, and he looks straight at me.

With killer sea-blue eyes.

PART
TWO

Sixteen

I realize the word I called out: *Nate.*

Around me people are shouting, shoving. Yet I'm frozen in a dream of unreality.

Nate stares at me for a few heartbeats, then whirls and jumps off the stage. Before his feet touch the ground, he's tackled by four hulking Uniforms. They punch him, viciously twist his arms, and drag him away.

My eyes burn like I'm crying fire. But there are no tears.

"Milly!" snaps a voice beside me.

I don't move. I can't. I'm in a dream, right? Nothing is real.

But my shoulder hurts, fingers dig into my skin, and when my thoughts clear, I realize Rosemarie has grabbed me. She jerks me around so we're facing each other, her usually sweet features twisted in fury.

"Come with me," she orders. "Now!"

The stage is a mob of Uniforms, barking out orders, and there are pink-garbed people too, kneeling beside Leader Sarwald. Hope surges through me at the sight of the skillful health workers. They'll know how to repair him.

No one ever dies.

Rosemarie pulls me away, but I look back at grim head shakes. The Uniforms have stepped back in a respectful line, their heads bowed. Health workers bend over the still figure, only they're using sharp cutting tools on his head, not saving a life. Retrieving memories.

"Do *not* say a word until we're alone," Rosemarie hisses at me.

I nod. I can't talk. Don't want to.

She marches me down aisles through people buzzing with shock and outrage. I keep seeing blood spread across Grand Sarwald's chest and the blow pipe in Nate's hand. A nightmare cycling on repeat.

Rosemarie leads me to the solar coach and shoves me inside. She slams the door then turns to me. "How do you know the hooded boy?" she demands.

I shake my head. "I don't know him."

Anger twists her face as she leans toward me. "I heard you!" she accuses. "You called him Nate."

I shake my head again, desperately. "I don't know what I said! I was too scarified to do anything."

"You know him," she accuses.

"No ... I don't."

"Liar!" Her hand whips out and she slaps my face.

I reel backward, touching my stinging cheek. No one has ever hit me. I'm gasping, hardly able to breathe. Rosemarie is my friend in a Family of strangers. But now she's a stranger too.

"Do. Not. Lie." Her nails dig into my arm painfully. "You may think I'm being cruel, but I'm trying to protect you. What if someone else heard you call out to the killer? Do you know what will happen if they think you helped him?"

"I—I wouldn't ... I didn't!" I start to shake.

"How do you know him?"

"I don't really!" I gulp in air, thinking fast for a convincing story. I can't tell her about my trips to my cave, so I create a near version of the truth. "I only met him once. A few weeks ago when I was walking on a trail."

"Why didn't you tell anyone?"

I shake my head. "I—I wasn't sure what to do."

"So you did nothing?" Anger steams under her words. But she pauses, takes a breath, then asks in a softer tone, "Exactly what did he tell you?"

"Only his name."

"You asked nothing else? You're the most questioning youth I've ever met. You must have asked him more."

If only I could have, I think sadly. "Someone else was coming down the trail, and he ran into the trees. I didn't think my Instructors would believe me if I told them of a youth not of my born-group. Where does he come from?"

"Not from ShareHaven, that's for certain."

"Then where?"

"Outside." Rosemarie scowls. "But he never should have been able to get past our Fence. Did you see which direction he went?"

I think of broken wire in the Fence. I thought Nate a friend … but I was wrong. I showed an enemy the way inside ShareHaven. I swallow guilt. "I didn't see where he went. I ran back to the Edu-Center."

She peers into my face, probably comparing me to her Milly—an obedient sister who would never hide truths. "Leaders need to know of outsiders."

"Are you going to tell them?" I suck in a nervous breath.

"I should. But I won't."

"Thank you."

"I've never lied to the Leaders before … but I can't lose

141

Milly again."

She embraces me like I'm the sister she loves. I stiffen at first, then relax into her comfort. It feels good to have someone care.

"I'm sorry … about everything," I say, overwhelmed with emotions. "I should have told someone … and now Grand Sarwald is … but he can't really be gone. The health-keepers will mend him, won't they?"

She shakes her head, tears in her eyes as she tucks a strand of my hair behind my ear. "We must keep what you've told me a secret. Understand?"

I sniffle and nod.

"Good," she says with a sigh. "I doubt anyone else heard you call that boy. All the focus was on the podium. If anyone does ask, I'll cover for you. And I'm sorry for that." She points to my cheek. "I shouldn't have lost my temper. But I was fearful the Uniforms would take you away."

I bite my lip. "To jail?"

"If they suspect you of betraying the community, they'll do worse." She glances down at her tightly clasped hands.

I think of what might happen to Nate and shudder. "Execution?"

"Not for youths. You would be punished differently than an outsider." Her lower lip quivers. "I can't speak of it, so don't ask again. Show only your very best behavior. Promise me?"

I nod, holding my breath.

I know what she's afraid to say.

The worst punishment is being Returned.

The cloudless sky shines springtime blue, although it's nearly winter. We drive by fields where wooly grazers wag their tails, hoxen munch on dark wilding grass, and red-winged birds flutter high from branches, singing sweet melodies. Life on our peaceful community goes on as if nothing has changed.

As if our Grand Leader hasn't died.

Rosemarie and I are the first to return from the Sunday Fair.

She slips her arm around my shoulders as we leave the vehicle barn, and we walk the stone path to our dwelling.

"Are you all right?" she asks, shutting the door behind us.

I nod. "Are you?"

"I'm not sure …. I can't stop thinking about … about …." Her voice trails off. She rubs her forehead, then says she's going to lie down.

I tell her not to be concerned with chores. I need to work, to stay busy, so my mind doesn't plunge back to the podium.

Humming a wordless tune that Lorelei taught me, I stare out a kitchen window across buildings, pastures, and gardens. It's beauteous here, I realize with surprise. Beauty isn't something I expected from the Cross Family, where most of them work in constructing and have callused hands. I look down at my hands, smooth except for my short, cracked fingernails. There's a burn mark on my thumb from the heatery coils, but it's already fading to pink.

I still wonder what would have happened if I told Scientist Lila how I really felt about joining the Cross Family. Would she have changed my future? Or was I only fooling myself? Scientists are above ordinary people, devoted to miracles and discoveries. I'm where I was born to be—in a Family.

Still, I'm uneasy with my new relatives. I peel carrots,

listening for hoxen clomping and rumbling carts. What will happen when Leader Cross and the others return? What has happened since we left Sunday Fair? Is Nate still alive? Why do I even care about a killer?

Where does Nate come from? "Outside" was all Rosemarie told me. But how can anyone survive outside the Fence? I've seen drawings of fearsome gorilla-panther hybrid beasts, and sometimes at night I hear roars. I'm safe, though, inside ShareHaven. At least I thought I was. Now I fear no one is safe. Murder is no longer an unreal concept, and this memory won't easily fade. Death's bloody fingers have left a mark on my brain.

Yet it's not Grand Sarwald's face I keep seeing in my thoughts. It's Nate. Stun-looking, smiling, fascinating Nate. Why did he do such a terriful thing? Every morning ShareHaven citizens recite words of thanks to our scientists, who gave us forever life. Life, so precious and sacred. Yet in one blow of a killing pipe, Nate ended a life. I should hate him, want him punished. Yet I can't find hate, only sorrow at the thought of his execution. Because he will be killed, a quick, public death. No one escapes the Uniforms. They're kill-trained, and when they shoot, their aim is perfect.

A door slams, and I hear thudding footsteps. Leader Cross has returned. I duck out of sight and into the kitchen just as he strides down the hall, followed by Arthur, Jarod and Rosemarie's sons. They move swiftly with grim expressions. No one speaks of Sunday Fair.

Cowering in the kitchen, I rinse dishes in the sink. I can't stop thinking about Nate. I see his face in the reflection of water. In that moment our gaze met, his blue eyes widened with surprise, shame ... fear? He stared at me, seconds spilling like blood drops until he ran out of time. If I hadn't called his name, he would have escaped.

I've started peeling potatoes when Rosemarie comes into the kitchen.

"Your appointment is tomorrow," she says as if announcing good news.

The peeler slips from my fingers. "Appointment?"

She catches the peeler and hands it back to me. "You're due at City Central at noon."

Her words steal my breath. I guess what this is about—my first memdenity. My whole childhood has prepared me for this important step into adulthood. I'm curious to know more about Milly but not ready yet.

"So soon?" I whisper.

"Not soon enough—unless you plan to take up nudity."

I gape at her. "What?"

Rosemarie pinches a corner of my white tunic. "We ordered your fabric, but you need to go to their shop for measuring."

I nearly collapse with relief—although it seems disrespectful to be concerned about fashionizing when our highest leader has been murdered. "But shouldn't we wait? Won't there be ... more important things going on?"

"You're important to me," is all she says. She picks up a knife and chops peeled potatoes with sharp thwacks.

Chills slither up my skin in the steamy kitchen. How can Rosemarie be so calm after witnessing a death? My mind spins with images of Grand Sarwald's cry, his fall to the podium, and the sea-blue eyes of his killer. When Nate looked at me, his expression wasn't that of a killer but of a friend in trouble. He seemed so civilized when we spoke by the sea.

145

Yet his blood must run cold like a fish.

There is no communal dinner that night. Rosemarie and I eat on the small table in the kitchen. She prepares food trays that she carries away, refusing my offer to help. The scent of simmering secrets mixes with the aroma of vegetable stew. Rosemarie says her head aches and leaves to get a healing tonic. When she doesn't return, I put away the last clean dish. I climb the stairs and hear soft snoring, so I open the door quietly.

Rosemarie is already asleep in her bed. I'm careful not to wake her as I slip beneath my blankets. I fall into an uneasy sleep and dream about Nate.

We're back in the cave, only he's wearing denim pantons, not breathing tubes, and we're swimming together in the Lavender Pool. We don't speak—we only swim in circles around each other. He's all human, with ripping muscles and faint dark hairs on his legs and arms. He reaches out for me, and our fingers entwine. The light water storms to darkness. His hands change, coarse, scaled, and monstrous. His fish-skin hands squeeze my neck. Panic screams through me, agony for a breath, and I'm ....

Awake. I clutch my blankets to my chest, over my pounding heart, and gulp air. My skin is sticky with sweat. But the only terrors in my room are lurking in my thoughts.

I can't go back to sleep. I slip soundlessly out of the room so I don't wake Rosemarie, who sleeps on her stomach with one arm hugging her pillow.

In the kitchen, I pour a glass of milk and sit alone at the table, shivering from my dream. It's a warning about Nate, I decide. He may seem like a friend, but he's a killer. I must forget about him.

After rinsing out my glass, I leave the kitchen. But as I pass the meeting room, I hear rumbling voices.

The door is partially open, so I peek inside.

Empty.

Where are the voices coming from? The rumble echoes from the walls and floor. But there's no breath of life in the room—only flickering shadows from a lamp on the meeting table. I listen carefully, unable to pinpoint the source of the sound.

Could it be a ghost? I wonder, not really believing unquiet spirits exist. But only hours ago, I saw a man die, which makes unbelievable things more real. Like a soul, which I imagine as a silvery orb of sunshine and stars, small enough to fit into my hand, yet huge with shimmery energy. Did Grand Sarwald's soul die with his last breath? Or did the health workers tuck the soul safely in the tubes with his memories? Will he come back in twenty-five years in the body of a youth?

I hear murmurs again. The noise buzzes like bees from an unseen hive. Only there's no one else in the room.

The curtain has been pushed aside, and a glow from outside draws my attention to the window. When I press my face to the glass, I notice the double doors to the vehicle barn are wide open. Usually there are three solar coaches and two solar cycles stored inside, but now there are several more coaches.

When I glance around the meeting room, something else bothers me. The chairs are at odd angles instead of tucked under the table, and there's a tea cup where Leader Cross usually sits. When I touch the cup, it's warm.

The voices rumble again.

Slowly, I turn in place, searching for the sound. Could it be coming from the cabinet? The huge wooden cabinet has double doors folded together like closed wings. When I hook my finger into the door handle, it opens into a dark tunnel.

A hidden passage.

SEVENTEEN

Stairs plunge down, disappearing into darkness. I hesitate, then step onto the staircase. The voices grow louder.

Curiosity draws me down, down, down. I've gone five steps and can barely see my hand gripping a metal rail. Halfway between safety and danger, I pause. I shouldn't be here. Yet how can I retreat now? My thoughts travel back to when I first discovered my cave, thrilled to explore the unknown. There's no thrill now, only foreboding.

Blackness lightens, and my eyes adjust. Golden light glimmers from the bottom of the stairs. My foot creaks on the next step. I stiffen and hold my breath. I count sixty seconds. When I breathe again, I continue downward, cautiously. My nose itches from musty smells, and I fight the urge to sneeze. Near the bottom, the dim shapes of shelves hug basement walls. No one is around. Only boxes and rows of canning jars fill the room.

I follow a slant of light to the back of the room. A lamp glows over a door.

Voices rise in anger—a man, then a woman—although I can't understand their words. Why would anyone meet in such a dismal place? A night-time meeting seems dishonest. Whoever is beyond the door doesn't want to be discovered.

And neither do I.

Chilled air shivers up my bare arms as I reach for the

door. At my touch, it swings open a crack. I jump back, ready to run. But nothing happens, and I sniff an acrid odor coming from inside the room. Leaning close to the crack, I hear a woman say, "Must do something about him."

I know the warbling voice: Grandmother Ida May. How did that feeble woman make it down the steep stairs?

"Have faith." Leader Cross's voice is distinctive. "It's for the best."

Another voice rumbles, but I can't tell whether it's a man or woman. As the voices continue, low and urgent, the frustration of not knowing what's being said is a rash I need to scratch.

I angle my face against the opening, and I stare at a strange room. The walls are covered in gold-framed paintings of bleak deserts, stormy seas, and winged people battling with swords. Beside a tray of biscuits, smoky tendrils swirl from candles in ornate bronze holders on a marble table. More candles glow on a raised dais painted with images of moons and stars. Perched on the stand are marble statues of figures in robes, some with wings, and a few kneeling with pressed hands, reminding me of the way Rosemarie knelt by her bed, her hands folded together.

At the heart of the room, chairs form a circle, and I recognize Leader Cross, Arthur, and Daisy, who sits close to Grandmother. I strain to see the others but can only see a few, each of them wearing gold chains with four-point stars—like the necklace I found in Milly's jewelry box.

"Why at Sunday Fair?" asks a stocky man who looks a decade older than twenty-five. His thick eyebrows blend together like a mustache in the wrong place. This would make me smile if I wasn't so tense.

"We never choose the time or place and must be grateful for the gifts we receive." Leader Cross sips tea then adds, "It's the will of our higher power."

"With a little help," Daisy adds, her eyes flaring like flames. When Grandmother frowns at her, she looks away.

"The timing was unfortunate," Leader Cross says in a superior tone I've noticed him use when speaking to women. "We can only pray for his spirit to find peace."

"He was a good man," Arthur adds soberly. Around the somber circle, heads bow in agreement. "He will be missed."

Grand Sarwald, that's who they're speaking of. Is this some sort of gathering to mourn his passing? But then why are so few people here? I only recognize one man from the Sarwald Family.

A tall man wearing a small round hat touches his heart. "We have comfort in knowing he's gone to a better place."

Better place? But nowhere is better than ShareHaven. Savages and beasts roam outside the Fence, and civilizations beyond our island were devastated by the mind-plague. What's going on here? Leader Cross makes the rules for our Family, so why gather with such secrecy with people from other Families? I bite my lip, wanting to hear more, yet afraid of being caught. If I back up quietly, I can leave without anyone knowing.

"What about the boy?"

This question is asked by Arthur—it's hard to think of him as my husband—and it startles me. Who are they talking about?

"He's no threat," Leader Cross insists.

"I must disagree, Ryan," Arthur says, frowning. "Many will wonder how he got through the Fence."

Daisy nods. "He'll be questioned."

"If he talks, my Family will never forgive me." A woman with tawny brown skin and high cheekbones twists her gold chain. "I'll be dishonored!"

"Nilene, calm down." Leader Cross reaches out to reassure her. "He won't expose us. He has sub-intelligence and gives no value to life—not his own or anyone else's."

"He could break under torture," warns a man in the back whom I can't see.

"Leading the Uniforms to our tunnel." Arthur drums his fingers on the chair, the intense depth in his gaze reminding me that my mere fifteen years is nothing compared to his centuries of experiences.

"The boy won't get a chance to talk." Leader Cross sweeps a commanding gaze around the circle, as if each person in the room is a piece on his chessboard and he's going for checkmate. "Execution will silence his tongue."

Execution! I jerk back, bumping my elbow against the wall. I suck in a breath, sure someone heard me. But the conversation continues, and I exhale. Although I'm sick inside, now I'm sure they're talking about Nate.

"Wouldn't it be more sensical to help him escape?"

This question comes from a woman sitting behind Arthur. When she stands, I'm stunned. I stare, not wanting to believe my eyes. Yet candlelight flickers across a face I know ... and love.

Instructor Penny.

How can she be part of this conspiracy? While other Instructors only saw my mistakes, Instructor Penny saw my heart. I never window-gazed during her lessons because I didn't want to disappoint her.

Now I'm the one disappointed.

"Penelope, you're being too emotional," Leader Cross says.

"The boy only did what he was told," Instructor Penny argues, lifting her head high and not allowing Leader Cross to intimidate her. I want to applaud.

"The savage got caught," the bushy mustached man complains.

"Still, he succeeded," Arthur says. "Also, his aim was impressive."

"True. He showed real talent. Unfortunately, he won't be around when we need those skills again." Leader Cross' words knife-twist inside me. He used Nate to kill Grand Sarwald and speaks of murder with no regret. Anger burns through me. No one is who I thought. Not Leader Cross, my almost-husband, or my favorite Instructor.

Daisy pushes back her hair to expose her disfigured cheek as she stands beside Instructor Penny. "This is all wrong. What have we become?"

"Never doubt why we gather here, child," Grandmother's gnarled fingers grasp Daisy's hand. "In your soul, you know what matters. Hold onto that."

"But I never expected something so public … so bloody." Daisy's voice is softer, vulnerable. "It was different last time—a quiet passing. The only one who suspected the truth was Rosemarie, and she'll never give us away."

Leader Cross nods. "Not after what we've given her."

"Against my wishes." Daisy glares. "I don't care what the scientists say, youths can't replace the dead. That girl will never be my mother."

"I won't argue with you," Leader Cross says. "But she

is a distraction that keeps Rosemarie happy. That's all that matters."

"Unless she flips out like the last one," Daisy warns.

"He was a DNA abnormality. The scientists assure it won't happen again."

"If you can believe them," Daisy says.

"Can we return to the real issue here?" Arthur lifts his arm, demanding attention. "What should be done about the boy? He could destroy us."

"I've spoken to the Civility Keepers," Leader Cross assures, "and they'll arrange the execution soon."

"Your solution to a death is more killings?" Instructor Penny stomps her boot on the floor. "How can you be so callous?"

"Is it callous to protect my Family? Turn your concern to your own Family. The savage was only a tool. No one will mourn him."

I cringe, wanting to defend Nate. He's intelligent, gentle, and his smile is far from savage. Why would Nate take orders from people who hate him?

Instructor Penny shakes her head. "Have you all forgotten why we meet in secret? Where's your compassion? The boy isn't much older than our youths."

Leader Cross snorts. "He's fortunate to have survived this long—those creatures rarely see age eighteen. We should have exterminated them long ago. One less Noc is no loss."

Noc? But that would mean .... Not Nate. No, he can't be. Yet it explains why he didn't tell me where he came from and how he can live outside the Fence.

Nate is a Nocturne.

EIGHTEEN

My thoughts are fog, so cold and dense that I'm sure I'll never find my way back to my room. But I do.

Rosemarie snores softly from her bed, a sniffly snort that often keeps me awake yet now rumbles reassurance. I'm glad she wasn't involved in the secret meeting.

Careful not to wake her, I don't turn on a lamp. Moonlight spills through the window—a silvery path I follow to my bed. I slip out of my clothes and underneath the covers. Sleep, though, is not so easy. My brain won't shut off and replays everything I've heard. I clutch my pillow, squeezing it so tight I'm surprised it doesn't burst and spill out feathers. What am I going to do? Why did everyone at the meeting conspire to kill Leader Sarwald?

Nate knows the truth, I realize. But he won't get a chance to tell anyone.

Execution. I can't bear to think of this. Leader Cross called Nate a "savage," as if he's less than human. But he's very human. I can't forget his stunning smile and the way he spoke my name, in that lilting yet husky voice that touched me in an unexplainable way.

My head aches, and my pillow is damp. I hadn't realized I was crying. Is it for Nate? Why do I even care? I can't help him. There hasn't been an execution in many decades. Death will be quick, that much I remember from my lessons. But

I don't know which method will be used. Poison injection, electrical wires, or a flame pyre? He'll be marched to a raised podium as if he were the playformer he'd pretended to be. But he won't speak any lines, and there's only one act.

If only I could save him, I think as I sink into sleep. If only ….

I wake to aching eyes and a sick feeling of dread. I glance over at Rosemarie's bed made neatly. She's gone.

Sunlight slices through the window. Hurriedly, I put on coverings and run a comb through my tangled hair, then wrap my hair in my scarf and hurry downstairs. I smell buttery toasted bread as I near the kitchen. Daisy sits at the table alone, sipping tea and biting into sourdough toast. Her hair looks different today, parted to one side so a soft curl waves across her scar, and her face is brighter with rosy lips, a soft lavender coloring over her eyes, and she wears a pink tunic with a lovely pattern of red roses.

Although I long to ask about her transformation, I know I'll be lucky to get a "good morning" from her. So I ask if she's seen Rosemarie.

"She's busy." Yup, the rudeness goes on.

"Doing what?" I persist.

"Not your concern."

"It is too." I stand my ground, giving her a hard stare. "Rosemarie's going to drive me to City Central for Family clothing."

"Change of plan. She can't, so I'm going to take you."

"Where is she?" I ask, alarmed. "Is she okay?"

"She's fine." Daisy sighs as if talking to me is a waste of breath. "If you must know, her son, Titus, sprained his ankle, so she's helping him today. We leave in a half hour.

Don't make me wait."

Before I can protest, Daisy stands up from the table to stride out of the room, leaving crust on a dish for me to clear.

I rush through breakfast, then quickly tidy the kitchen. I'm wiping my damp hands on a cloth when I hear footsteps. Daisy has returned, standing in the doorway with folded arms, frowning in a clear message of "time to go."

Tossing the cloth aside, I follow her.

Daisy leads me to a three-wheeled cycle. It's smaller than a solar coach, with a glass bubble over a padded bench and space only for two. I watch Daisy turn a knob on the wheel then pump a foot pedal until a panel light shines blue and the engine hums to life. *I could do this*, I think, and wonder when I'll be allowed to drive alone.

"Sit," Daisy commands, tapping a sequence of four buttons on the panel.

Daisy is speaking to me, which raises hope that she'll get over her resentment. Was it my idea to become her mother? No. So why does she hate me? When I have Milly's memories, I'll love Daisy. Hard to imagine now.

Once we're on the main road, Daisy returns to ignoring me. I look out the window, eagerness rising as I remember my last journey to City Central. As a youth, coming to City Central was rare. I pressed my face against the window, fascinated by how quickly we traveled and by all the glimpses of flat-roofed dwellings and hybrid work-animals penned in corrals. I tried hard not to blink, afraid to miss anything.

It was especially thrilling to tour the Retro-Museum, spilling with questions as I followed the Instructors from one exhibit to another. So much to see! Displays, photos, and relics from retro-century covered the walls and dangled from wood beams high on the ceiling. Retro devices like cameras, music on disks, and hand-sized computers were displayed behind protective glass. And there were rare paper relics: shoe boxes, cereal boxes (for some sort of morning meal), and newspapers with tiny faded printing. Paper made from trees, not the hemper grown in heat-domes, was as common as dirt back in long ago. Murder was common too. In a back room, a wall of photos showed scarifying visions of riots, wars, gangs, and even violence among families.

"Let this be a warning," Instructor Ivan told us, "of what happens in societies that don't respect Family and follow rules."

Of course, today is about fashion, not history.

The first building we see as we enter City Central is constructed with steel and bricks, towering like a doomed castle. Instead of curtains on the windows, there are iron bars.

The prison, I realize with a twist in my stomach. I frown at the gray-garbed Uniforms standing guard at the entrance. I know who they're guarding. His execution will take place within days.

And I will join my Family to watch.

Daisy drops me off at the fashionizing shop, a rectangular dwelling in a dark wood hue, with shuttered windows like most buildings. The plaque over the door glitters with bright purple writing: *Ying Coverings*.

"If you finish before I return, wait on the front steps." Daisy actually smiles, probably because she's glad to get rid of me. She hurries away, her step light with eagerness. Where is she going?

When Lorelei leads me into a back room, I tell her about Daisy's strange behavior. "She seemed so joyous," I add.

"Not at all like her usual sourness."

Lorelei shrugs. "I'm not surprised."

"What do you mean?"

"Daisy is your daughter and you don't know?" She arches her brows in an exaggerated way.

I shake my head. "I'm the last person Daisy would confide in."

"It's not a very secret secret." Lorelei's braid brushes against me as she leans to whisper. "She's in love with a man from a different Family. But she can't marry him because he is committed to his wife partner."

I think of Marcus and how he wanted me to Choose a Name that would leave me free to marry. "Why doesn't Daisy find someone to love who's free to marry?" I ask.

Lorelei giggles. "Don't you know anything about love?"

"As much as you know. We had the same edu-lessons."

"But I paid attention in class, not only to the books but to what went on with our mates and Instructors," she says in her annoying know-everything tone. "Remember when I told you that one of our mates was in love with an Instructor?"

"I didn't believe you. Who was it?"

"Clark. Didn't you notice the flowers on Instructor Serenity's workstation?"

"Those flowers were from a student?" I asked, surprised because I thought Instructor Serenity picked the lovely vase of wildflowers herself.

"If you didn't stare out windows so much you'd notice what's going on in front of your face," Lorelei teases. "It ended badly, though. Because of Clark's obsession with our teacher, her Leader gave her a different work assignment."

"But it wasn't her fault," I object.

"Love isn't fair ... it just is. You're clever, but you know little about romance."

"I know more than you think." I turn from her, pretending to admire a pink silk fabric while I bite back anger.

Lorelei wouldn't mock me if I'd told her about my one-and-only kiss with Marcus. It happened during a game of seek-hiding. When I crawled into a hollow beneath a willow tree, I found someone already hiding there. In the darkness, I wasn't sure who it was until he whispered, "Quiet!" I recognized Marcus's voice. We huddled close, barely breathing. I could smell his lemon-washed hair, feel the fine hairs on his arm, and hear the quick thuds of our heartbeats. He started to speak, but I heard a footstep outside our hiding hole, and I silenced his words with a kiss. My body softened, heated and tingling at his nearness. But Marcus pushed me away. I'd confused him—but it was confusing for me too. The kiss made me wonder if I loved Marcus, yet afterward he avoided me. We didn't speak for two miserable weeks.

I began to understand why, when Head Instructor Ivan held a special lesson for all youths. "You are reaching an age where your bodies will turn traitor on your sensical natures. You must resist these childish feelings. Immature emotions create a false love that can be as destructive as the mind-plague. Those under twenty-five are in most danger of losing their minds to love. When you are sixteen and protected by the sterilization process, you may explore your physical natures. But always remember that the purest love is for your Family."

For a long time, I thought if I got near a boy I'd lose my mind. Retro people lost memories because of the airborne disease that attacked their brains. Love sounded like a disease too, when not controlled in a Family. It was reassuring to learn the urges would go away with medication and maturity.

Yet Daisy has been a mature twenty-five for over a century, and she's "exploring her physical nature" with someone she can never marry. It would be more sensical to find someone unmarried in the Cross Family.

I turn back to Lorelei to ask about the man Daisy loves, but we're interrupted by Lorelei's "daughter" bustling into the room, a cloth measuring tape dangling from her fingers and the fabrics Rosemarie selected for me at Sunday Fair.

Over the next hour, I am swathed in soft, lovely fabrics. Lorelei and I are watched closely by her daughter, so our conversation stays polite, but we catch each other's glances, communicating in subtle gestures. Her daughter glares at me when I forget to call her Flavia. So I make a game out of saying her name with an exaggerated FLA-via or Fla-VEE-ah. It's very, very hard not to giggle.

I'm standing like a scarecrow with my arms stretched out and pins holding together the seams of a silky fabric when a man rushes in and declares a "stitching emergency!" I try not to laugh at the large rip in the rear of his pantons. Lorelei offers to help the man, but her daughter shakes her head.

"You lack the skills, Flavia. I'll attend to this and finish Milly later. Reschedule her for tomorrow."

Lorelei's shoulders droop, but she doesn't complain. Her lips are tight, angry, as she yanks the pins from my fabric. I try to comfort her, but she won't talk to me. I know she's longing for memdenity so she'll never again be accused of lacking skills.

Outside, I sit on a brick planter, looking up and down the

paveway for Daisy. I lean forward with my elbows propped on my knees and my head resting on my palms. I think of Lorelei's sadness at not being allowed to help. Why couldn't her daughter give her a chance to show what she—not Flavia—can do? Lorelei is an amazing needle-weaver. She's saved me by repairing torn pantons so well the Instructors never suspected I'd damaged them. I believe in Lorelei's skill, but she doesn't believe in herself. If only I could convince her she doesn't need someone else's memories to be skilled.

I hear the whirl of a solar cart and look up expectantly. Not Daisy—another Family's cart. Daisy asked me to wait and I gave it a try, but waiting rips.

Time to explore, I decide. I'll be back before Daisy returns.

City Central dwellings have wood plaques tacked over business entries to identify their services. Instrumental music sails through the window of a documenter office. Next door another building has large round windows and grand sculptures climbing up the steep brick steps. *Civility Keepers*, I read on the plaque over the door.

Across the road a door is wide open, inviting customers. *Fooders* reads the plaque. Cinnamon smells brings a memory from when I was age seven and going on my first lesson trip with Instructor Penny. The shop dazzled us with crates and crates full of sweet treats, like being inside a rainbow that had burst into candy pieces. Cakies, dough twists, sticklets, and sugar orbs shimmered like treasure. Charity Lawson, a sticklet-thin woman with freckles like cinnamon sprinkling her pasty face, invited me to choose one sweet for my own. I knew immediately what I wanted—a blueberry sugar cakie.

Now as I inhale a whiff of sugar, my mouth waters with

delicious memory. I would give anything for a cakie but have nothing to barter. After memdenity is complete and I'm accepted fully into the Cross Family, I'll receive a bartering allowance. But today I have nothing.

Charity Lawson has the cinnamon-freckled sameness of my long ago visit. I was half her height then, but now we stand at the same level.

"You're Milly—the Cross' youth," she says with a smile that stretches wide across her face. "But why are you out alone?"

"I finished my fashionizing appointment early," I say.

"I loved getting new coverings when I was Chosen by the Lawsons."

I look at her surprised. "You were a youth?"

"I was one of the first. Since then my Family has welcomed three more youths. I've been Charity Lawson so long I don't even remember my born name."

I stare at her, my mouth falling open. "How can you forget your name?"

"It started with an M, or was that an N?" She shrugs. "It doesn't matter."

"But you had that name for fifteen years. You had Instructors and youth mates and many experiences."

"I remember what's important." She gestures around the candy shop. "I'm a Lawson with a wonderful husband, parents, two sisters, dozens of cousins, and five children. Now my Family has Digger too, and he's a fine young man."

Digger? Oh, yeah. Ted wasn't a close mate, although I like him well enough. He has a disgusting habit of chewing with his mouth open.

"I'm glad for Digger," I say politely. "He's a great match

for your Family."

"He enjoys eating, perhaps more than store work, but he has an eagerness for learning."

I sniff the sweet air and think enviously of Digger going to such a welcoming Family.

Charity Lawson smiles at me. "What would you like?"

"One of everything," I tease, then shake my head. "But I can't today. I have nothing to barter."

"Pick your favorite sweet as a gift from me," she says, coming beside me and leading me to a case. I can hardly choose with so many delicious sweets, finally pointing to a blueberry sugar cakie.

As I walk slowly, savoring the flavor of blueberry, my thoughts circle from Nate to Rosemarie to Daisy and back to Nate. I'm not paying attention to where I'm headed, as if my feet have thoughts of their own. When I look up, I'm in front of the dismal brick building that towers over the paveway like a dark cloud. The sweetness in my mouth goes sour as I gaze at the jail. Its oppressive grayness chills my skin. Two Uniforms guard the entry, allowing no one in or out without permission.

Nate is in there, I think. A tool—that's what Leader Cross called him. Not a human with feelings and fears, but an object to be used, then discarded. How long before his execution?

I don't know why he killed Leader Sarwald, but he didn't act alone. My Family was involved. I stare up at the brick building and long to see Nate. But I won't see him until his execution when I join my community to watch him die.

Sighing, I turn away from the jail.

I've only taken a few steps before the sound of a door opening causes me to whirl around. The Uniforms standing guard slide aside and bow with respect as a woman leaves the jail. She lifts a corner of her shining gold and purple robe as she descends the stairs. Her hair is pulled back, her skin showing fine lines of age, and her expression is distant, as if her thoughts are far away.

What is Scientist Lila doing at the jail?

NINETEEN

Lila shouldn't be here.

It was strange to see scientists at the Celebraze and Sunday Fair, but visiting the jail? This goes against all I've been taught about the separation of Families and scientists. The scientists' compound is a community of its own, with secrets and locked doors. Scientists take no active role in the community.

"Jennza, is that you?"

Lila Farrow's commanding voice stops me before I can move away. She smiles at me as if we're close friends. I can't smile back. Did she see Nate in the jail? Has he been tortured? Did he tell her about Leader Cross and the others who conspired to kill our Head Leader?

"Jennza, what a nice surprise." Lila comes up beside me, putting a gloved hand over my arm. "But why are you out alone?"

"I had a fitting." I glance toward the fashionizing shop, plucking at a corner of my faded white tunic. "Rosemarie says I lack suitable coverings."

"You deserve new tunics and much more. I hope you're adjusting well to your Family."

Her mouth twists when she says "Family," and I wonder if she still disapproves of me being Chosen by the Cross Family. I don't understand her interest, but a burst of hope rushes through me. Scientists are all-powerful, and if they make a decision, even if it's against rules, leaders must obey. If Scientist Lila asks again if I want to be in the Cross Family, I'll tell her the truth.

She points to my head. "The Cross Family scarf looks good on you."

"I'm not so sure." I hesitate, searching her face for a sign that she might still want me. "The black cross on red fabric isn't very … um … interesting."

"It depends how you wear it."

"I'd rather tie my hair with colored bands or wear it loose … is there a way to … to wear my hair however I choose?"

She arches her brows. "You'll have to ask Rosemarie. She knows more about fashions than I do."

There is a closed door in her expression. She gave me one chance and I ripped it. There are no second chances.

"I'll ask her," I say with a forced smile.

"I hear you are becoming a skillful house-crafter. You have a long, useful life ahead of you." She looks back at the jail, and her lips purse as if she's thinking of something distasteful. "I'm glad for you, Jennza."

I hide my disappointment with politeness. "Thank you. But I'm called Milly now."

"Of course … Milly." She studies me. "Where are you headed?"

"My ride hasn't come yet, so I'm taking a walk."

"Rosemarie is late?" she asks. "She's usually more responsible."

"Not Rosemarie. Daisy drove me."

"Ah … Daisy. You may have a long wait," Lila says with a

sly smile, so I know she's heard the rumors about Daisy too.

"I don't mind. I enjoy seeing more of City Center," I say.

"What's to see? Dull boxy dwellings."

"It's not dull to me. I like exploring."

"As I do too. But I'd rather explore a natural vista of sky, trees, and sea. All the buildings here look alike."

"Except the one you left." I point at the jail.

She nods solemnly. "It's a grim place I'd rather stay far from."

I raise my brows in question. "But you were inside."

"Sometimes it's necessary to get involved with the community." She tilts her head, studying me. "Yesterday we witnessed a shocking tragedy, but the Nocturne is behind bars, so there's no reason for you to be afraid."

"I'm not." At least not for myself.

"Of course not, fearless Jennza." She touches my cheek softly. "When I first saw you on the stage at the Celebraze, I could tell you were strong-willed and independent. I think you would find my compound interesting, and someday I'd like to take you there for a walk along the sea cliff trails."

"Really? Could you do that?" I ask, surprised because no one *ever* visits the scientists.

"I usually get what I want. But don't speak of this to anyone." Her brown eyes brighten to yellow-gold as she brings her finger to her lips. "My fellow scientists didn't want me to come here, but I feel a responsibility to our community and wanted to offer my support on behalf of all scientists."

Something in her tone, an urgency mixed with excitement, makes me ask, "Did you see the prisoner?"

She peers at me as if she can hear my thoughts, and I squirm uneasily under her golden gaze. I shouldn't have asked a scientist something so rude. But nothing I've been taught about scientists fits the way Lila treats me.

"What do you know about the Nocturne?" Lila asks me.

I shrug. "Nothing."

"Are you sure? At the playformance, when Grand Sarwald fell, everyone focused on helping him—except you. You were fixated on the Nocturne," she says in a tone too casual for her barbed-wire words.

"I don't remember that—only my shock. I stared at Grand Sarwald too, until I was too sad to look anymore."

"There's something more you aren't disclosing."

I make a face of complete innocence, which I've perfected from childhood. Wide eyes, arched brows, and slack mouth. Even Instructors who know I did wrong doubted my guilt. But Lila peers intently into my face.

"I feel a connection with you, Jennza," she says softly. "When we met, I sensed we were very much alike—adventurers, leaders, not followers. I know most Instructors were tough on you, not understanding your need to question rather than conform. I understand how that feels, and I will honor any secret you share with me."

Her silky words spin a web around me, and I'm tempted to unload all my worries on her steady shoulders. Still, something holds me back.

"I don't have any secrets."

"You can trust me," she says. "Speak freely about whatever is on your mind. Are you troubled by Grand Sarwald's death?"

I glance away, sighing. "It doesn't seem real."

"Sadly, it's too real." Lila shakes her silvery head. "Grand Sarwald was a dear friend, and I'm sorry that I'll never speak to him again. I already miss him."

"But his memories were saved," I say, wanting to comfort her. "He can be born again in a youth."

"Perhaps ...." She bites her lip, then glances up at the sky. "Scientists believe the essence of a person is stored in memories."

"Essence?" I repeat. "Is that the same as soul?"

She touches my cheek softly. "What does a youth like you know of soul?"

"Not much." I shrug. "What is it?"

"No one really knows, not even scientists, although we may say we do. It all comes down to faith." She sighs. "You would think a long life would mean knowing the meaning of everything, but time only gives us more time to ponder over questions."

I look at her curiously, having no idea what she means.

"Apologies if I've confused you," she says. "What happened yesterday has shaken me. I can't forget the look on Grand Sarwald's face as he collapsed. "

"I can't either," I admit, although it's not Grand Sarwald I can't forget. It's Nate—his cloak falling back, his shock to see me, and his gaze pulling me in like an undertow.

Lila glances again at the jail, frowning. "We need to protect ourselves from outsiders. Apparently the Gate and Fence aren't enough. The Nocturne's execution will send a strong warning to others like him."

I shift uneasily. "Has he ... um ... told anyone why he killed our leader?"

"He hasn't spoken a word."

I nod, struggling to stay calm. "Has it ... the execution ... been scheduled?"

She nods. "Two days."

I can barely breathe. I want to plead with her to save Nate. He may be a killer, but there's good in him too, or he wouldn't have offered to help Petal, or saved me from the vampfish. I owe him my life.

I'm trying hard to hide my emotions, but tears sting my eyes. I turn away.

"What's wrong?" Lila's arm comes around me tenderly. "Is there something you want to tell me?"

"Seeing one death was bad enough ...." My words trail off in a sigh.

"I've never approved of the Leaders' insistence that all citizens witness executions—not that we've had very many. Only three in this century. I would gladly excuse you from going, but I can't interfere in such matters. Don't waste sympathy on our enemy."

"But he's so young," I say. "Isn't there a less violent punishment?"

"The laws state that punishments match the crime. You have a kindly heart, Jennza," she says with a deliberate emphasis on my youth name. "I hope you'll think of me as a friend."

She leans so close I inhale her flowery perfume, the scent that made me realize she spied on me after the Celebraze. I know I shouldn't trust her, yet she makes me feel valued, as if my thoughts and feeling are important. But why did she show unusual interest in me? Scientists don't notice youths—not without a reason.

I look down to the paveway, where a scraggly weed has broken through a crack in the hard surface. If I told Lila about the conversation I overheard in the Cross cellar, she'd know Nate didn't act alone. But would she help him?

"Are you afraid of the killer?" Lila asks, mistaking the reason for my silence. "I assure you, there's no way for him to escape."

"Has anyone ever escaped?" I ask hopefully.

She shakes her silvery head. "Uniforms are posted at all entrances and cells have locked steel doors. The prisoner is in the most secure cell at the far back of the prison. Even if someone tried to help him escape, they'd never get into the jail. So be assured, there won't be any more killings."

Except Nate's, I think sadly.

She glances at a time piece on her wrist. "I'm late for an appointment, so I must leave. It's been lovely seeing you, and I promise it won't be the last time. Take care, dear Jennza." She surprises me by drawing me close in a hug.

Her touch lingers on my shoulders as I watch her leave. She moves in a brisk manner, her head high and her arms swaying at her sides, and I imagine walking beside her on a rocky cliff path.

I should return to the fashionizers. But doing what I should has never interested me. My gaze lifts to the jail.

Nate's in there.

Lila spoke of his cell as inescapable, deep in the prison— as if he's already dead and buried.

An idea jumps into my mind. Crazy. Too risky. I shouldn't even think about it.

But I'm already moving. I make sure no one is watching, then step off the path, ducking into the dense bushes alongside the jail. Shadows swallow me. I have the odd sense of leaving society and entering a wild new world.

Dying leaves crunch beneath my feet, the sound echoing

like thunder. Branches twist and tangle around me. A gnarly branch grabs my hair, pulling painfully as I jerk away. I keep going, slowly. I push away a branch, but when it flings back with thorns as sharp as arrows, I drop to the ground, tasting dirt. I start to rise, but I spot a faint animal trail that disappears beneath the bushes.

Crawling on my hands and knees through the bushes, I feel more animal than human. Sounds fade to my own ragged breathing and the skittering noises of tiny creatures scurrying up branches or down into holes. When I come through the bushes, I blink at the sudden brightness.

I stare at the wild ivy spiraling up the wall. A dark stain of metal bars slashes against the brick building.

Nate's window.

TWENTY

I'm here. Now what?

I imagine Marcus asking, "Why don't you ever think before you act?"

The barred jail window is just beyond my fingertips. Vines twine up the walls like a ladder that would snap under my weight. Aside from the risk of pain and bone breakage, a crash to the ground would alert Uniforms.

There are so many reasons why I should leave. Nate's an enemy of ShareHaven. I saw him holding the blow pipe that struck down Grand Sarwald. I need to know why he did it. But will he tell me the truth?

There's a chill in the air, not from the darkening clouds, but from the jail. As if brick can exhale ice and danger. Worries storm through my mind: What if Nate isn't alone? If the Uniforms find me, what will they do to me?

I bend down, pick up a small rock, and fling it at the barred window. It's swallowed by a maze of vines. I try another rock, throwing it so high it bangs against the window and bounces into the ivy. I jump at the sound, diving back into the leafy shield of bushes.

When it seems safe to step back out into the opening, I search the ground for another rock. I find twigs, thorns and weeds—but not any rocks. I dig into the pocket of my tunic and pull out a patch of red fabric, a dried potato peel (how'd that get there?), and my star-shaped sand shell. I rub my thumb over my favorite shell before slipping it back into my pocket. Tossing the peel aside, I see an acorn on the ground and grab it. I aim carefully, then throw as hard as I can. The acorn soars through the window.

Muffled sounds echo from inside the jail. I stand alert, ready to move fast if a Uniform comes to the window. There's movement. A figure clasps the bars. Hidden in shadows, I can't see his face.

"Who's there?"

This raspy voice sounds nothing like Nate. Am I at the wrong window? I slip back into the bushes, peering at the figure leaning against the window. Clouds shift; sunlight slices through the bars. The sky reflects sea-blue eyes.

"Is someone there?" Nate rasps again.

His rough hand tightens around the bars. There's a scar from his left thumb to wrist, jagged and deep red like fire burns inside. Infection, I think, angry the health-keepers haven't treated his injury. But I know why and am sickened. Why heal a condemned man? He won't live long enough to die from an infection.

I step out into the light.

"Jennza!" he chokes out.

I nod and say softly, "Nate."

"I'm hallucinating. You can't be real," he says shaking his head.

"I am." I move closer so I'm clearly in his view.

"How did you ...? What are you doing here?"

I'm drawn into his gaze and can hardly think or breathe. How can I explain why I'm here when I don't really know? Is it only to satisfy my curiosity, or is it the thrilling rush

I get when I look into his eyes? He makes me feel like I'm teetering on the edge of a cliff, poised to dive into an unfathomable sea. I know he's dangerous, and yet I don't care.

"You're hurt." I gesture to his purpling bruises.

"Damaged but not dead." He grimaces. "Yet."

"So you know you're going to be ...." I stop, unable to finish.

"Executed," he finishes in an empty voice, as if part of him is already dead.

"I'm so sorry! If I hadn't startled you by calling out your name, you could have escaped."

"I know what will happen. What I don't know is why you came here."

"I'm not sure either." I glance down at scratches on my arm. "I just ... um ... wanted to see you."

"Not much to see."

Wrong, I think. Even with cuts and bruises, Nate fascinates me. I'm drawn to him in an unexplainable way and could stare into his eyes forever. But only one of us has forever.

"Jennza, it's dangerous for you to be here." He glances uneasily over his shoulder. "The Uniforms will check on me soon."

"I can't leave yet. Not without knowing ...."

"What?"

"Why you ..." I suck in a deep breath. "Why you killed Grand Sarwald. I saw you holding the pipe and couldn't believe it was you."

"Believe it," he says with a bitter edge in his voice. "Killing is what I do."

"But you saved me in the cave."

"I killed a bloodsucking fish. That should prove to you I'm violent and not worth your pity."

"I'm not here because of pity. I want answers."

He shakes his head. "You're safer not knowing."

I strain my neck, looking up at him. "You're concerned for my safety? Trying to protect me? That doesn't sound like the behavior of a killer."

"No person is only one thing." He sighs. "I'm also a map maker. It's what I have a talent for, and I'm good at it."

"Leader Cross said you were good at killing. He also said he used you, so I know you didn't act alone. Leader Cross and his group convinced you to do this. But why did you agree? Did they threaten you?"

He pulls back so his face is half in shadows and half in light. When he speaks again, his voice is as hard as brick. "Our talk is over. Leave."

"Why not tell me? Maybe I can help you if I know the truth. I know it's some sort of conspiracy. I heard them talking about you. They want you dead. But I don't." Frustration grips me as tightly as his fingers grip the bars. "I want—need—to understand why you did it."

"Jennza, it's not my secret to tell."

"Why protect them? They won't protect you."

"They're not the ones I'm protecting." He pauses. "Your concern means a lot. If I could have requested a last wish, you just fulfilled it by coming to see me. Only now, please go." Weariness weighs down his words. "You shouldn't be here."

"Clearly not," I agree with a stubborn purse of my lips. "I'm ripping all kinds of laws. If I'm caught, they'll toss me in jail too."

"They won't harm a Topsider."

"Topsider?"

"You." His finger aims at me through the bars.

"So it's true … where you come from." I frown. "You really are a …."

"Nocturne," he finishes. "It's what your people call us."

"But the drawings I've seen of Nocturnes are nothing like you." I shake my head. "Half-human, clawed, wolf-jawed beasts."

"Sounds terrifying," he says wryly. "You should avoid them."

"I should, but I won't."

He moves into the light, looking at me with something close to a smile. "A Topsider concerned for a Nocturne. My friends won't believe it."

"Your friends must not know many Topsiders."

"Oh, they know them," he says wryly. "Topsiders seek us when they need special skills. The first Topsider I met was a woman with soft, dark skin as youthful as a babe, who spoke of being born before the Fence went up. Hundreds of years ago. I was amazed anyone could live so long and look so young. I wondered what it would be like to live in sunshine, rather than underground. I longed to be like Topsiders—with flawless bodies and a relaxed way of moving, as if they're all listening to the same music. It wasn't until I met you in that cave that I realized not all Topsiders were alike."

"Why?" I ask defensively. Is my rule-breaking nature so obvious that even a Nocturne knows I'm flawed?

"I'd never met a Topsider my age and so full of independence, like an untamed creature. You were brave too. I knew you were scared, yet you were ready to attack me."

"Not when I realized you saved my life. Why did you?"

"You were worth saving," he says simply.

"So are you." I purse my lips. "It's my turn to help you, only I don't know what I can do."

"There's no saving me."

"There has to be some way to get you out of here."

He shakes his head. "Save yourself. Leave now before someone catches you."

I don't want to, but I've already stayed too long. Daisy will return soon.

Before I can move, I hear voices from the road beyond the thick bushes. Deep, male voices. Through the shrubs, I glimpse figures in gray clothing walking down the paveway.

Whirling back to Nate, I whisper, "Uniforms!"

"Hide," he whispers back.

Shadows are deepest by the ivy, so I press against the wall. I'm shaking, and my heart pounds. I expect Uniforms to burst through the bushes and drag me to jail. But I don't hear anything except a murmur of voices fading away.

Still, I'm afraid to move until I hear Nate whisper, "They're gone."

I glance around uneasily. "I'll wait a little longer."

"Not too long," he warns. "Forget about me, and don't return. There's no hope for a dead man."

"There's always hope," I argue.

"Hope is a luxury for Topsiders. My people are realists. Our lives are short, so we're grateful for each day. Even now I'm glad for this window which shows me daylight." He reaches out, his hand cupped up as if reaching for the sky. "Also, I'm glad for an unexpected friend."

"I meant what I said about wanting to help you."

"Your being here has already helped. I'm tired of my

own thoughts and miss the noisy conversations of home. We love laughter, dancing, and stelling."

"Stelling?" Most of his words are like my own, as if in the past our people were friendly. But I've never heard this word.

"Storytelling," he says.

"I love stories too. Tell me a story—stelling—about you," I ask, my hands still shaking. "After that I'll leave."

"What do you want to know?" I can't see his expression behind bars, but I hear the hint of a smile in his words.

"About your tubes. When we first met, you wore a tubed costume. Why?"

"My air suit allows me to breathe underwater." He pauses. "We can't go outside during the day because poisonous snakes stalk us. We're trapped underground without sunlight, except that I found a tunnel to the sea."

I stare at his pale, scarred hands. "How did you find it?"

"My father, a master map maker, taught me his craft. Normally, sixteen-year-olds are assigned to the night hunting crew, but my father is too ill to search out new tunnels, so I explore for him. Months ago, I found one that opened in a steep cliff above the sea but below land. When I told my father, he warned me to stay out of the sea because of water snakes. But I couldn't stop thinking of that endless blue water. So I made a pulley system to lower myself down to the sea in a tube suit with enough air for me to swim around the cliffs. It's amazing to breathe in sunlight and sea breezes."

"I know that feeling," I tell him. "Once I discovered the sea, I couldn't stay away. I'd make up games like jumping before waves touched me and throwing sticks that always came back. I wouldn't have found the cave if not for a stick."

"A stick?"

"I threw it so high the wind blew it against a huge rock, and it disappeared."

"Into the cave," he guesses.

I nod, moving so close to the ivy wall he could almost reach through the bars to touch my head. "How did you find the cave?" I ask in a whisper.

"I followed a gull wing."

"Gull wing? Oh, you mean a storm gull."

"I was swimming in my tube suit when I spotted a gull wing on the shore. The bird flew away as I drew close. I was angry because I'd hoped to bring back fresh food to my family."

"Family?" I ask, surprised to hear a Nocturne use the word.

"My father, sisters, brothers, nieces, nephews, and many cousins. I am fortunate to still have my father. Few of us live past twenty. If the creatures don't kill us, sickness does."

"But sickness can be cured."

"Not for us. Sickness comes with pain, weakness, then death."

"But that's awful!"

He shrugs. "It's our life."

The math saddens me. If he's sixteen, he only has a quarter of his lifetime left. Yet he's accepting it with no anger in his voice. I like the sound of his voice and want him to keep talking, so I ask, "Did you catch the gull wing?"

"I saw it perched on a high rock. I pulled out my blow pipe, aimed—but the gull disappeared. I didn't know where it went until I spotted a rocky cliff that was darker near the top. I climbed up and found the cave. I thought it was a tunnel that would take me beneath your Fence. But even better—the tunnel took me to you." His smile touches my heart.

"When I first saw you, I thought you were a sea monster," I admit.

"I thought you were a siren, a beautiful sea creature. I've never seen one, only read of them."

I feel my cheeks warm, stunned to be called *beautiful*. I've never given any thought to my physical appearance, although I've read many retro books where beauty is valued above hard work and intelligence.

"You have books where you ... uh ... live?" I glance down, wondering how anyone can survive underground. How can he appear so human when his people burrow like moles? A life without sun and sky would be like being buried alive.

"Our books are ancient and stored in protective cases," he says. "My mother was a master steller before the sickness took her. My best memories of her are being held on her lap and listening to her read to me. She loved mythology stories of flying horses, sea monsters, and a powerful king, Neptune. The sirens were mysterious women of the sea who sang sailors to their—" He gasps, pulling away from the window. "Footsteps! Outside my door. You must go. Now!"

I hesitate, my heart twisting. The next time I see him will be at his execution. I wish I could be the opposite of a siren and save his life. I don't want to leave, but what else can I do?

My throat tightens. All I can do is say good-bye.

I turn away but have a sudden thought and reach into my pocket.

"Wait," I call up to Nate. "Here's a piece of the sea."

I throw my favorite seashell through the bars.

My aim is perfect.

TWENTY-ONE

"There's a leaf in your hair."

That's all Daisy says when I sit beside her in the solar cycle. My cheeks burn as I pluck the leaf from my hair. It's brittle and crumbles to the floor beside my mud-splattered shoes. I glance over at Daisy, and while her gaze doesn't shift from the road, a sly smile crosses her face.

What does she suspect?

My heart jolts with each sway of the cycle. She can't know where I've been. I looked up and down the paveway before leaving the bushes, and I returned to the fashionizers before Daisy.

I'm ready if she accuses me. "I'll tell you where I was if you tell me where you were," I'll say. But miles pass, and Daisy doesn't even glance at me.

Silence stales the air. I roll down the window, inhaling cool breezes that have a faint taste of salty sea. I reach into my pocket to touch my shell but remember it's not there. I think of Nate and sigh.

Wheels rumble on a rough patch of road, and the cycle lurches, tossing me sideways. My elbow bangs against the door, and I cry out.

When Daisy laughs, I glare at her. "If you were a more skilled driver, you wouldn't hit so many bumps."

"You think you could drive better?" she snaps.

"I know I could."

"I'd let you prove yourself wrong, except you'd crash, and I happen to like this cycle very much."

"As much as you hate me?"

She jerks the wheel sharply, and I grab tight to the door handle. "You're only a shell, not a complete person."

"That's not true!" I dig my fingers into the seat cushion, so I don't strike her. "You don't know anything about me."

"Nor do I care to," she says coolly.

She sits calmly, as if she's a superior species, and my dam of anger bursts. "You hate me because you think I want to replace your mother—which I don't. Also because of what the last youth did to you."

Her hand flies up to her cheek. "Who told you about him?"

I immediately realize my mistake. I can hear Marcus's voice saying, *Jennza, will you ever learn to control yourself?* I won't betray Marcus, so I retort, "Why didn't you have your scar healed?"

Fury flashes in Daisy's eyes. Finally, I've gotten to her. If she's going to hate me, I should deserve it.

"As a reminder and a warning about youths. But nothing changed. You came here anyway."

"I'm not going to become violent. No matter how much you rip me with insults, I won't attack you."

"The last youth wasn't violent until after."

"After what?"

"His first memdenity."

"I don't believe it." I gulp in a deep breath. "You're trying to scarify me."

"The memories hurt his head. He woke up screaming,

184

shouting for the voices to go away. Then he grabbed a knife and did this." She lifts up her hair so I get a clear view of the jagged red scar down her cheek.

"The scientists swear memdenity is safe, but memories turned that gentle boy into a monster." She glares into my face. "And it could happen to you."

The house is eerily quiet when we return, so I wander outside where gray clouds hint of rain. I find Rosemarie in the garden, kneeling beside a woven basket half-full of pumpkins. The red sash at the waist of her bark-brown pantons trails to the ground as she stabs a sharp spade in the dirt.

"You're back," Rosemarie wipes sweat beads from her forehead. "How was your sizing?"

"Unfinished." I explain about the postponement. "Will you take me tomorrow?"

"Tomorrow will be another busy day. But I can drop you off before I deliver lunches to the laborers working in City Central."

"Thank you. Can I help here?"

"Catch," she says as she tosses a fist-sized pumpkin at me. "Add that to the basket. Did you know before the mind-plague pumpkins grew larger than this basket?" I glance down, then shake my head. "Petite pumpkins were created to conserve space. They're seedless and quick-growing. But even small pumpkins make for exhausting work."

"Why don't your sons help you?"

"They're constructing a platform. I'm almost done here anyway." The thump of another pumpkin landing in the basket muffles her sigh. "Oh—I spoke to Arthur about your covering problem."

I cringe at the image of her discussing me with Arthur, especially my personal coverings. Even though he'll soon have the right to see me *without* anything on. My skin crawls.

"I finally convinced Arthur to give me the key to Milly's storage crate. Since her clothes don't fit you, there's no reason to keep them in storage. Most coverings will be shared among Family, but some things you'll find useful."

Wearing the coverings of a dead woman chills me. "I don't need anything."

"You need everything." She chuckles.

"But not Milly's."

"They belong to you," she says with a finality that ends the discussion.

To Rosemarie, I'm already Milly.

Bending down to work beside her, I grasp a pumpkin vine and pull until it breaks free of the ground. Cradling the small pumpkin in my palms, I admire the smooth curves and orange shimmer. If I hadn't ripped the roots, the pumpkin would keep growing and thriving. Instead it'll become soup, bread, and pies. I frown at the torn vines and my dirt-splattered hands, overwhelmed by a sense of loss. Life shouldn't end so easily, even for a pumpkin.

I squeeze my eyes tight and think of Nate. Beaten, bruised, and hopeless. Memories, like ghosts, wisp alongside me as I work in the garden. It's Rosemarie talking, yet its Nate's voice I hear. His joy for sky and sea, his longing for home, his acceptance of death. I can't bear to think I'll never hear his voice again.

Rosemarie and I leave the pumpkin patch, taking a path between tall stalks of corn. She explains the canning process we'll tackle soon, readying for winter's barren cold, a time of cleaning, cooking, and serving my Family daily. How do people live forever without going crazy with routine? I can see why some join groups like the playformers, smack sticks in sporting competitions, or like Leader Cross, strategize with games of chess.

We return to the house, pulling a wheeled cart of baskets heaped with the day's harvest, and set to work in the kitchen. It's dark when the house rumbles with footsteps and voices. The smell of pumpkin soup steaming on the burner fills the kitchen as Rosemarie and I pour it into a ceramic tureen for dinner.

I'm distracted by my own thoughts, so it's not until the salad has been served that I notice the strangeness. No one says anything directly. But shifting glances are as subtle as dust particles in the air. Leader Cross challenges Arthur to chess after dinner. Jarod and Rosemarie's sons discuss construction supplies. No one speaks to me as I take my seat beside Rosemarie.

Have I done something wrong?

When Rosemarie and I wash and dry dishes, I whisper, "I haven't poisoned or dropped hot soup in anyone's lap lately. So why am I being avoided?"

"It's because ... well, I can't say. But there's no cause for worry. Everything is fine." She has tears in her eyes as she drops her rag and embraces me. Her hug is so tight I know I'm in trouble.

When we're finished in the kitchen, Rosemarie excuses herself to visit Grandmother. She doesn't invite me to come along, which adds to my uneasiness. Even Rosemarie is acting oddly, and fear clenches my stomach that this could be my last night with the Cross Family. Every step I take up the stairs to my room is as heavy as stone.

I unwind my red scarf from my neck and gently smooth out the creases, then place it in my top drawer. There isn't much else in the drawer. My belongings will fit easily in one bag. I wonder if I should pack now.

A cool breeze chills my bare neck. The window over my bed is cracked open. Who left it that way? Not me. Surely not Rosemarie who wears extra layers to stay warm. I cross over to the window and push it shut. The last time I found the window open, I also found Petal curled on my bed.

But my bed is undisturbed.

Changing into my night covering, I slip under the blankets. My pillow is lumpy, and when I lift it up, I find a square package. There's no label, but I know it's meant for me since it was beneath my pillow. Who would leave a gift? Rosemarie? Arthur?

I dig my fingernail into a corner of the package to rip it open. Inside I find a small packet and a folded note.

Unfolding the paper, I read a scrawled, blue-inked message:

Only you can free Nate.

I won't do it.

I can't do it.

How can I *not* do it?

I'm tempted to open the small packet, but it's sealed with glue-wax and addressed to Nate. I read the note again and again, tormented by each word. Someone knows that I know Nate.

Daisy. Of course it's her. Her sly glances hinted that she knows my secrets. But even if she does, why would she care if Nate lives or dies?

When my doorknob jiggles, I shove the packet under my pillow and pretend to be asleep. I sense Rosemarie's gaze on me. Soft footsteps come closer, and her hand brushes across my hair. "Sleep well, Milly," she whispers.

Her tone has the finality of a good-bye.

I want to grab her arms and beg her to tell me what is going to happen to me, but she goes into the privacy room, shutting the door behind her.

I'm so tired, my body aches for sleep, but plans whirl in my head. Somewhere between dreams and thoughts, ideas take shape, transforming into a bold plan that will break more rules in one day than I've broken in all of my fifteen years.

When I awake the next morning, I know what I have to do—even though it's more dangerous than climbing the Fence or sneaking Petal to Marcus.

I'm going to give the packet to Nate.

With this decision made, dread lifts from me. I move through my chores, lighter with hope. Rosemarie seems in high spirits too, humming a cheerful melody as we prepare to leave for my sizing.

When Arthur says he's going with us, my dread returns. Even last night, when everyone else ignored me, he still pulled out my chair and offered to butter my bread and refill my water glass. And often, when he doesn't realize I'm aware, I find his gaze sweeping over me like I already belong to him.

Now Arthur takes the driver's seat, inviting me to sit beside him, but I pretend I don't hear and slide into the back beside Rosemarie. She pats my shoulder, then hums happily like when she's baking pumpkin bread. Arthur raises his brows at Rosemarie and they share a meaningful look.

I'm too anxious to puzzle over them, each wheel-turn bringing me closer to Nate. I go over my plan, scheming how to sneak away from my sizing. I'll need Lorelei's help, but will she agree? She has to! I'll plead until she gives in. I only need about fifteen minutes to follow the path beneath the bushes, throw the packet through Nate's window, and hurry back before I'm missed. Timing is important. Luck would be useful too, and I wish I still had my favorite sand shell. But Nate has it, and he'll need more than luck to escape.

The drive into City Central blurs until we approach thick bushes, and I see the brick walls of the prison. The packet for Nate is tucked in my pocket.

I think of Nate's face, shadowed by irons bars. I can help him, if I can only get to him. Somehow I'll find a way. I'm so lost in thought that I don't notice where we're going until I glance out the window.

"Arthur!" I cry, pointing. "You passed the fashionizing shop."

"Yes, I did." He grins at me.

"Why would you do that? Make him turn around," I urge Rosemarie. "I'll be late for my appointment."

She shakes her head. "I postponed your appointment."

Arthur slows the coach cycle in front of a square stone building with a pink engraved plaque over the entry door.

"I've been bursting to tell you since yesterday, but Leader Cross didn't want anyone to ruin the surprise." Rosemarie grasps my hand. "You're getting your first memdenity."

TWENTY-TWO

Nate will be executed tomorrow.

And today, a part of me is going to be buried beneath Milly's memories.

I'm numb as I climb down the steps of the solar cart. Arthur grins at me, his head lifted high with pride and something else—maybe ownership. Will he be in Milly's childhood memories?

"Come along, Milly." Rosemarie's cheerful tone is a smothering blanket.

Arthur comes around to open my door and offers me a hand. Already the attentive husband, he is kind and will be good to me. I know this and appreciate his kindness. I have heard of husbands who strike in anger, so I'm lucky to have a gentle man for a husband.

"The insertion won't hurt," he says as he opens the entry door for me. "Don't be afraid."

"I'm not." Pain is brief. It's the permanent changes I dread.

Rosemarie slips her arm around my shoulders. "You'll do fine."

I enter a small room with a desk and rows of chairs. No photos, paintings, or decorations on the walls—only stark blankness.

A deep-voiced man in white pantons and a pink shirt

strides on long legs through double doors. He's tall, with skin a shade lighter than mine and thick, flaxen hair. "You must be Milly," he booms in a deep voice.

"Not yet," I say like it's a joke. But it's not.

"Wait here while I see if your room is prepared," he says, then goes down a back hallway.

Rosemarie squeezes my hand. "No worries, okay? It won't take long, and afterward you'll be pleased with everything you know."

I nod, but Arthur frowns. "Actually, she won't gain much from the first memdenity. Childhood memories have little substance," he says with a dismissive shrug. "Nothing useful."

"She learned many skills as a youth," Rosemarie argues. "Milly's cooking talent started young. I should know—I was with her."

"And I wasn't." Arthur draws in a deep breath, then blows it out. "I'll wait over there." He sits in a hard chair, alone.

"Poor Arthur," Rosemarie says, guiding me to a chair on the opposite side of the room. She sits beside me, leaning close to whisper, "He didn't marry Milly until she was age twenty, and while they were happy together for the first century, there was a time when they stopped talking … and unfortunate things happened. You will ease more hurts than you know when you bring Milly back to him."

But I don't want to be Milly, I think with panic, wanting to run somewhere far away where I can make my own memories.

The yellow-haired health keeper returns.

"The insertion room is ready," he says.

Rosemarie rises to go with me, but the health keeper

gives her a stern look. "Only the youth is allowed," he says.

I'm led down a narrow hall and through a steel door. A lock clicks behind me. I'm told to sit in a leather chair with steel clamps on the arm rests. Wire devices twine around a tray like silver snakes. I want to gag at the sterile chemical odor. My heart thumps.

It's happening. The moment my whole life has led up to.

The flaxen-haired man reminds me of a giraffe, long necked and lanky. "I'm Rachid," he says, cranking a knob that reclines my chair so I'm staring up into a ceiling of twisted cords. "It's good to see you again."

"We've met before?"

His chuckle rolls in a faint accent. "You won't remember; you were only a babe. I never forget the babes, and I noticed you because of your curiosity. You always knew what you wanted too, grabbing toys from your born-mates. I knew you wouldn't be one of the discards, so I cuddled and played with you."

"Discards?" I've never heard this term before.

"The scientists always supply us with extra embryos." He reaches for my wrist and slips it in a clamp. "Only the most healthy make the final fifteen. I remember them all, and you were a favorite."

This should please me, but the word *discard* is troubling. What if I'd been born with a flaw or an illness? Would I be here? Would I be anywhere?

The snap of an arm clamp startles me. I jerk but can't move.

"Relax, Milly," Rachid says calmly, and my long ago memory stirs at his voice. "It's a simple procedure, and you'll sleep through it."

"If it's simple, then why are my arms restrained?"

"A safety measure. You won't feel anything."

That's what worries me.

Clamps fit over my ankles too, and my tunic bunches up to my thighs. I glance at the knee I scarred as a child, smooth with no trace of the scar. I hold tightly to the memory of being age one, stumbling, pain and blood. The scar will never fade as long as I remember.

A cone mask comes down over my face, eclipsing light. Strange, sweet smells wisp up my nostrils. Hands lift my hair. Cold metal presses on the back of my head. There's the flash of silver and a shining needle aiming at my face. I'm drifting somewhere beyond water and land. My last thought is clear, strong, and determined.

I am Jennza.

Images flood my mind with sounds, smells, and strange sights, bright lights and tall ceilings. Someone holds me tight, murmuring soft words. I'm helpless to do much except cry and suck and sleep. Tiny hands, my tiny hands, reach up to grasp larger hands. I'm content, safe and loved.

I'm rushing forward, small legs stretching into first steps. Learning letters and reading on my own. I laugh with a small girl with long black curls. We're bundled in heavy jackets and gloves—no, the word is *mitten*—and we're excited about something. A door opens and a whoosh of icy air stings my cheeks. The other girl runs ahead, and I run after her, stumbling in thick, soft white ground. A word comes to me: snow.

Time leaps. I'm riding on a leather seat beside the black-haired girl. I look at her now, recognizing the smile that tilts unevenly at one corner and the thick brows over serious brown eyes. Rosemarie: my sister.

We're at the sea, but we call it the Pacific Ocean. The sandy shore shimmers like white-gold cloth. Confusing strings of words and images tangle in my thoughts. Rubber-wheeled vehicles—cars. Tiny boxes flash pictures and make sounds—phone. Something large and metal roars into the sky, shrinking in the distance like a tiny flying bird—airplane.

The car stops in a paved square—a parking lot. We're swallowed into a dizzying crowd hurrying into shops, whirling flashing lights, music and buckets flying high in circles—Ferris wheel. The screams and crowds make me clutch tight to Rosemarie's hand. She says we should skip the rides and go to the beach, so we race to the shore, where people ride boards in high waves. Sand tickles my bare toes. We laugh, chasing waves and dancing in seaweed. "Race you!" Rosemarie shouts, and my little legs can't catch her.

I'm calling her name, "Rosie! Rosie!" when stinging salt water crashes over me, sweeping me away from shore. Can't breathe. I'm swallowing salt water, choking, slipping deep into darkness.

A hand grasps my shoulders, pulling me from the water. I'm on my side on the ground, still sinking, drifting away. A man stands over me, water streaming down his face ... or tears? "Milly, baby! Breathe!" I spit out water, sucking in air, sobbing "Daddy!" as I cling to him.

Another scene flashes by. Noisy streets and honking, like geese, blares from cars, trucks, buses, taxis, and even horns on bicycles. I'm riding in the back of a car, strapped on a cushioned box. Booster seat. The Daddy man is driving and a woman sits beside him, her hair dark with braids like

Rosemarie's. Mom. I look to the side and see my sister. Rosie. There's a car seat with a crying baby, a boy with a squishy face. He spits up on me, but I still like him. Brother.

Towering buildings reach for the clouds. I peer out windows at chaotic sidewalks of people riding, walking, and skating. Wiggling in my belted seat, I ask again and again how long before we're there. We're going to climb a tower. Rosemarie says she'd rather see a museum, and the Daddy man says we will after we climb the tower. There are many, many steps that go up, up, up. My legs hurt from the climb. "Carry me," I beg the Daddy man. But he's holding the boy baby. I'm not liking the spit-up baby so much now. Rosemarie takes my hand. "Stay with me," she says.

Numbers race up and down in my mind with each step. 26, 27 … 35 …. But the number steps never end and my legs burn. I want to go back to the car. I let go of Rosemarie's hand and look down, down, so far down. Rosemarie shouts at me to hurry up. But I can't stop looking at the distant ground. My head is spinning and I'm rubbing my eyes because I'm crying. My foot slips. I'm falling … until Rosemarie pulls me to safety.

More images blink by.

Tall buildings shining like rainbows in the night. Traffic honking and red-green-yellow lights flashing. Swarming sidewalks. Towering aisles at stores with more toys than I could ever play with, balloons floating over a banner spelling out, "Happy 4th Birthday, Milly!" and so many gifts that I don't know which to open first, until Rosemarie points to the one she wrapped all by herself.

"Do what your teacher tells you," the Mommy says on my first day of kindergarten. I hear "kind garden" and look for a garden. When I ask the teacher, she laughs and says,

"What a good idea, Milly. We'll make our own garden." I love school and my teacher and the garden where carrots, tomatoes, and herbs grow. I take some home and Rosie shows me how to bake spaghetti sauce and carrot cake.

Sunshine, wind, blossoms, rain, and snow spin away the years. I'm taller, and the Mommy and Daddy change too, deep lines worrying their faces. They whisper at night, and I creep forward to hear odd words like "insanity," "epidemic," and "plague." At school the next week, there's an empty desk. I cry when I learn my friend Haley won't be coming back.

Lessons, homework, recess games. We wear gloves and paper masks to school like an every-day costume party. We paint pictures on the paper cones that fit over our mouths and noses. I get the idea to sprinkle glue and sequins on mine, but Jeremy grabs my mask and stomps on it until the sequins are dead on the floor. My teacher quickly gives me a new mask to wear.

There are three empty desks at school now, including Jeremy's. I should be glad he's gone, yet a tight squeeze hurts my chest. I understand now about the "Mad Mind" disease that hurts people, especially children. I wake one night to flashing red and blue lights out my window and my brother screaming.

Now we're a family of four. Rosie and I don't go to school anymore. Strong locks protect our doors and black sheets cover the windows. The Daddy man warns me never to go outside after dark. Rosemarie and I play together in our room, pretending we're princesses trapped in a castle, waiting for handsome princes to rescue us. When I hear strange noises from outside at night, I climb into Rosemarie's bed.

We pack and drive a long way to a huge place called

an airport. I wear my face mask that's covered in red heart stickers. While we wait in a big room for our flight, a woman rushes by, screaming. She points out a huge window up at the sky. A plane blazes with fire, falling. "The pilot lost his mind!" someone screams, then others scream too. The sound hurts my ears, so I cover them with my hands. When a big boom shakes the building and cracks windows, Mommy, Daddy, Rosemarie, and I hold each other.

We don't take an airplane. Instead, we ride on a boat for so many days that I forget what land looks like. We leave the big boat for a smaller one that rocks my tummy so much I vomit on Rosemarie. We switch to an even smaller boat crowded with luggage and people wearing masks and gloves. I hear stories of family and friends who have died from the mind-plague. Mommy speaks softly of my brother. I want to talk about him too, but words are swallowed by sadness.

At nightfall, Mommy wraps a blanket around me and pulls me closer to her on the hard bench. "We're going to be safe," she whispers. "My new job assisting scientists is in a safe place where sickness can't find us."

"I feel sick now," I say with a sour taste in my mouth.

"But you're not sick here." She bends down to touch the top of my forehead. "And you never will be."

Images shift to travels in an even smaller boat, until an island rises from the sea with trees so thick the land is smothered. There are no houses or highways or cities. The boat captain dumps our luggage and us on the shore and leaves. Rumbling shakes the ground, and a tank rolls on thick wheels out of the woods like a monster.

When I'm told to climb into the tank, I cry.

Rosemarie clasps my hand and whispers, "Don't be afraid."

But I am afraid—of the darkness inside the tank, the wild jungle outside, the roaring engine, and the uniformed man at the wheel. When the roaring stops, the uniformed man flips open a ceiling hatch, and we climb out into sunshine.

We stand before a massive steel gate.

ShareHaven.

TWENTY-THREE

"Milly ... Milly ..."

Someone shakes my shoulders.

When I open my eyes, there's Rosemarie, looking the same as when we arrived at the health-keepers, yet so much more familiar to me. I see a shorter, round-cheeked girl with wispy black curls sharing birthday cake, popping balloons, playing princess games, and holding my hand tight when I'm afraid. She's always there for me, strong and loyal and true. I love my sister.

"Are you all right?" Rosemarie asks.

I can't find the words to answer. My brain is a sponge, overfilling with images. Faces, objects, and places swim like finless fish through my mind. I can't grasp the slippery images that squirm out of reach. My head feels like a pressure cooker ready to burst. Reaching up, I lift my tangled hair and rub a rough patch of skin on my neck.

"Would you like a pain tonic?" Rosemarie caresses my cheek, her hand warm.

"I'm not in pain," I say in a voice that doesn't sound familiar. I look down at my hand too, and it's all wrong; the fingers too long and thin. Panic swells. Not my hand! I hit the hand against a chair, over and over, wanting to rip it from my arm.

Rosemarie grasps the hand gently, entwining her fingers

200

in mine. "Milly, relax. I'm here for you. It's natural to feel confusion after the first insertion."

"I—I just want …." I try to finish this sentence, but I can't.

"Would you like to go home?" Rosemarie slips her arm around me.

Home. A dark brown house with a large picture window over a planter blossoming with flowers, and two metal coaches—no, *cars*—parked inside a—a *garage.*

"There are no cars here," I say, rubbing my forehead.

Rosemarie chuckles. "No traffic or pollution either. Solar energy is much more efficient than dinosaur fuel. I'd almost forgotten cars."

"We had a blue Chevy with four doors and a sunroof."

"I don't remember," she says with a shrug. "It was so long ago."

"Your hair is shorter and you finally got boobs."

She laughs. "Oh, Milly, that sounds so much like you. I can hardly believe it … and I'm so glad. What else do you remember?"

"We had a mother and father and little brother—but he died."

Rosemarie nods sadly. "Gregory. He didn't have a chance. The early stages of the mind-plague struck little kids the hardest. We moved to ShareHaven a few months after that and were very happy here until …." Her voice trails off.

"Until what?"

She sighs. "You'll get those memories next time."

Next time. I cringe, not sure I want memories that make her so sad.

"Dwell on the happy things," she says. "What else do you

201

remember?"

"Voices and pictures spin in my mind, and most don't make any sense. But one thing never changes."

"What?" she asks in a hushed voice.

"You." I squeeze her hand. "You're always with me."

"And I always will be, Milly."

She leads me outside to the solar coach, where a man who looks familiar but somehow out of place jumps to greet us. Dizziness buckles my feet, and the man rushes to catch me. He has kind eyes and I think … I think ….

I struggle through memories, like being half asleep and trying to wake up from a troubling nightmare.

The man rushes to open the back door for me. "Milly?" He bites his lip as he peers into my face. "Do you remember me?"

Milly only sees a stranger. I concentrate hard, pushing Milly away. "Of course I do, Arthur," I say, and he relaxes into a wide smile.

Rosemarie reminds me about my fashionizer appointment, triggering an uneasy sense of forgetting something. I sort through Milly's whirling thoughts, frustrated until we drive by a platform being constructed in the middle of City Central. A ladder leads up to a high, narrow stage—the execution podium.

Memory jolts into place. The packet for Nate! Do I still have it?

My fingers slide into my pocket. Graces good, it's still here! I need to give it to Nate. Only how? I have a plan, surely I do, but my thoughts are bubbles, floating out of reach.

"Are you hurting?" Rosemarie scoots closer to me in the solar coach. "You're rubbing your forehead."

"I'm trying to remember ... something important."

"Allow your memories to settle. Don't push them."

"They're pushing me," I complain.

"Mems are like newly planted seeds, nurturing in the ground and connected by roots. They need time to grow into shape."

There's not enough time, I think anxiously. We're almost to the fashionizer shop, and looming above rooftops in the distance is a building of bricks

The solar coach stops. I don't move, though, clasping the packet in my pocket, struggling to piece together memories. A plan ... to go to Nate ... give him the packet. Sneak to the jail, crawl through the path in the bushes, and ....

Bushes, branches, darkness. Sirens scream and the Daddy warns, "Never go outside without your mask!" I reach up to my face and feel for a breathing mask that isn't there. I have to find it! Daddy will be angry.

"What's wrong?" Rosemarie says gently.

I blink. Visions shift back to the solar cart where I'm sitting beside Rosemarie. "Nothing," I say with a shake of my head.

"If you're not feeling well enough, we can cancel your fitting," she says.

"No. I have to do it."

The world tilts as I walk into the fashionizer shop. It's strange to see Lorelei. She's not part of my new memories. The usual click of connection I feel with her is missing. Rosemarie and Arthur say they have an errand to run and ask Lorelei to take care of me.

"Surely," Lorelei says, gesturing for me to follow her. "Come back to the style room."

I go with her, but when I step into a room lined with fabric, tools, and cabinets for clothing, I look up at Lorelei and see a different girl—dark-skinned, with short, straight, ash-brown hair and freckles. Naomi, my best friend. She smiles as she places a half-heart bracelet around my wrist. "A friendship bracelet," Naomi says.

"Why are you staring at me so oddly?" Lorelei asks.

My gaze shifts to a shelf of stitching needles. I see a building with sick people and healers. *Hospital.* "This won't hurt," a man wearing a white jacket says as he pokes a sharp needle into my arm.

"No needles!" I jump away from the shelf.

Lorelei's mouth falls open. "What are you talking about?"

"I hate needles!"

"No, you don't. Remember our mini sword fights with needles? You made up the rule of first one to bleed is the loser—and you nearly always won." She leans close to me. "You're acting odd. What's wrong, Jennza?"

Jennza.

My name.

Instantly, the fog in my mind clears. "Sorry, Lor, it's just so confusing. All the memories make me dizzy. I'm not myself."

"Oh. My. Graces!" Lorelei's hands fly to her cheeks. "You did it. The big M! The huge leap from youth to adult. I can't believe you didn't tell me."

"Don't shout ... it makes it worse." I rub my forehead.

"When I heard you had to change your appointment because of another appointment, I never thought it was The Appointment. Tell me everything! What was it like? What are your memories? How does it feel? I am so jealous I can hardly stand talking to you."

"If your head ached like mine, you wouldn't be jealous."

"Your first memdenity!" Her gaze shines. "I still have weeks before I get mine. You're so lucky to have yours early. Are the memories amazing?"

I pause, trying to come up with an answer. But there's no way to describe the voices screaming in my head, the overlapping of Jennza and Milly. My first steps; her first steps. My age celebrazes; her birthday parties. Her parents; my Instructors. Her best friends; my best mates. One face forms, then another colors over it with a different mouth, nose, and eyes. The emotions are so confusing. I'm happy to see Lorelei, yet I'm shy because Milly doesn't know her. Also, Milly feels a terror of needles, even though my Jennza thoughts know these needles are for sewing, not for medicine shots.

"Are you alright?" Lorelei asks. "Tell me what you're thinking, Jennza, or are you Milly now?"

"I'm ... I'm me." But I bite my lip, not sure of anything.

"Then stand still so I can measure. Arms out and legs slightly apart." She purses her lips, giving me a look mixed with envy and fear. "Does it hurt?"

She's asking about the memdenity. "No, not really. But it's crowding my head with pressure like a canning jar close to bursting. My thoughts spin conversations and pictures and events from retro-century. They're *my* memories as if I was there ... although I'm only age fifteen so I couldn't have been. Yet it feels like it's happening now."

She takes a step back, frowning. "You're in pain?"

"No, not the way I'd feel if your needles jab me." I glance uneasily at the stitching pins. "It's like when you eat too much and keep eating even though there's no more room. My head is exploding with thoughts."

"I can't wait to explode with Flavia thoughts," she says with a huge smile.

"You say that now, but wait till it happens." I rub my head.

"I will rejoice when that day comes. Once my head is full of knowledge, my braggy daughter won't roll her eyes at me like my head is full of cotton. I'm going to ask my Family to schedule my mem soon. You didn't have to wait, so why should I?"

"Don't rush …. You don't want to …."

My thoughts jerk me to a summer evening without a breeze. I'm sweating as I chase after Naomi. "You're it!" she taunts as she runs down the street with other kids from our neighborhood. I know all their names and where they live, who I hate and who I like. They're heading for Dead Man's Dump, a deserted house surrounded by an orchard of tangled trees and thorny bushes, where a man died alone and wasn't found for months. When I reach the orchard, it's as creepy as a graveyard. Weeds climb to my knees and the bushes grow thick. Tree branches grab at my hair and mosquitoes sting my skin. Sounds fade away too, as if I'm lost in a nightmare. I don't know which way to go, and no one is here to help me. I'm swallowed by darkness and bushes. I start to cry ….

"Aren't you listening? I said turn around."

Lorelei's impatient voice snatches me back from a distant century to a lit room where I'm not alone. I'm so glad to be here with Lorelei, I don't complain when she orders me to stand on a pedestal and hold my arms out so she can hem a covering.

We only have one more covering to pin when her daughter comes into the room. "Flavia, I need your assistance in my styling station." She turns to me apologetically. "I'm sorry, but this won't take long. Do you mind waiting or would you rather reschedule?"

I sink on a chair, tired from standing so still. "I'll wait."

"She'll be back shortly," the daughter promises. "If it wasn't urgent, I wouldn't interrupt. Leader Hale will be here soon to pick up the executioner's uniform. I worked most of the night, but it's not finished yet and still needs to be sized before tomorrow."

Tomorrow. Every nerve in my body flames.

"I won't be long," Lorelei says, hurrying away.

I wait long minutes until I'm sure I'm alone. I couldn't have arranged this better if I'd planned it. I open the door slightly and peek into the other room, where Rosemarie has dozed off in a chair and Arthur stares out the front window. They'll never know I'm gone if I sneak out the rear door and go to the jail. I touch the packet in my pocket, but I don't get up from my chair.

Move, Jennza! I urge myself. I don't understand why my heart pounds and I'm so reluctant to leave. The rear door isn't locked. No one is watching me.

Don't go outside, a voice in my head warns.

Milly's voice, I realize. She'd never break a rule or disobey her sister.

But I must help Nate before it's too late. So I shut out her voice and push through the rear door. Outside, the sky is cloudy with gusty winds. Chill bumps shiver up my arms. I sneak around the building to the paveway, nervously looking around. I hurry past the sweetery shop, then suck in a sharp breath when the jail looms tall, dark, and scarifying.

No, I'm not scared. It's Milly who trembles inside my

thoughts.

Leave me alone, I think as I keep moving forward. I go around the corner of the jail, where trees offer dark shadows and thick bushes cluster like a squadron of uniformed guards.

My hand is deep in my pocket, clutching the packet. I'm so close now. I only need to crawl through the trail I took yesterday. Nate will probably be at the window, staring up at the sky. He'll be so glad to see me, especially when I throw him the packet. He'll know how to use what's inside to escape.

But my feet won't move. Time is slipping away.

Go! I tell myself. *Hurry!*

The nightmare orchard of trees and darkness surrounds me, closing in, stealing my courage.

Dangerous. Don't go outside alone.

Not my thoughts. I fight to think clearly, breathing hard like I've been running for centuries. Bushes clench together into thorny fists, and I draw back. Milly's fears pummel me from the inside, storms of screams hailing to be heard. I clutch my chest, gasping. I must to go through the bushes. Must help Nate ….

But I stop. My legs turn to stone, refusing to go into the tangled trees.

When my body finally moves, it's with a will that's no longer my own.

Tears fall down my cheeks as I turn from the jail.

Milly is going to let Nate die.

TWENTY-FOUR

"He'll walk up thirteen steps, his unlucky number." Leader Cross chuckles, ripping off a chunk of the buttermilk bread I placed on the table moments ago.

He's speaking of Nate, and I forget how to breathe. It's been hours since I left the jail. I can't bear to think or feel anymore. Yet I crack open the door between the kitchen and dining room and listen to Leader Cross, Jarod, and Rosemarie's sons calmly discussing Nate's death.

Arthur glances up from his potato broccoli soup. "Have they chosen a death mode?"

"Beheading would suit the compost scum," says Rosemarie's son Titus.

His brother Tyler snorts. "Electrocution would be more ripping to watch."

Leader Cross nods. "True, but too damaging for the scientists. They want the corpse whole for clinical study. They should leave ShareHaven decisions to Leaders." I'm shocked by his disrespect to our scientists.

"So how will the Noc die?" Arthur wipes his mouth with a napkin.

I go rigid with this question, my fingers clamped to the partly open door.

"Venom," Leader Cross says cheerfully. "From a rattfin snake—the deadliest. He'll die writhing in pain, which is fitting for the subhuman monster. We'll need to arrive early to secure good observing seats."

I want to shout that Leader Cross is the monster, not Nate. But when I think of raising my voice against my Leader, I envision Milly breaking a glass, milk dripping down into her lap. The Daddy yells at her, his face angry red and his voice so loud she cringes in her chair, soaking in shame.

Heat blows behind me as Rosemarie opens the oven. She sets a steaming pan of baked chicken on the counter, then comes over and slips her arm around my shoulders.

"The memories hurting?" She strokes my hair. "My poor Milly. I shouldn't have let you work today. You've been so brave, and I'm proud of you."

Don't be proud, I want to tell her. I'm a coward—running away when I could have saved Nate. I hate myself. I hate Milly.

"Would you like a pain tonic?"

I deserve worse than pain.

Rosemarie is looking at me with such concern that something inside me cracks. "I don't want a tonic ... I want it all to go away ... it's too much at once."

"Take deep breaths and relax your mind," she tells me.

I try, but the images are striking lightning-fast with no warning. I'm afraid to wade in the sea, yet I feel joy when I dive into the Lavender Pool. My first kiss was with a guy named Paul who has pickle breath. Yet that's wrong because my first kiss was with Marcus. A confused voice questions, *Marcus who*?

"You'll feel better after a good night's sleep. You'll wake knowing all about Milly. It's overwhelming at first; that's why it's split into three parts. You won't go through this again for several months, and it'll be easier next time."

I rub the tender spot at the back of my neck. It's not physically painful, but pressure rises inside like a balloon ready to pop. *Balloon.* An object Jennza has never seen, but Milly had bunches of them every year at her birthday parties. Decorated cakes, wrapped gifts, and youths singing "Happy Birthday." Memories push and pull against me.

Rosemarie insists I sit while she finishes serving dinner. I don't join the others but stay in the kitchen. Rosemarie brings me a steaming bowl of soup, buttered bread, and baked chicken. When I finish, she takes me up to our room and tells me to rest. It's too early for sleep, but the war in my body is exhausting. It's much easier to nod and agree.

Lying on my bed, my eyes are closed, but my mind keeps whirling with Milly thoughts: school, friends, arguments, laughter, fears. Her world seems so much bigger than my island, with cities and traffic and elevators whooshing high into sky-touching buildings. It's more than I imagined from viewing the history museum. Smells, sounds, and sights suffocate me. My brain can't breathe.

From a faraway place, I hear someone shout for Milly to go away. My Jennza voice. She's … I'm still … here. But I can't reach her through the darkness, as if I've plunged deep into a sinkhole and can't climb out. *Leave me alone, Milly.* A surge of anger rises like a ladder with rungs I can grasp. Each rung is a knowing of my real self. Jennza. I start with my name and move to images of people who belong to me. Marcus, holding a swizard in his dirty hand; Lorelei, wearing a tunic décored with shell buttons as she bosses me around; Instructor Penny, hugging me when the other Instructors aren't looking; Nate, catching the shell I've tossed up to him, grateful for a small token from a sea

211

he'll never see again.

I left him to die.

Gasping, I sit up in bed. Sweat drips from my forehead, and I wipe it away. My room is silent, dimmed in darkness. I don't know how long I've slept, but many hours have passed because Rosemarie is snuggled under her covers, softly snoring. She curls toward the wall, her back to me.

I need my sister. So I leave my bed to crawl into hers. Warm covers—warm memories are comforting. So natural—something I've done since I was a little girl.

"Have a bad dream, Milly?" She draws me into her warm arms.

"Dreams are easy. Reality hurts."

"I told you the memories will be easier with time."

"It's not the memories … it's what I've done … or haven't done."

"What are you talking about?"

I purse my lips. I've said too much already.

"Come on, Milly. You know you can tell your big sister anything."

The word *sister* flashes so many scenes in my mind: sharing an umbrella on a rainy day, somersaulting on freshly mowed grass, and her arm around me as we huddle together on a rocking boat heading for a remote island.

I can't tell her about Nate, but there's something she can tell me. My memory flies down a flight of stairs to a private meeting in the dark of night. "Do you know why Leader Cross and others meet in secret?"

Her arms around me stiffen. "It doesn't concern you."

"But I heard them speaking … and they mentioned Na— the killer. They knew he was going to kill Leader Sarwald."

"Our Leader would never be involved in something so terrible."

"He wasn't the only one. Daisy and Arthur were in the underground room too. And people from other Families. The room was strange, with candles and pictures of winged people ... angels." In a whirl of images, I see a huge building with a temple, statues, and stained-glass windows. And I see myself ... no, the other me ... Milly. Kneeling before an altar, hands clasped in prayer, giving thanks ... not to scientists.

"Church," I whisper hoarsely. "That's why they were meeting in secret ... they were worshipping ...."

"Do not speak of this!" Rosemarie's expression darkens like she wants to slap me. "Our faith is based on science. Remember that."

"But I've seen you do it too," I remember suddenly. "That's what you were doing when you thought I was asleep."

"What I do is no business of yours," she says with such anger I know I've struck the truth.

A timid voice inside me warns me not to argue. Don't do anything to cause trouble; it can only turn out badly. But it's going to turn out worse for Nate—unless I can help him.

"It's not just curiosity. It's not right for the ... the Nocturne to take all the blame if others were involved."

"Your interest in him must end now." Rosemarie grasps my arms and looks into my face. "And stay away from the secret meetings."

I bite my lip, not sure I want to know the answer to my next question. "Are you ... part of the secret meetings?"

"I'm not in the group, but my husband was." She lowers her voice, clutching at her covers. "They trust me to keep quiet. But they won't trust you until all three memdenities.

If they find out you know about them, I won't be able to protect you. So much is at stake. It's taken over a century to achieve our perfect life."

Perfect? I almost laugh. "If it's so perfect, why does Daisy sneak out to be with someone from another Family?"

"She has free will to see who she wants, as long as the Family isn't shamed. Physical needs are natural and allowed, although not to be confused with love for our Family."

"But I am confused. And I don't want to do anything physical with Arthur. He seems nice enough, but he's so much older."

"Milly, I know you better than you know yourself, and you and Arthur are perfect for each other."

"Soul mates?" I question, still not really understanding this concept.

"Friends, partners, lovers." She peers into my face, smoothing away strands of my hair from my eyes. "You're lucky to have a wonderful man like Arthur. When your memories return, you'll be the wife he deserves, giving him what I … what no one else can," she adds, with a look on her face that gives away her heart.

"Graces good!" I gasp. "You love Arthur."

"Don't be ridiculous!" she says sharply. "He's my sister's husband. Why would I work so hard to bring Milly back if I loved her husband?"

It's because she *does* love Arthur. I'm not sure how I know this, but somehow I do. She wants him to be happy, even if it means he'll never love her the way she loves him.

My own feelings for love are confusing. At the Celebraze, if I'd been able to Choose one of the names on Marcus's list, I'd have no husband and would be free to marry Marcus. I'd join his Family or he would join mine. And we would have been happy together. But when I close my eyes, as I'm doing now, I see Nate's face—the scar at the corner of his mouth, his tight, muscled arms and those eyes ... those dazzling sea-blue eyes.

"Milly, you're not yourself," Rosemarie says, the anger fading from her face as she leans close to me.

I almost laugh. Milly is definitely not herself, because she's me too. But she's going to have to stand aside, because I have important things to do.

"Get some rest," Rosemarie urges. "We'll talk more tomorrow, and I'll teach you what you need to know. But please don't ask any more questions now."

Small black hairs in her braids fray loose around her face, and her eyes pool with shadows and sadness. I want to comfort her, to promise anything that will bring back her smile.

Stop thinking like Milly, I order myself.

So I think of Nate. Saving me from the vampfin, his stunning smile, the lilt in his voice, and the scars on his hands. I sit taller, confident and determined.

"Tell me about the meeting," I demand. "It's about faith, isn't it? They meet in secret because it's illegal to worship outside of our community's faith."

"Go to sleep, Milly," she urges, pushing me away.

"I can't sleep until I understand what's going on in my home."

"Fine. But you must never repeat this." Rosemarie whispers, although we're alone with no chance of being overheard. "They mean no disrespect to the scientists, but there are so many different beliefs and different shades of god. They gather together to share a belief in a higher power. My husband wanted me to join, but I refused. I was too afraid of breaking community rules."

"Still, you kept their secrets," I accuse. "Isn't that breaking rules too?"

Instead of denying this, she studies me, searching. "Do you remember when we were small and went to church?"

Memories jostle for attention, one surfacing of a glorious building with a slanted roof topped with a white cross. Crowds file through double stained-glass doors, and we're led to a cozy room with other children. "Sunday school," I say, nodding. "Mrs. Cox told us stories, and we sang songs."

"I'd forgotten Mrs. Cox."

"She had a mole on her nose and painted her lips bright red," I add, hearing our girlish voices giggling. I search for more images of the woman but find none. There weren't any more of church either.

"Mom had a strong faith, but Dad didn't, so we stopped going," Rosemarie explains. "My husband, Jed, though, had a strong Catholic background. He'd considered becoming a priest for a while, but he married me instead. He never missed a Sunday service—until ShareHaven was attacked and our churches destroyed. When we rebuilt our community, the Leaders decided on one church with one faith based on science. Share and share alike, the Leaders agreed, not only our food and chores, but our beliefs too."

I think of the Unity Pledge: *I pledge to honor Family, respect community, and give thanks to the miracles of scientists. Peace and safety forever.*

Rosemarie's gaze drifts down to where she's twisting a corner of her pillow. "But giving up religious beliefs proved difficult—especially for my husband."

I lift my brows, encouraging her to go on.

"Jed told me his soul would die if he kept denying his true beliefs, not in science but in a higher power. I reminded him that dissenting beliefs resulted in wars, destruction, and the mind-plague disease."

"But the mind-plague was an accident of nature," I point out.

"That's what your Instructors taught you, but those of us with longer memories know the disease was spread by a terrorist group who believed that anyone who didn't follow their religion deserved to die."

Milly's thoughts click in: faces talking from a box—TV—warning us to wear breathing masks and showing crowds of running people and burning buildings. I hear a TV woman say a word which sends chills through me: *bioterrorism.*

The mind-plague infected the world, destroying brains, societies, and my baby brother. Milly's brother, I remind myself. Not a random disease like I was told but airborne hate designed to kill. I lean against Rosemarie, remembering a tiny boy with chubby cheeks and a laugh that made me laugh with him.

"Beliefs are complicated, both uniting and dividing people," Rosemarie says sadly. "I warned Jed not to join the Believers—that's what they call their group—but he did anyway. I always knew where he was going when he left our bed at night. One night he came back acting strange. He held me tight," she said, her voice cracking, "and he said he would love me forever. Then he—he made me promise not to save his memories if he had an accident."

"You said he was murdered," I remind her.

"My husband died while working on a construction

project, when a nail gun misfired and pierced his brain." She glances over at a dresser where an old-style photograph of a bride and groom is framed. "But it wasn't an accident." She swallows hard. "Jed was going to ask the Leaders to allow freedom of religion in ShareHaven. The day before the appointment with the Leaders, he was killed quickly in such a way that his memories couldn't be retrieved. It was called an accident—but he knew he was in danger."

"How could he know?" I ask solemnly.

"He wouldn't tell me, but I suspect he was threatened."

"By who?"

Her eyes swell with tears. "Our Leaders."

I shake my head. "ShareHaven Leaders are against violence. They would never commit murder."

"That's why someone outside of ShareHaven had to kill Jed." She wipes a tear from her cheek. "Someone like your friend Nate."

TWENTY-FIVE

Rosemarie falls back to sleep, but I lie awake, staring at the ceiling and thinking of Nate. Locked away. Condemned to die. Nate's guilty, surely, but he was only a tool. I don't know why Nate allowed himself to be used. I only know he's not a savage and doesn't deserve execution.

I have to do something.

When I climb out of bed, each step I take toward the door is heavy with Milly's fears. *It's too dark. Stay here where it's safe. Night creatures will attack. I'll be caught. Rosemarie will lose me. I can't do this ....*

But I will, a stronger part of me shouts.

Rosemarie's breathing is even as I slip on my pantons, long-sleeved shirt, and jacket. I climb downstairs, entering the night.

It would take 'til daylight to walk to the jail. A vehicle, especially a solar cycle that rolls quietly, would travel more quickly. One small problem: I've never driven a vehicle. It seemed easy when I watched Daisy, but what if I lose control and crash? As fear shocks through me, I realize these are Milly's fears, not mine. Jennza would leap into the cycle and thrill with the ride.

While Milly's fears are paralyzing, there's wisdom into thinking first before jumping into danger. Too often I've jumped without checking for a safe landing. So I swallow

219

my impatience and pause to think how to operate the solar cycle. It takes many tries before I learn to twist a button and pump the floor pedal at the same time. A green light flashes. The engine rips to life. I locate the reverse handle, and roll out the barn door in a rush of triumph.

I don't flash on the front beams. There's enough light from a full moon and the glowing vehicle panel. On the main paveway, I increase my speed, my pulse racing with each mile. I only slow when I near City Central, recognizing dark building shapes. Bricks tower high, like a storm cloud against night stars—the jail.

Reaching into my pocket, I touch the packet, hoping it contains a miracle to save Nate. I park the solar cycle a fair distance from the jail, then sneak down as silent as a night creature. I stay in the shadows. As I near the hulking brick building, lights shine on a Uniform guarding the entrance to the jail. I hold my breath, not daring to breathe. Heart thudding, I creep to the bushes and crawl along the dirt trail beside the jail. Weeds brush my face, snagging my hair. It's slow going, but I know this path well now.

Milly's fears threaten when a bat swoops close to my head. I slap my hand over my mouth before Milly can scream. But I think of Marcus teaching me about crawlies and know the creatures around me are harmless—grass snakes, leaper frogs, and long-tailed rodents. Minutes seem like hours when I step out of the bushes and peer up into Nate's window.

The bars reflect silver, seeming oddly beauteous. Nate's inside, but I doubt he's asleep—not in his last hours. What are his final thoughts? His family, I guess. I always imagined Nocturnes living beneath ground in total darkness, a grim, desolate existence. But when Nate spoke of his home, friends and their sharing of stories—stelling—his words were made of light. I'm curious to see his home, but that's impossible. The most I can do is help Nate return safely.

I withdraw the packet from my pocket, running my finger over the bumpy paper. What's inside? But even more puzzling, who left it for me? Someone else wants to save Nate. That should be reassuring, but it means someone has watched me. Who knows that I know Nate? Rosemarie knows of my friendship with Nate, but she'd rather see him dead than help him escape.

When I toss a pebble at the window, it bounces off a steel bar. The ping echoes like gunfire. I dive back into the bushes. Milly's voice warns me to leave, but I'm learning to quiet her. I imagine Nate's face. I'm concentrating so hard that I'm startled when Nate appears at the window.

He scowls down on me. "I told you not to come back."

"I came to help you," I retort, annoyed and hurt he's not happy to see me. "But if you'd rather die in a few hours, I can turn around now."

"Don't risk your life for me."

"My choice." I raise my arm. "Here. Catch."

When I throw the packet, he catches it in a pinch of two fingers. Awkwardly, he draws the package through the bars.

When I hear him groan, I call out, "Are you alright?"

His leans forward, his blue eyes catching moonlight. "I almost dropped it." I hear a rip of paper. "Oh my god!" he cries. "Where did you get this?"

"Someone left it for me."

"Who?"

"I don't know. I found it in my room with a note that

said I could save your life. Do you know who left it?"

"No. All Topsiders want me dead."

"I don't, and at least one other person cares about you." I stare up curiously. "What's in the packet?"

"You didn't open it?" His voice is light, almost teasing.

"I wanted to, but it was addressed to you," I admit. "What is it?"

"Rubber strips and a bottle."

I'd expected something more useful, like a steel saw or weapon. "How can rubber and a bottle save your life?" I ask.

"Watch," he says.

He winds the rubber strips around the window bars like he's winding a bandage. "Now for the igniter," he tells me, holding up the small container. He drips green liquid on the rubber, a few drops spilling down the ivy wall. Nothing happens at first … then I hear the sizzling.

Everywhere green drops drip, including ivy leaves beneath the window, green flames spark. There's an acrid odor and soft, popping explosions.

"Are there Uniforms near your cell?" I call up to Nate in a tense whisper.

"No. They come hourly to check on me." His gaze fixes on the flames. "The acid fire will quickly burn through each bar."

"How did you know how to do this?"

"Acid fire is one of many means used to enter locked dwellings—part of my training before coming here."

There's a coldness in his words that chills me. He's trained for killing, I know this. There's so much more I want to know but no time to ask.

Flames scorch through each bar as easily as a brittle stick. The bars twist outward like fingers pointing into the night sky. Nate presses on the bars and they snap off, tumbling to the ground. I jump out of the way.

When I look up again, there's a wide gap in the window.

A miracle! I think, and wonder again who left the packet. Someone was able to sneak into my room and knew enough about Nate's training to give him the tools to escape. Whoever it was also knew I'd help Nate. But how could anyone know so much?

Nate jumps to the ground with the grace of a gull wing, landing softly next to me. As he smooths back his hair, I study him. I stare into his face—the scar over his brow, determined chin, strong shoulders, and curve of cheekbones. I imagine tracing my finger over his scar, down his cheek, to his full lips ....

"Thank you, Jennza," Nate says softly. "I won't forget what you've done for me."

When he starts for the bushes, I swing around to block him. "*We* leave together."

"Not possible." He glances around furtively. "A Topsider could never survive beneath the ground."

"If I wanted to, I could," I argue. "But I have no plans to leave, only to help you get away. You need my help."

"I travel alone." He shakes his head. "You can't come with me."

"Actually, you're coming with *me*." I gesture to the path through the bushes. "Unless you'd rather wait for the Uniforms to find your cell empty and call an alarm."

"Are you always this stubborn?" he demands.

"Worse. Drop to the ground. It's going to be a tight squeeze."

"Keep your voice down. There could be Uniforms

nearby," he says as he crouches low and follows me into the tangled bushes. His attitude irks me. I rescued him, yet he's ordering me around? When I pull a branch away, knowing it will rebound on Nate, I don't warn him.

"Ouch!" he cries out. "Why did you come here?"

"Why have I done anything? To save your annoying life, which makes us even since you saved me from the vampfin."

"You would have survived without my help."

"The stinging illness would have made me unable to attend the Celebraze. You helped me, and now I'm sticking to you until I know you're safe."

We reach the paveway, slowing our steps. The Uniforms might not notice a girl in dark coverings, but a prisoner wearing yellow won't be hard to miss. I turn back to Nate, putting my finger to my lips.

Night is a silvery cushion of quiet. No people or vehicles on the road, nor breeze of wind. Nate glances back at the jail, his strong shoulders taut like an animal prowling in the dark. He could probably move faster without me. But his blue eyes light up when I show him the solar cycle.

"Why walk when we can ride?" I say. "I'll take you beyond the Edu-Center to the Fence. We'll have to hike through the woods to avoid being seen. I'll show you how to get over the Fence. Or do you already know?" I add suspiciously.

He hesitates, then nods. "I saw you unwind the top wire, but that's not how I entered ShareHaven."

I climb into the solar cycle driver's seat, scooting over to make room for him. "The Fence is the only way in or out of ShareHaven."

"Except for the main gate."

"Do you plan to go up to the Uniforms and politely ask

them to open the Gate for you?" I almost laugh at this crazy image.

"There's a tunnel beneath the main gate." He slides beside me, so close that I'm warmed by his body heat. "Drive toward your compound—it's not far from there. After you drop me off, hurry back so no one finds out you've helped me."

Morning is creeping up on darkness, a curve of dawn lightening the sky. We're running out of time. A flash of Milly trembling in the dark, frightened of shadows, makes me tremble too.

We say nothing as I drive the solar cycle away from City Central. I want to rip with speed but am still learning the levers and pedals. I crank a lever forward, but it shoves us into reverse. Quickly I crank the other direction. Nate chuckles until I glare at him. I don't admit I've never driven a vehicle before.

"Hurry." Nate taps his fingers on the door.

I slam my foot on the speed pedal. Sweat drips from my forehead. My mind spins with images of a city with crowded building towers—skyscrapers—and speeding cars. I smell an acrid odor—exhaust—and hear honking.

Nate lunges across the seat to grab the wheel. "You almost crashed into that tree!"

"Sorry." I take a deep breath to clear my head, gripping the wheel.

"What just happened?" he asks.

Milly would be too scarified to admit the truth, but I won't let her influence me. So I say, "The memdenity confuses my thoughts."

"You've done *that*?" His voice drips disgust.

"All youths get them."

"Not where I live." Nate scowls. "I won't let anyone mess with my brain."

I feel the same way but find myself defending the process. "How else can useful skills be learned?" I ask.

"By reading or listening to stelling."

"Why use a spoon to fill a bucket when you can dip the bucket into a lake?" I repeat a phrase Instructor Penny used to explain memdenity. "I experienced Milly's childhood in one morning. While I learned about retro-century from the Instructors, *living* it is so much more real. Jennza has never seen a car but Milly rode in them. I heard songs, tasted foods, tapped my fingers on a com—com—" I search the word for the magical device.

"Computer," he says, which surprises me, because he's right.

"Yes, and there's much knowledge that is mine now. My next memdenity will show me house-crafting skills, marriage, and natural birth."

"Marriage? You have a husband?"

I nod. "Also a daughter, sister, nephews, and grandmother."

"But you're not really Milly." He looks at me with a puzzled frown.

"No ... she died a long time ago. I'm expected to become more like her, a gentle person who is much loved by her Family."

"And you're okay with this? A husband? What if he wants ... well ... to act like a husband? He must be much older than you."

"He ceased aging at twenty-five, so in ten years we'll be the same age." I hear my voice, calm and accepting, but when I think of Arthur touching me, I shudder.

"Twenty-five forever," he says with a sarcastic edge. "My people are lucky to survive past twenty, yet you'll never grow old. Even your memories are eternal."

I stare at the road, my speed steady, but my thoughts uneasy. It's not fair for my life to be so easy while his people battle creatures and die young. And why have I been told lies about Nocturnes? Nate isn't subhuman or a beast, and there's gentleness in his face that stirs my heart.

Nate touches my arm, his fingers callused but gentle. "Jennza, I will never forget what you've done for me tonight."

His tone echoes with good-bye. I slow the cycle as we near the turnoff to my compound, letting my gaze linger on his face for the last time—the scars of bravery, full lips, and sea-blue eyes. His gaze meets mine, and although I quickly look at the road, I thrill at his nearness. And I wonder: when he's safe with his people beneath the ground, will he think of me?

"Almost there," he says.

Almost gone, I think.

I peer ahead at a tangled landscape of trees, recognizing the row of trees leading into the Cross compound.

Soon Nate will return to his people. I'll never see him again. My emotions plunge down an endless hole. I shouldn't care about a killer. He admitted his guilt with no remorse, and he'll probably kill again.

Don't trust a Noc. Never leave the Fence. Stay safe in ShareHaven.

I'm not sure if these are Milly thoughts. Or mine.

"The Uniforms must know you've escaped," I say anxiously. "Be careful."

"They'll be too far behind to catch me. Don't worry."

"I never used to worry about anything until I met you."

He reaches out as if he's going to touch me, and I'm disappointed when he pulls away. "Before I met you, I thought all Topsiders were arrogant and cruel."

"I thought all Nocturnes were monsters."

"Your Fence isn't only to keep claws out but to keep us out too. While creatures stalk the woods, we're forced underground. It takes a dozen hunters to kill one claw. We've tried to destroy them, but they multiply faster than we do, so we're forced to live underground."

His words crawl under my skin. "I've never seen a monster—but I've heard their growls at night."

"You live in daylight when they sleep."

I push the pedal with a burst of anger, and the solar cycle nearly careens into a ditch. "Sorry," I say quickly, righting the cycle. "I'm just so angry at our leaders. They should help you, not shut you out. We should all work together to defeat the claws."

"You can't change the world," he says sadly. "Or even one island."

"I can try," I insist. "If the leaders won't do anything, I'll go the scientists."

"They won't listen, and you'll only endanger yourself."

"Danger is my normal."

"I wish all Topsiders were like you—with more heart than hate." He reaches across the seat, touching my arm. "You're special, Jennza."

I like the sound of my name from his lips.

The Cross entrance looms ahead. To the right, beyond shadowed trees, is the only gate in the Fence, its high sentry platform a dark silver smear against night.

"Stop here," Nate says. "I can walk the rest of the way."

I slow to a stop, resisting the urge to keep driving so he can't leave. He's looking at me. And I'm looking back, losing myself in blueness deeper than the sea. I should just tell him what I'm thinking ... feeling ... wishing ....

Nate suddenly points to the Cross compound entrance. "What's that?" he asks tensely.

Twin lights shine from a vehicle leaving the compound, heading our way.

"Hide the cycle!" Nate barks. "Over there. Behind the trees!"

Dirt spits from the tires, hitting my arm as I swerve off the smooth road. The cycle bumps and lurches until I stop it behind a thicket of trees. I jump out and start running with Nate. "Go to your tunnel!" I cry. "Hurry!"

"What about you? It's not safe here."

"I'll hide until I can sneak back into the compound."

"The alert may already have gone out about my escape. Uniforms will search for me with guns and sniffer beasts. The sniffers will find you. Come with me!" He grabs my hand and pulls me deep into the shadows.

Trees swallow us. I nearly fall over a log, trying to match his long strides. Towering in the near distance are the iron spikes of the Gate. As we draw closer, I count seven Uniforms patrolling the Gate: three on the ground and four perched on the high sentry platform, poised to destroy enemies.

Nate rips aside hanging vines and squeezes through a narrow, rocky gap. Brittle branches crunch beneath our feet, each sound sharp like breaking bones. Nate stops by a gigantic blackened oak that's twisted and burnt, as if struck by lightning not once but over and over.

A slant of moonlight shines on Nate's pale, sweating face. His jaw sets with purpose. In a swift jerk, he grabs a burnt branch and pulls it sideways.

There's an odd grating sound, and the ground beneath my feet quakes. Branches yawn and stretch, sliding apart to reveal a gaping, dark hole.

Nate steps into the hole, and I start to follow until Milly's terror tugs and rips my thoughts, her fears stinging like whipping branches.

No, not now, Milly. I have to be strong.

Before I lose courage, I plunge forward, following Nate into the unknown.

TWENTY-SIX

Concrete steps disappear beneath the ground.

Nate is a shadow blurring down the steep staircase, and I hurry to keep up with him. I envy his ability to move swiftly in the dark. Tunnel-dwelling is his normal, I remind myself. When he turns back to urge me to hurry, his voice is clipped and anxious.

I brace my hand against the side of the tunnel, which isn't rock or dirt as I expected but metal. At the bottom, lights flicker from the low ceiling. Nate touches his finger to his lips.

Looking around nervously, I search for any hint we aren't alone. But no one could hide in this cramped room, and the door up ahead is fortified with steel and bolted shut. There are two chairs beside a wooden desk, a metal cabinet that looks retro-century, a blanket on the narrow cot, and a plate with a dried apple core and bread crust on a dusty table.

"No one's been here in a while," Nate says, blowing out a deep breath.

I eye the cot uneasily. "What is this place?"

"It's called the Threshold, a meeting place for trading beneath the Gate."

He frowns as he says *trading,* and I know he doesn't mean trading frivels at Sunday Fair. Lives are traded.

"Who met you here? Leader Cross?" I guess.

"We didn't exchange names." His expression hardens. "Why should they give anything but orders to a Noc?"

"What orders?" I hold my breath.

"You already know."

"But I don't know why." I bite my lip, aching over the differences between us. "What can they give you in return? What's worth more than a life?"

"Hundreds of lives. We barter for medicine." A shadow crosses his face. "Living without sun causes illnesses, mostly in our young. But they survive much longer with vitamins and medicine."

"Why not ask for our help? Health-keepers can heal any illness."

"But they won't. Not for us." He slaps the table, the dried apple core rolling close to the edge. "Your people hate mine."

"Not all of us," I say.

"I'm learning that." He sighs. "But you'd be safer to stay away from us ... from me."

"Why?" I clench my fists in frustration. "I know my Family Leader was involved in Grand Sarwald's death and that others wanted him dead too. They bribed you to kill him, probably with medicine. But there's so much I don't know, and you're my last chance to get answers."

"You won't like the answers," he warns.

"I have to know how Grand Sarwald was killed."

"They told me the target wanted a quick death because he was dying from a slow, painful disease."

"Ridiculous!" I shake my head. "We have medis to cure all illnesses. No one sickens or suffers with pain. Grand Sarwald was a brave man who would never dishonor his Family by asking to die. Whoever told you that was lying."

He turns his head so I can't read his expression. "I wish things were different, that life had more value than barter."

"No one can force you to kill."

"And no one can force you to take someone else's memories." He looks hard at me. "Yet we do what we're born to do."

I touch the memdenity scar on my neck, frowning.

"More than a fence divides us," he continues with an upward glance. "I've wondered what it would be like to be one of you, to wake every morning to the sky and have long, peaceful lives." The wistfulness in his voice aches inside me.

He rubs his thumb over a jagged scar on his arm. "But I'd rather be with people whose scars are shown outside, not hidden beneath smooth skin. Your people are even cruel to their own if they aren't perfect—leaving them outside the Gate to be devoured by beasts."

"What are you talking about?" I demand. "No one is ever put outside."

"Are you sure?"

His question startles me. Not even the Uniforms would be so cruel. Yet I wonder if this explains why youths who've been Returned are never seen again.

"Believe what you want." Nate frowns. "But don't trust anyone."

I step closer to him. "Including you?"

"You know what I've done."

"But you didn't want to."

His blue eyes harden like stone. "I volunteered."

"You ... you wanted to kill?" I'm begging for him to say no.

"I did what I've been trained to do. The medicine I earned will keep many children alive."

"Until they grow up and become killers too," I say

sarcastically.

"If they're lucky." He points to the steel door. "I can't stay any longer. I must go now."

He taps the door, and blue-gray light floods down over us like silvery moonlight. I watch as Nate taps a numbered sequence on the panel.

"Go back the way you came. There's a panel on the inside of the door," he says, pointing behind me toward the tunnel. "Touch numbers 4, 8, 4, 0."

I repeat the numbers over and over again until they're firm in my memory.

Click. A light flashes red. The door slides sideways into the wall, revealing a deep tunnel.

"Leave now," Nate urges. "Follow the steps back exactly and press the numbers. Forget you ever saw this place."

"But what about you? Will you be safe?" I whisper.

"Life isn't about being safe; it's about surviving to live another day." He gazes deeply into my eyes. "You've given me more days. Thank you, Jennza."

He reaches for my hand, and I should pull away, yet I curl my fingers through his. Our hands melt together. His are callused and scarred, mine soft and smooth. I long to lean against his chest, lift my face toward his and ...

Abruptly, he drops my hand. "I—I have to go."

I nod, unable to speak. It's like I'm being ripped apart from the inside. Exposed, my emotions raw and bleeding.

Nate reaches into his pocket and pulls out a star-shaped shell. "Here's your shell."

"No, it's yours now."

Like my heart, I think. I'm swept into the brilliant blue of his gaze that touches something deep inside, something thrilling and scarifying. Whenever I look at the sky-reflecting water, I'll see his eyes.

He leans close, and I inhale his woodsy scent. "I don't know how I'll do it, but I'll come back to see you. I promise."

Then he's gone.

Without Nate, the underground room is suffocating. Concrete walls close in, and there's no sound except for my heartbeat. I glance at the table where someone left the crust of bread and apple core. A wrinkled blanket covers the empty cot. Who slept here?

No one from ShareHaven would need to hide, so it must be here for "tools" like Nate. Outrage burns inside me, and even though Nate is safe, I am determined to find out who gave the orders for Grand Sarwald's death.

As I climb back up the stairs, I go through the list of Believers at the secret meeting—Leader Cross, Arthur, Daisy, Grandmother, and members from other Families, including Instructor Penny. It hurts to think badly of Instructor Penny. I need to talk to her, to find out her truth.

The stairs seem steeper climbing up, and I'm breathing hard by the time I reach the top. There's no knob or handle, only a small square panel like the one on the door Nate left through. The panel glows eerie silver in the dark, numbers zero to nine gleaming like demon eyes. I try the sequence that Nate told me. Click. The light flashes from red to green.

I push at the door and it opens easily.

As I step into chilly air, strong hands grab me.

A harsh yet familiar voice shouts, "I've got her!"

Twenty-Seven

I'm under house arrest, confined to my room with no visitors—until the leaders can decide my fate.

Leader Cross nearly twisted my arm off when he dragged me from the tunnel. "Where's the Noc?" he demanded.

"Gone," I told him with satisfaction.

"How did he get out of jail?"

I wouldn't answer.

"Did you help him escape?"

Milly's thoughts pulled at me, warning me to apologize and beg for forgiveness. But I rushed on, too angry to be scarified. "You bribed Nate to kill Grand Sarwald," I accused. "You would have let him die so he couldn't tell the other Leaders about your meetings!"

He fist came at me so fast, I hit the ground before pain exploded.

Hours later, pain still burns my face. But worse is the sting of my own foolishness. I should have kept quiet and said nothing.

Outside my locked door, Rosemarie's voice rises angrily.

"You can't keep me out of my own room!" she shouts. "What have you done to Milly? What's happening? I don't understand any of this."

"She knows too much," Leader Cross snaps.

Rosemarie gasps. "She's won't tell anyone. You can trust

Milly."

"She's not Milly—and she never will be." His words slam hard like his fist. "Leave this matter to me."

"I will not!" she shouts back. "Release her right now. I won't let you hurt her."

"I won't do anything to her. They will."

There's a pause. No one says anything until Rosemarie begins to cry. "No," she sobs. "Not again. Please, don't do this. She's only a young girl and means no harm."

"There's no other option."

"She won't tell anyone. I'll watch her so she doesn't leave our dwellings."

"You didn't even know she'd left your room," he scoffs. "There's too much at risk to trust her. There's only one way to ensure her silence."

"No!" Rosemarie gasps.

"It's the right punishment."

"It was bad enough with *him* … but something was wrong with his mind. Milly is healthy, intelligent, and a sweet youth."

"Your *sweet youth* destroyed steel bars to release a killer from jail. She betrayed ShareHaven and shamed our Family."

"Surely there's a mistake."

"Yes—but I won't allow any more. They're coming for her tonight." I hear Rosemarie's sharp intake of breath. "She'll be Returned."

PART THREE

TWENTY-EIGHT

I sit by the window, watching dying autumn leaves twist in the wind and fall from the large oak tree by the vehicle barn. The door to the barn has been left open, and I glimpse visiting vehicles. Is this another not-so-secret meeting of Believers? Are they discussing me? Leader Cross will twist the truth, turning even Instructor Penny against me. Will he say I went crazy like the last youth? I have only a few hours left in the Cross Family.

What will happen by nightfall?

If Nate is right, I'll be thrown over the Fence to the claws. My born-mates, usually Clark and Homer, exaggerated rumors of youths being devoured by claws or dissembled—limbs, organs, bones—into nothingness. The R word strikes fear bone deep. Even the Instructors, with their vast knowledge, would only say that Returned youths are sent to the scientists' compound. All I know for sure is that they're never seen again.

Rosemarie will protect me. I cling tight to the slim string of hope she'll convince Leader Cross to let me stay.

When I hear footsteps outside my door, I jump from my bed, eager to see Rosemarie. Instead it's Arthur—like I've never seen him before. His usually smooth black hair is untidy, stubble rough on his chin, and there are furrows in his forehead as if he removed his cease-aging patch.

"Milly … my Milly!" He pulls me into his muscular arms.

"What's happening?" I slip out of his arms, going over to peer through the opened door. I expect to see a Uniform, waiting to arrest me, but no one's there.

"They say you know too much."

I shake my head, feeling as if the more I know, the less I understand.

"Leader Cross says you must go but I can't—" His voice cracks. "I can't lose you—her—again. You're only one memdenity away from remembering our life together. Our wedding in the City Center garden, the pink roses I gifted you every birthday, and the miracle of watching our daughter's birth. Daisy was the last natural birth on the island, and we were so proud of her."

"Daisy will be glad I'm gone," I say bitterly.

"But Rosemarie and I need you." He comes so close to me I can feel his breath on my skin. "Once I thought I loved someone else, but I couldn't forget you. Only one more memdenity, and you'll remember loving me."

I can't imagine loving Arthur. Even though he's tall with a muscled body and pleasing face, we're centuries apart in age and experiences. And I feel no stirring of emotions. Not like when I think of Nate—his eyes, his face, his hands—and heat thrills through me. Did Milly feel like that with Arthur? If I'd gained all her memories, would I feel those emotions too?

Now I'll never find out.

"They can't take you away after I've waited so long," Arthur says with a wild desperation. He grabs my wrists, staring into my face. "I can't lose you."

"I'm … I'm sorry." I'm aching inside with pain that stabs sharper than needles. I didn't want to be in the Cross family, yet now I'm desperate to stay.

"I tried explaining to Leader Cross that you're not a threat, but he wouldn't listen." Arthur runs his hands through his hair.

"Rosemarie tried too." I press my lips tight so I won't cry.

"This can't happen!" Arthur stomps the floor, rattling the shells I'd placed on my dresser. "If they take you away, my wife's memories will go with you." The softness dies in his eyes, narrowing in accusation.

"Only the first fifteen years. Another youth can have her other memories."

"That's not how it works." His frustration shifts to fury. "The health-keepers don't allow division of memdenity. Milly's memories will be destroyed—because of *you*."

"I'm sorry," is all I can say.

"'Sorry' won't bring her back. You have to save her!" His anger burns my wrist as he pulled me close, his breath hot and sour. "You stole my wife."

I try to pull away, but he holds my wrist tight. "You're hurting me."

"You've hurt me far worse," he growls. "I'll do anything to get my wife back. You must save her!"

His fingernails dig into my skin, and I cry out with pain. I give a fierce jerk, finally pulling away from him but losing my balance. Falling, I slam against the floor. The impact, hard and stunning, takes my breath.

"Milly!" Arthur sobs, reaching out for me. "I'm so sorry, Milly."

"I. Am. Not. Milly!" I slap his hand away so hard that he stumbles, teetering off balance.

When he grabs for me again, I shove him away, and he

reels backward. His head thuds against a bed post. I scramble to my feet, gasping. Through the window, the crimson curve of daylight is falling fast into night. The Uniforms will come for me. Soon. I must escape while I have the chance.

But why is Arthur so still? I stare at him, lying on the floor, not moving. Why doesn't he move? He can't be ....

His eyes flutter open and he moans, "Milly ... please ... give me ...."

I don't wait to find out what he'll say next.

Yanking open the door, I rush into the hall. No one is there, and I nearly fly down the stairs, having no plan, only desperation to get away before the Uniforms arrive. When I hear voices from the main floor, I grab hold of a banister rail, panicking. This way is blocked.

Doubling back to the second floor, I glance around desperately for a way out. I look at the doors down the hall. Three lead into bedrooms and one is a supply closet. My only chance is to crawl through a bedroom window.

But if I get away, where will I go?

No time to come up with a plan, only to run.

I race down the hall, trying the first door and finding a sleep room with only a bed and dresser—nowhere to hide or escape. I check in the next room—which isn't empty. Grandmother's wrinkled eyes widen at the sight of me, and her mouth opens. Sure she's going to shout out an alarm, I slam the door, then run down the hall. The next room is the one I would have shared with Arthur as his wife. I look past wedding photographs and the jewelry box to the balcony.

Expecting shouts and thudding footsteps any second, I push open the door to the balcony. A roof slopes down to a tall, leafy oak with strong branches.

Milly's fear of heights slams into me. *Get down, don't climb, it's not safe. You'll never make it, you'll fall and break your bones.* I'm paralyzed with her terror and start to back out of the room.

"No!" I say, then shove aside her fear with images of myself playing climbing games with Marcus in a tree so tall I couldn't see the top branches. I pretended to be a furry monk-lee, swinging from branches and never once losing my grip.

I am not afraid, I tell myself. Determination pushes me forward. I grip the edge of the shingles; my knees crouch as I take small steps at a slanted angle. The air is misty with the darkening clouds and the acrid scent of rain.

Climbing down the tree takes only a few heartbeats. I hide in shadows, considering my next move. I have to get far away quickly. Once they know I'm gone, they'll lock the gates, then search until I'm found.

It'll be dark soon, with claws stalking the night outside the Fence. I can't survive out there, yet I can't stay in ShareHaven—not without a Family. If I wait too long, the Uniforms will arrive with boar sniffers.

Should I go to Marcus or Lorelei? Surely, they'd hide me. But if they get caught, they'll be punished—Returned?—too, and I can't do that to them. I need a safe place to hide until I can decide what to do.

The answer is so simple I almost smile.

My cave.

Petal will be so joyous to see me. She'll purr her tinkling sound and give me lick-kisses. She taught me how to find edible plants and sweet fish and fresh water seeping from a wall crevice, so I'll have food, water, and safety in our cave. And Petal will be my Family.

But how will I get to the cave quickly without being caught?

My gaze shifts to the vehicle barn. I borrowed a solar cycle once; can I do it again? Glancing around furtively, I stay low as I creep to the vehicle barn. I slip inside, heading for a Cross Family solar cycle. I change my plan when I see the Edu-Center solar coach. Instructor Penny must be inside the house.

Hmmm ... . When she returns to the coach, she'll drive back to the Edu-Center. I know she would help me if I could talk to her alone, but she might be with other Instructors. Besides, she's one of them—the Believers—and they want me gone. Still, her coach will take me close to my cave. If I hide in the rear compartment and stay quiet, she won't know I'm there.

I move toward the coach but stop at the sound of a creaking door.

Whirling around, I stare at Daisy. Her arms are folded triumphantly across her chest and she's smiling. Not a nice smile; it's the sort a spider might give to an insect struggling in a sticky web.

Caught.

TWENTY-NINE

Daisy's taller than me, but she lacks the muscles I've gained from cookery work and climbing trees. I bend my knees, ready to tackle her. I'm poised to spring forward when the sound of growls and grinding wheels startle us both ....

"Bad news for you." Daisy smirks as she points beyond the door. "The Uniforms are here."

Here for me.

Panicked, I look at hay piles, vehicles, crates and high windows. Plenty of places to hide but nowhere to run.

"She's in here!" Daisy shouts with a wave of her arm. Triumphantly, she flings the doors wide, welcoming the Uniforms.

Five figures in imposing gray clomp out of the jail coach. This coach is similar to a solar coach, only it's domed, with impassable metal bars separating the front and back seat. There are no doors or windows in the back. An attached wagon holds chained boar sniffers. The bloodhound-hog hybrids growl and gnash spike-sharp teeth.

The tallest Uniform challenges me with a "go ahead and run" expression. I won't make it a meter before the sniffers take me down. I won't beg or sob. Lifting my chin high, I shove against Daisy and step out of the vehicle barn. Returned ... soon I'll know what it means.

One of the Uniforms is familiar—long black hair flapping

like a wing over his forehead and a thin mouth set in a forever frown. He was posted at the jail entrance when I first visited Nate. He grabs my arms, twists them roughly behind my back. I hear the metal clip of a restraint. Pain squeezes my wrists.

"Inside," he barks, shoving me into the back seat.

The sniffers growl and snort in the cart behind me.

I take one last look at the Cross dwelling, tears spilling hot down my cheeks. The cart door slams. Locked. I fall backward, crying out as my elbow smacks against hard wood. Wheels creak as I'm driven away. I hear sobs that sound like Rosemarie. I'll never see my sister again. I'm dead to ShareHaven, yet I'm still breathing. Is this how Nate felt waiting in jail for his execution? At least he knew what was going to happen. I have no idea.

The bearded driver glances through the steel bars, his gaze cold. He snorts, then turns away. When the coach lurches over a road bump, I stumble sideways. I can't push back up with my arms shackled. Despair chokes my throat. *Don't think about what's happening ... what could happen.*

I send my thoughts back into Milly's memories, needing to think of a happy moment so I don't lose control. The happiest time was before life turned sad, before we lost our brother and left our home. A morning of sunshine and turning six. A special birthday gift. The present I longed for since I rode a pony at a kiddie carnival—my own horse. We couldn't keep a horse in our suburban backyard, so my horse stayed at a ranch. I wanted to name her Ariel after my favorite Disney cartoon, but my parents said she already had a name: Sunrise. So I called her Sunny. She was so beautiful—reddish brown with a white mane, a small Arabian with a long swishy brown tail. I took riding lessons. Mom said I was a natural rider. When I sat tall on Sunny, I felt confident and fearless.

I smile at Milly's thoughts, riding Sunny through golden fields instead of being jostled in my rolling prison. Metal cuffs dig into my skin.

Although there are no windows to see through, I smell salty air. We're not headed for the Gate to toss me like raw meat to vicious claws. Instead we're nearing the sea and climbing up a steep road into hills that conceal the most mysterious part of ShareHaven: the scientists' compound.

The rumors are true. The scientists punish the Returned. Does that mean Lila, who called me her friend, will be the one to end my life?

Wheels click-clack as the road grows rougher. The coach stops abruptly, and I slam against the floor. The door bursts open. Two Uniforms yank me out.

Stumbling, I fall on my knees. Pain shoots through me as the black-haired Uniform yanks me to my feet. Another Uniform pushes me forward. I'm surrounded by cruel hands and imposing hills that rise into twilight. Scientists dwell in these hills, shrouded in mystery. Lila described rocky cliffs and a vista of sea and sky, and I hoped to walk with her along sea cliffs. I can only hope that being Returned is quick and painless.

Wood creaks like a gate opening, but I only see tall grasses sweeping up a steep hillside. A light seems to float in the air. A figure made of shadows and moonlight comes forward holding a torchlight. The pale, white-haired woman is apple-round, with a doughy face drooping oddly to one side. Her feral eyes glint dangerously at me.

"Here she is, Frost," the bearded Uniform says in a clipped tone. "We've brought her directly to you as requested."

"She doesn't look dangerous." Only half of the woman's mouth moves, her words hard to understand.

"The youth betrayed ShareHaven by releasing the Grand Leader's killer from jail, and she also attacked her husband. Leader Cross suggests you Return her immediately."

"Humph," the droopy-face woman snorts. "Scientists don't take orders. But we can always use another droll."

What is a droll? I think, sick with fear.

She points a sharp-nailed finger at me. "Come along, girl."

I glance around at wild grass stretching across rolling hills. Where are the buildings? I breathe in a salty breath, my heart syncing with the rhythmic rumble of the sea, and I long for the safe haven of my cave.

"Follow," she barks. Her torchlight moves with the sweep of her hand pointing behind her.

"Where?" I'm puzzled because there are only endless hills. "Are we near the scientists' compound?"

"Very near." Her words come from only one side of her mouth, garbled and hard to understand.

"What will happen?"

She raises her hand, silencing me. "No more questions. Must I ask the Uniforms to escort you or will you come with no resistance?"

I glance back at the Uniforms. One wrong move and the sniffers will be set loose. I imagine their hot breath and sharp teeth sinking into my flesh.

"I won't resist," I say, as if I've given up.

But I'm studying the misshapen woman—"Frost" the Uniform called her—searching for weaknesses so I can escape. A Uniform hands Frost a key, which she pockets. Once I enter a building, I'll never leave.

Deliberately, I stumble, my legs buckling as I fall to my knees on ground.

"I can't move … not with the chains." I hang my head, moaning. "I won't be able to walk. Could you unlock my hands?"

"Do I look brain-lacking?" Frost asks as if amused, pocketing the key.

"I promise to do whatever you say." I rattle the chains and exaggerate moaning. "The pain is too much. Please unlock my hands."

"You won't feel pain much longer," she says in a bored tone. "You'll stay in chains until we reach the lab."

Lab. This word pierces my hopes.

The woman has a chain of her own, which she clips to my restraints, like leading ropes for the hoxen. She jerks me forward. "Follow."

As if I have a choice!

Behind us, wheels rumble and sniffers whine, probably disappointed to miss out on a human snack. I bite my lip, not wanting to think about what lies ahead.

We go a few meters before Frost stops at an impassable thicket of thorny bushes at the base of a towering hill. She reaches through the bushes. A shrill beep makes me jump. She drags me through the bushes that move aside like sliding doors. I shut my eyes at the burst of blinding light. When I open my eyes, I'm staring at a doorway concealed in a hill.

"Where are we?" I ask.

"Don't speak to me," she says coolly.

We step into a hallway—not made of dirt or grassy roots

but walls so white I blink and a high ceiling that shimmers as bright as daylight. She tugs me to the right down a narrow hall that twists snake-like until we stop at a dark wooden door.

The room we enter has walls a golden shade of sunshine. There's a dining table, bookcase, large-screened viewing box at the center of a grouping of chairs, and cookery with double burners and large sinks.

Frost jerks me to another door, and once again, we're traveling through a twisty hallway. She won't talk or look at me—as if I'm not worth the effort of speech. In her cloud-white coverings, she reminds me of a half-melted ice statue. She's not a scientist, so she must work for them, an assistant to the scientists—like Milly's mother was when we—they— moved to the island.

"The Uniforms are wrong about me," I tell her in my sweetest tone, hoping she'll realize I'm non-threatening and unshackle me. "I'd never hurt anyone, especially someone in my family. I'm not dangerous. Please let me go."

"Quiet." Her clipped tone invites no questions. But if I waited for invites I'd never learn anything.

"I'm friendly with Scientist Lila Farrow. If she knows I'm here she'll want to see me." *But will she?* I worry.

"Her brother is eager to welcome you." She chuckles, then shoves me forward. "We're almost there."

Burnt hope is bitter to swallow. Frost jerks on the chain. I stumble, falling to my knees, which are bleeding through my pantons from my previous fall. They leave a stain on the white tiled floor as I struggle to my feet.

"Clumsy," Frost mutters angrily as she yanks my chain again. I want to hail her with insults, but I get a memory of

Milly losing her temper and throwing a dish at her mother. Blood trickles from a cut on her mother's arm and Milly sobs, "I'm sorry." But her mother shouts and confines her to her room without dinner.

Frost could do far worse to me.

I hold my temper.

We enter a passage where the walls are less bright and high ceiling lamps seem to hang in the air. The rush of activity visible through an opened door startles me. Rows of figures garbed alike in loose gray shirts with hoods and pantons in rough black fabric sit at stations, working with tubes, bottles, and mechanical devices. Most are youths I've never seen before, quicksilver hands moving with precision, synced with each other like playformers on a stage. They gaze straight ahead without glancing at me. Blank eyes, expressionless.

A narrow-faced boy with a crooked nose and thin lips, though, isn't quick or precise as he pours yellow liquid into a thumb-sized black tube. He hunches over at his table, his elbows poking out and his movements jerky. When I am only a few meters from him, his gaze shifts toward me—not with the vacant stare of the others but with a shock of awareness. A tube slips from his hands to the floor, shattering, yellow liquid spilling.

"Carlos!" Frost pulls out a slim, pencil-like device from a shirt pocket. "I warned you!"

He says nothing.

Frost aims the device, and a shock of blue electricity shoots out, striking Carlos in the chest. I smell burnt flesh. The boy's black eyes widen. His body convulses, a stream of liquid darkening his pantons. He's wet himself, but he doesn't move or utter a sound.

The flash of awareness is gone from his face, like flipping to a blank page in a book. He stares straight ahead, joining the rhythm of the other workers.

"What happened?" I ask, sickened by the burning smell.

"Punishment," Frost says with a smile on half of her face.

"Is something wrong with him?" I keep my gaze on the electricity device in her hand as she slips it back into her pocket.

"The droll won't cause any more trouble."

"Trouble? But he only dropped a tube."

"Cease speaking, or I'll rip out your tongue." Frost yanks on my chain, dragging me into the next door.

My arms burn with pain. But I won't cry. My thoughts keep going over the boy's name. Carlos? Haven't I heard it somewhere before?

Frost shoves me into a gray room that makes me feel like I'm being swallowed by fog. A tall, familiar man wearing a gold and purple robe sweeps across the tile floor toward me. Scientist Daniel Farrow.

"So it is you," he says, with a narrowing of dark eyes. "My dear sister will be so disappointed to miss this."

"Please," I say, swallowing salty tears. "Tell her I'm here."

"And ruin all my fun?" he says with a tight, pleased smile. "I think not."

He stands beside a steel table with circular metal loops at the bottom and top. Not loops—restraints like the ones twisting my arms. There are no chairs, only the table and shelves of tubes, jars, coils, and gleaming sharp tools.

Nightmares come in many forms: some evolve from fears of falling, getting lost, or losing a loved one. Tools for cutting into skin are now my worst nightmare.

Carlos.

Now I remember where I heard his name. He was the youth who attacked Daisy and was Returned. Only he isn't dead. Are the others in the room Returned youths too? Still alive and working for the scientists? Or are they alive? What did Frost call him? *Droll.* Empty shells of the people they once were, like zombies in retro-century scarytales.

And soon I'll be one of them.

THIRTY

"Prepare for surgery," Scientist Daniel orders Frost, holding a cutting tool between his bony fingers.

"So you're going ahead as usual?" Frost asks. "What about your sister?"

"She has already retired for the night, and I won't disturb her," he says firmly. "Tomorrow I shall take pleasure in introducing her to the new droll."

"I understand, Daniel." Frost's voice is softer, her lashes fluttering, and the smooth half of her face is transformed with a feminine smile.

"Secure the subject to the table," he orders, as if Returning is routine and I'm no more interesting than a test tube. But there's a look of satisfaction on his face, similar to Leader Cross when I've watched him play chess and announce to his opponent, "Checkmate."

Metal clangs behind my back as Frost unfastens my restraints. My arms collapse to my sides, aching. Frost shoves me roughly toward the table. Her hands clamp on mine. I struggle, but she's stronger than she looks, and she tosses me to the table like I weigh no more than air.

"No! Wait!" I try to think of something—anything!—to stop this insanity.

When I try to roll off the table, Frost pins me down. I'm facing a tray with tools—assorted sizes and shapes, silver gleaming and sharpened to slice skin. Fear jolts me. I realize what they're going to do. Cut into my brain—turn me into a worker droll like Carlos. That's why Arthur accused me of stealing Milly from him. I won't only lose myself, but I'll lose Milly too.

"Stop thrashing." Scientist Daniel scowls as if I should be ashamed for such rude behavior. Well, excuse me for not wanting to become a zombie!

I strike a fierce kick at Frost's chin. She swears, then slams me against the table with such force that all the breath rushes out of me.

"Frost, sedate her," Scientist Daniel orders in an annoyed tone.

"Gladly." Frost aims a sharp needle at my arm, but I twist away. "Stay still!"

"Can't you handle a youth?" His eyes narrow with focus as he arranges instruments on a metal tray.

"She's more trouble than she looks." Frost jumps back from my kick. "And stronger too."

"You should have been better prepared."

She gestures around the room. "The tools are organized on the tray. The sedative is in the syringe, and I've switched on the solar power."

"But you shouldn't have unchained her until she was sedated. Surely the other assistants would show more foresight. You disappoint me."

Frost presses her lips together, glaring down while she aims the needle at me.

"No!" I beg, writhing on the table. "Don't do this ... please. Get Lila—she knows me."

"Pathetic." Frost purses her lips in disgust. "Hold still."

I answer by kicking her elbow. She cries out, nearly dropping the needle. "You're no better than that savage you broke out of jail," she growls. "Returning you is going to be my pleasure .... There!"

A pinprick stabs my shoulder. Everything spins and blurs. Voices swirl around me. Fingers press against my skin, tilt my head back, push me on my side. A light shines too bright. I try to shut my eyes but can't.

"Her hair is in the way," a voice ... the scientist ... says. "Should I tie it back?"

"Just get rid of it."

"Gladly."

Somewhere inside me, a girl is sobbing. I'm aware of the creak of an opening drawer. The ice woman lifts scissors, fitting her fingers through the handles. Cold metal presses against my skin. Snip, snip, snip. Curls of brown tossed away like trash.

"What can I do for you now?" Frost asks.

"Pass the Number Three for a prelim skull scan. If her bones show a high density, I may need Number Five."

"It's ready, sir."

"Administer the pain medi drip."

Frost snorts. "Why waste medis on a Return?"

"It's your decision." He squeezes his hands into stretchy gloves.

"She won't remember the pain—or anything else," Frost says.

Her half-smile dooms me.

"One moment while I adjust the setting." Scientist Daniel turns a crank on a metal wheel device.

"No rush. She's not going anywhere." Frost leans so close

I can smell her breath, a sour odor, as if she's recently eaten something unripe or rotted.

"Would you like to know what's going to happen?" she asks me.

I'd rather spit in her face than admit my curiosity. I don't want to care or feel, and I long to float so far away that her noise is smaller than an insect's buzz. But her words hold me in a tight grip, ripping away my wings ....

"You're still numb, so the pain won't come quickly. Not until the scalpel cuts deep into the base of your neck ... right here. Oh, what's this?" Chill seeps through me at her touch. "You've already had a memdenity? The improved skin-seal is so natural I didn't see the small incision. What we're going to do is similar to the memdenity procedure—only reverse. Instead of pouring memories into your brain, we'll withdraw memory cells, suctioning your memories like water through a straw. Sadly, there are risks. It's an evolving procedure, so you may lose the knowledge for speaking, eating, and bodily functions."

"That only happened once." Scientist Daniel frowns at Frost, rubbing a cloth over a spiked tool. "It was during the experimental stages and has never happened again. The procedure is 97% perfection."

"Isn't that reassuring? You won't drool or soil your clothing," Frost says, as if this is worthy of a celebraze. "You'll be as you were before this procedure—except you'll remember nothing. Not even your name."

I won't forget. I won't.

"Your life here will be simple without the burden of memories. You'll contribute to ShareHaven in a useful role as a droll. Haven't you wondered who prepares the cease-age patches and medi treatments? Scientists and assistants like myself have far more important duties."

Fight, fight, FIGHT! I struggle to release the screaming in my head. But my mouth can't open. My legs and arms are stone. *Lift, lift, move!* I can't. Nothing happens. Frost looms over me, half of her face smooth with contempt and the other half twisted like a monster. She murmurs something to the scientist as she reaches for a sharpening tool. My focus shimmers to the gleam of silver tools, jumping my thoughts somewhere else ... another time ... a memory.

I'm lying back in a chair with my mouth open—no, not my mouth, but Milly's—and I'm with someone with an oddly name: dentist. A health-worker for teeth. He promises, "This won't hurt." But he lies.

A paper napkin is strung like a white scarf around Milly's neck. She trembles, but pain doesn't scarify me; it's the fear of nothingness.

Without memories, will I exist?

Silver slashes across my eyes. A sharpened cutting tool, poised in the scientist's hand, aimed at my neck, coming closer ....

A door bangs and someone shouts, "Stop!"

THIRTY-ONE

"Daniel, put down that scalpel!"

Lila's voice. High-pitched, forceful, and furious.

White-gloved hands fall away and a flowery fragrance swirls around me. I'm floating somewhere between dreams and memories, and I wonder if Lila is really here or if my mind is playing tricks. I drift on shimmering clouds until the voice jerks me back again.

"Why wasn't I told Jennza was here?" I open my blurring eyes and see purple robes and silvery coiled hair.

"A Returned youth has no identity." Frost's words are wind gusts battering my head. "Who she was doesn't matter."

"It does to me." Lila's words are hard-edged, but her fingers, gently grasping my hand, are soft and gentle.

"I can handle this without your help, dear sister." There is no warmth in this statement. "It's only a routine operation."

"Like hell it is!"

"Why are you so agitated, Lila?" her brother asks calmly.

"You know damn well!" she shouts. "Put down your tools and get away from her. This procedure is cancelled."

Scientist Daniel points the tool's sharp tip at her. "Leader Cross ordered this youth Returned."

"I'm giving you a new order. No one touches her. I'm taking full responsibility for her."

"Lila, it's not wise to oppose the Leaders."

"Would you rather oppose me, brother?" she challenges. "You couldn't stop me from doing what I knew was right when we were kids. Don't try to stop me now."

"It's been a long time since we were kids, and I don't appreciate you bringing our personal lives into the operating room." His face darkens.

"This is personal, and we both know it. You warned me to stay away from the youths, but I didn't. So this is how you get back at me—by harming an innocent youth."

"Innocent?" he barks. "Leader Cross said she broke the killer Noc out of jail."

She gasps. "He escaped?"

"Not only did she help him get away, she also attacked a Family member. She's demented, like the last youth."

"You know nothing about her. Stand aside, Daniel."

The screaming in my mind silences as Lila's arms lift me, holding me close. I inhale a perfume of flowers and safety.

"Are you all right, Jennza?"

I want to nod, but I'm floppy as a willow limb. I fear Scientist Daniel will force me back to the table or Frost will clamp me into chains. But no one stops Lila as she half-drags me to the door. I hold onto my consciousness until the lab door slams.

My legs buckle and dizziness spins me away.

A child's toy scissors cutting paper dolls, clipping around the black-drawn outline of legs, feet, arms, shoulders, and the sunflower-blond head of a smiling paper girl. A princess made of paper. *Paper doll,* the word comes to me. I watch Milly playing with paper figures.

"I'll call you Lissalynn and cut out a prince for you to

marry so you can live happily ever after," five-year-old Milly tells the paper girl. I'm holding a waxy stick—*crayon*—a yellow color for the prince's golden hair. The crayon breaks in my hand, smearing a muddy trail across the paper. A wave of seawater splashes the prince's eyes sea blue. The paper prince swells bigger until he's taller than me, with long legs that spring from paper to life.

Nate. He reaches for me, and I try to run to him. But when I look down at myself there are no legs, arms, or body. He's flesh while I'm less than a paper drawing. I'm no one anymore, and he can't see me.

A door creaks.

Snapping upright, my fingers brush a smooth silk pillow. Not my pillow. The darkness is too dark, without the comforting sliver of light peeking through window shutters. I'm in a room so silent I can only hear the *beat-beat* of my own heart. No soft snores from the bed on the other side of the room. No Rosemarie. Where am I?

My eyes adjust, and I see the faint shape of a lamp. Fumbling on the smooth oval surface, I touch a knob and twist. Light flashes on, illuminating blankets, a downy soft pillow, fawn-brown oval rugs, curtains the color of mustard, and a glass vase blooming with lilacs on a table in a room I've never seen before.

But I know the person sitting in a chair beside my bed.

"How are you feeling, Jennza?" Scientist Lila jumps to her feet, coming over to my bed.

After weeks of "Milly," I love the sound of my name. Something like hope rises in me as I lift my chin, meeting Lila's gaze. I can remember each time we've spoken. I still don't understand her interest in me, but I'm grateful. If not for her, I wouldn't know my own name.

Lila's purple jacket billows around her as she smooths a corner of my blanket, sitting beside me. When she squeezes my hand, her skin is tough yet gentle, weathered by sun and life. I study the fine lines around her lips and silver strands of hair sweeping across her forehead. Her eyes are like the darkest corner in my cave, with depths beyond my knowing.

"I'm so sorry you suffered, Jennza. This never should have happened," she says fiercely. "My brother went too far."

"You ... you saved me."

"I wasn't soon enough," she says sadly. She reaches out to touch my head. "Your hair ... so lovely ... cut."

My arms are heavy as I feel the jagged edges of my hair—or what's left of it. Instead of falling past my shoulders, it stops high over my neck. I won't be able to hide Petal anymore. But if she comes looking for me, I won't be a zombie-brain who doesn't remember her.

"Hair grows back—memories don't," I say gratefully.

"You're safe now. I promise nothing like this will ever happen again."

"They would have turned me into a droll if you hadn't stopped them." I lift my gaze to hers. "Why did you help me?"

"I couldn't let them do that ... not to you."

"Why am I different than other youths?"

"It's because you *are* different that sets you apart."

"But if it had been another youth, like my mate, Lorelei, would you have saved her?"

"It was you," she says, brushing her hand across my cheek.

I shake my head, still not understanding.

Scientist Lila scoots close to me on the bed. "You don't fall into step with the others and have a unique sense of curiosity. At your Celebraze, even when you stood in a line of youths, you stood apart, restless and curious."

"And scarified," I admit. I am tempted to add that I know she spied on me after the Celebraze, but I'm so grateful to her for saving me and don't want to cause trouble between us.

"While I am still furious at my brother for what he almost did to you," she tells me, "I am glad you are here. I see much potential in you."

Potential for what? Her words should comfort me, but they're like being given a gift box I can't open because it's sealed shut. Something wonderful or something terrible might be inside, but I have no way of knowing.

"What will happen now?" I peer into the dark, unfamiliar room.

"You'll rest until you feel better."

"But after that?" My fingers dig into the silky pillow. "Frost said a Returned youth has no identity. Where will I go?"

"Nowhere. You'll stay here."

"How can I? I have to be in a Family."

She glances toward the window, where the curtains are as closed as her expression. "You can't go back ... not to any Family."

"But there's no other life for a youth," I argue.

"If you step outside this compound, the Uniforms will arrest you."

"Arrest me?" Hot fear grips me. "Do the Leaders know I wasn't Returned?"

"Yes, but they have been informed you're my guest."

"What if they come after me?"

"They have no authority here and can't enter the compound. No one can unless we invite them—which is rare."

She twists her lips wryly. "Scientists and leaders have been differing for over a century. We conflict over progress versus conformity and choose to stay separate from ShareHaven. They resent us yet need our miracles for immortality. While you're here, they can't harm you."

"And if I leave?" I ask uneasily.

"They will order your execution. I can't interfere with their laws."

"My Family will be angry that I wasn't Returned," I say with a shudder. "Not about me, but about Milly. I have her childhood memories."

"Already?" Frowning, she leans close to my neck. "They should have waited longer for your first memdenity."

"Rosemarie was eager to have her sister again. We ... I mean, they ... went through a lot together, surviving the mind-plague and coming to this island."

Milly's past and my present blend in my foggy mind. I rub my head to push away the confusion. "Did you know Milly?"

"Not well, but this isn't a large island, and we were much closer before the Attack. I was at her wedding to Arthur—a pleasant man who suited her well."

I cringe at his name, remembering his hands on me. "He is ... I mean ... would have been my husband."

"A good reason for starting a new life." She smiles. "Forget the Cross Family. They deserve to lose you."

"It's not me they lost ... it's Milly."

Milly's memories spin through my head—sunshine, sandy beaches, and white-tipped waves. Pacific Ocean. Gliding storm gulls ... no, they're called seagulls. Long, mournful horns from boats and buildings spiraling into the sky. A neighborhood of colorful houses pressing against each other. Naomi, my best friend, lived across the street, and we had tea parties with our stuffed toys. Summer smells of cut grass, splashing in a plastic pool, my dog Sadie licking my face, bike rides, school, backpacks, birthday parties, and horse rides on Sunny.

"Are you okay?" Lila asks.

I suck in air, then exhale away the images. "Milly's memories are so vivid I have to remind myself I've never lived outside ShareHaven. I know what it's like to travel in the sky on a plane and to be part of a retro-family—with biological parents and siblings." I sigh. "My little brother ... I mean, Milly's ... died in the mind-plague. Remembering his smile and how he loved dinosaur toys makes me hurt inside. He never made it to age six."

"If it's too sad to remember, I can fix that."

I sit up straight. "What do you mean?"

"If you choose, Milly's memories can be removed."

"I can't go to the health-workers. You said I'd be arrested if I left here."

"That's true. But there's no need to go anywhere." Her dark eyes dance with humor. "Scientists created memdenity. We taught the health-keepers how to administer the process. I can easily remove every thought of Milly's."

"Can Milly's childhood memories be saved for another youth?" I think of Arthur, sobbing over his lost wife, and I wince with guilt.

"Memories can only be transferred once."

"So Arthur was right." I sigh. "Milly's childhood will die outside of me?"

"You must decide what's best for you. I can free you of

267

Milly's memories."

It seems so final—like a double murder.

"It's your choice. What do you want?" she persists.

"To keep them … keep Milly. She's alive to me, even though she died long before I was born. I don't want her memories to be lost because of me."

Lila pats my arm gently. "Worthwhile endeavors require sacrifice. Don't blame yourself."

"I am to blame, although I don't regret helping …." I glance down before I say too much.

"The Nocturne," she finishes for me. "I wondered why you risked so much to help a subhuman."

"He's as human as I am," I argue. "I couldn't let him die."

"In retro-century an accused person would have a fair trial and lawyer, but that practice has been abandoned by ShareHaven's justice system." She taps her finger to her chin as if thinking deeply. "Did the Nocturne convince you he was innocent?"

"No." I shake my head. "He's guilty."

"Yet you helped him anyway. You must care much for him."

Heat rushes to my face. "I barely know him."

"No need to defend your actions to me. Long before I came to this island, there was someone I loved so much that I left my home, job, and family to become his wife and live on this island. I never regretted one moment of our time together. The only thing I regret is not having children. We tried … but it didn't work out. He wanted a little girl with my dark hair and eyes, and I'd tease back that I'd rather have a boy with his blue eyes." She touches my cheek softly. "You remind me of him. You have the same curious, determined spirit."

She means this as a compliment, but I turn away, reminded of my shame. I don't regret helping Nate, but I'm sorry I hurt Rosemarie. I never even told her good-bye. And because of me, she's lost her sister. Forever.

I glance at the closed window, wishing there was a way to repair my mistakes. Not being connected to a Family is like tumbling through the blackness of space, aimless without gravity. As a youth, my role was to learn from the Instructors; as a Family member, my role was to resume a Lost One's role; and even being Returned would have given me a role as a mindless worker droll.

Who am I now? I spent my childhood training to replace someone else, learning pledges of safety, respect, and honor. But while my born-mates planned for a future with a Family, I ran with the wind and climbed trees to the sky. Always looking, searching, and yearning for a future of my own.

Now my thoughts take wing, flying to new possibilities. For the first time in my life, I can be anybody. Even myself.

THIRTY-TWO

Lila promises to come back after her morning work hours and tucks my blankets up to my chin, softly touching my cheek. "Sleep, dear Jennza," she whispers. Surely my mind will never relax enough to sleep. But when I awaken, the curtains have been parted, prisms of golden light shine across the wooden floor, and I smell fresh-baked bread and fried eggs.

"Goodly morn," a cheerful voice greets.

A petite girl with short brown hair sets a tray on my bedside table. She's several years younger than fifteen (how can that be possible?). With the fidgety movements of a squirrel, she stirs a sugar cube into root coffee and arranges a fork and spoon precisely on each side of an oval dish of honey-frosted bisks, strips of flacon, and eggs. There's also a steaming bowl of cinnamon-swirled hot oats.

"They told me not to talk to you, but wouldn't that just be terribly rude?" she says in a high-energy voice. "I heard you almost got brain-sucked. Did it hurt? Oh, probably not since Lila stopped them and brought you here. I saw her brother just now in the passage, and he's steamed stinkin' mad. Usually Scientist Daniel is all snitty superior to everyone, even the other scis, but Lila can right snap him in his place. I'm Visla Summers."

I've never heard of a Summers Family. Is she a sister-niece-cousin-daughter-mother of a scientist? Do scientists even have Families?

270

"Thank you for this." I gesture to the tray, my mouth watering at the delish smells. "I'm Mil—Jennza."

"Oh, I know who you are—or at least who you were. I wasn't sure what name to use due to the awkward Return situation. Maybe a combo of both names such as Millza or Jennzy. But I'll call you whatever you prefer. Did you really break that savage murderer Noc out of jail?"

The question slams a fist to my stomach. "He's not a savage."

"But he's a Noc, isn't he? All of them are as savage as claw beasts. I can't believe you're friendly with one. Does he have fangs and a furry tail? Can he speak our language?"

I shake my head, then firmly change the subject. "Where's Lila?"

"She's conferencing, and you can guess the topic." Visla doesn't wait for my guess. "You. But rest assured—you're safe with Lila protecting you. She won't let her brother suck out your brains."

This is reassuring ... I think. "Is Lila in trouble for helping me?"

"She's always at the nucleus of trouble but can smooth-talk her way out of any conflict." Visla giggles. She's a puzzle—her eyes big but her mouth and nose small, as if she's not finished growing. She's short too. If I were standing, not lying in a bed, her head would only reach my chin.

I sit up higher, readjusting the pillow behind my back, then giving in to my growling stomach and tasting a honey bisk. It's even better than it smells, honey melting sweetly on warmed bread. I'm aware of Visla watching me, eager to slam me with more questions, so I ask her one instead. "Why is Lila being so nice to me? Do you know?"

"No one does. You're a mystery among us sistas."

"Sistas?"

"Assistants. Each scientist has one or more sistas. You can't think this place runs itself, do you? The scis are clever but lacking everyday smarts for menial chores. Without us, they'd starve and stink in unwashed clothes."

"I thought drolls did all the chores."

"Drolls only follow orders. Sistas tell them what to do. Drolls are more like machines than human. Nothing up here." She taps on her head.

"They almost did that do me."

"Sucking out brains is so repulse! Once Sci Daniel made me hold a vial of brains and I nearly spewed my guts out. You're lucky Lila saved you. She's the nicest sci. Daniel is puffed up with arrogance, Martyn rarely speaks or leaves the lab, and Kataya prefers animals and plants to people."

I nod, curious about the scientists. I've never thought of them as ordinary people, believing they were almost magical, brilliant and as dazzling as stars in the sky. Lila still seems magical to me, but I realize now that scientists aren't lofty gods; they're human too.

"I could tell you plenty about what goes on here," Visla says, her little voice huge with pride. "I've been working with the scis for eighty-three years as a sista."

"After so long, why are you still an assistant—a sista? Why not become a scientist?" I ask.

"Oh, that could never happen."

"Why not?"

"The scis don't share secrets—not even with each other."

"How does anyone become a scientist?"

"It's never happened. Although in theory it could." She

tilts her head as if considering this concept. "It's highly unlikely, but possible with memdenity."

I rub the tiny scar on my neck. My neck is exposed, no longer covered with thick hair. I miss the warm feeling of hair tumbling down my back. Hair grows back and the scar will fade (or be removed), so I'll appear no different than anyone else on the outside. But memories have changed me in ways that no one can see.

Visla gestures impatiently at my tray. "How can you eat so sluggy? Ramp it up!"

"I've had enough—and it was delicious. Thank you." I lick honey from my lips, then push away the tray. Looking down at myself, I pluck at the sheer fabric gown I've never seen before and don't remember putting on. "Do you know where my coverings are?"

"If you mean the filthy tunic you had on last night, don't even ask." Her childlike face scrunches with distaste. "You won't see it again."

"What will I wear? I don't have any other coverings."

"You do now." She goes over to a drawer and opens it in a swift yank. "Pantons, tunics, privacies, boots—everything you'll need."

"Graces good!" I come beside her. "All of that for me?"

"And much more. You'll find out." She smiles mysteriously, then glances down at a timepiece on her wrist. "Sci Lila has precise instructions for today."

"What?"

"I'm to give you a tour. Starting now, if you're ready."

Ready and eager! I grab coverings and hurry to the privacy room, changing into slate-gray pantons, a blouse the shade of ripe grapes, and a warm black jacket which falls to my knees. The coverings smell of lavender and newness, as if they were stitched especially for me.

Visla explains that we're on the second level, with rooms for Lila, Kataya, and their assistants. I follow her down a short hall to a door with no handle, only engraved numbers. She taps a "1" and the door slides open to reveal what I think is another room, until I step inside and the whole room moves sideways, then down. *Like the elevator in the Haunted House ride,* I think, remembering a vacation at Disneyland with my parents and little brother. Sunny skies, excited crowds, and ride after ride of joyous whirling, plunging, and splashing. I smell hot buttered popcorn and hear my delighted screams as I careen down a roller coaster. Such a happy memory ... I wish I'd really been there.

Visla cranks a lever that slowly lowers us to the first floor. She tells me the compound has three levels; the first floor is where the drolls work and sleep. She opens a door to a room with three rows of crude beds.

"The drolls sleep here. They're permitted six hours each night. They can fall asleep on command."

"Why don't they have blankets or pillows?"

Visla shrugs. "They never asked."

How can they when their memories have been stolen? I think with a surge of anger. I wonder who they were once and where they came from. They can't all be Returned youths, because many are aged more than twenty-five. Unless—and this thought chills me—they *were* youths when they came here but aren't given cease-aging patches, slowly aging till they die.

"The kitchen is also on this floor," Visla says with a "follow me" gesture. Her smile is so sweet, my anger shifts back to curiosity. I hurry after her.

The huge kitchen lacks the warmth of Rosemarie's kitchen; the walls are gray, without windows to invite sunshine. Was it only yesterday I worked alongside Rosemarie in her sunshiny bread-smelling kitchen? *Rosemarie.* Is anyone helping her peel potatoes and pick vegs from the garden? She must be so sad—losing Milly again. I wonder … will she miss me too?

Visla gestures for me to follow her down a low-ceilinged passage with shining white walls. "Instead of ceiling lights, our walls are coated in a solar glowing paint," Visla explains.

"Clever."

"Sci Martyn created this paint. Come on, we'll start with the kitchen and laundry. Wait till you see how the dishes wash themselves!"

I walk briskly to keep up with her, wishing I could tell Lorelei and Marcus I'm touring the scientists' compound. They'd be stun-smacked. We often spoke of scientists, imagining they lived in a castle floating above clouds and rode unicorns every night. Once we thought we saw their "castle." The three of us snuck outside at night to our tree platform. I was telling a scary-tale about a wolf-shaped constellation that chased the moon until it grew weary and leapt to the earth in the form of a fiery dog-beast. Marcus shot me that skeptical look, where his brows knit together and his mouth puckers. "Stars are giant, luminous spheres of plasma," he said. "It's unsensical for stars to transform into dog-beasts." Lorelei interrupted by pointing into the sky. "If dog-beasts don't exist, what are those lights?"

We stared, open-mouthed, at light flashing from the highest point on the island.

"The scientists," I cried. "It has to be the scientists!"

When the lights vanished, Marcus declared, "I'm going there someday."

Lorelei scoffed. "Don't be demental. No one ever goes there."

"I will," he insisted. "I'll find the secret way inside their compound."

"If anyone uncovers scientist secrets," I said, trying to sound mysterious, "it will be me."

We all laughed, no one taking me seriously, including myself.

Now I'm living with the scientists—although I'd rather be with my best mates in our favorite tree.

There's a tug on my arm, and I blink to find Visla scowling at me. "Did you hear anything I just said?" she demands.

"Sure," I lie. "I'm just more interested in seeing where the scientists work."

"The lab isn't on this level," she says.

She leads me into a room with large metal containers similar to the chillers Rosemarie uses for storing perishable food, like goat milk, butter, and meat slabs. It's so cold my breath comes out in puffs, and I wrap my arms around myself.

"We always keep a year's supply of food," Visla explains.

She points to the chillers, but I'm more curious about the dull-eyed man of advanced age lifting boxes to a shelf. He isn't wearing a jacket or gloves and his skin is mottled purple-blue. He's obviously cold but doesn't know it. I want to grab him and shout, "Don't let them do this to you!" But what good would it do? No one is at home in his mind.

Visla chatters on about daily food preparation, seeming

unaware of the droll, as if he's no more alive than one of the boxes he carries.

With a pitying look at the man, I follow Visla. As we turn left down another passage, she says, "I'll show you the laundry."

"I can already feel the heat."

"Isn't it brutal?" She tucks a honey-brown curl behind her ear. "Laundry frizzles my hair."

"My hair used to frizzle too." I reach for my curls but only find jagged edges. "Not anymore."

Visla opens a door, releasing a cloud of gray mist. A tumbler machine cleans coverings—Milly would call it a washing machine—and overhead, soggy coverings sway on twine strung across the ceiling, swirling fans blowing hot wind to dry them. Two drolls lift sopping clothes from baskets—women with hair even shorter then mine, their blank faces dripping sweat.

"It's so hot and uncomfortable in here," Visla yells in my ear.

"Uncomfortable," I agree, but I'm looking at the drolls. "Can we go to the lab now?"

Visla nods.

Once we're in the elevator, far from noisy tumblers, silence curls around us. I can't stand the curiosity any longer. "Can I ask a personal question?"

"Took you long enough." Visla smirks. "You want to know my age."

"You're younger than me. But youths haven't been born in fifteen years."

"Physically, my body is eleven," she says proudly.

"How is that possible?" I ask.

"I was born in ShareHaven six years before the Attack."

"But ... but ...." I stare at her, puzzled. "Why did you cease aging before twenty-five?"

"I was the first to try out the patch—well, the first to survive." She shrugs. "Early stages of new procedures are always unpredictable."

"The scientists experimented on you?" The elevator rises smoothly, yet I'm jolted inside.

"How do you think they perfected the cease-aging patch?" She puffs out her scrawny chest with pride. "Only the most trusted sistas participate in experimental research. There was a celebraze when it was proven I'd stopped aging."

"But you stopped too soon!"

"It was a risk the scis were willing to take. They were able to determine the prime age to cease growth because of me. This was a key breakthrough in the development of the cease-aging patch."

I shake my head. "How could you allow them to do that to you?"

"I'd do anything for Sci Lila." We've reached the third floor, and the elevator stops, but we stand still looking at each other. "You'd understand if you'd been here when ShareHaven was attacked. An explosion killed my parents—Dad was a custodian and Mom a chemist. When ShareHaven shifted to a ruling of Families, I had no Family. The Leaders wanted me to leave like they forced others to do, but Sci Lila made me her assistant. I owe her my life."

I think of Frost's cold hands on my neck and the cutting tool in Scientist Daniel's hand. I owe Lila my life too.

"Still, you were so young—couldn't you have joined a Family?"

"None wanted me. I was injured and too weak for hard work, another burden to a ripping chaotic community. Even though Lila was dealing with so much, she healed me." Visla holds out her arm and wiggles her fingers. "Can you tell this arm and hand are mechy? I lost my real arm in the explosion that killed my parents. But Lila and Martyn—he's brilliant with circuitry—fixed me so good no one can tell it's mech-flesh. The only dif is my digi-clock." She touches the gold band encircling her wrist. Not jewelry as I first thought, but a timepiece embedded into her skin. At a tap of her finger, the time flashes: 9:36A.

"We're late," she says, frowning. "Sci Lila will be waiting for us."

Visla presses a wall button and the elevator doors slide apart. We enter such brightness, as if we're stepping outside. I glance down a narrow hall and count three closed doors. Visla says two of them are Daniel's and Martyn's rooms, and the other is the lab. Like trapped sunshine, neon-white walls illuminate the place with painted symbols swirling across the ceiling in a mysterious language.

We stop at a large metal door.

As Visla turns the brass handle, the floor rumbles. I turn around to the opening elevator. A golden-haired woman in a white lab coat runs out, screaming. Her arm dangles oddly at her side. Her eyes are wild with panic. As she rushes by, I gasp at the deep jagged slashes on her mangled arm.

Still screaming, she races into the lab.

Spilling a trail of blood.

THIRTY-THREE

I'm too stunned to move, wanting to help but having no idea what to do.

"Tamsin!" Visla's voice shrills with panic. She lunges for the lab door. She twists the knob, but it doesn't open. "Let me in! Please!"

"What happened to her?" I point to the blood drops on the floor.

"I don't know, but I'll find out. Poor Tamsin. She'll need me." Visla pounds on the door and calls again to be let inside.

"Who's Tamsin?"

"A sista for Lila ... like me." Visla's voice shakes. "I can't believe this happened .... She knows the risks and is always so careful."

Visla turns away from me, pounding on the door with her mechy hand, calling out for Lila and Tamsin over and over. "Why won't they let me inside?" Visla sags to the ground, her back against the locked door. I kneel to slip my arm around her trembling shoulders. "I have to see Tamsin ... make sure she's okay."

"Lila will heal her," I say gently. "Have you known Tamsin long?"

"We were raised together, playing all over the island before there were Family compounds or beasts in the woods. Tamsin lost her parents in the Attack like I did, and she helped me recover from this." She lifts her mechy hand.

"Tamsin's arm looked ... so bloody .... What do you think happened?"

"I don't know. She's cautious when she works in the restricted—" Visla stops.

"Restricted what?"

"Nothing." She stares at the door, her lower lips pressed tight. "I could help if they'd let me inside .... She needs me."

"Have there been other ..." I search for the right word. "... accidents?"

"No," she says quickly. Too quickly. "I can't talk about this. Please go back to your room. The tour is over."

I start to argue, but there's a metallic click. The lab door opens. Lila's purple robe falls apart like curtains as she looks at us. "I thought you might still be here."

"You must let me in!" Visla jumps to her feet, peering beyond Lila into the dimly lit room. "How's Tamsin?"

"She's healing well."

"Are you sure? Her arm looked ...." Visla flexes her own mechy hand, frowning. "Will it be usable?"

"There's no lasting damage. The injury appeared worse than actuality."

"How did it happen?" I ask.

Lila and Visla exchange a meaningful glance before Lila answers, "Tamsin was clumsy while cleaning tools. Fortunately, the cut didn't go too deep."

Not deep? Are we talking about the same injury? A tool doesn't chew flesh like a savage beast. Something alive attacked Tamsin—with sharp teeth and claws. But how could a beast get inside the scientists' compound?

"Tamsin is fine," Lila assures, with a calmness that

makes me want to scream for her to tell me the truth. "I sealed the wound with curing cream, and she's resting in cubicle eight."

"Can I sit with her?" Visla asks anxiously.

"Of course, but first bring a droll to clean this mess." Lila gestures to the floor, distaste flickering across her face. "You're free of duties for the day and may stay with Tamsin. She'll be cheered by your presence when she awakens."

"Thank you so very, very much." Visla exhales deeply, then hurries to the elevator.

I move to follow, but Lila stops me with a firm hand on my arm. "Jennza, you haven't finished your tour."

"But Visla said—"

"Visla is no longer your guide." Silvery purple sleeves brush against my arm as she clasps my hand. "I am."

I hardly know what to say when she invites me into the lab—a door that only moments ago was locked. "Would you care to see where I work?"

"More than anything!" My glance flickers to blood drops. "But don't you have more important things to do?"

"No more important than you. If you're concerned about Tamsin, be assured she's healing and resting comfortably in a rear room."

"Won't I be intruding on the other scientists?" I think of Scientist Daniel aiming a sharp cutting tool at me while I lie helpless on a table. And his assistant Frost, with her icy cruelness. I never want to see them again.

"You may go anywhere I say." Scientist Lila lifts her shoulders defiantly. "Only Martyn is working here now, and he rarely looks up from his microscope. He's busy with research and documentation—nothing exciting."

A lab—with experiments and secrets—is exciting to me. While my born-mates invented stories about their future Families, I dreamed of exploring beyond boundaries and discovering universal secrets. The broken Fence wires were my first discovery, then the cave and the best discovery of all—Petal. And look where I am now: the most mysterious place on the island, where Instructors, Leaders, and Uniforms aren't even allowed.

"Come inside," Lila says with a swish of her elegant purple robes as she holds the lab door open for me.

I follow Lila into the lab.

Compared to the luminous hall walls, the lab seems dark, with stenches of chems. Lila was right—the lab is dullness. There's no décor on the walls—only metal shelves. The ceiling slopes toward skylights, which do little to brighten the room. I count four work areas divided by partitions—one for each scientist—consisting of a desk, chair, and document cabinet.

"Nothing elaborate, but it's a good working space." She makes a sweeping gesture around the room. "Kataya is the chaos queen," she adds, pointing to a desk cluttered with stacked jars, over-full files, boxes, and a tray piled with tiny yellowed (animal? human?) bones.

"Over there is Daniel's desk," she continues with a nod to the plainest desk in the room; there's not a pencil, paper, or dust mote on the flat wood surface.

"And there's Martyn, the most brilliant man I know, yet he forgets to sleep and eat." A scientist with gray hair on his egg-shaped head is hunched over a thick retro-book, flipping through pages, his glasses slipping down his thin nose. He's aged like Grandmother Cross. He mutters to himself, showing no more attention to us than Frost gave the drolls.

"Lastly—an oasis for my cluttered mind—my desk," Lila finishes, crossing over to a U-shaped desk in the center of the room. It's organized precisely, paper, pens, folders in perfect alignment. There's a framed picture of Lila beside a goodly looking man with fawn-brown hair, blue eyes, and a close-shaven beard. They're staring into each other's faces as if no one else exists in this moment. Something about their expressions—longing, joy, and sadness combined—makes me think of the way Nate looked at me before he left through the tunnel.

"This is the Sharing Bloom." Lila's voice pulls me from the picture. I follow her gaze to a flowering vine enclosed in a glass dome with tiny air holes. The plant has dark-purple stems, four-pointed green leaves, and shoots of yellow blossoms that shimmer as if on fire.

I sniff the blossoms, surprised to smell nothing. "Do you know why it's odor-lacking?" I ask.

"Nature is a trickster, using beauty to lure in prey and odors for defense. There's a scent, but it's only obvious when boiled in salt water. I doubt you've ever seen one before today."

"But I have." In my cave they dangle from the ceiling, growing down instead of up. I'm sure it's the same flower I call rainbells.

Her brows arch. "Where?"

I hesitate, not ready to share this secret. "I don't remember."

"You've probably confused it with the lillsy, which is similar and grows near the Edu-Center," she says, reaching out to lift the glass dome. "Daniel's wife—she died many years ago—discovered the Sharing Bloom quite by accident, which is often the way for scientific breakthroughs."

"It's lovely—like bubbles waving in the air."

"It's much tougher than it appears and never withers like common flowers—not in rain, heat, wind, or icy winter. In fact, adversity makes it stronger. The flower does have a weakness, though, which makes cultivating it very difficult."

"What?" I reach out to touch the bloom.

She slaps my hand away and lets the glass dome fall back into place. "Human touch," she answers. "Our skin oils are like acid to the Sharing Bloom, so we must handle them with gloves. Ironically, while human touch damages them, their oils heal us. Without the Sharing Bloom, we wouldn't have the cease-aging patch, healing creams, or memdenity."

"They come from a—a flower?"

"Not an ordinary flower—it grows in a location only known to scientists. This isn't common knowledge, so do not repeat it."

If it's so secret, why is she telling me?

Slipping back in her tour tone, Lila points across the room to a closed door and says that's where Tamsin is recuperating. I'm curious about Tamsin, but Lila leads me away.

Before exiting the room, I get an odd feeling. I glance over my shoulder to find Martyn scowling at me. He quickly looks away, but I sense resentment. I turn to ask Lila about him, but she's already moved ahead. I hurry after her.

This narrow hallway has three closed doors to the right and one to the left. Contrasting odors swirl in the air— sweet sea-mist grasses and harsh, acrid chemicals. A flash of memory comes to me, of running through the street, clinging to the Daddy's hand, while behind us buildings burn. "Your mask!" the Daddy man shouts, so angry that I start to cry. He looks back, then sweeps me up in his arms and helps me slip the breathing mask over my head.

"Jennza?" Lila's voice snaps me back.

"I—I'm coming," I choke out, my throat aching as if on fire, although the cool hall is temperature controlled.

"Our file room." Lila gestures to floor-to-ceiling rows of metal cabinets.

A hunched-over, aged droll sits in a chair, his hands folded on his knees and his gaze straight ahead. There's no sound in here, not even the breathing of the droll, although I'm sure he's alive. The second room we enter is a startling contrast, echoing with electric humming and beeping. I stare curiously at machines, boxy steel containers, and shelves with odd-shaped jars of tools and wires.

"Only scientists and assistants have access here," Lila tells me, which makes me wonder—and secretly hope— she'll ask me to be an assistant.

As I draw near the largest steel container, a chill reaches out like icy fingers. Flesh-bumps slither up my skin, and I rub my arms for warmth. Lila isn't fazed by the brutal chill, dipping her hand into her robe pocket to withdraw gloves. She taps a keypad on top of the container, entering numbers so fast I can only remember that they begin with 372. A puckering sound echoes like an icy kiss. Misty air puffs icy clouds as the lid rises, revealing hundreds—thousands—of frozen tubes.

"What are those?"

"Life," Lila says proudly.

"Medicine?" I scrunch my forehead.

"Medis sustain life; these tubes are the genesis of creation."

286

"They look like popsicles," I say, with an image of sweet iced desserts dripping on a very hot day.

She chuckles. "I haven't thought of popsicles in eons."

"I didn't think of them—Milly did."

"Focus on your own memories," she scolds. "Did the Instructors teach you how youths are created?"

I nod, remembering a hot, sweaty day where Instructor Ivan caught me window-gazing and shut all the windows, adding to the stuffy misery of learning. My born-mates blamed me, shooting angry looks my way, even Lorelei. But I forgot about heat-misery when Instructor Ivan gave a lecture on creation. He said youths began as tiny liquid drops. I laughed because this seemed so unsensical. But as he compared the process to growing seeds in a hot-house, I listened with rapt interest—not glancing out the window even once.

"Youths are created by the health-keepers," I say, hoping to impress Lila.

"No." She shakes her head. "The health-keepers finish the process that the scientists begin. These vials contain genetic matter, mostly donated by scientists working here before the Attack. We came from all over the world, ensuring a diversity of genetics so youths aren't biologically related."

"Where did you come from?" I ask.

"I was born in India, then educated in America," she answers, her musical accent more obvious. "I met my husband, who was British, in college—which didn't please my very traditional family. Thankfully, such matters are no longer important, and our goal in youth creation is for good health and high intelligence." She gestures to the glassy frozen rows. "Scientists safe-hold all genetic matter and supply health-keepers with male and female DNA every twenty-five years."

"I was … a DNA popsicle?"

She laughs. "You began life in this lab, as did those of all the youths."

I did, but not Milly. In my mind, I see our mother's stomach unusually large. Pregnant with my little brother. When Mom's stomach is smaller, she holds a blanketed baby. And the look on her face—so content and joyous—is the most beauteous smile ever.

"I would have liked to have my own baby," Lila admits, frowning.

"The retro way?" I ask, then redden at my rudeness. "Sorry, I shouldn't have asked something so personal."

"I don't mind. When I came here with my husband—also a scientist—we aspired to save humanity and create a perfect world for our future children. But when ShareHaven was nearly destroyed, our dreams died. How could we save the world when we couldn't save ourselves?"

"You survived."

"I was one of the few." She sighs and I wonder if she's thinking about the husband she lost. "The discovery of perpetual youth restored hope—until we learned the cease-age patch caused infertility. Women rushed to have babies before we realized the need to control our population. After that, girls were sterilized at age sixteen, and youths were created in our lab—until Leaders shifted this task to the health-keepers."

"Why did they do that?" I ask, puzzled at the bitter twist to her lips.

"They can't control us, so they try to control our influence on ShareHaven. We could have objected, but it's a simple procedure even a droll could perform. We're still caretakers of genetic matter, and I take that responsibility seriously." She points to a panel with several buttons. "If the yellow light flashes, we're alerted to a malfunction in the cooling module."

"What does the red light mean?"

"If it flashes—which has never happened—we have sixty seconds to restore power or the frozen vials will thaw and be destroyed. While the green light flashes, youths will continue to be born every twenty-five years."

Born from glass tubes. No fathers or mothers—only liquid.

I'm not sure why this saddens me. I've always known I was created in a lab. But Milly has changed me. Her memories of laughter, hugs, and parents makes lab-creation seem unnatural.

Lila taps an indented panel on the cold box. "Inside are two thumb-sized solar batteries. Sun-based energy keeps the vials frozen—sun and ice working together toward the goal of life. I love ironical twists of science."

I nod, fascinated. I imagine Lorelei yawning with boredom, and while Marcus would be interested, he'd rather be digging in the dirt for crawlies. But I'm the far opposite of bored. Science reminds me of mixing recipes in Rosemarie's kitchen; even when you know the outcome, there are always surprises.

"This ends our tour." Lila taps a wall switch and the room goes dark except for the pulsing green light on the frozen box.

"Now what should I do?" I'm not only asking about today but also the larger questions about my future. Can I stay here without a work-role? I've only seen scientists, assistants, and drolls. Luckily, I escaped being a droll. And while it would be coolsome to become a scientist like Lila, that's impossible. As Visla said, you're either born a scientist, or you're not.

But an assistant—I could do that. I'd work hard for Lila and be the best "sista" ever. I hope, I hope, I hope ....

Lila studies my face. "I suppose you're wondering at my interest in you."

Uncertainty lumps in my throat. I can only manage a nod.

"Don't look so fearful." She smiles. "I'm on your side. Remember when I promised to take you for a walk along the cliff trail?"

"Yes—but I never expected it to happen."

"I don't make idle promises. The night of your Celebraze, I asked if you wanted to join the Cross Family. If you'd said no, I would have taken you from the Crosses and brought you here. No Leader would have stopped me."

I'd suspected this but never really believed she'd want me. If only I'd told her the truth that day. I wouldn't have shamed the Cross Family and become an outcast. But I wouldn't have saved Nate either. I can never regret that.

"I never fit into the Cross Family—except with Rosemarie," I tell her.

"I suspected as much. But I couldn't interfere once you joined a Family. Everything changed when you came here." Her face shines. "I can't repair what's happened, but I can give you a new start—beginning with three surprises."

An assistant. Please! I think, crossing my fingers.

She regards me with a searching look. "You need to

290

consider your future. You can't go back to the Cross Family or anywhere else in ShareHaven. If you step outside our boundaries, the Uniforms will arrest you."

My memory slams with the sound of hammers building an execution platform. "I'll watch my step," I tell her.

"You're only safe within our boundaries."

"Does that mean I can work for you as an assistant?" I ask hopefully.

Scientist Lila shakes her head. "No."

"Oh ... but I thought ...." Disappointment rips through me.

"I have no need for another assistant."

"There's nothing else for me." I reel back, sickened. "Not a droll!"

"Never a droll." She tenderly strokes the uneven edges of my shorn hair. "I want you here, working with me."

"But not as an assistant?"

"No. I'm offering you the memdenity of my sister-in-law, Angeleen Dupree." She holds my gaze. "A scientist."

THIRTY-FOUR

Me? A scientist wearing purple and silver robes? I'll make amazing discoveries like bread that never molds, unstainable fabric, or a weapon to destroy all claws and snakes so the Fence can come down. Instead of being enemies of ShareHaven, Nocturnes will be our neighbors. Also as a scientist, I will cure all ills and bring peace to the world.

I want to shout, "Yes!" but Lila cautions me to think it over before giving my answer. What's to think over? Compared to my other options—a droll or execution—becoming a scientist is a yes-plus.

"This would be a good time for that walk I promised you," Lila tells me.

She leads me out of the lab and back to the hall, where the floor shows no sign of Tamsin's blood, as if her injury never happened. The elevator swooshes open, and Lila presses *one* on the keyboard. We enter a hall I've never been in before and pause at a locked door. Lila quick-fingers a code, which I memorize, and we step into brilliant daylight. I glance back at the door we came through, and it's camouflaged so well it seems to disappear into the sloping, grassy hillside.

"This way," Lila says, her purple robe flying around her in the sea breeze.

We step into dazzling sunshine and a sweeping view of a cloudless blue sky. I walk with Lila up a trail rising into rugged rocky cliffs. I suck in salty mist and delight in the panorama of sparkling sea.

The dirt trail follows the cliff's edge and is surrounded by wildflowers that wave like flags and windblown grasses. Someone must tend to this trail often, clearing away debris. No bristly weeds like on the cliffs near the Edu-Center. With high cliffs like a fortress, there's no need for the Fence. Far below, the sea foams against the rocky shore. My heart swells with the rushing waves, hope in and dread out, a future stretching on like the diamond-sparkling sea. We walk in silence, although there's nothing silent about my thoughts.

A scientist! It's more than I ever hoped! But if a clever assistant like Visla—trained alongside scientists—can't become a scientist, how can I?

Yet Lila says it's possible. I'll be Angeleen Dupree, smarter, important, respected. More than anything I ever imagined—more than Jennza.

I have so many questions: Memdenity wasn't created until *after* the Attack, so how were Angeleen Dupree's memories stored? Did she die in an accident? How long ago did it happen?

My thoughts spin as I walk beside Lila on the cliff path. I'm uneasy about getting another memdenity so soon. How much can my brain hold? And is it fair to cover Milly's memories with someone new?

Yet I want this more than I've ever wanted anything. My yearning for adventure, feeling out-of-place, always longing for more from life makes sense now. I'm not good at following rules because I'm not meant to be a follower. I'd rather lead so others can follow *me*.

Lila stands at a cliff jutting over the sea, her toes slightly over the edge. I come up beside her. "What do you see?" She points at the blue-green horizon.

"The sea," I say.

"I see infinite possibilities," she says. "Each water drop is an element united into a cohesive mass stretching around the world. Ideas sail like boats, carrying us to new places."

"Boats?" I repeat with a queasy feeling, remembering the miserable boat rides when I came to this island. But that wasn't me. "I've never ridden in a boat, although Milly did. She lived near San Francisco."

"A lovely place—at least it used to be." Lila sighs. "When I visited San Francisco, I took a boat ride out to Alcatraz Island—where prisoners were once locked away from civilization. It seems ironic now; we're here safe in our island utopia, while the outside world is trapped in destruction."

"Do you ever wonder what's outside our island?" I ask.

"Devastation and disease." Her lips press together. "We're safe here—that's all that matters."

I'm glad for her kindness but aching too, for the people I may never see again. Marcus, Lorelei, Instructor Penny, and Rosemarie. The ache grows into a lump I can't swallow. And I feel guilty too, for how badly I hurt Arthur. All he wanted was his wife back, but because of me, that won't ever happen.

I turn to Lila, picking at my thumbnail like Marcus does when he's troubled. "Lila, can I ask you a question about something that might be … um … a forbidden topic?"

"Of course. But I can't promise to answer," she says.

"Does someone's soul come back with memdenity?"

Her eyes flash, surprised. "As a scientist, I should answer no. Theoretically, soul does not exist. But recently I had a dream where Angeleen, who died centuries ago, talked to me. It was too real to be a dream. And when she hugged me good-bye, I felt warm arms around me. How can that be possible when her memories are saved in a tube?"

"Were you close with Angeleen?"

"Very close." Lila nods. "She was my friend before she was my sister-in-law. Since the dream, I've had a sense that she's with me—not in body but in spirit. If you bring back her memories, I think her soul might stay elsewhere. It's been very confusing to me. I shouldn't admit this to you, but it feels good to talk."

"You can tell me anything," I assure, which makes her smile.

"It was easier when I believed science was the answer to everything. But lately I've had opposing thoughts about science versus religion. Where does spirit go when people die? Into a tube or some place beyond this?" She waves her hand from cliff's edge to sea to sky.

"You're smart—can't you figure out the answer?" I ask her.

She laughs wryly. "If only it were that easy. Answering the complexity of existence would be like explaining how to bake an apple pie to an ant. To us, baking apples into a pie crust is a simple process, but an ant only sees its path in the dirt. Yet if a scrap of apple fell in the ant's path, it would recognize the apple as food. No understanding of making the pie, only knowing the bite of apple can give sustenance. Am I making any sense?"

"Um ... not really. But I love apple pie."

"Simply put, as humans facing a giant apple pie of a universe with unanswered questions, we can only be grateful for the scraps of sustenance—knowledge, food, and love—

that come our way."

"I am grateful," I say solemnly. "To you."

Lila touches my chin softly, turning my gaze to hers. "Are you ready to give me your answer? I will only ask you this once, and no matter what you say, I will keep you safe and you can stay here." She sucks in a heavy breath, then asks, "Do you want to be a scientist?"

My gaze is like a breeze blowing in every direction, from Lila's solemn face to the sea, then back to the hill that conceals the scientists' compound.

All of this can be mine.

"Yes," I say, agreeing to the sea, Lila, and myself.

Lila opens her purple-sleeved arms wide and draws me close into her sweet perfume. "Welcome, Angeleen."

THIRTY-FIVE

"Since that's decided," Lila says, "are you ready to learn your second surprise?"

"I don't need anything else," I protest. "You've already done so much."

"Because I chose to. This is an appropriate place to share this with you—both of us poised at the edge of possibilities."

Or the edge of disaster, I think with an unexpected foreboding. My gaze drops to the distant rocky shore below, where boulders are under attack by relentless crashing waves. I shake off these dark thoughts, rising on a tide of hope.

"Do you know of the retro concept of birthdays?" Lila asks me.

"Yes," I say, as the memory of balloons, gifts, and laughing faces singing, "Happy birthday to Milly" floats through my head.

"The custom was abandoned since no one ages anymore, and most don't care to count their years. But I have fond memories of my childhood birthdays and want to share this tradition with you." Her dark eyes shine. "Your second surprise is a birthday party."

The following week thrills with new experiences, although I rarely see Lila. She busies herself in the lab, leaving me with Visla. I enjoy being with the energetic assistant who talks fast, jumping from topic to topic like a busy squirrel climbing branches. We fall into a routine of breakfast together, where she talks so much I'm saved from thinking deeply. Her face always softens when she speaks of Tamsin's improving health. They're best mates like I am with Lorelei and Marcus.

Except for noon walks on the cliff trail with Lila, I stay in my room. I've yet to meet the other sistas, although I know much about them from Visla. I asked why no one else is allowed near me, and she says it's for my protection. She won't say any more, but I know it has something to do with Scientist Daniel and Frost. Surely any threats will end once I become a scientist.

Lila brings me two retro-books with stiff backs and thin, yellowed pages: *Tanglewood Tales* and *Pippi Longstockings*. I treasure these books, reading them carefully so as not to rip the pages. When I ask Lila for more, she says she'll look around, but paper books usually are stored at the Edu-Center or protected in glass at the museum. They're fragile because they come from the pre-digital era. Technology failed during the mind-plague and all digital books were lost.

Every afternoon on our walks, I ask Lila how much longer 'til my memdenity. Her answer is always the same. A head shake and "soon." Since I can't go to the health-workers, Lila will perform the procedure. She warns me that this is a secret and I must not tell anyone, not even Visla. I trust Lila—still, I'm nervous. I've grown to enjoy the random images and conversations from Milly's memories, and I'm adapting better, recognizing the shifting in my mind warning me that my thoughts are tumbling into Milly-life. I vow to hold onto to both Milly's and my memories, even after all three of

Angeleen's memdenities.

The night before my birthday party, my mind whirls and I can hardly fall asleep. I read until my eyes ache, and when I do drift off, it's to a dream—or memory—of Milly before she came to the island, when she turned thirteen.

Rosemarie is in the dream too—a younger version of her, but there's no mistaking her gentle smile or her skill in the kitchen. She carries a cake that trails a plume of smoke from thirteen candles. I'm sitting at a large table— my parents added a piece to the middle so it could fit all of my friends. My most recent best friend, Mandy (she's left-handed so I call her my Leftie Bestie) sits beside me. There's an empty seat on my other side saved for Rosemarie. My parents sit across from me with my brother between them, licking frosting off a mixer beater. In a corner of the room, gorgeous wrapped packages cover a table. Rosemarie saves wrapping paper for recycling—but I'd rather rip them open. She can't keep a secret and has already told me I'm getting new boots for competitions.

Competitions? The word gives an image of a spirited quarter horse jumping barrels, and I'm leaning tight in a saddle, flying with hoofbeats. I taste dust and the musty scent of a sweaty horse. I hear applause, from an audience sitting in bleachers, and in the front row, my family stands and applauds for me.

I wake up with a wistful longing, missing Milly's family and a world that no longer exists. When I cross the room and pull back the yellow curtains, I'm warmed by sunshine slanting into my room. I belong here.

Opening drawers, I try on pantons, shirts, tunics, and privacies. There are fresh flowers too, in shades of morning—

orange poppies and yellow lilsies. Visla must have left them for me.

That's not all she's done. Reaching up, I touch the smooth edges of my short hair. After Visla left my evening meal, she took scissors to my hair, shaping my curls into soft layers above my shoulders. When she held up a mirror, I almost didn't recognize myself, but I was pleased with this new me. *Angeleen*, I thought.

I reach for the brush Visla gave me and run it through my hair. Did the real Angeleen have long or short hair? In what shade? Were her eyes brown, green, blue, or hazel? I remember the surprise of seeing a picture of Milly, how different she was to my imaginings. And Milly was shocked by our new appearance. Will Angeleen be a surprise too? I'll gain the first memdenity soon, but I'm impatient to know everything now.

Why not ask Lila? I think as I button the laces of my tunic.

Lila has told me she has root tea in her lab every morning before beginning her work. So I head for the lab.

This is the first I've entered the elevator alone. My hand wavers uncertainly over the numbers. I reach for number three button, but hesitate when I notice a number four. *Four?* But there's no fourth floor. Curious, I tap the number four, expecting it to stop on the third floor as usual. But it continues to rise, slowly. I'm positive Visla said there were only three floors. So why is there a fourth button?

My curiosity rises with the elevator. When the elevator stops, the red lit number four goes dark. But I don't move.

In my head, Milly's voice warns me to leave. Jennza would stay to investigate. But Milly thinks before diving into trouble. There could be a danger on the fourth floor that Lila doesn't want me to risk, like poisonous chemicals or Lila's brother and his cold-hearted assistant.

The elevator stops and the door slides open.

Quickly, I push the close-door button. The elevator swooshes back down to level three. I blow out a deep breath, proud of myself because I thought before rushing into trouble. If there's something on the fourth floor that Lila wants me to know about, she'll tell me.

When I tap on the lab door, Lila opens it with a startled expression that widens into a smile. "I expected someone else, but this is even better. Would you like a cup of root tea?" she asks, pulling up a chair beside her desk.

"I'd love it," I say.

She crosses the room to the cabinets, then returns a moment later with my hot tea. I blow on my hot tea, inhaling rich, earthy scents, before asking her about Angeleen. "Is there a picture of her?"

"Hmmm ... there must be. Now where would it be? I'll have to look." A knock at her door brings her to her feet. "That must be Visla."

When Lila opens the door, she lowers her voice to a whisper. Visla bounces back and forth on her feet, even more excited than usual. *What are they talking about?* I wonder, biting my lip so I don't rush over and demand to know what's going on.

After much whispering, Lila closes the door, turning to me with an excited grin. "Are you ready for your surprise?"

"Now?" Relief mingles with curiosity. "Is it the birthday party?"

"Not yet. That's your second surprise—there's a third

also." She stands aside and opens the door wide. "And they've arrived."

When I look past Lila, my mouth falls open.

I stare at two people I never thought I'd see again.

THIRTY-SIX

"Marcus! Lorelei!"

I'm so happy to see them that I've blurted out their youth names. But they'll always be Marcus and Lorelei to me, and I'm overjoyed to see them.

"Surprise!" Lorelei lifts her arms in a twirl.

"Heya, Jennz," Marcus says quietly.

I open my mouth to say "heya" like always, only I can't speak. Tears prickle my eyes, blurring my vision so my mates appear like ghostly imaginings. Yet Lorelei's hug is real, and I reach out to draw Marcus into our hug.

When I step back, I'm startled by the changes in Marcus. He's wearing formal pantons with a buttoned, long-sleeved white shirt. While I saw his shorter hair at Sunday Fair, now his hair is unnaturally darker and parted to the side with gloss gel. He seems taller too.

Lorelei, though, looks much the sameness. Her long black braid brushes against my cheek as we embrace, her scent fresh like spun cotton. She's bubbling overfull with emotions so easy to read on her expressive face.

I love them both so much.

"I can't believe you're here," I say with a catch in my throat.

"Imagine how stunned we were to receive invites from scientists! No one ever visits them! And to be invited to *your* party is wondrous. I've been so worried about you."

She bites her lower lip. "We thought you … you were …."

"Gone," Marcus says, frowning. "We were told Jennza no longer existed."

"I was Returned. Almost." I glance over at Lila and Visla, who are quietly watching our reunion. I cover my mouth to whisper, "More later."

"I have much to say to you too," Marcus whispers back.

"For being almost Returned, you look well." Lorelei pushes between us, hugging me again. "But what happened to your hair? It's ripping short!"

I reach up, having forgotten that Marcus isn't the only one with shorter hair. "It'll grow back." I force a smile, not ready to talk about how close I came to becoming a droll. I swish the smooth edges of my hair. "And it's easier to manage. No more tangles or tying it with a scarf."

"I like it." Marcus looks at me in a deep way.

My cheeks heat as if sun-flamed, and I can't think what to say.

"Lila, I can't believe you did this for me," I say with a grateful glance for Lila.

She smiles. "What's a party without friends?"

"I didn't think it was possible to bring anyone here from outside."

"There's little I can't accomplish," the scientist says proudly. "Since you can't go outside our boundaries, I brought your friends to you. It required covert arrangements. Today is the only day their absence won't be noticed."

"Why today?" I ask.

"Sunday Fair." Lorelei nudges me like she thinks I'm teasing. But I had no idea it was even Sunday.

"It was all very hush-hush. I pretended I was going to

Sunday Fair. But beneath this covering is your gift." Lorelei runs her fingers over her velvety jacket. "I sewed two hidden pockets inside this jacket."

"I can't even tell there are pockets," I say.

"My own design," she says proudly. "Our invitations warned us to tell no one our true destination."

"Your born-mates can only stay three hours," Lila explains. "That's enough time for your party."

"Best. Surprise. Ever," I say, remembering Milly's reply for a favorite gift.

"*J'ai eu des fêtes d'anniversaire magnifique*," Lorelei says in a rolling accent I've never heard her use before.

"What did you say?" I think she's teasing me.

"Pardon, I forget myself. I said your birthday party will be magnificent. When I lived in France—a language I can now speak fluently—I had many splendid birthday celebrazes. My twelfth was *magnifique* in a hotel with over a hundred guests. Not long after, though, Maman was ill with the mind-plague."

"France? Maman?" I stare until comprehension strikes. "Graces good! You've had a memdenity!"

"Three days ago! My mind is spinning with pictures and conversations and experiences. I love being Flavia!" She holds the edge of her braid like a dancing partner and gives a twirl. "It's more amazing than I imagined, and now I know much about retro-century. I remember parents, cities, airplanes, horses—a much smoother ride than hoxen—and I used to play the piano."

"You did?" I say enviously. Milly and I both lack musical talent.

"I performed at recitals and received thunderous applause. I can't wait for my next memdenity. Then I can ask permission to play the museum piano."

Marcus puts his hands on his hips, frowning. "You're gabbering faster than magbirds. Slow down. I can't understand half of what you're saying."

"Poor Marcus hasn't had his memdenity yet," Lorelei teases.

"It was delayed."

I start to ask why until I remember that his Leader was killed—by the boy I helped escape. Does he know what I did?

"Don't be jealous because we're more advanced than you," Lorelei tells Marcus in a lofty tone.

"Climb off your high perch." Marcus playfully swats her arm. "New memories don't change anything—you're still the same fluff-brain who shrieked at harmless wormlings."

"You threw one in my hair," she accuses.

"Your hair never looked better."

"You're a jerky-toad."

"Flavia fluff-brain."

"Don't call me that!"

Marcus dodges Lorelei's kick, laughing. I laugh too. Lorelei shoots me a scathing look, then starts to giggle, and we're all laughing.

I hug this moment, dearer than gifts wrapped with ribbons. Despite new names and separate lives, we're still best mates.

That will never change.

The first floor dining room is transformed with strings of silver ribbons and paper flowers floating like clouds in the ceiling. A large table is covered with a purple tarp painted with images of Sharing Blooms, and in the center is a three-tier cake, iced with yellow frosting.

There are gifts too, wrapped in a rainbow of shaded papers—except one which is sewn with cloth and buttoned closed—Lorelei's crafty gift.

We are a party of eight: myself, Lila, her three sistas, and my best mates. Two drolls stand at the door like stone statues. Marcus and Lorelei glance at the drolls curiously. I whisper that drolls are harmless. With some guilt, I realize I'm beginning to ignore them too.

My first birthday party is better than Milly's lifetime of birthdays combined. My friends, my cake, my gifts. And such lovely gifts!

Visla insists I open a flat box first—a lace-trimmed night covering from Visla and the other sistas. Lila hands me a box, and when I lift the, lid I *ahh* with delight at the framed photo of a woman with dark hair piled high on her head, bow-shaped lips, and green eyes. I don't need to be told her identity: Angeleen Dupree.

"Angeleen was thirty-two when this was taken," Lila tells me with warmth in her voice. "She survived the Attack only to die years later from a fall off a cliff. For a long time, I avoided the cliffs, but now I think of her when I take walks. We worked together on the early stages of cease-aging. She was brilliant."

I'm overwhelmed with gratitude and don't know what to say. If I could pile my thanks to Lila, they'd vanish into a horizon of sky. She's not just giving me a new identity—she's sharing her friend.

Lorelei picks up a gift and plops it in front of me. "*Dépêchez-vous! Ouvre mon cadeau.* A Flavia creation. "

While I unbutton her wrapped gift of hair frivels, I

glance up to find Marcus studying me with an intense expression. Is he feeling left out because Lorelei and I share the memdenity experience? I vow to talk less of my new memories and warn Lorelei to be more sensitive too.

Marcus shifts in his boots awkwardly as he hands me lavender-scented goat soap. "It's not much. I churned it myself and added lilac petals."

I sniff the soap and smile. "It smells lovely. Thank you, Marcus."

"Soap from dirt boy?" Lorelei teases.

"I prefer to be clean." He shows off his tanned but spotless hands.

He laughs, but he isn't smiling. Something isn't right with him. Whenever our gazes meet, he quickly looks away.

Lila orders the drolls to clean fooder plates and to clear away wrappings. The sistas gather my gifts and carry them to my room.

"You have two hours left with your mates," Lila tells me. I ask for permission to take Lorelei and Marcus walking on the cliffs. Lila not only agrees but orders a droll to prepare a lunch basket.

Outside in fresh air, beneath a cloudless sky with the rushing sounds of sea, everything feels more natural between us. I imagine we're walking the familiar Edu-Center trail, our feet falling in step, like we've done so many times.

At the highest point, we prop up rock slabs like seats, sitting in a tri-circle. My gaze meets Marcus, and once again he turns away.

"Is everything all right?" I ask him.

"Why wouldn't it be?" He shrugs, looking at the ground.

"You just seem ... I don't know ... different. Are you

getting along with your Family?"

"I've earned their trust." He hesitates. "But what you did caused suspicion of all youths."

"So you know." I suck in a deep breath, then blow it out.

"I don't believe any of it." Lorelei scoots between us. "We heard you helped the killer escape, but rumors are hardly ever true. You'd never betray your Family."

I hang my head, shamed. "I did it. Please, don't hate me."

"I could never hate you," Lorelei says with no hint of anger. "You must have had a good reason. That's why we've been working on a plan to help you. Tony found out something stunning."

"Tony?" I repeat. "Who?

Marcus slowly raises his hand. "Me."

I stare at him. "What happened to Neil? That's the name you Chose."

"My Family has decided I'll be more useful as Anthony Sarwald."

"I've heard that name before." I rub my chin, then gasp. *"Grand Leader Anthony Sarwald!"*

"Marcus will be our highest Leader." Lorelei shakes her head. "Isn't that ripping weird?"

I nod, half expecting this to be a joke. But they're both serious.

"Marcus—I mean, Tony—will be the most powerful person in ShareHaven," Lorelei adds. "You'll be able to see him more often since he'll consult with scientists. Isn't that ripping weird?"

Marcus frowns. "I'll get the first memdenity in a week. It's an honor with much responsibility. I doubt I'm the right person for this role, but I'll do my best."

"You always do, and it's more than enough," I say, squeezing his hand.

"I'm unsure, though, about Grand Sarwald's character," Marcus says uneasily. "I moved into his dwelling, and when I was putting away my shoes, I found a loose floorboard in the closet. I pried it up and found ...." Marcus picks at his clean fingernails. "I found a locked steel box. I didn't have a key, so I used a twisted wire to open the lock."

"Wait till you hear what he found inside!" Lorelei adds, with a jump so close to the ledge I grab her arm and pull her away.

"This." Marcus (not Neil or Tony ever to me) reaches under his shirt and brings up a four-pointed symbol on a gold chain—exactly like the one I found in Milly's jewelry box.

The symbol of the Believers.

THIRTY-SEVEN

"I've seen other necklaces like that," I tell Marcus.

Lorelei lifts her brows curiously.

Marcus asks, "Where?"

"The first one I saw was in Milly's jewelry box," I answer. Then I tell them about waking up at night when I still lived with the Cross Family and discovering a secret meeting of Believers in a hidden room. "Some of them wore these symbols too, and they spoke of Nate—the boy who killed Grand Sarwald."

"The Nocturne you helped." Marcus's tone sharpens with accusation.

"I couldn't let him die—not after what he did for me."

They both give me "what haven't you been telling us?" looks, and I can't hide my secret any longer—not if I want to keep their friendship. So after two years of keeping my cave a secret, I tell them everything: sneaking off to the cave, swimming with Petal, and how Nate saved me from the vampfin.

"You understand why I had to help him?" I ask, then hold my breath.

I exhale when their expressions soften, and they both nod. "Leader Cross was angry when Nate was caught," I continue. "They wanted his execution to be quick, so he wouldn't expose them. The Believers planned Leader Sarwald's death."

"Not Instructor Penny!" Lorelei's eyes widen. "She'd never do anything against ShareHaven laws."

"She was at the meeting," I say sadly. "But she was the only one who defended Nate. Leader Cross, Daisy, and the others said he was a savage who deserved to die, but Instructor Penny felt sorry for him."

Marcus frowns. "Being at the meeting makes her as guilty as the others."

"Secret friendships are common," Lorelei says with a dismissive wave of her hand, her voice slipping into a French accent. "Like Daisy's romance." She sighs. "How sad to love someone not of your Family."

"Romancing outside a Family is allowed," Marcus says. "But an illegal meeting led by a Leader is disturbing. What is the purpose?"

"It has to do with faith." I tell them what Rosemarie said about her husband being murdered because he was going to vote for freedom of religion.

"If people want more churches, give them more." Lorelei picks up a shiny black rock and bounces it in her hand. "What's the ripping problem?"

Marcus shakes his wheat-brown head. "We begin our mornings with a pledge to honor our Family, society, and science. Science is why we live forever, not an invisible belief in a higher entity. Worshiping higher powers would shift the power in our community. The Leaders won't allow it."

"Unless the Leader is part of it," I point out.

"Grand Sarwald had a Believer necklace, which means he was part of the group too." Marcus stares down at the star-shaped necklace around his neck.

"Then why did they plot against him?" I wrinkle my brow.

"I don't know, but the answers may be in the papers he hid. Perhaps he joined the Believers to get proof of their guilt. He was going to expose them, so they hired the Nocturne to kill him. I'll know the truth when I receive memdenity."

"You may not like what you find out," I warn.

"And you only get childhood mems at first. I still can't stitch a perfect hem." Lorelei tosses her rock over the cliff, and I strain forward, listening, but there's no thud or splash. "It'll be two months and twenty-six days before my second mem. Way too long!"

I pat her shoulder. "Marcus has more patience."

"While I'm waiting, I'll seek answers," Marcus says with a determined press of his lips. "If I find proof of a murder plot, the guilty will be punished."

The fierceness of his expression is different from the carefree youth who gently cradled crawlies in his hands. I can't take my eyes from him, noticing small details like how the wind barely stirs his shortened hair, the commanding lift of his shoulders, and how his hard muscles fill out his moss-green shirt. No longer the youth but a man who will become Grand Leader.

"Jennza, when I'm officially Grand Sarward I'll clear the charges against you." Marcus tells me. "You can return to ShareHaven."

"How can you clear the charges when what I did was wrong?"

"You only wanted to help a friend, which shouldn't be punished so severely. Some things are out of our control and mistakes happen that you regret. But there's nothing you can do except go on." He glances away from me with a troubled expression. "I wish things were different ... that none of this ever happened."

"You're a good mate," I tell him, touched by his concern.

Lorelei gives me a hug. "You're missing out on so much—and I'm missing you even more. We won't give up until you can return to your Family."

"Not the Crosses!" I shake my head. "I will *never* go back."

"If Leader Cross is proven guilty of conspiracy, he'll be jailed and you can choose a new Family." Marcus speaks with the confidence of a future leader. "You'd fit well with my Family. You'll enjoy working with crawlies and natural resources."

"My Family is more fun," Lorelei says, with a defiant look for Marcus. "We sing while we sew and create interesting crafts. It would be so wondrous to have you for a sister, cousin, mother, or some other Ying relation."

"I'd love to be with both of you." I bite my lip. "But I like it here too—and there's something more. Scientist Lila asked me not to tell anyone here, but you're only visiting. So I can tell you."

"A secret?" Lorelei says eagerly.

"Swear you won't repeat it."

"Criss-cross thumb promise." Lorelei presses her thumb against mine.

Marcus offers his thumbs too, criss-crossing against ours.

"Scientist Lila wants me to work with her." A burst of pride rushes through me as I announce, "She offered me a memdenity!"

"An assistant?" Lorelei puckers her face. "You'll get bored following scientists around like puppets. And what about those creepy drolls?"

"I almost became one." I shudder then explain what happened.

"That's terriful! Aren't you afraid Scientist Daniel will try again?"

"Lila assured me he'd leave me alone. Besides, I'm not going to be an assistant." I give an excited squeal. "Lila asked me to become a scientist."

Lila flips back her long red braid. "Ripping impossible."

"No one can become a scientist," Marcus says.

"I will. My new name will be Angeleen Dupree."

"Sounds French," Lorelei says, a little more interested. "*Nous pourrions parler français ensemble.*"

"I have no idea what you said, but maybe Angeleen will know French, and then we can have fun conversations together," I say, smiling.

But when I glance over at Marcus, his expression is darker than the blackest thundercloud. "Jennz, don't do it." Marcus kicks at a clump of grass. "You belong with a Family."

"I'm a criminal in ShareHaven. If I leave here, I'll be executed."

"Not after we clear your name," Marcus says with fierce determination.

"You can become whoever you want—like a Ying." Lorelei gives a playful tug on my hand. "We can have such fun together. You'd love it."

Marcus shakes his head, and I think he's going to insist I join his Family. "Be yourself," he says.

I'm touched by his understanding. I can't go back to my youth or the Cross Family. Will I fit in with the scientists? Martyn ignores me. I haven't even met Kataya. Daniel almost turned me into a droll, and his assistant Frost hates me simply because I exist. But a memdenity will make me one of them. They'll have to accept Angeleen once I become her, and this will be my forever home. Surrounded by sky, sea, and my best mates, hope rises within me.

We pull out the picnic lunch, sharing chicken sticks, fried potatoes, and spiced asparagus. Marcus, who loves to eat, chews, while Lorelei shares the latest ShareHaven gossip. I'm never sure how much is truth, and it's hard to follow some of her stories because she keeps slipping into French. When she does, her mouth twists down in a way I've never noticed before, and she moves her hands in jerky excitement.

Glancing up at the fading sun, I'm sad our time together is ending.

When we're finished eating, I pick up the woven basket. We turn our backs on the sea. Trees and tall weeds rise on each side of the path, and as I reach for the camouflaged door, it appears like a flat rock against dark earth. I lift a clump of moss and pull a lever.

We slip from daylight into a false brightness of illuminated walls. I take the now-familiar passage to the elevator and level one. The room where Lila held my party only a few hours ago is empty of gifts, cake, and guests.

Marcus leans close to me. "Need to talk," he whispers. "Alone."

The urgency beneath his words tightens my heart. I've sensed something troubling him. Now I'll find out. But first I have to distract Lorelei.

"Want to see my room?" I ask them.

"Would I ever!" Lila's velvet jacket twirls with her enthusiasm.

I lead them back to the elevator and rise to the second level.

When I push open my door, Lorelei is all about the fabrics—as I expected. After examining each of my party gifts, she opens my drawers, admiring and insulting my coverings. "This fabric is fine, with a thick weave, yet it breathes so you won't sweat. But this tunic isn't purple—it's the color of puke. Burn it now, because if you have to wear it, you'll hate yourself."

I glance over at Marcus, expecting him to tease Lorelei. But he's staring out my window, frowning.

Lorelei flits like a hummingbird, lifting pieces of clothing from drawers and waving them in front of her. She flutters over to my closet, yanking it open. "Now this is more like it! Capes, tunics, and scarves! This scarf is *très jolie*. I wish I could try it on."

"Why don't you?" I suggest.

"Oh, could I?"

I gesture to my privacy room. "Go in there. Take as many coverings as you'd like. We'll wait here."

As if she expects me to change my mind, she grabs scarves and tunics, then practically dances into the privacy room. When the door shuts, I touch Marcus on the arm. "Talk. Fast."

His head droops. "It's not—I mean—I don't know how …."

"What?" Crossing my arms to my chest, I give him a fierce look.

"Nothing."

"Your eyes shift when you lie, Marcus."

"Don't call me by my youth name."

"Don't avoid the topic," I retort. "What's wrong?"

He rakes his fingers through his hair. "I can't tell you ... you'll hate me."

"Me, hate you? Never! You can tell me anything."

"Not this." Shoving his hands in his panton pockets, he looks down.

"Are you nervous about your memdenity?" I guess. "I was too, but it wasn't painful. The memories confused me a lot at first, with voices demanding to be heard in my brain. But now instead of fighting the voices, I listen and wait till they stop. The memories sort of tickle my mind. I've learned so much about retro-life, and you'll be amazed at how different things were before the mind-plague. People climbed inside metal planes and flew in the sky."

He blows out a deep sigh. "This isn't about memdenity. There's something else ... I have to tell you ... only I couldn't around Lorelei."

I've never seen him look so miserable—and guilty. But what does he have to be guilty about? I'm the one who freed a killer. He never broke any rules except helping me by returning Petal to the sea ....

"Petal!" A sharp fear pierces me. "Is this about her?"

Marcus winces, the color fading from his face. "I—I'm so sorry."

My heart squeezes. "You took her to the Fence. Didn't you?"

"I ... I meant to." Misery hangs heavy with his nod.

Sick inside, I can hardly speak. "But you promised to keep her safe! Please ... tell me she's alive."

"I think she is ... I hope."

"How can you not know? I gave her to you and you promised to take her to the sea. I warned you she needs salt water or she'll die."

"I tried." He hangs his head. "There's a sea pond on our compound for cultivating salt for spices. I poured salt water in a bucket and Petal dove right in. Her health improved immediately. She splashed and made tinkling sounds."

"She still needed the sea," I say accusingly.

"I meant to take her!" he cries. "But I had to wait till morning. I rose early and hid her in the bucket. I was ready to take her to the sea but then …." He stops, rubbing his forehead as if in severe pain.

"What?" I demand.

"The shed door opened. Uncle Sean—he's temporarily taking over Leader duties —stood there. I thought he was angry until he slapped me on the back and congratulated me. He was excited because he'd never seen a creature like Petal. He thanked me, then took Petal away."

"You let him steal Petal!"

"I'm not the Leader yet. I couldn't stop him. Besides, I thought he'd return her to me. When he didn't, I searched everywhere in our compound. But I couldn't find Petal." His voice chokes. "She's gone."

THIRTY-EIGHT

I'm shaking with waves of fury rushing through me. My hands clench into fists. I want to strike at Marcus, punish him for betraying me ... for losing my sweet Petal. I clamp my lips shut to hold in my rising anger.

Petal will be okay, I assure myself. Didn't she make her way miles to find me at the Cross compound? She even found my window and waited in a curl of sweetness on my pillow. She's tiny but large with bravery. She will have found a way back to the cave.

But I imagine her lost, hurt, crying for me. And I want to cry too.

"What do you think of this scarf as a belt?" Lorelei exclaims in a flurry of gauzy mauve as she twirls from the privacy room.

My arms are folded against my chest. I ignore Marcus's pleading look and turn abruptly from him. I force a smile for Lorelei, a volcano boiling beneath my calmness. "The scarf is lovely," I tell her.

Marcus says nothing, and Lorelei glances between us curiously.

"Is something wrong?" she asks, unwinding the scarf from her waist.

I shake my head, and Marcus murmurs a low "no."

Lorelei asks again, knowing us too well. But neither of

us will talk about it. If I speak Petal's name, I'll break down in tears.

There's a knock at my door. Visla arrives to escort Marcus and Lorelei to the solar cart. My birthday surprise—which started out so wondrous—is over.

"I hate leaving you." Lorelei throws her arms around me. "What if I never see you again?"

"You will," I say, although I'm unsure.

Marcus moves toward me, but I hold back, unable to look at him. He murmurs, "I'm sorry," then hurries out of the door.

I'm tempted to run after him and mend the hurts between us—until I think of Petal's trusting eyes.

The door shuts. Footsteps fade to silence.

Flinging myself on the bed, I give in to the tears. How could Marcus betray me? And poor sweet Petal, where is she? What did that terrific man to do her? She could be locked in a cage, crying out for me to help her, or lost too far from the sea, withering to bones, dying alone.

She's too clever to get lost or caged. If she can make the long journey from the Edu-Center to the Cross compound, she can travel the short distance from the Sarwald compound to the sea. Petal's probably in our cave.

I won't know unless I check the cave. Lila will surely offer to help if I explain about Petal. But if I tell her the location of my cave, it won't be my secret anymore.

I'll have to search for Petal alone, even if it means risking arrest and execution. But I won't rush out without thinking like the old Jennza. I'll wait till it's safe to slip out of the Gate, then I'll go to the ocean path beyond the Edu-Center. It's not an impossible distance, closer than when I lived with the Cross Family. When I know Petal is safe—she has to be!—I'll return before I'm missed.

I'm impatient to leave, but my Milly memories warn me to be cautious. I rise from my bed and pick up the hair frivels Lorelei crafted for my birthday gift. My fingers trail along the velvety bows, and I think how no other ShareHaven youth has ever had a birthday celebraze. Lila has done so much for me, bringing my friends here, my party, and the picnic by the sea. I'll show her how much I appreciate her kindness by becoming the best scientist ever. Even if Marcus and Lorelei clear my name, I won't join a Family. My future is here with Lila.

Slipping on socks and shoes, I cross the room. My hand is poised on the knob when I hear a sound. Shuffling from beneath my bed—like a snake or swizard or … Petal!

I rush toward my bed, then draw back with a gasp.

A dark shape rises from the floor.

Nate.

THIRTY-NINE

"Hi, Jennza." Nate brushes dust from his shirt and stretches his arms and legs. "I thought your friends would never leave."

My mouth hangs open. Although he wears the stiff gray uniform of a droll, his blue eyes shine with so much life there's no mistaking him for a mindless slave. I hardly know which of the questions spinning in my head to ask him first.

"Why ... why were you under my bed?"

"Not the best hiding place. So dusty I had to pinch my nose to stop from sneezing. Cramped too. My leg fell asleep." He smacks his foot on the floor.

"Why did I go to all the trouble to help you escape if you're brain-lacking enough to come back?"

"I had to see you."

His words tug at my stomach in a not-unpleasant way and heat rushes through me. Being so close to him, I'm dizzy with feelings I don't understand. I want to be angry, yet I'm thrilled to see him again. He's risking his life, I remind myself. If he's caught, I won't be able to rescue him.

Yet he came to see me, and I'm smiling.

"They'll execute you if you're caught." I try to sound angry.

"It's worth the risk to speak to you again," he says. "I like the sound of your words, how they rise and fall soft like calm waters on the beach."

I like his sounds too, and I admire the contrast of his dark brows over his blue eyes and how his mouth curves into dimples. His face is so unlike those of my born-mates—rough, pale, with faint, paler lines of scars—a jagged line on the side of his nose and a deeper line along the curve of his left cheekbone. It's as if his face is a map of a life very different from my own.

"Happy birthday," he says, sitting on the edge of my bed. He gestures to the boxes piled on my dresser. "Sorry to miss the party, but I wasn't invited. Still, I can give you a gift."

"It's not really my birthday."

"Would you like this?" He reaches beneath the heavy droll robe and withdraws a folded paper—retro paper, yellowed and sturdy. He unfolds the single sheet, then hands it to me. "It's only a copy I drew to find my way here. I have no further use for this, but you might find it interesting."

I look down, marveling at black lines spreading across the paper like the dark veins of age on Grandmother's arms. The oblong dark mass of land surrounded by curvy lines of waves is our island. A map, I realize, recognizing the tiny symbols for rivers, trees, low and high lands. Only it's unlike the maps I saw in the Edu-Center, showing not only ShareHaven but the whole island. I look beyond the Gate where Nate escaped, following a line running beneath the ground to an arch symbol with a word: *Home*.

"Is this where you live?" I lift my eyes to meet his and he nods.

"Far different than your sunlit room," he says, shrugging. "But it's safe."

His tone hints at pride, and I understand that he loves

his home, even though it's beneath the ground. By giving me this hand-drawn map, he's sharing a piece of himself.

"Thank you," I say softly. "I'll treasure it."

He shrugs. "It's only a rough drawing. Map-making is what I do, and I find even crude sketches like this useful in finding my way without waking sleeping beasts or being shot by your Uniforms."

"How long have you been hiding here?" I ask, amazed he not only entered the most protected, secret place in ShareHaven but found my room.

He glances at the sky through the half-open curtains. "Three hours."

"How did you get here?"

"By boat, foot, and hoxen."

"You rode a hoxen?"

He grins. "Borrowed one."

I start to argue that hoxen were genetically engineered to pull carts, not for riding, when I get a memory of galloping bareback across a field. I'm riding a sleek, dusky-brown horse while my sister Rosemarie trails far behind on a gentle mare named Buttercup. "Slow down!" she shouts, but I pretend not to hear. With a nudge of my boots, Rebel, the half quarter horse, half Arabian speeds ahead, kicking up tufts of grass as if racing against the wind.

Horses don't exist, at least not in ShareHaven. I'll never see one of these retro-creatures, yet I have memories of riding them since I-she-we were a child. I jumped barrels competitively and won beautiful ribbons and trophies. I hear applause, smell the ripe odor of hay and manure, and caress silky horse hair. Milly isn't sweet or obedient when astride a spirited horse—she's in control and confident. We hold firm to the reins, head high, heart racing with each hoofbeat.

"I wasn't sure I could stay on a hoxen," Nate is saying. "After the fifth time he threw me off, I figured out how to grab the mane and hang on tight. I stayed off roads and out of sight since I'm not in a mood to die today." His words should be heavy with fear, yet he's grinning.

"How did you get into my room without being seen?" I ask, worry twisting inside me.

"I found this hanging up on a wall hook." He plucks at the fabric of his droll robe. "It hides my clothes, and no one looks in the faces of the zombie-workers."

"Drolls. They're called drolls."

"They don't blink. That was the hardest part, trying not to blink." He smooths his hair back so it's similar to the male drolls, except for a curl that waves around his ear. "Are they human?"

"They used to be," I say sadly.

I think of the droll I saw on the first day—Carlos. I'm sure he's the Cross Family's last youth—and I almost ended up like him. I haven't seen him since Frost zapped him with her electricity gun.

"How did you find my room?" I ask Nate.

"Snuck inside your friends' cart," he says, moving to the window and glancing through the curtains at a view of sky and wild grasses. "I've been hiding outside for two days, watching and waiting. I found the hidden entrance but didn't know how to get inside until the cart stopped at the door. When the driver pushed a button that opened the door, I jumped into the back and hid beneath a blanket."

I wag my finger at him. "You could have been killed."

"If I had, would you mourn for me?" He raises his brows

teasingly.

"Don't be demental." I try to sound angry.

"You must care a little. You broke me out of jail."

"Something I'm starting to regret." I cross to the window and shut the curtains. Doesn't he realize the need for caution? What if someone saw him?

"Admit you're glad to see me again," he says.

"Stop talking nonsense, or I'll kill you myself."

"Nah, you don't have it in you. But I could teach you how to fight." He raises his hands into fists, playfully punching the air. "I've spent years practicing combat, weaponry, and hunting."

I shake my head. "I have no cause for fighting."

"Are you sure?" he challenges. "The world outside is dangerous."

"But for you it's more dangerous inside our Fence. Do you wish to be executed? Leave before someone sees you."

"Not until I get what I came for."

"What?" I glance away, picking up a small unwrapped box and plucking at its green bow. I thought he'd come to see me.

"Medicine." He sucks in a sharp breath. "I can't sit by and do nothing while people I care about die."

"You came to steal from the scientists?"

"I'll do whatever I need to." His lips press with determination.

"Too dangerous," I warn. "You can fool the drools with your disguise but not the scientists. How will you get into the lab?"

"The same way I broke out of the jail." He reaches beneath the droll covering, then pulls out a small green bottle and rubber strips.

I remember how the green liquid exploded rubber strips into fire that destroyed steel bars. Still, I shake my head. "Lab doors are larger than the jail's window. You'll never get into the lab."

"I could with your help."

"I can't betray Lila's trust—not after everything she's done for me." Green ribbon rips beneath my fingers.

"I understand," he says, but I can tell I've disappointed him. He jumps to his feet. "I'll find it on my own."

"And die before you reach the third floor." I toss the ripped bow aside and move quickly to block his way to the door.

"Better than watch my father die from a snake bite," he blurts out.

"A viper got him?" Shuddering, I sink beside him on the bed.

"The monsters grow in unnatural numbers, and they're harder to kill."

"But you told me his mapping skills kept him out of battles."

"While I was imprisoned, my father went into battle to prove he could still fight even though he's quite old."

"How aged is he?" I ask sympathetically.

"Thirty-six." His eyes shine with tears, and this touches me deeply. The trained killer, who showed no emotion when he was hours from execution, cries for his dying father.

"I'll ask Lila for the medicine you need," I say.

"As if a scientist would help a Nocturne," he scoffs.

"She's very kind, and I'm sure she'll help you." I think of the map he showed me, where squiggles of lines are all that separate our communities. We share the same island and shouldn't be enemies.

"Topsiders put up the Fence because they want us dead."

"No, it was only to protect us after the Attack. But it's wrong for us to be safe while you're forced underground," I say with rising anger. "The Fence shouldn't divide life and death. If we all worked together, we could destroy the snakes and claws."

"Topsiders would rather the monsters live and we die," he says bitterly. "They blame us for the actions of our ancestors."

"What do you mean?" I knit my brows.

"Have you wondered how we came to live outside your Fence?" When I shake my head, he continues, "Many of our ancestors were fishermen living here peacefully long before scientists divided the island. But we're also descendants of soldiers from the militia group that attacked ShareHaven. After the Attack, the ones who were too injured to escape by boat survived in the woods. They joined with the fishermen when claws and snakes forced them to go underground. "

"You're descended from our attackers?" I step back from him.

A wary look crosses his face. "Does it make a difference to you?"

"No," I say without hesitation. "And if people in ShareHaven could know you, they wouldn't be afraid. My born-mates Lorelei and Marcus would like you."

"The boy who lost Petal?"

I wince. "You overheard that?"

"Hard not to hear when I'm squished under here." He pats the bed. "If you'd asked me to protect Petal, I would have died before allowing someone to take her away."

"Marcus will search until he finds her." As I say this, I realize it's true, and I wish I could take back the harsh things I said to Marcus. "You must have also heard that my friends are trying to clear my name so I can be part of ShareHaven again. They never stopped caring about me."

"Like a family." Pain crosses his face. "My father will die soon without medicine. If he lives, he'll do great things for my people. He mapped the route to a new tunnel that contains ancient tools and electronics from when the tunnels were part of a military station. These devices have already led to communication with the outside world."

"What outside world? The mind-plague destroyed everything. There's nothing civilized beyond our island. The mind-plague devastated the world."

"Centuries ago," Nate says. "My father knows civilizations exist because he got one of the old machines he found to work briefly—he says it was called a computer—and he heard voices in another language. He's hopeful that if he can make contact again we'll be rescued from this island."

"Rescue?" I ask, confused. "But this is our home."

"Only for those free to live in the sunshine like you," he says bitterly. "Monsters will keep killing us until we're gone."

I shudder. "Isn't there any way to destroy them?"

"We kill them every night, but they just keep coming back. Unless we can kill all of them, our only hope is to leave this island. My father can help—if he survives. I need that medicine to save him. Will you show me how to find it?"

I bit my lip, thinking of Lila. "It's too risky for you to go into the lab."

"Please, Jennza."

"If you're caught you'll be executed or worse." I point to his droll clothes. "Do you want to become a droll for realness? They cut into your brain and steal your memories so you can't even remember your name."

He's quiet for a moment, plucking at the fabric of his stolen clothes. "I'll risk anything for my father," he finally says.

I can't turn from his pleading gaze.

"It's not safe for you to go," I say. "I'll get the medicine for you."

FORTY

No matter how much I argue, Nate insists on coming with me.

He moves stiffly through the corridor, his gaze as blank as a droll. When we pass a droll leaving the elevator, it's like I'm seeing double—until Nate slants a sly smile my way. We step into the elevator and rise up to the third level. I am firm that Nate must not enter the lab. I take him into a storage closet and won't leave until he hides inside.

"If you want your father to live, you must stay alive," I say. "It's safer for me to get the pills. What do they look like?"

"They're orange and round, in a bottle with a snake symbol. Please … find them." Nate's voice cracks. "My father is so weak. I—I can't lose him."

I flash to a memory of Milly's small hands, clasped in her father's larger hands as he tucked her into bed, bending down to kiss her cheek, his lips cool and soft. "Sleep tight, Silly-Milly," he whispered, making her feel safe. Loved.

"I'll find the pills," I promise Nate, with the same determination that pushed me to climb a forbidden fence, explore a hidden cave, and lose my heart to Petal.

I cross my fingers for luck, an old custom of Milly's.

The door shuts behind me without a sound. The hall is eerily quiet too. Taking a deep breath, I go to the lab and punch the entry code on the outside panel. Lila has trusted me with this code.

Where are pills stored? I wonder as I peer around the desks—all empty. Even Martyn's desk, which is surprising because he's usually there. Where's Lila? She told me she planned to work in the lab after my party.

But after searching each room in the lab, I don't find Lila—or the snake medicine. I wonder at the lack of experiments and devices. I haven't even seen the operation room I was brought to my first night here. Only the room with the frozen life vials holds anything interesting. Desks, a cold box, and storage shelves don't fit my idea of a fully functioning lab, lacking the soul of experiments and discoveries. And none of the bottles in the storage room has a snake symbol.

Still, I keep searching. I'm opening drawers in a desk when I heard a soft swish of robes. Whirling around, I'm face-to-face with a man in purple and silver.

"What are you doing here?" Scientist Daniel demands in his deep yet oddly calm voice that shivers ice through me.

I slam the drawer shut, staring into accusing black eyes. "I—I … um … I'm looking for a … a medi Lila wants." Gulping terror at the man who wanted to carve out my brains, I look over his shoulder to the door—my only means of escape.

"What medi does she seek?" he asks.

I think fast, recalling a few days ago when my head ached and Visla brought me a medi. "Caput Achey," I answer. "But I couldn't find it."

"How very unobservant of you," he says with a sly smile. "Why are you backing away? You don't seriously think you have anything to fear from me."

"Don't I?" I reach back for the desk, feeling for a sharp pen or anything that could become a weapon if he should grab me.

"I have far more important things to deal with than a youth." He smiles in a superior manner. "Besides, my sister has convinced me you'll be useful to her as an assistant."

"Assistant?" I don't correct him.

"Lila and I may appear at cross purposes, but we're both scientists who care deeply about the betterment of ShareHaven. She can be vexing at times, but still, she is my sister, and I can't forget her kindness after my wife died. During that painful time, Lila and I put our professional differences aside, both grieving—until she claimed credit for discoveries that should have been mine. But that's her nature—always trying to prove she's superior to me."

She is superior, I think.

"I didn't trust her motives for wanting to bring a youth here," he adds with a narrowed look at me. "When I found out you were being Returned, I offered to perform the surgery. Nothing personal, my dear," he adds in a pleasant, almost friendly tone. "But Lila won out, and you're still here. Since then we've come to an agreement, and you have nothing to fear from me."

"Um … thank you?" I say uncertainly.

He shakes his head at me, then walks to a shelf and reaches for a small bottle. "I believe this is what you're looking for," he says, offering me the bottle.

I read the label: Caput Achey.

"Hurry back to Lila. I have research to do here and don't want to be interrupted." He waves his hand, dismissing me.

Holding tight to the bottle, I waste no time scrambling past him to the door.

As I open the door, a thought startles me. *No, that can't*

be true, I tell myself. Yet the possibility spins his words like a cycle in my mind. Impossible. Lila wouldn't do that to me. I'm sick inside, wondering. I have to know ....

"Scientist Daniel," I call out with forced calm as I turn back toward him.

"What now?" He glances up impatiently from a file.

"You mentioned your wife ... and I just wondered ..." I clasp my hands tightly around the bottle so they won't shake. "What was her name?"

"Angeleen Dupree Farrow."

I toss the Caput Achey bottle at Nate as if it's on fire and will engulf me if I hold it for another second.

I'm not able to speak of this. I must talk to Lila first, to find out if it's true.

And I thought being married to Arthur was bad. This is far, far worse.

Nate grasps the bottle, hope shining in his blue eyes for a moment until he looks closely at the label. "But this isn't—"

"Sorry," I say quickly. "They aren't the right pills. I looked and looked ... but I couldn't find a bottle with a snake symbol."

"You searched everywhere?"

"Yeah, although ..." I pause, wondering why only Daniel was in the lab. Where were the other scientists?

"What is it?" Nate raises his brows.

"I'll show you." I lead him back to the elevator and point to the control panel. "Do you notice anything odd about the numbers?"

He lifts his brows. "One to four. So?"

"There are only three floors. I thought it was an error, but what if there really is a fourth level? It would explain why I can't find Lila and how I've never met Scientist Kataya. I thought Scientist Daniel and Frost were avoiding me, but maybe the fourth level is the *real* lab?"

While I'm excited to realize this possibility, I'm hurt too, because it means Lila and Visla deceived me.

"Let's find out," Nate says with eagerness.

My hand shakes as I push number four.

When the door slides open, I cringe, expecting to be met by angry scientists or hulking droll guards. No one is there, but I notice the familiar chemical smells of a lab. A door lies ahead, identical to the lab entry on the third floor. I warn Nate to stay back while I touch the panel, trying the third floor level code.

The door falls open—into a tunnel. Milly's thoughts flash fear through me "Maybe we should go ...."

"I'm not turning back," Nate says firmly.

Swallowing fear, I force my feet to move forward, our footsteps echoing as we go deeper into the tunnel.

At first I think we're going to come out on the other side of the hill, and that this is another way in or out of the compound. But we're going up, not down. Abruptly, the tunnel stops at a door. Like the other door, an electronic panel flashes, awaiting the entry combination.

I hesitate, then tap the same number combination I used before.

The door slides open.

We enter a huge domed room where light streams onto a round table surrounded by a dozen chairs. A discussion room, I guess. Floor to ceiling cabinets line the walls. The room is empty, but noises murmur from an adjacent room, whines of machines and low rumblings of conversations. I stare at the metal door leading into this room. My pulse races, and my hands clench at my sides. There's nothing special about this door, but I'm jerked back in memory to shackles dragging me forward and sharp cutting tools.

"What's wrong?" Nate whispers, coming up beside me.

"This is the *real* lab," I whisper. Another voice fights to be heard in my thoughts. *Leave now!* Milly orders.

I back away from the door, fear ripping through me. But instead of turning around and running away, I walk past the lab into a hallway. Nate stays close to me, as if he's protecting me instead of the other way around.

I sniff as the air changes from a chemical smell to something dark, wild, and dank. My stomach churns. The smell intensifies as we near a solid metal door. I try not to breathe too deeply.

"Definitely not the smell of medicines." Nate pinches his nose with his fingers. "It's familiar, but I'm not sure why."

The door has no viewing window, and the stench hints of dead things, not bottled medicine. The hairs on my skin prickle. I hurry past this door to the room at the end of the hall. "Let's try the other room first," I suggest.

Nate follows me to the last door. It has a small window, and peering inside, I see rows of metal shelves. I turn the handle, and the door creaks open. I stare excitedly at shelves crammed with boxes and bottles.

"Medicine!" Nate pushes past me, his expression so animated that no one could mistake him for a droll.

I read labels—cures for itching, aging, soreness, broken bones, sleeplessness, bleeding, and hiccups. Nate systematically searches too, starting with a top row and working to the bottom. Bottles are organized by ailment, I quickly realize. Head ailments on a top shelf. Stomach pain preventatives on the next shelf. Animal stings, allergies, bites: bottom shelf. My gaze flies fast to a bottle with a snake on the label.

"Graces good!" I cry with triumph. "I found it!"

Nate grasps the bottle, rubbing his finger across the snake. "It's strange to think this small bottle can save my father. How can I thank you, Jennza?"

"Be careful, and don't get killed," I tell him.

He grins, pocketing the bottle. I check the corridor, and it's empty, so we hurry out of the room. Nate moves quicker, and I remind him I'm supposed to be leading him. He spreads out his arm, inviting me to move ahead. But after I've taken a few steps, I look back. He's not following me. He's staring at the door to the room with the dead-thing odor.

"That smell is familiar." He sniffs, then gasps. Disbelief and shock show on his face.

Before I can ask what he's remembered, he lunges forward and twists the knob. His mouth falls open, and he reels back in horror. I come up beside him, putting my hand on his arm, and lift my gaze.

I slap my hand over my mouth to bury my own gasp.

From floor to high ceiling, the shadowed room is stacked with dozens—hundreds!—of metal cages full of miniature beasts.

The nearest cage holds a scaled snake with circular rows of teeth and spikes rising across its twisty worm-like body. Above it is a claw so tiny its talons are smaller than my teeth—but sharp like needles. A fanged snake slithers on the ceiling of his cage, whipping a barbed tail through the bars. Beside this cage, a wolf-like creature howls and grips leathery claws around the bars. These are creatures of nightmares, with wiry fur, barbed skin, and growls. The largest claw in a giantness cage hangs by its massive tail, hissing as its steel claws slash, its demon eyes fixed on us hungrily. The floor of the cage is littered in bones.

"What is this place?" I move closer to Nate, clutching his arm.

"Shhh!" Nate looks furtively in every direction. Grasping my hand, he pulls me farther away from the beasts.

I want to block my senses—the putrid smell; monstrous images sure to torment my nightmares; howling, growling, horrible sounds; the acidic taste of fear; and the foreboding sense of worse horrors to come. My only comfort is touch—Nate's gentle, callused hand on mine.

"They're not even grown beasts—they're youths. Why are they in cages?" I shout into Nate's ear so he'll hear over the chaotic din. "Did the scientists capture them for research or to be destroyed?"

"No." Nate's face darkens. "This isn't about destroying. It's about creating. It's obvious what's going on here."

"Not to me."

"They weren't captured and brought here—they were born here."

I shake my head. "But the scientists hate monsters!"

"Then why are there so many? And some look only days old." Nate's voice is as hard as a slither's bony spine. "I always wondered why Topsiders didn't try to destroy the creatures."

"No one can defeat them—they're too fierce," I say, dodging the spit from a snake. "They can't be stopped."

"That's what I thought." Nate narrows his gaze at the creatures. "But I'm looking at the truth."

"No! There has to be another explanation. The scientists would never breed monsters. Their discoveries prolong life, not destroy it."

"For ShareHaven only."

I can't bear for him to be right, yet the evidence howls around me. I point to the bottle in his hand. "You have the pills. Forget this place, and let's leave."

He shakes his head. "I thought beasts were our worst threat, but they're only weapons."

"Most of these are too little to be dangerous."

"They'll grow and join the other beasts," he says with a narrowing of his brows. "They stalk and kill us—just as the scientists want them to do."

"Lila would never," I argue, but my voice is lost in the growls.

"People I care about have been ripped apart by beasts. Beasts created here." He clenches his hands to fists. "Now I understand why, no matter how many we kill, there are always more to fight. The monsters were bred to kill us. Topsiders want us dead, yet when they need killing skills, they bribe us with medicine," he adds bitterly. "We're no better than beasts—because that's what they've forced us to be. The proof is in this room. The beasts aren't natural to our island. They're created to hunt us."

"No! No!" I can hardly speak, horrified. "The scientists—not even Daniel—wouldn't do something so terrify. There has to be a reason, noble and scientific."

I can't bear looking into Nate's hard blue eyes and turn away. I stare at a door almost hidden in a gap between towering cages. Through a window, I see bursts of yellow. Curiosity pushes me forward.

Opening the door is like leaving a chilly day for one of humid warmth, not uncomfortable but damp, like a sunny day after rain. I blink at the brightness of golden flowers stacked in pots along a wall, lacy plastic coverings dripping inside with moisture for the blossoming flowers.

"Blooming Flowers," I murmur, realizing this is where the life-giving flowers are nurtured and protected. Scientist Lila said they only grew in one place, and I just found it.

"What are those for?" Nate says, tapping my shoulder.

I glance up to follow his gaze to the other side of the room.

He's pointing to a large sub-temperature container like the one used for storing frozen youth DNA in vials. If I lift the lid, I doubt I'll find vials of human DNA.

Nate is right.

Monsters are created here. I frown at the frozen box, imagining droplets of liquid growing into fierce monsters, set free outside the Fence to kill Nocturnes.

I jump at a touch on my shoulder. "Footsteps," Nate says in a hoarse whisper. "Coming down the passage!"

Tilting my head, I listen but can only hear the caged monsters.

"My hearing is sharp ... from hunting," he adds in a rush. "We must go!"

I shut out growls, snorts, and hisses and hear a distant click-click of footsteps. There's something else too, a sound like bells. Only this sound isn't far away; it's in this room. I look beyond the frozen box to a shadowed corner, where a cage is draped in black cloth. A tail whips through the bars, pushing aside the cloth. I hear the sound again, and my heart jumps.

It can't be!

Nate calls my name, but I ignore him, reaching for the cloth. I whip it from the small cage, where a tiny scaly creature curls in a shallow bowl of water.

Petal.

FORTY-ONE

I murmur Petal's name over and over, hugging her to my chest. She's beauteous and healthy, not withering to dust. She tinkles her happy sound, wiggling excitedly and giving me lick-kisses. With a shake of her feathery tail, she showers salty drops on my face, but I don't care. I love her so much.

Relief overwhelms me—yet I'm furious too. All this time Petal has been so close and I didn't know.

"My poor little one." I kiss her bristly head. "Who locked you in here?"

Nate touches her water bowl, then brings his finger to his lips. "Someone clever enough to know she needs salt water—like a scientist."

"Not Lila, but maybe the others," I spit out. "Now I know why Marcus couldn't find her. She was brought here."

"Why?" Nate shakes his head. "She's not a dangerous beast."

"She's unique and unusually smart. They probably want to study her. But I won't let anyone put her in a cage ever again." Petal curls her long tail around my arm, her way of hugging me back. "She belongs in the cave."

"I'll take her there," Nate offers. "She'll be safe with me."

I melt into Petal's liquid black eyes, my heart breaking at her suffering. I can't leave her. Not yet.

"We'll take her together," I decide. "Then I'll come back

and talk to Lila."

"Will you still become a scientist?"

I can't answer his question.

Leaving, even though I intend to come back, will betray Lila's trust. And there's the risk of capture too. If Uniforms find me, I'll be the one in a cage—unless they kill me first.

How could so much change in a few short hours? I'd been so joyous at my party, surrounded by friends and excited about a future as a respected scientist. Now I don't know if I even have a future … but I have Petal.

I trail my fingers along Petal's bristly skin, and I consider Nate's accusation about the scientists. He's right; one of them—or more—bred the baby monsters. I can't believe Lila is involved. She's too kind to harm humans or beasts. But Daniel and his assistant Frost thrive on cruelty. And the evidence against them hisses, howls, and thrashes in cages.

Like a zoo, I think with a leap of memory to a place with animals squawking, roaring, and bellowing from cages. I'm small but quick, running ahead of my mother, who pushes a stroller, and my father calls out, "Milly, come back!" I giggle and run faster, turning around a corner and suddenly looking around … to find myself alone. I turn around in circles, bumping legs and not seeing anyone I know. A lion roars so close I can almost feel its teeth sinking into me. I sink to the ground, shaking and crying for my—

Stop it, Milly! I shout inside my head. *I don't have time for your fears. I have to be strong.*

Petal whimpers, and Milly's thoughts shrink to only a buried whisper.

"You're safe with me," I tell Petal, kissing her on her whiskery nose.

I lift her up to my hair to hide her but only feel the coolness of air on my neck. No long hair, I remember sadly. So I slip her inside my tunic, and she curls into the deep pocket. Only the tip of her dangling tail is visible.

Nate waits at the door, mouthing, "Hurry!" and gesturing for me to come on.

As we make our way through the cage room, sharp-toothed beasts growl and swipe their claws through the bars. These small beastlings will mature into killers. If ShareHaven wasn't protected by the Fence, there would be a fourth danger for Edu-Center Youths: Do not risk being attacked by flesh-eating beasts.

Nate and I hurry through the room, staying far from the cages.

"We'll make sure the hall is clear, then go to the first level," I tell Nate. "If anyone sees us, I'll say I'm going for a cliff walk, and you pretend to be a droll."

He rolls his eyes back and moves his arms stiffly. "Yes, miss. I'll do anything you tell me to because I am here to serve and not to think."

"You do that too well." I shudder. "If you ever want a new role, I'm sure Frost would gladly suck out your brains."

"Not interested." He scowls, adding in a hushed voice, "Even with my mind intact, I would never live in a place where science is a tool for killing."

"The scientists gave us health and immortality," I point out.

"They also send beasts to destroy us and destroy healthy minds to create slaves who serve them. They're the monsters," he says angrily. "I'm ashamed I used to envy and want to be like Topsiders."

"It's natural to want to live forever," I say.

"I just wanted to live. Period." He traces a mottled red scar on his forearm. "It's torture losing people I love to claws and snakes. I hated yet envied people like you."

"And now?" My breath catches. "How do you feel ... about people ... like *me*?" All the beasts seem to go silent as I wait for his answer.

"I wouldn't trade my father and friends for the chance to live forever." He stares into my face. "But I'll miss you."

"I'll miss you too," I tell him. "If only there was a way ...."

Nate reaches out to stroke Petal's skin, his callused fingers brushing against mine. "Come with me."

"Underground?" I suck in a shocked breath.

He nods. "Topsiders may think of us as savages, but we're far from it. Beneath the ground we create our own light—not only in electrical devices that brighten our homes but in a joyful respect of the value of life. I can show you the tunnels, and we'll go to the sea every day and be with Petal. After evening super, we'll gather together for stellings. You'll be part of a family that welcomes all who need sanctuary— it's been our tradition for centuries. I can't promise you a forever life, but every day will be worth living."

I imagine following him into a strange world of dark tunnels and pale moon skins that have never seen the sun. I'd like to see the electronic relics and thrill in voices from distant places. Every day would be an adventure and much more, since I'd be with Nate. I look into his blue eyes and sink into an undertow of emotions. I want to be with him, feel the touch of his scarred hand on my skin and press my lips against his.

But I shake my head. "I can't. This is my home."

"You'd rather stay with scientists who created these

monsters?" He gestures around the room. "They locked Petal in a cage."

"Not Lila. I'm positive she doesn't know these beasts were being used as weapons against innocent people. She'd never allow something so terriful. You can trust Lila."

"I'll never trust a scientist."

I cringe. Will he hate me when … if … I become a scientist?

Nate stares at me for a long moment, then sighs. "I'll check the hall to see if it's safe," he says, reaching for the door.

But before he can touch the knob—it turns by itself. Nate stumbles as the door shoves him backward.

"You!" Frost snaps.

I say nothing, stepping back until I'm up against a wall.

"How did you get in here?" She glares at me but doesn't notice Nate, although he's standing only a few meters from her.

"I—I took a wrong turn," I stammer.

"Through locked doors and a tunnel?" Her pale brows narrow. "You're not allowed on this level—especially in this room."

"I'm going now. It was a mistake."

"Your mistake." She lifts something small and black from her pocket—the electricity weapon she used to punish the droll Carlos. She aims the weapon at my face. "I'm going to find out exactly what you're doing here, and you're not going to move until I say you can."

"Please, just let me go." I can't take my gaze from the weapon.

"You've compromised our secrets." Her cold gaze sweeps past me. "Droll, why did you fail to sound an alert when you found this intruder?"

I follow her gaze, expecting to see a droll—but there's only Nate, his face half-hidden beneath the droll cap. Nate's eyes glaze over with no life. In the dark robe with no facial expression, he looks eerily like a droll. If Frost looks closely, she'll see his battle scars and notice that his hair is slicked back, not sheared short. But like everyone else, she doesn't waste more than a glance at him.

"Useless droll," Frost gripes. "Must I explain everything? Contain her."

Nate grabs my arms, holding firm but not roughly. I cry out and pretend to struggle, hoping to keep Frost's gaze on me and away from Nate.

"Finding you here could work out quite well." The half smile on the smooth side of her face is worse than her scowl. I shiver.

"Lila will be wondering where I am," I say with growing fear. "I didn't mean to come here. I got lost."

"This room is off limits for all but scientists and trusted assistants like me."

"I'm going to be a scientist," I blurt out, then realize my mistake when her cold eyes ignite with anger.

"Liar!" She raises her hand as if to strike me. "By breaking in here, you've betrayed us as you did your Family. Not even Lila will forgive this."

"She'll understand," I say, hoping it's true.

"Lila's attachment to you is pathetic. Youths can easily be replaced. There will be more in twenty-five years. Lila shouldn't have stopped us from Returning you. And the way she manipulates her brother disgusts me. She bosses the most brilliant scientist in the world around like he's a mere youth. Lila is a fool!"

"No, she's not. She's kind and sweet and clever."

"You know nothing!" she growls with the fierceness of one of the caged beasts. "You're only an ignorant youth."

Her smugness snaps something inside of me. "I'll know more than you when I get the memdenity of Angeleen Du—"

"Dupree!" She waves the gun at me. "What do you know of Angeleen?"

I purse my lips, angry with myself for saying too much.

"Angeleen is long gone and will never come back. She died too violently for her memories to be retrieved—I made sure of that. She never deserved Daniel, and his devotion to her sickened me. He only had eyes for her perfect face, while not even science could repair mine." She touches the sagging, frozen side of her face.

I stare, horrified not by her face but by her words. *I made sure of that.* A confession of murder? Did she kill Angeleen because she wanted Scientist Daniel for herself?

"Lila is no better than Angeleen," Frost goes on with a stomp of her foot. "She shows me no respect because I'm not a scientist. When I asked to be trained as a scientist, she told me that scientists are born; no one can learn knowledge of such magnitude. But if what you say is true, Lila saved Angeleen's memories and plans to give them to *you!* I won't allow it!"

"If you talk to her—" I start to say.

"Angeleen will never come back." She cuts me off. "Daniel is finally noticing me, not as an assistant but as an intelligent woman who appreciates him. Lila only cares about getting what she wants. But this time she'll get nothing." Her glare burns through me. "You'll become *nothing.*"

"Lila knows I'm here," I lie. "She'll come looking soon."

"Not soon enough," she says, with a calculating look on the smooth side of her face. "Even if she searches here, the beasts will hide all traces of you, including bones and hair. Thorough, useful creatures."

I wince at her words. Nate circles his finger in a gentle motion on my palm, curving up then down ... spelling a word! T-A-L ... R? No ... K. Talk. He wants me to keep Frost talking.

"Lila will suspect Daniel if I disappear," I say nervously.

"Let her suspect." She shrugs, the gun still aimed directly at me. "Or perhaps I'll tell her I found you in here and had to protect the beast experiments."

"She knows about these ... these monsters?" I ask in horror.

"Lila designed them."

I gasp, staring at the stacks of cages with screeching monsters.

"Lila's area of expertise is genetic hybrids. After her breakthrough with gentle animals like hoxen and monklees, it was the natural step to experiment with hostile creatures," Frost says. "But it was Daniel who had the clever idea to use the beasts to keep strangers from the island. It's taken over a century to reproduce the perfect combinations of beasts. The first few decades, they became attached to humans and were helpless when released into the wild. The ones that adapted taught us which species to breed. Introducing the beasts to the island created an intriguing balance of nature. The strongest beasts survived—and each breeding group grows stronger and deadlier. If Nocturnes hadn't gone underground, the beasts would have exterminated them long ago."

I'm stunned by her lack of remorse. How can she speak

of murder as casually as discussing a change in weather?

"Nocturnes are a plague on our island," she sneers. "The beasts saved us the nuisance of having to eliminate the sub-humans by doing it for us." She points to the cages. "The claws grow more vicious with each born-group. See how that yellow-striped beast strains at his cage, eager to dig his claws into our flesh? He's only a few weeks old, but his knife-like claws and fangs will bring down prey four times his size."

Prey. Nocturnes. Like Nate.

Behind me, Nate's body is taut. I can feel the heat of his anger.

"Do you see that cold box?" Frost points as casually as an Instructor giving a lesson. "It stores genetic matter from the beasts. Lila has been experimenting on a more efficient hybrid she calls a slither-claw. The combination of claws and venoms has resulted in the ultimate killing creature. This slither-claw will bore through dirt, creating tunnels to seek out prey underground." Her half smile shines with malice. "The sub-humans will have nowhere to hide."

"Not Lila."

"You think your precious Lila is too kindly?" Frost mocks. "Has she won your adoration with a party and special attention? Do you think if you ask her to stop creating beasts that she will listen to you? You are wrong. Lila cares about her work above all else."

Frost's words sting to my core, although I'm sure she's lying, trying to turn me against Lila. I don't believe her but need to keep her talking. "Lila trusts me more than anyone. She asked me not to tell anyone about her hybrid experiments," I say, pleased to see a startled look on Frost's face.

"Not even Lila would tell a youth a scientist's secrets," Frost argues.

"I'll be a scientist soon. If you don't believe me, go ask her."

"You will never be Angeleen!" She eyes me suspiciously. "Did Lila send you here to spy on our progress?"

"I can't divulge her plans," I say, as I slip my hand in my pocket, caressing Petal and sending her thoughts of *stay quiet* and *don't move.*

"What plans?" Frost's hand on the gun shakes with her anger.

I purse my lips, refusing to say any more. I've never hated anyone so much. If I had claws like the caged beats, I would gladly rip out her throat.

"Tell me now or the droll will throw you in a cage with a slither-claw," she threatens. "The beast is small but deadly. He'll shred your skin, then dissect you bone by bone and swallow every piece."

Frost steps toward me, so close with her gaze fixed on my face, unaware this droll is more than a breathing pair of handcuffs.

"If what you say is true about Angeleen's memories, then Lila must be stopped. I should have eliminated her long ago." Frost strokes the smooth side of her face, deep in thought. "Daniel will mourn her for a while as he did with Angeleen, and I will comfort him. With no wife or sister to interfere, he'll turn to me and finally realize we belong together." The gun still aimed on me, she snaps her fingers at Nate. "Droll, kill her now."

Nate doesn't move, but I feel the jump of his pulse through his hand.

"Droll, I gave you an order!"

Her gaze shifts to him, and her eyes widen. "You're not a—"

Nate withdraws a small pipe from his pocket. Raising it to his lip, he blows.

Frost realizes what's happened only a second before the swift dart strikes her neck. Her weapon clatters to the floor. Her mouth moves but nothing comes out. Swaying, she thuds on the floor.

"Did you … Is she … ?" I ask, peering down.

"Only stunned," Nate says. "It's a mild poison, but if you want her dead, I can do that too."

With Frost dead, no one will know I'd found this room. Her death will be blamed on the beasts. I can leave here and no one will ever know what really happened. I can become a scientist—if I want to. Is it worth being married to Scientist Daniel, a man who turns youths to zombies and is so full of his own importance he doesn't realize his assistant killed his wife? Scientists don't live by ordinary rules of marriage, so I can stay with Lila as a scientist—unless Frost destroys everything. She would have killed me, and she wants to kill Lila. Eliminating her would be self defense.

Kill her, a voice hisses in my head, and I feel Milly's fear *She's crazed and almost killed us. She deserves to die.*

Milly's fear and mine overlap, so I'm not sure whose voice I'm hearing. It would be so easy to let Nate kill Frost. To him, killing is survival, not a crime. He'd feel no guilt at killing an enemy.

But I would. And so would Milly.

"Don't kill her," I tell him.

I hurry into the room with the cold box containing vials

of DNA, the womb of all genetic monsters, thousands of beasties waiting to be born. I can't kill another human, but I can stop more beasts from being created.

I unplug the cold box.

When I return to Nate, he's staring at the walls of cages, growls and hisses echoing around the room.

"They will grow to kill hundreds of innocent people. I don't have enough poison shards for all of them. But I do have this." He takes rubber strips and a green bottle from his pocket.

He wads papers into a pile near the cages, douses the papers with green liquid, then trails a snake-like rubber strip through the center of the room. When he ignites the rubber, a slow spark burns toward the papers.

"We only have minutes before smoke poisons the room," he says in a rush.

I imagine smoke filling the room, silencing the creatures as it steals their last breaths. When the fire engulfs the room, they will already be dead. I never thought I was capable of killing—not even monsters bred to kill humans.

Yet Frost's death won't be on my conscience. As the door shuts behind us, silencing growling and hissing monsters, Nate and I drag Frost's limp body down the hall, a safe distance away.

"Let's go." Nate holds out his hand to me, and we run.

It's not until we've passed the room where scientists' voices murmur, fled through the tunnel, and taken the elevator back to level one that the ground rocks with an explosion.

We keep running.

FORTY-TWO

No one stops us—a sista we pass is running toward the explosion and doesn't even glance at Nate. It's almost too easy to leave the scientists' compound. Security measures only prevent intruders from getting inside, not from getting out.

I try not to think of the destruction and death we left behind.

When I breathe in fresh, salty air and a breeze smelling of wild grasses blows through my hair, I feel a rush of hope. I may have no home with scientists or a Family, and the Uniforms will grab me and drag me off to jail, but for the first time in my life I'm free to make my own choices.

"We made it!" I shout into the sky as if my words are young birds flying for the first time.

"Yes, we did," Nate says with a smile that lights up his blue eyes. "Thank you, Jennza. Without your help, I wouldn't have the medicine for my father."

"He'll be better soon." I stare up into Nate's sweet, scarred, wonderful face and am overwhelmed by emotions. "You risked your life to save your father, but by stopping the growth of more monsters, you've saved all Nocturnes."

"We both did it," he says. "But you risked more. Where will you go now?"

"The cave." Petal musically tinkles from inside my pocket, and I'm reminded of the urgency to get her to seawater.

355

"But after Petal is safe, where will you live?" His voices softens. "You can't go back to the scientists or a Family."

"Petal has taught me how to find food and stay safe in the cave. I can live there."

"Or you can live with me." He holds out his hand. "There is much beauty beneath the ground—my people have brightened darkness. You would be welcomed there, and eventually—when there is no threat from monsters—we will make a new community aboveground."

I stare at his hand, tempted to take it and agree to a future with him. Thoughts tug for attention in my spinning head. *Go back to Rosemarie,* Milly begs. *I'll clear your name so you can be in a Family,* Marcus offers. *Please don't leave. You're my best born-mate ever,* Lorelei sobs. The only thing I know for sure is that I have no future with the scientists. By now, Lila knows I'm responsible for destroying her beasts, and instead of becoming a scientist, she'd Return me to a droll.

Blinking back tears, I shake my head. "Once Petal is safe, I'll figure out what to do. If we head for the Edu-Center, we can cut through the woods to the Fence. It'll be a long walk since we can't use the main road."

"Why walk when we can ride?" Nate grins.

I don't know what he means until he leads me down a wooden path to a towering oak. A hoxen is tied with a long rope to the oak.

"I'll get on first, then lift you," Nate says.

I back up, not sure about climbing on such a giantness creature.

Ride with the wind! There's nothing to be afraid of when I'm tall on a horse. Milly's thoughts push into my own. She's offering courage, not fear. A vision of her galloping on a horse gives me a burst of excitement. Milly soars confident-ly on the back of a horse. A hoxen isn't a horse, but it's close. Before Nate can climb on the hoxen, I dig my fingers into the thick mane and swing myself up as if I've been doing this forever.

"Impressive," Nate says. "I thought you said you'd never ridden a hoxen."

"I haven't … not exactly."

"You look comfortable up there." He lifts his arm. "How about giving me a hand up?"

I stretch my fingers toward his reaching hand. Touching. Lightly. Then a firm grip, our fingers weaving together. A long moment stretches, like we've both jumped into deep water and are holding our breaths. Sizzling warmth spreads through me. I'm pulled into his blue-sea gaze. I notice every curve and angle of his face—scars from a life lived mostly sub-ground. His lips tilt up at the corners.

"Ready?" he asks, and I'm startled he's still on the ground, waiting for me to make room for him on the hoxen.

I boost him up. His strong arms slip around my waist. He leans close, his breath hot on my neck, and I'm burning and wonderfully shivery at the same time. I smell a scent like the sea and sweat, and I glance down at his hands wrapped around my waist. Can't think. Emotions racing fast, although we hav-en't moved yet. His touch … his scent … his everything. These feelings must be the dangerous hormones my Instructors warned against. Yet they're nothing fearful; they're wondrous.

I dig my heels into the side of the hoxen and shout, "Giddy up!"

We ride through dense trees, far from the road. Despite having to detour around rocks and deep gorges, we're quickly at the Edu-Center boundaries. When I see the shadows of the buildings where I spent my childhood, I smack my feet against the hoxen and command, "Whoa."

I'm flooded with memories here: climbing trees, chasing flutterlings, hiding so well in games that my born-mates couldn't find me, crafting hair decorations with Lorelei, and my secret kiss with Marcus. These buildings held more than lessons; they were my home. My memdenity.

Yet if any of the Instructors who chose to stay here rather than join their Families see me, they'll have me arrested—unless Marcus and Lorelei find evidence to clear my name. Is it possible? To gain my freedom, I'd have to expose the Believers' "trade" with Nate. But only a Believer can prove that Nate was a hired weapon.

There's one Believer who might help.

I stop on the trail, unsure whether to turn back or go forward to the cave. Is clearing my name worth the risk of being arrested? Yes, I think with a rush of certainty. No matter what happens today, I don't want to be an outlaw in my own community. I love ShareHaven, my born-mates, Instructors, and Rosemarie. I want the choice to be in a Family and perhaps even bond with a husband.

Keep going with Nate. Don't go back into danger. Milly's thoughts push me to keep walking, but I won't listen. *Silence,* I tell her, not sure if I'm speaking to a soul or layers of memories, and it doesn't really matter because ultimately I'm the one who makes decisions for this body.

Lifting Petal from my pocket, I hand her to Nate. "Take her to the cave."

"But I thought you'd come with me ... at least that far."

"I'll meet you there. I need to talk to someone first."

"Who?"

"Instructor Penny."

Sneaking into the Edu-Center is child's play, and I excel at it. It's easier too, because only a few Instructors choose to stay here after youths have left. Most Instructors have returned to their Families—but not Instructor Penny. She confided to me once that she feels closer to youths than her actual Family. I find her in the reading nest, her head bent as she reads a thick book.

When I shut the door behind me, she looks up, gasping. "Jennza! "

I nod warily.

"Graces good! I thought you were … but you aren't!" Her book skids across the table as she jumps to her feet with her arms outstretched. "I'm so relieved! I've been worried about you, Jennza—I mean, Milly."

"You were right the first time." I don't move into her arms, holding stiff and sturdy like the door my fingers clutch for support. "I'm not Milly."

She sighs sadly. "I know."

"Then you also know why I can't go back to the Cross Family and what they tried to do to me."

"Yet you've survived."

"Only by luck—I was almost turned into a brainless zombie." My words blow like poison darts from my lips, accusing. "That's what Returned means, although I'm sure you know that too."

"Please don't hate me. I wasn't even aware you were gone until it was already over. I was devastated, more than you'll ever know. I'm overjoyed to see you, yet afraid for you." She bites her lip. "You shouldn't have come here."

"Are you going to turn me in?"

"I would never!" She speaks with such ferocity that my doubts about her fall away. "I'll hide you and keep you safe. Ask me for anything, and I'll help you. I love you, Jenny."

The nickname softens my heart, and when she opens her arms, I melt inside her hug. She's warm and smells of honey-lemon soap. I want to tell her I love her too, but the words lump in my throat.

"I wanted to help you, Jenny," she goes on. "But by the time I'd heard what had happened, you were already gone. There wasn't anything I could do."

"Except tell the truth." I pull out of her embrace and stare at the glint of gold peaking out from her tunic collar.

"What do you mean?"

"I know why you wear this." I grasp the golden chain around her neck, tugging so the star symbol dangles. "You're one of *them*. You say you want to help me, but you kept their secret. You could have cleared me by telling the other Leaders who was really behind Grand Sarwald's death."

"The Noc killed him. You were there when it happened."

"Yes, I was. But I was also in the Cross compound when the Believers—including you—met to discuss what to do about the killer … my friend Nate."

She reels back with a choked cry, clutching the necklace. "You couldn't have been there. I never saw you."

"No one did. I was listening outside the door. I heard you talk about killing Grand Sarwald. You defended Nate, and I'm grateful for that. Still, you knew our Leader was going to die. I don't believe you'd be part of a murder conspiracy without a strong reason, but I can't think of one … and I desperately want to, because you mean so much to me."

Her eyes fill with tears. She glances down at her necklace; the four-point symbol catches a reflection of sunlight and shimmers like a night star.

"I'm guilty," she finally says, the word *guilty* echoing off the reading room walls. "But it's not what you think. Grand Sarwald's death wasn't murder."

I put my arm out to balance against the table. "How can it not be murder?"

"Please don't ask me to explain." She sinks into a chair, her tawny brown skin paling. "I swore never to speak of this."

"If you really care about me, you will—and you'll tell the other Leaders too, so I can walk freely in ShareHaven without fear of being jailed or executed."

"No one will arrest you if you stay with the scientists. Their compound is the best place for you. Go back there where you're safe."

"I can't go back." I shake my head.

"Oh, Jenny, I want to help, but I can't betray the Believers."

"You'd rather I die?"

She looks deeply in my face, and I study her too, saddened by the shadows beneath her eyes that make her look far older than twenty-five. "Have you ever wondered what happens when we die?" she asks me with a seriousness beyond the conversations we shared during lessons.

The question is so unexpected, and if she'd asked me when she was my Instructor, I would have automatically said, "No one dies." But now I know of conflicting beliefs, souls, and murder.

"I have no more idea of what happens to souls after death than an ant knows how to bake an apple pie," I tell her, glancing around at the reading nook I've enjoyed so often, a place of stories, and longing for the comfort of childhood. "But I do wonder ... especially about souls .... What happens to a soul after death?"

"Does anyone really know?" she says with a wry smile. "Scientists assure us we can live again with memdenity in a youth. But Believers would argue our souls go to a higher power. Do you know the word *religion*?"

I nod as if we're in a lesson room and she'd called on me. "A retro-concept which led to many wars and suffering."

"It also led to hope, faith, and miracles," she says. "Before the Attack, I wore a symbol of a cross around my neck. Now I wear this." She gently touches the chain. "The Believers are a mix of religions, so we created our own symbol. This necklace represents all our religions united in a mutual goal—to restore freedom of beliefs in ShareHaven."

"Rosemarie told me her husband Jed was killed because he wanted to build more churches."

"He wanted *real* churches for all faiths, not only the glorification of science. But even more, he longed to go on to his next life—beyond this existence. He worried about Rosemarie though, and didn't want her to bear the shame if he committed suicide. He preferred that Rosemarie think someone killed him rather than tell her the truth—that he chose to die."

I shake my head, confused. Jed wanted to die?

"It's complex," Instructor Penny says. "We maintain peace in ShareHaven by following laws. If a law is broken, the Uniforms deal a fair punishment. But breaking some laws is common—trading work roles, black-market bartering, hoarding food, and relations outside of marriage. If no one asks, no one tells what really goes on in Families. But worshipping old faiths in secret meetings would result in severe punishment."

"Execution?" I ask, gulping.

"I don't know ... and don't care to find out."

"Then why join the Believers?" I ask.

"Daisy invited me into the group after I made a reckless comment about needing to go to confession. I missed attending traditional church. When the cease-aging patch gave us a forever life, it also meant never leaving this earth. Why worship a higher power you'll never meet? At least, that's what the scientists decided. But those of us who disagree met in secret to worship."

"And to plot murder?" I challenge.

"Grand Sarwald and Jed asked to die," she says.

"That's unsensical."

"Not if you're a Believer. Both Leader Sarwald and Jed longed to meet their God. But suicide isn't only against religious beliefs; it would shame the Family. There are two ways to die in ShareHaven: accident or murder. Since most people survive accidents, the only guaranteed method for death is to die by the hand of a skilled killer."

"Nate," I say, finally understanding. He'd been told he was killing someone who wanted to die, and that was the truth. It was still murder; but it was also compassion.

"We traded the Nocturnes medicine for each death," she adds. "Grand Sarwald's death was too public, but it was quick, which is a blessing."

"What about Jed?"

She smiles. "His death was beautiful. One swift, skillful hit. He died with no pain or shame to his Family."

"But Grand Sarwald's death wasn't as easy," I say angrily.

"It was unfortunate the Noc ... Nate ... was captured. Leader Cross worried he'd expose us if he was tortured. You may not believe me, but I was relieved to learn Nate escaped. I worried, though, when you were blamed. When they told me you'd been Returned, I was heartbroken and furious. I quit the group ... although I can't give up wearing my necklace." She glances down at her necklace, then back to me. "I'm so glad you're safe."

"Nate helped me. A Nocturne cared more for my safety than my own people." I look deeply into her face. "I need your help to make things right. Please, go to the Leaders—except Leader Cross—and tell them the truth."

"I can't." She purses her lips. "You're safe with the scientists. You've always had an inquisitive mind and potential for great things. Use your mind to make new discoveries to keep our island safe. I've heard rumors there are problems with the Sharing Bloom—which risks memdenity and immortality."

I glance away, thinking of the flowers growing in the room next to the caged beasts. Did the flowers survive the explosion?

"You can shape the future of ShareHaven," Instructor Penny adds.

"As an outsider," I say angrily. "You might as well toss me out of the Fence and leave me for the claws and snakes."

"The Believers will be ruined if we're discovered."

"Nocturnes fight every day just to live another day. You call yourselves Believers—so stand up for your beliefs and fight for your future."

She looks as me as if I'm someone she doesn't know, and

maybe that's true. When she shakes her head, I know I've lost.

"I'm not brave enough," she admits. "But I have faith in you, Jennza—more than you'll ever know. And I love you like you're from my own flesh, the daughter I never had." She glances up uneasily as if she's heard a sound. "If someone comes, I can hide you. You'll be safe with me."

"When have I ever chosen safety?"

"My dear rebel youth." Her smile is bittersweet.

"I have to go now." I gaze around the room, fixing every detail in my memory.

"Take care, sweet Jenny," Instructor Penny says, squeezing my hand.

I swallow hard. "Could you deliver three messages for me?"

"Of course I will."

She gives me hemper and a writing tool. I write first to Lorelei.

Dearest Lorelei,

You are my best born-mate, and I will treasure all the memories we shared together. Thank you for coming to my birthday. Always remember that you don't need someone else's memories to be skillful, kind, funny, and clever. You are wonderful inside and out. And I will never forget you.

Love,

Jennza.

Writing to Marcus is harder; there's so much to tell him, but while I trust Instructor Penny to deliver my notes, I can't be sure she won't read my words.

Marcus,

Our small friend is safely back in her home. You are very dear to me and I'm sorry we parted in anger. I'm honored you wanted me to join your Family, but I don't know what my future holds. When you rise to the role you have Chosen, embrace justice. Use your inner strength to be a fair Leader. Do not follow in the path of others. Make your own path.

Break a few rules and think of me.

Jennza

The third note is short and bittersweet.

Rosemarie,

I'm sorry I couldn't be the sister you deserve. I never meant to cause trouble, and I regret that I've hurt you. Milly will always be a part of me, and we both love you very much. Tell Arthur how you feel about him. Milly would want you both to be happy.

Love,

Milly and Jennza

Tears swim in my eyes as I fold each letter twice, then slip them in separate envelopes.

"Here." I brush a tear away and hand the envelopes to Instructor Penny.

"I'll deliver them safely," she promises.

When she opens her arms, I fall into them, hugging her one last time—then I leave my youth home.

FORTY-THREE

I go to the Fence, my shoulder still warm from Instructor's Penny's hug. I move quickly, strength growing inside me. I'm not sure what will happen now. I might be captured and executed. I could live in the cave. If my name is cleared, I can join a Family. Or I could go with Nate.

I reach up to climb the Fence as I've been doing for two years. Wire bites into my skin, and I breathe in the tangy freshness of salty air. The sun has lowered since my ride here with Nate, and by now Frost has been found and told the scientists what I did.

Did Lila really create the beasts so they would kill Nocturnes? I can't believe someone who's been so kind to me would kill innocent people.

As my fingers curl around the highest wire, I catch a whiff of flowering perfume and hear a voice behind me speak my name. It's as if Lila sprang from my thoughts, purple-gold robes blowing around her—only the edges of her robes are singed from fire, and her usually perfect hair falls in tangles around her dirt-smudged face.

When she calls my name, I hesitate. I'm so close to escape, but she'll find a way to follow me. She might even find my cave. Besides, there's so much I need to know.

She's not holding a weapon and wears an expression of sorrow, not anger. So I jump to the ground, then spring to my feet to face her. "Those horrible monsters would have killed innocent people. I'm not sorry I destroyed them."

"You did more than destroy them," she says sadly. "It's all gone—DNA, centuries of research, and the Blooming Flowers. I don't know what we're going to do now ...." Her words trail off as she stares out beyond the cliffs and the horizon of endless sea.

I think of the flowers in my cave, but I say nothing.

"Do you expect me to be angry and punish you by turning you into a droll?" she asks with a bitter twist to her words.

"It occurred to me," I admit. "How did you find me?"

"When Frost told me you and your Nocturne friend had destroyed the lab, I had a feeling you'd return to this place." She shields her eyes from the sun as she frowns up at the Fence.

"You followed me here once before," I accuse.

"Yes, I did. It was an enlightening moment," she admits with no shame.

"Frost told me things about you." I swallow. "Did you create the beasts?"

Clouds part overhead so sun shines onto Lila's lined face, and she nods. "Yes. I did."

I bite my lip, glancing at the Fence, wanting to join Nate and Petal but needing to know the truth. "You knew people were being killed, yet you created even more deadly beasts?"

"No. That's Daniel's research project, but I can't deny that I was involved in creating the hybrids." She drops her chin as if ashamed. "After the Attack, we all felt so vulnerable and afraid that having beasts roam outside the Fence seemed a good idea. But when I found out beasts were killing people, I tried to end the project. Only I have no control over my brother, and he continued breeding beasts. I know many in ShareHaven regard scientists as miracle-performing gods, but we're only humans. And we make mistakes."

She sounds so sincere, and my anger fades—until she narrows her gaze at me. "So where is he?" she asks, glancing suspiciously at the Fence.

"Who?" I blink, puzzled.

"The Nocturne boy you call Nate."

"What do you know of him?"

Her arms fold across her chest, studying me. "The day of the Celebraze, I saw you here with him."

"I know," I say, breathing in her scent of lavender perfume. "That's why I didn't accept your offer. I couldn't trust someone who spied on me."

"I had been considering molding a youth into a scientist deserving of Angeleen's memories for a long time. I meant it when I told you I noticed you right away during your Celebraze. You stood apart, and I was intrigued. But I heard from your Instructors that you were uncontrollable, so I followed you because I worried you were flawed like the youth who attacked Daisy. I had to ensure you'd be suitable." Her foot crunches on a twig, the crack sounding like a slap to my face. "But what I saw was much more enlightening and changed my plans drastically. Can you truly communicate with the webbed specimen?"

"Petal isn't a specimen," I say accusingly. "I thought she was safe, until I found her caged in the lab with the other beasts. Did you know she was there?"

"I didn't capture her," Lila says evasively. "It was someone from the Sarwald Family—he brought her to Daniel. My brother wanted to dissect her, but I convinced him to keep her for study."

"Yet you didn't tell me she was in the lab."

"That lab is restricted to only scientists and their assistants. I planned to take you there after your memdenity. The others would never allow a youth there, but they wouldn't be able to keep out a scientist."

A scientist. Angeleen Dupree. Me.

"You also didn't tell me who Angeleen was married to," I add.

"How could I after what Daniel almost did to you? I was waiting till the right time. Please believe me."

"I ... I want to," I whisper.

"And I want many things from you." She steps toward me, and I meet her halfway. I should never have doubted her. She's always been on my side and even after what I've done today, she came to find me.

A glistening of tears shine as she gently grasps my hands. "I've only wanted the best for you—a party, your friends, and a new identity. I know you think I'm angry because you destroyed the lab, but you only did something I'd long wished I'd had the courage to do. I hated knowing Nocturnes were being killed by our creatures."

"You could have stopped it."

"I'm only one of four scientists. We have an agreement never to interfere in each other's research. I won't deny that I'm worried about losing the Blooming Flowers. But perhaps it's time we returned to the natural way of life and death. Flowers start from a seed, live, then die, and new seeds blossom into new flowers. I'll deal with that later ... for now I'm more concerned with you." She squeezes my hands. "I was hurt that you left without telling me."

"I had … had to see a friend."

"The Nocturne?"

"No," I say firmly. "Instructor Penny."

Her dark brows arch with surprise. "Why?"

I won't betray Penny's secrets. "I missed her."

"I can tell when you're telling half-truths," she accuses.

"I thought Instructor Penny had information that could clear my name, but I was wrong. She told me to stay with you."

"Wise advice." Lila lifts her head, smiling. "You'll make an excellent scientist."

"You want me back even though I destroyed your lab?" I ask incredulously.

"Labs can be rebuilt." She waves my protest away. "But if you want to work with me, no further secrets. You must accept, too, that progress comes with sacrifices. You can't afford sentimentality like your attachment to the webbed specimen."

"I love Petal," I insist.

"You must love your work more than anything. Wait until you feel that first thrill of discovery—then you'll understand why I've had to put aside my own emotions for research. You can't let sentiment prevent you from making new discoveries for the betterment of ShareHaven. Once you have the mem-denity, your knowledge and new memories will guide you."

She makes it sounds so clinical—no emotions, only science. But there has to be more to my future, not just fulfilling a role but finding soul and meaning to my life. Will I find that as a scientist?

"I regret what has happened to the Nocturnes," Lila continues. "They don't deserve to be killed, although they are genetically beneath us."

"But they aren't!" I argue, shocked at her words. "They're like us."

"Listen to me, Jennza." She moves beside me. "I've grown fond of you and care about your future. In my long life, I've had to make difficult choices. It wasn't easy to leave my family to come here with my husband. After the Attack, my husband and I stayed to rebuild and improve ShareHaven. Then he had an accident, leaving me alone. The world outside was chaotic and dangerous, so there was no option of leaving. Still, I was lonely, so I came up with a plan to fulfill my deepest dream." Her voice drops sharply, catching with emotion. "And it almost worked. But fifteen years ago, something went wrong."

"That's when I was born."

"Yes. It's no coincidence."

An idea of what she means shocks through me. Could it be possible?

"You're the only one who can give me what I want desperately." Scientist Lila gazes into my eyes. "You know that the cease-aging patch causes infertility. Only DNA material saved before a body stops aging can be used for reproduction. Early experiments were fraught with errors. Misshapen bodies, diseases, and deaths. Once we perfected the embryonic process, we decided to create fifteen youths every twenty-five years."

"But extra youths are created," I say, remembering what I found out when I had my memdenity.

"Exactly!" Her face lights up. "Only the strongest grow into youths."

"What happens to the others?"

Her gaze shifts to the Fence, then back to me. "I could lie to you, but I want to prove that you can trust me. You must understand what it takes to maintain a peaceful society. Unnecessary youths are left outside the Gate."

"For the beasts to kill!" I reel back, my hand to my chest.

"Scientists are no longer in charge of youth creation and have no control over what the health-keepers do," she says bitterly. "While we store the DNA, it's ultimately the health-keepers who create youth-borns. They decide which youths stay or go. Still, I have some influence and had a unique plan for your group of youths. I wanted my own child."

My knees almost buckle, and I reach out to grip the Fence to steady myself. "There's another youth?"

A flicker of sadness crosses her face. "I created a youth from my husband's DNA and my own. A health-keeper was to deliver the youth to me, but my child was stricken ill and discarded outside the Fence. By the time I discovered what happened, my child was gone and not seen again until your Celebraze."

I think back to the Celebraze and how flattered I'd been when Lila told me I was different than other youths. She made me feel special. Her talk of science discoveries inspired me to do more than follow a map of someone else's life—to learn, dream, and discover my own road.

"After the Celebraze, I followed you to the Fence," she says. "That's when I realized my child had survived."

Chill bumps rise on my skin.

"I'd know those eyes anywhere. Deep blue, like the sea blending into the sky." She gestures beyond the Fence to a dazzling blue horizon. "Like his father."

"Blue?" I frown.

"The boy you met, Nate. He isn't a Nocturne—he's my son."

FORTY-FOUR

"But I thought you … you said I was … that you wanted …." Hurt rips through me. I pull away from her like her touch burns. Lila made promises and told me I was special. Only I'm not. This was never about me.

"I was interested in you for all the reasons I've said," Lila speaks quickly, reaching for me, only I draw back. "But after I saw you with my son, I hoped you would lead me to him. I suspected he'd find you again. I could never go to the Nocturnes on my own, so I waited for him to come back to you."

"You used me?"

"I'd do anything to get what's mine. My poor boy, living among savages. What if he'd been killed before I could even talk to him?"

"Killed by beasts you created," I accuse.

"When I saw him, I realized the Nocturnes had taken him and raised him as their own youth. I kept an eye on you, hoping he'd show up again. And he did." She sighs. "But he was arrested."

"You visited him at the jail," I remember. Something else clicks in place. "The packet I found in my room. It was from you!"

She nods. "I couldn't help him directly, so I planned for you to rescue him. I was waiting close by, ready to bring him here. But you waited a day to give him the package, and he escaped before I could talk to him. It was a stroke of luck you were brought here, so I had another chance to find my son. I have to save him from those savages."

"Those savages kept Nate alive—his own people tossed him outside the Fence like garbage."

"That should never have happened!" She clenches her hand into a fist, her ring glinting like fiery skies. "I want to give him the life he deserves. He's my son and belongs with me."

"He knows scientists bred the beasts. He'll never trust a scientist."

"You'll be a scientist soon, Jennza," she says, her dark eyes narrowing at me. "I warned you there would be sacrifices to make. When you gain the memories, you'll also gain guilt. Angeleen worked on beast experiments. She understood that protecting ShareHaven is the most important goal."

"Well, I don't understand, and I can't be like you or Angeleen." I step back toward the Fence. "I'm not going back with you."

"You're rather be arrested and executed? I'm the only one protecting you. Did your friends, Family, or Instructors offer you protection? No—only me. Everything I promised can still happen—but better, because Nate will join us. As Angeleen, you'll have a future—as Jennza, you have nothing."

Frost called me a "nothing," too. But they're both wrong.

While I would enjoy working in a lab—a miraculous place of discoveries—I won't trade compassion for scientific breakthroughs. Yeah, scientists achieved immortality and can even bring back the dead—at least their memories.

They've invented cures to save lives, but they've selectively destroyed lives too, spilling bloody death outside the Fence. I used to think they were superior beings, and I wanted to be like them. Except it turns out they're only ordinary humans. Do they deserve worship more than Instructor Penny's higher power? The Believers don't think so, yet they have their own guilty secrets.

ShareHaven is unraveling beneath the seams.

And I don't belong here anymore.

"Good-bye, Lila," I say sadly and start to climb the Fence.

"Don't turn your back on me! You can't leave!" She grabs my arm, jerking me to the ground, then forcing me to my feet to face her. "I need you to bring Nate to me."

"I won't."

"Do you care for him so little?" she demands. "Would you prefer he die in battle when he has the choice here? He'll be given his father's memories and work beside me. He'll never have to hide underground, and he'll live in comfort and safety forever."

"Forever?" I question. "The Blooming Flowers were destroyed."

"Angeleen once hinted that she knew where more grew on our island, and I will find them. Scientists can accomplish anything we set our minds to."

"But you can't force Nate to come with you. He won't leave his family."

"I'm his family." She rubs her lined forehead, her expression softening. She holds out her hands in a pleading gesture. "I'm not your enemy. I'm simply a mother who longs for her son. Can you understand that?"

I would do anything for my parents, Milly thinks.

"I want you both with me," Lila says with a sincerity that rings true. "Go to Nate. Tell him what I've told you, and if he agrees to come back to me, I'll ensure you're free to see your friends and go anywhere in ShareHaven. You can become a scientist or join a Family of your choice. I can make it happen."

"I don't want anything from you."

"All I ask is a chance to talk to my son."

"I—I don't know ...." I bite my lip, unsure.

"Tell him I love him and am offering him safety, immortality, and a fulfilling life role. Let him decide. If you don't, his death will be on your conscience. He'll return underground to the savages where he'll be lucky to survive another year. Nate's life is in your hands," she says, then whirls around abruptly and walks away, leaving me with choices that feel like I have no choice at all.

I climb to the top of the Fence, savoring what could be my last look from this viewpoint. The sea will still be here tomorrow, but where will I be? Who will I be? Milly's memories remain with me, warm like blankets wrapped within my own memories. We're two separate people, yet we're partners too. Her cautions and riding skill were there for me when I needed them. I'm glad she's with me.

It's a quick climb over the Fence, then I walk along the beach, stopping to flip a crab that's rolled on its back. It scuttles away, safe in its shell world. I stumble forward, unsure of anything except how much I want to see Nate.

He's in the cave. Waiting for me.

Petal crawls from his arm to his shoulder, then leaps across a rock shelf to scamper to me. I hug her to my chest and kiss her bristly head.

"Everything okay?" Nate asks, giving me a long look.

I nod, my emotions going crazy at his nearness. I'm in a chilly cave surrounded by mossy rock and slithering, swimming creatures, yet my body is warm. I stare into Nate's face, concerned and sweet, and I long to be closer, to lean against him and feel his heart blend with mine. I'd like to stay safe in the cave and hide from choices.

Without speaking a word between us, I suddenly know what I must do.

"Take me with you," I tell Nate.

"Underground?" He looks at me, questioning. "Are you sure you want to give up the sunlight?"

"There won't be new monsters. When they're all gone, Nocturnes can live in the sunshine too."

"But until then we have short, violent lives—no one lives underground forever."

"At least I'll be living," I say, thinking of prisons of steel and lies.

His mouth twists wryly. "It's hard to watch people you love die too soon."

His tone is wistful, like when he confided he once longed to live on my side of the Fence. And I consider telling him Lila's offer. If he knows who she is, will he go to her? She can give him so much—but she would own him.

Petal curls in my lap, and I stroke her leathery fur, calmed by her tinkling purr. I shift slightly on the rock where I'm perched at the edge of the Lavender Pool. "Nate, tell me more about your home," I say.

"What would you like to know?"

"You've told me there's light below the ground. What's it like living there? There's a fondness in your voice when you speak of your home."

"There's much to love," he admits. "Strange, I suppose, considering that we were driven underground by beasts. But like this cave of yours, there's beauty in the darkness, especially when I'm seeking new tunnels. My father taught me how to read maps almost before I could walk, and I can draw them too. Discovering a new passage is amazing, like the one which opened into the sea and ultimately led me to this cave, you, and Petal." He playfully tugs on Petal's tail, and she squeaks a protest, springing from my hands and diving into the pool. "We have rivers and ponds too. Most are too cold for swimming, but I know of a spring where the water bubbles with natural heat from the earth itself. The underground is vast, with tunnels and rooms from when it was a military fortress. We have electricity in all homes, strung from wires from retro-centuries and powered by rushing streams. No one has explored it all—but I plan to someday."

His words create images, as if he's sharing memories with me. Not the grim darkness of the underground I imaged, but the light of curiosity and adventures. Still, I can't forget Lila's words. I owe him the truth.

"Nate," I say looking into his blue eyes. "If you had the chance to live in ShareHaven, would you do it?"

He frowns. "You speak as if it's a possibility, but there's no way a savage like me could live with Topsiders."

"But what if … if a scientist welcomed you?"

"The beast breeders?" He spits on the ground. "Never!"

"Are you sure?" I search his face. "Not even if you suddenly found out you weren't … that you belonged aboveground?"

He shakes his dark head. "Nothing could make me leave my father. I am content with my life, but it might be hard for you."

"When have I ever chosen the easy way of anything?" My laugh is a sharp, bitter sound.

"You never do," he says meeting my gaze in a way that shoots heat through me. "But you have no idea how difficult life is beneath the ground."

"I'm eager for a challenge—if you want me to come with you."

"More than anything," he says, his strong, pale fingers entwining with my darker ones.

"So take me with you."

"Are you sure you want to live in a place stalked by beasts?"

"The beasts will be gone soon. And eventually the Fence will be gone too," I say as a wild thought jumps into my head.

Nate's eyes widen. "The Topsiders will never take down the Fence."

"They may have no choice." I smile. "Without the Blooming Flowers, there won't be any more memdenity or immortality. They will be desperate to find new flowers."

"How does that help us?"

"I know where the flowers grow." I smile slowly and point upward, to the dangling bubbles of flowers covering the cave ceiling. "If the scientists and Leaders want my help, they'll have to make some changes. No more dividing this island; it's time for both communities to live as one. I'll start a new war—Jennza seeking justice for all who live on this island."

He grins. "I love the way you talk."

And I love how the skin around his sea-blue eyes crinkles as if with wisdom lines when he smiles. I may even be falling in love with him … unless I'm already in love with Marcus. I have much to figure out about love and many other things.

But there will be time later for decisions, discoveries, and sharing truths. Before I tell Nate who he really is, I need to see his home underground—what he'll give up if he goes to Lila. And I'll discover much for myself too.

A new life, a new community, a new kind of family.

I hug Petal, but it's not a good-bye because I know I'll see her again.

Standing, I reach for Nate's hand. He meets me halfway, and we begin a journey to a place where darkness may hold more light than a forever life under the sun. Although I'll miss many things, I will come back to ShareHaven, not as a Nocturne or even Milly.

I am Jennza.

Always.

DISCUSSION GUIDE

1. Why does Jennza dread joining a Family? What sets her apart from other youths who accept their future roles in ShareHaven?

2. What are the pros and cons of a traditional family structure compared to ShareHaven's Families?

3. Are memories who we are or what we've done? If you woke up one morning with no memories, would you still have the same interests and personality? What if you were inserted with the memory of committing a terrible crime—would that make you guilty?

4. Each character reacts differently to memdenity. Lorelei sees it as a way to improve her flaws with enhanced memories. Marcus is eager to learn new skills. Jennza wants to be herself. If memdenity were possible, would it be beneficial or dangerous? Would you want it?

5. Jennza puzzles over the concept of "soul." *There is no physical organ on the human body labeled "soul,"* she thinks. What do you think?

6. Nate is both a killer and a hero. Is he the victim of his own crimes? And does Jennza help him because of romantic feelings or a sense of justice?

7. ShareHaven considers Nocturnes "Subhuman" and abandons them on the dangerous side of the Fence. Is this reminiscent of other prejudices in history?

8. The Believers meet in secret to worship many different religions. How does the belief in an afterlife fit into a society where no one ever dies?

9. If Jennza had all three memdenities, do you think she would gradually become Milly? Would she love her daughter and husband? How much influence do our memories have on our feelings?

10. How does aging define who we are and our friendships? Could you be best friends with someone the age of your parents?

11. Jennza has strong feelings for both Nate and Marcus. Which boy is the best for her? Does she make the right choice?

12. Jennza quotes the Unity Pledge: *I pledge to honor Family, respect community, and give thanks to the miracles of scientists. Peace and safety forever.* Why do you think ShareHavenites are taught to recite this daily?

13. At the end of the book, should Jennza have told Nate who he really is? Would you have told him? And if so, how do you think he would have reacted?

14. Photos are unnecessary in ShareHaven. What other things would be unnecessary in a forever society?

15. Would you rather be who you are now with all of your memories or be a youth forever in ShareHaven with someone else's memories?

ABOUT THE AUTHOR

Linda Joy Singleton is the author of over 40 YA/MG novels, including the YALSA honored *The Seer* and *Dead Girl Walking* series. She started writing at age 8 and kept her stories, poems and other keepsakes in memory boxes—realizing even at a young age that memories are precious and fragile. She's a longtime member of the Society of Children's Writers and Illustrators and Sisters in Crime. She and her husband live in Northern California on 28 acres with a lovely view of oaks and pines.

For more: www.lindajoysingleton.com